THE *Jade* NOTEBOOK

THE *Jade* NOTEBOOK

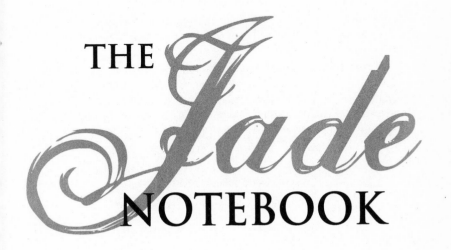

LAURA RESAU

Delacorte Press

Text copyright © 2012 by Laura Resau
Jacket photographs © 2012 Sergey Borisov for iStockphoto (girl in water);
Ben Osborne for Nature Picture Library (turtles in water);
Doug Perrine for Nature Picture Library (turtle on spine)

All rights reserved. Published in the United States by Delacorte Press,
an imprint of Random House Children's Books, a division of
Random House, Inc., New York.

Delacorte Press is a registered trademark and the colophon is a trademark
of Random House, Inc.

Grateful acknowledgment is made to Coleman Barks for permission to reprint Rumi
excerpts from *The Essential Rumi,* translated by Coleman Barks, copyright © 1995
by Coleman Barks (HarperSanFrancisco, an imprint of HarperCollins Publishers).

Visit us on the Web! randomhouse.com/teens

Educators and librarians, for a variety of teaching tools,
visit us at randomhouse.com/teachers

Library of Congress Cataloging-in-Publication Data
Resau, Laura.
The jade notebook / Laura Resau. —1st ed.
p. cm.
Sequel to: The ruby notebook.
Summary: After down-to-earth Zeeta and her flighty mother, Layla, settle in the
idyllic beachside town of Mazunte, Mexico, where Zeeta's true love, Wendell, has
an internship photographing rare sea turtles, Zeeta discovers that paradise has its
dark side as she and Wendell dig deeper to unearth her elusive father's past.
ISBN 978-0-385-74053-1 (hc)—ISBN 978-0-375-98953-7 (Gibraltar lib. bdg.)—
ISBN 978-0-375-89941-6 (ebook)
[1. Missing persons—Fiction. 2. Secrets—Fiction. 3. Mothers and daughters—
Fiction. 4. Single-parent families—Fiction. 5. Mazunte (Mexico)—
Fiction. 6. Mexico—Fiction.] I. Title.
PZ7.R2978Jad 2012
[Fic]—dc23
2011034861

The text of this book is set in 12-point Adobe Caslon.

Book design by Heather Daugherty

Printed in the United States of America

10 9 8 7 6 5 4 3 2 1

First Edition

Random House Children's Books supports the First Amendment
and celebrates the right to read.

To my mother, Christine Resau

Acknowledgments

I've been fortunate to work once again with the wonderful people at Delacorte Press, especially my bright, warm editors: Krista Vitola, who has provided valuable revision guidance throughout the entire Notebooks series; Françoise Bui, who has been a complete delight to work with on this, our first book together; and Stephanie Elliott, my longtime editor. I've been enormously grateful to Stephanie from the moment she pulled my first manuscript from the slush pile. It's truly been a privilege being your colleague and friend, Stephanie—you have changed my life!

A big thank-you to my beloved agent, Erin Murphy; to the fabulous women of Old Town Writing Group—Sarah Ryan, Leslie Patterson, Molly Reid, Dana Masden, Carrie Visintainer, and Laura Pritchett; and to my young adult writer friends—Todd Mitchell, Victoria Hanley, Amy Kathleen Ryan, Ingrid Law, and Lauren Sabel—who all offer creative nourishment. Gloria Garcia Diaz, *querida amiga,* *gracias* for your Spanish help and your soulful rendition of the folk song "La Llorona," which always brings tears to my eyes. *Gracias* for conversations with the gracious experts at Mazunte's Turtle Center and with the sweet family who runs the eco-resort El Copal.

My mother, Chris, has been essential to my writing; not one of my books would exist without her intelligent feedback and unwavering support. Both my mother and my father,

Jim, are as steadfast and helpful as the sea turtles in this book (but not as ancient)! Thanks, Dad, for the fantastic, dusty sea turtle book you dug up for me, probably at the Goodwill—you are my eternal source of treasures. I'm grateful to my brother, Mike, whose love and talent for photography inspired aspects of Wendell's character. Finally, thank you, Ian and Bran, for your big hearts and hugs and patience as we bumble through this delicious mess called life!

❖

A glossary and pronunciation guide for Spanish words used in this book can be found on page 359.

❖

One must have chaos within to give birth to a dancing star.
—Friedrich Nietzsche

Chapter One

At sunset, Comet Point feels like the tip of the world. Far below, the water churns, slapping against the crags, spraying my skin. I gaze past the jagged rocks, where the sea smooths into silk and spreads out to touch the sky. And there on the horizon, the sun dips lower and lower, setting the clouds on fire.

Here at the cliff's edge, the tiniest details are magnified: every fine hair on my arms moving in the breeze, every pebble pressing into my palms, every speck of dirt clinging to the backs of my thighs. A tiny pink boat, upside down on a patch of sand. The silhouette of a fisherman, his line catching light.

After the sun slides through the last puddle of flames and disappears into the sea, I stand up, brushing the dust from my dress. My eyes stay fixed on the fading line where sky meets water as I walk toward the mainland, weaving around hardy shrubs and a huge saguaro cactus. Soon sky and sea are the same shade of twilight blue with a hint of silver, indistinguishable.

Once I reach the steep part of the path, I scramble up the rocks, looking for safe footing. Comet Point, not surprisingly, is shaped like a comet, the head being the tip of the peninsula. I make my way up the comet's fiery tail, which ends in jungle high above the beach.

When we decided to move to Mexico, I had no idea that this little beach town would feel like a shoe that fits as if it were made just for me. Mazunte is the home I'd given up on ever finding. Why does this place, of the dozens of breathtaking places I've lived, feel so exquisitely perfect? I can't pinpoint a reason—not a logical one, anyway. Maybe, somehow, the silvery strands of the comet pulled me toward Mazunte from far across the ocean.

When I reach the top of the sandy path, I leave the sea behind, following a narrow trail that slices through dense foliage. The moon is just rising, its light barely filtering through the leaves, just enough for me to make my way back toward the cabanas. Knowing the route by heart, I fly through the insect songs and tree shadows.

Instinctively, I slow down as I pass the first in a ring of signs around a section of jungle about a kilometer in circumference. These signs give me the creeps. The first, I can barely make out in the moonlight, but I know what it says: ¡TERRITORIO PROHIBIDO! ¡SE DEVORAN LOS INTRUSOS! Forbidden territory! Trespassers will be devoured! More hand-painted signs around the perimeter of the property offer variations on the theme: Trespassers will be cursed/taken prisoner/eliminated. Disconcerting, but I like to think that whoever made the signs just has a somewhat twisted sense of humor.

As I walk, I peer beyond the signs, curious. It's our mysterious neighbors' property, but it looks just like the rest of the area—enormous leaves, vines, branches, occasional flowers. I haven't yet dared to cross the line, and I'm not quite brave enough to do it alone at dusk. What I do instead is shout past the sign, loud, in English, on some kind of impulse: "Fine! Devour me!"

As soon as the words come out, even though there's no one to hear, a little wave of embarrassment washes over me.

And then, a noise shatters the night. A deep, vibrating noise that seems to tear through the forest, rumble the earth. It comes from what feels like just meters away. It's so loud it makes me jump, sends my heart racing.

I freeze. What *was* that? A motorcycle engine? A chain saw? Motionless, I hold my breath and listen. The only sounds are my pounding pulse, the insects, the distant waves, a breeze through the leaves. All I see are shadows in hues of green and blue and purple. I breathe out and take a tentative step down the path.

Then it thunders again, filling my ears, resounding through my body. The noise wakes some primal fear in me. I barely resist the urge to run away at top speed.

I reassure myself under my breath. "Don't be crazy, Zeeta. It's just a noise."

Silence again; only the familiar hum of the jungle at dusk. My muscles relax a little. The TRESPASSERS WILL BE DEVOURED sign must have put me on edge. I bet the noise was just a car engine that my imagination transformed into something monstrous. Again, I exhale, try to steady my legs and slow my racing pulse. Then I suck in a deep breath and take a step forward on the path toward home.

This time, when the sound rips through the darkness, I run. I tear through the trees, the branches scraping my skin, catching on my clothes. After a few minutes, my lungs are burning and there's a stitch in my side. I stop and lean over, gasping, my hands on my knees. Then, tentatively, I peer into the shadows behind me. Nothing. My ears alert, I half walk, half jog toward the cabanas.

I settle on an explanation. It was something rational—like thunder in the distance, or a particularly loud wave crashing. The cliffs *can* produce unusual echo effects. The farther I get from the Forbidden Territory, the easier it is to shake off the creepiness, even tip my hat to whoever posted those signs. After all, they're effective.

A few minutes later, as I round the bend to the cabanas, my heartbeat has calmed, my trembling subsided. Emerging from the jungle, I enter the yellow glow of the kitchen hut. There in the candlelight, beneath the woven grass roof, Layla and Wendell are eating fresh fish and laughing with the guests.

I hover at the trees' edge and savor this moment, watching my mom and my boyfriend—the people I love most in the world in this place I already love most in the world. Which is saying a lot for someone who's lived in seventeen places in her seventeen years on earth.

Here, safely outside the jungle, wrapped in the aura of my perfect new home, it's easy to let go of the strange noise, hope I don't hear it again. Why bother even mentioning it? Why make waves in an otherwise smooth sea? Even paradise has to have a few flaws, right? It's part of the package. Like the stinging jellyfish off Phi Phi Island when Layla and I lived in Thailand. Or the pickpockets in Marrakech. Or the deadly single-lane mountain roads in Nepal.

Wendell catches my eye, his face lighting up with his cute half-smile. He comes to me, folds me in his arms, wraps me in his cinnamon-soap smell. I press my lips against the comforting pulse of his neck, nestle my head on his shoulder. Yes, this is it. Paradise.

❖ ❖ ❖

Within minutes, Layla whisks over, kisses my head, and sets down a steaming plate of fried fish and cilantro rice, a dish of flan, and a glass of *agua de sandía*. "Eat up, Zeeta, love!"

My mother is surprisingly skilled at running these cabanas. It was a good decision to branch out from her usual stints teaching English. With Wendell's and my help, Layla is managing fourteen little palm-thatched bungalows—checking people in and out, tidying the rooms, cooking meals, giving yoga lessons at sunrise, orchestrating Mayan flower baths and sweat lodge ceremonies, hosting bonfires on the beach, hanging out with travelers from all over the world. She's thrown herself with blissful abandon into every little task . . . except for cleaning the bathrooms, which she usually leaves for me.

Layla is voluntarily washing dishes now—a first for her. In previous countries, the crusty plates would sit in the sink for days until I'd give in and do them myself. But here in Mazunte, Layla seems to actually enjoy the task, chattering with adoring backpackers as she works.

As I dig into my fish and rice, Wendell and I talk—a comfortable, meandering conversation about which flowers to plant in our garden. "Birds-of-paradise," I say. "Heaps of them."

He considers this, then, with a playful grin, says, "How about something carnivorous? Venus flytraps—you know, to devour any trespassers who slip through the cracks."

I smile. Now's the time when I could mention the sound in the jungle—a roar that might have come from something truly carnivorous. But I keep the conversation light, happy. "I'm thinking more along the lines of passionflower," I say, taking a bite of my lavender flan.

In response, Wendell leans in and kisses me—sweet and golden. Then he begins clearing plates, pausing to chat with guests. Whenever he passes, he bends down and lets his lips brush against mine ever so lightly, sending a delicious shiver through my body.

After my last bite of flan, I bring my dishes over to the sink and lean against the counter, satisfied. For once, my existence has roots, stability. Everything and everyone I need is here, now. My mother's usually the gushing one, the flowery, rose-colored-glasses one, but now I can't help spouting, "We've finally found it, Layla. Paradise."

"I know." She plunges her hands into the soapy water. With no electric lights on the grounds, we use only candles and lanterns, which make the suds glow orange. She playfully flicks bubbles at me. "This place . . . it's *bien padre, güey.*"

Mexican slang seems to have endless ways of saying "cool, dude." We use some variation of "really cool" constantly because everything here is indeed *bien padre.* Which literally means "really father."

Layla grins. "Or, in Rumi's version of really cool, *What souls desire arrives. We are standing up to our necks in the sacred pool. . . .*"

It's poetry from her favorite thirteenth-century mystic. She never tires of quoting him. Normally, I'd roll my eyes, but this time I finish the line in a rare moment of complete agreement. *"Majesty is here."*

She lifts her hands from the dishwater. Iridescent bubbles cling to her forearms like bits of pearly sea-foam. Before I know it, she's giving me a soapy hug.

And I let her.

It was right in this spot, a week ago, that she said, while washing dishes, "You know, Z, I could stay here forever." And without missing a beat, I said, "Let's do it! Let's stay here, Layla. For good." I kept going, letting myself lapse into extreme sappiness, speaking her language. "I belong here,

Layla. It's like . . . It's like . . ." I searched for words to describe the precise feeling this place gives me. "It's like I'm finally home." An otherworldly look swam over her face. She pushed her hair from her eyes, leaving a trail of bubbles.

"Maybe we both are."

"Really, Layla?"

She nodded. "Let's do it, Z! Let's settle here. For good."

"Promise?"

"Promise," she said, sealing it with a kiss on my cheek.

Unbelievable. After seventeen homes, Layla has finally agreed to let us stay in one place.

Of course, she's famous for her flightiness and flakiness. She's fallen in love with all of our homes, especially during the first few months—the honeymoon phase. And then, when the first year in a place is drawing to a close, she grows restless and fantasizes about distant lands. Her wanderlust always propels her—and me—on to the next country, our next home. It's exhausting.

I want to think that this time it's different. Maybe it is. She's never actually promised that we could stay in a place for good—not until now. I guess that's something. I wish I could believe her, but I know her too well. Her promise feels as beautiful and fragile as these soap bubbles. At any moment it could pop.

Knowing I'll be leaving for college in two years makes me even more determined to protect this dream. I'll need something that's a constant. A home to come back to on semester breaks. And not just any home. My home here, on the cliffs near Punta Cometa, on the magical border of sea and jungle.

After Layla releases me from the hug, I wipe off the suds and notice a scratch on my forearm. I must have gotten it in my mad dash through the jungle. I nearly forgot about the weird noise. For a moment, I consider mentioning it to Layla. Maybe she heard it and has a logical explanation.

But already, the incident has gained the dusky quality of a nightmare quickly dissipating. I don't want to tell Layla about anything that might jeopardize our new home. Anything that might burst this precious bubble.

No, I decide. I will tell her nothing that suggests this place is anything less than a shimmering piece of heaven.

Chapter Two

After we finish the dinner dishes, I do a couple of hours of trig homework by lantern light in the kitchen hut. Between problems, I look around in appreciation, wondering again what it is about this place that feels so right. Now that I know we're staying for good, the feeling is intensified. I can't help smiling to myself, shivery-happy with the knowledge that I'll actually get to see these bushes and trees grow over years. I'll get to plant flowers and build paths and form long friendships. For the first time in my life, I won't have to tear myself away after a year. *If* Layla sticks to her promise.

Wendell's sitting next to me, updating the cabanas' website on his laptop. His just-washed hair, usually braided, is hanging loose and damp over his shoulders. The computer screen's blue light bathes his face, his strong jaw, his soft eyes. After my last equation, I lean back and rest a hand on his leg.

Five months without seeing each other, and now, even after two weeks together, it feels like a miracle every time we touch.

We arrived here on the same day—January first—when Layla's new job started. It was serendipitous that Layla and I came across the job posting. Back in France, where we lived last year, I did an online search for Punta Cometa and found an ad looking for a multilingual family to manage cabanas. Layla was game, so we left France earlier than planned and came here. And the luckiest part of it—Wendell had just finished up all his credits for high school graduation in Colorado. He scrambled to get an internship for his last semester at the Turtle Center down the road from the cabanas.

The precise, ordered new path of my life with Wendell stretches before me like a shiny ribbon. Layla has agreed to give him his own cabana and meals in exchange for maintaining our website and helping with chores. He'll stay for the next year and a half, with a few short visits home to Colorado. He'll focus on building up his nature photography portfolio while I take online classes for my last year and a half of high school. After I graduate next spring, we'll go to college together—the University of Colorado in Boulder, where he'll pay in-state tuition and we can live with his parents to save money. His parents are disappointed that he isn't going to a fancy art college and is taking a year off after high school, but they haven't tried to stop him. Secretly, I suspect they like the idea of his going to college close to home.

Finally, Wendell and I will be together for more than a few months at a time. Finally, I'll have a home to come back to. Finally, there will be no more wandering into the unknown.

I tuck my trig notebook and pencil into my bag, stretch my arms. Wendell shuts down his laptop and takes my hand. "How about a walk?"

It's past midnight, but that doesn't matter. Time flows differently here. "Sure." I reach out and he pulls me up. "Sounds perfect."

Twenty minutes later, we're hand in hand, walking on Playa Mermejita, where moonlight and starlight melt together on the dark water. Usually, we go to the busier, well-lit beach of Mazunte, near downtown, but tonight, on an impulse, we've chosen this more solitary beach. There's not an electric light in sight. There are no restaurants or bars. No bonfires or drum circles. Only an overgrown jungle path and a single-lane dirt road lead here. We've heard that the currents are rough for swimming, with hidden rocks and riptides. That must be why no one comes here. It's remote, risky, and at night, eerily dark.

The moon illuminates the beach, reflects off the water, just enough for us to see our way. Waves rush, gather strength, slap against the shore, and retreat again. With every step, sand squishes between my toes and sea-foam licks my heels. Wendell moves my hand to his face, lets his lips run up the sensitive inside of my arm. Tiny shocks of pleasure ripple across my skin.

When he looks up, his eyes glisten with an idea. "Hey, Z. Let's meet here for the handfasting."

I stare, surprised. Surprised in a good way, a *bien padre* way. Last year, when Wendell spent the summer with me in France, we did a Celtic handfasting ritual, a promise to be together for a year and a day. We were told to choose a special meeting place for our next handfasting, on August second. If we both show up, then we renew our promise. If one of us doesn't come, our bond is broken and we agree to move on. I didn't realize he'd taken it so seriously, that he'd actually been on the lookout for the right spot.

My gaze sweeps over the beach, at our moon shadows stretching far in front of us. We're standing beside a huge driftwood log, exactly in the middle of a long crescent of sand. One side is lined with jungle, rising into the majestic cliffs of Punta Cometa, and on the other, the surf forms a scalloped lace pattern at our feet. Yes, this is perfect. I mark an X on the sand. "Right here," I say, smiling. "This very spot."

"August second, at midnight," he says, wrapping his arms around me.

"Midnight," I repeat, raising my face toward his.

Our lips are on the verge of touching when that noise thunders from the forest above. It's not as close this time, but it's clearly audible over the pounding waves.

I squeeze my eyes shut, waiting for the sound to fade into the rush of surf.

Wendell pulls away from me, scanning the cliffs. "What was that?" His eyebrows furrow. "I heard the same sound at dinner, Z. When you were on your walk. I was a little worried about you, actually." He squints up at the trees. "What do you think it is?"

"I don't know. But I'm not letting it scare me." I twist my finger around my wind-tangled hair, deciding how much more to say. "I heard it earlier tonight, too," I admit. "Loud. And close."

"Why didn't you say something?" His voice is full of concern. "Where'd it come from?"

"The place in the jungle with those weird signs."

"The Forbidden Territory?" he asks, frowning. Up to now, whenever we've mentioned the Forbidden Territory, it's been to joke around. As in, *If you don't help me take out this trash, I'll banish you to the Forbidden Territory.* But now, his voice is serious, worried. "What did it sound like up close, Z?"

I shrug. "Just—loud. And deep. Kind of rumbling. It's probably some crazy echo from the cliffs."

He doesn't look convinced. Chewing on a fingernail, he stares up at the jungle. His wariness puts me on edge; he's not a person who scares easily.

I'm almost angry at that noise for breaking the mood. Determined, I set my jaw. "Listen, Wendell, just forget about it. Let's enjoy ourselves, okay?"

And to prove the point, I sink to the sand, pulling him down with me. Easily, he surrenders.

"As long as we don't get devoured," he murmurs, kissing my ear.

"Or eliminated," I counter.

"Or cursed."

"That would be the worst. . . ."

Within minutes, we've lost ourselves in salty skin and sea spray, and after a while, we fall into a delicious half-sleep induced by ocean waves.

❖ ❖ ❖

Some time later, my eyes open. Wendell is nudging me gently. I prop myself on my elbow, brush the sand from my cheek. With a finger to his lips, he motions to an enormous dark form in the surf just meters away.

"What is it?" he whispers.

I rub my eyes and stand up, brushing more sand from my dress, my legs, my shoulders. Wendell's already walking toward the thing. Following him, I squint in the faint moonlight. In a sleep-scratchy voice, I speculate, "Some kind of sea creature?" When he stops at a distance, I stand beside him, blinking, sensing that we're witnessing something extraordinary. "Is it alive?"

He studies it. "I think it's coming ashore."

The ghostly form emerges from the surf, impossibly slowly. I take a step closer, make out its heart-shaped body, wide flippers like wings, tiny slits of eyes, glinting. Now I grasp the size of this beast. It's as big as a car.

"A sea turtle, Zeeta," Wendell whispers. "It's so huge, it must be a leatherback. Endangered for years, hunted nearly to extinction."

I watch the creature's arduous trek from the surf, letting the magic wash over me. There's something ancient about this animal, something that humbles me, mesmerizes me.

And I feel the presence of my father. Whenever Layla talks about their one-night stand nearly eighteen years ago in Greece, she tells how he emerged from the sea like a creature from another world. Despite my eye-rolling, I started to think of him that way, somewhere out there, living his own deep-sea life. Then, last year in France, he began to emerge, only to retreat again before I even saw his real face. He worked as a mime, part of a troupe of street performers appropriately called Illusion. I'd met my father at last, met him without knowing it was him. Briefly, an image flashes in my mind—my father lost in dark waters, swimming in circles, aimless.

Disturbing. I shake off the thought, just as Wendell says, "Look, Z!," gesturing up the beach.

There are more turtles ahead, although none quite as big as the first one. About seven or eight of them, most in various stages of dragging themselves from the surf. A couple have already started digging their nests, their flippers alternating, right, left, right, flinging sand.

"These leatherbacks migrate thousands of miles to feed," Wendell says, his soft voice growing animated. "Down to South America. Every couple of years they swim all the way back to the same little stretch of beach here to nest. They'll lay a few clutches of eggs throughout the nesting season, then head back to the waters off the coast of Chile, or Peru, or Ecuador. Isn't that *padre*?"

I nod, grateful to focus on sea turtle factoids instead of that strange, underwater image of my father.

As we tiptoe around the leatherbacks, Wendell spouts off more facts, and I find myself becoming surprisingly absorbed. He's always been most interested in the art form of photography. But something happened over the fall, as he was preparing for this internship, reading books and articles and watching videos back in Colorado. He apparently developed a fondness for sea turtles. More than a fondness. A passion.

Eventually, we reach the rocks at the end of the beach, then turn around, passing by the six turtles and stopping at the largest one, the one we first spotted.

"It's instinctual," Wendell is saying, "finding their nesting place—something to do with magnetic particles in their brains. After sea turtles hatch, they spend over a decade wandering, but they're drawn to come back to the beach where they were born, where their mothers and grandmothers nested. They've been doing this for over a hundred million years."

I take this in. "Maybe my dad is a merman after all." I'm attempting to joke, but my words end up sounding almost grave. "A turtle merman."

"A turtle merman?" Wendell looks at me, skeptically at first, then tenderly. "You think he's really somewhere around here?"

I shrug, trying to figure out what I think, how to put the underwater image of my father into words. Back in France, I'd been certain this was where my father had gone, to his home town of Mazunte. But now that we're here, and there's no sign of him, I don't know what to think. In fact, I've been trying *not* to think about him, and to focus instead on the perfection of this beach town. But tonight I can't shake this picture of my father, lost in a dark place.

"Hey," Wendell says, "we'll find him." He studies my face, trying to look inside me. "I'm sure he's fine, Z. And I'm sure he'll be happy to see you."

After a moment, I whisper, "Then why hasn't he contacted me?"

It's the first time I've spoken the question aloud. Wendell knows the facts: My father has my email address. I check my account daily, just in case this will be the day the email comes. But day after day, there's nothing.

Wendell pulls me close. "I don't know, Z. But there's still hope."

"Maybe," I concede.

"I read a story about a sea turtle," Wendell says under his breath. His arm tightens around me; his lips graze my ear. "A Native American myth."

"Tell me," I murmur, keeping my gaze fixed on the creature.

"Ages ago," he says, "nothing existed but darkness and sea, so Turtle dove far down into the water to retrieve the Earth. He disappeared for many years, swimming all the way to the bottom. By the time he resurfaced, all the Earth had washed away except for a tiny bit of mud under his toenail. But it was enough. Once the speck of mud was placed on Turtle's back, it grew and grew and grew and became our Earth."

After a pause, I say, "So you think my father's just taking his time? That he's out there somewhere?"

Wendell nods. "Maybe he's holding on to a muddy little piece of hope."

"Hope for what?"

Wendell thinks. "A new life, Z. One with you in it."

I watch this enormous creature, imagining the depths it's come from. It's so hopeful, so slow and persistent, dragging its body up the beach to find the perfect nesting spot. I close my eyes and send a message to my father, wherever he is. Tell him to hang on to that sticky speck of hope.

"Good luck," I whisper to the turtle.

I lean into Wendell, appreciating the way his body fits mine perfectly. At least he's a sure thing in my future. I don't have to worry about him leaving and returning. He's with me, and he'll stay with me. The most essential ingredient in my paradise.

❖ ❖ ❖

Once we start walking back along the beach, I realize I'm utterly exhausted. It's the deepest middle of night, and my eyelids are drooping, my legs heavy. Soon we leave the stretch of sand and enter a path that winds through a hillside of jungle, heading back to our cabanas.

A noise rumbles through my grogginess. I jump, thinking of the strange jungle sound. Then I catch a glimpse of headlights through the trees and my muscles relax. It's just the roar of a truck engine. Now hip-hop salsa beats, heavy in the bass, are pounding through the night.

Wendell turns his head too, then gives me a puzzled look. "Weird," he says, rubbing his eyes. "The road's a dead end. Who'd be coming here at this time of night?"

I yawn. "Probably tourists looking for a new place to party."

Wendell stares a moment longer, his eyebrows furrowed. "They're over near the turtles. Maybe we should warn them about the nests, tell them to stay away."

Walking all the way back there seems entirely unappealing. I tug on his hand, pulling him toward the cabanas. "Come on, let's get a little sleep before sunrise. Remember my plan? Just enjoy paradise."

Taking one last, reluctant glance in the direction of the music, he turns to follow me.

❖ ❖ ❖

After a drawn-out kiss good night, Wendell disappears into his cabana—a small, octagonal wooden structure with giant windows and a palm-frond roof. I head into my own cabana, just past his. They're nearly identical except for the starfish painted on the door of mine, the iguana on Wendell's. His parents' one condition for his staying here was that we have separate cabanas. At first I rolled my eyes, but now I'm secretly glad. I love having my own space, an entire little house to myself, even if it is just a room and bathroom. I've always had to share tiny spaces with Layla, put up with her propensity to throw silk scarves over everything—windows, lampshades, toilet tanks—but I get to decorate this place however I want. I've settled on minimalist decor—just a few carefully arranged shells and stones and pieces of driftwood.

And a jar of sand. I unscrew the lid, run the fine white grains through my fingers. My father gave me this sand. He'd saved it from the Greek beach where he fell in love with Layla—the beach he was sleeping on when, after one night together, she left him, without their ever having exchanged last names. His initials, J.C., were all she remembered. I later discovered they stand for José Cruz, which I suspect to be a fairly common name in Mexico.

I brush the sand off my fingertips back into the jar and secure the lid. Then I move on to the packet of carefully folded papers beside them. In France, he had these letters delivered, as he did with all his gifts. I untie the ribbon and flip through the letters, some crinkly and yellowed, addressed to Layla, written years ago, before I was born. Since he didn't have her address, he couldn't send them. Not until our paths crossed in France. My gaze sweeps over the words I've memorized, words that make my insides feel tender, sometimes in a good way, sometimes not. The letters are full of heartache, and grow increasingly heavy with despair. They capture my father's illness—bipolar disorder—and remind me that he can become dangerously lost in cycles of depression.

I shuffle past the older letters to the two most recent ones, written half a year ago in France and addressed to me. I glance over the words for the hundredth time, idly searching for some clue—not so much to how to find him, more to why he hasn't contacted me.

Please do not try to find me. Please just
know that you have always been loved. And

Zeeta, know that you will always have the love of a father, even if you don't know me.

I move on to the second letter, written after I continued searching for him, against his wishes:

I admire your spirit, your strength, your resolve to find me despite everything.... It's not that I don't want to be part of your life. I'm working hard to become a father who would make you proud. Please be patient. I will try to find the courage to introduce myself.

I'm tired of being patient. Part of me has the urge to crumple up the letters and throw them against the wall. Instead, I run my hands over the worn paper in a kind of prayer. I imagine a muddy speck of hope—hope that this is actually my father's hometown, for starters. The clues that led me here weren't airtight—just random memories my father shared with our mutual friend back in France. He mentioned that his childhood was colored gold from sunsets at Comet Point, that it was a famous nesting place for rare turtles. Which makes sense, since his nickname is Tortue— "turtle" in French. After online searches, I deduced that he must have been describing this little coastal village of Mazunte. But even if I'm in the right place, finding him won't be easy if he doesn't want to be found.

I press Play on the ancient CD–clock radio and my father's music begins, undulating guitar melodies that seem in sync with the waves crashing on the beach below. Undressing, I shake off the last grains of sand, then slip on pajama bottoms.

On an impulse, I pull on the threadbare black Jimi Hendrix T-shirt my father gave me. I inhale the scent of the soft fabric—the musty, salty dampness that pervades everything here, a comforting smell. I breathe in again, trying to distinguish any last traces of my father's smell, even though the shirt's been washed a dozen times. I try to conjure up his voice, its warm tenor. I spoke with him in France without realizing he was my father. If only I could picture his face—but it was always hidden under mime makeup. I wonder what his sister looks like, the one who's supposedly the mirror image of me. I try to subtract Layla's features from my own face and imagine the part of me that came from my father's genes. A frustrating task.

Finally, I crawl between the white sheets, make sure the mosquito net is tucked firmly into the mattress, and let my head fall onto the pillow. I'm just drifting off when a thundering sound makes my eyes fly open. My heart races. Am I imagining it? I listen, holding perfectly still. All I hear is my father's song and the waves and crickets and frogs outside my window. The regular rhythms of nighttime. I do some deep breathing and, after what seems like ages, manage to sink into sleep.

But when I do, my dreams are strange. A giant turtle

is crawling out of the dark surf. He transforms into a kind of merman who reaches out flippers that morph into arms. For a long time he holds me, and I let my eyes close. I feel like a little girl, sinking into his embrace, and then, when my eyes open, I find myself in a bright, dazzling world of sunshine. All night, I try to recapture that feeling, but every dream ends with me swimming in the blackest sea, searching for the turtle merman, who somehow has slipped away once again.

Chapter Three

Early the next morning, Layla makes her rounds past the cabanas, ringing a bell to wake the guests for sunrise yoga, belting out bits of mystical poetry. *"Rise with the sun. Turn away from the cave of your sleeping. That way a thorn expands to a rose. . . ."* She chooses a different verse each morning, always Rumi.

In the past, I was the one she woke up unreasonably early, but now she has our guests to keep her company in her predawn spiritual questing. I disentangle myself from my mosquito net, splash cold water on my face, and change into a sundress. I don't bother brushing my hair. Bristles won't penetrate its stiff coating of sea salt—nature's hair spray, Layla insists. Her blond hair is rapidly heading toward ropey dreadlocks. Just her style. I pull my dark hair back in a blue silk scarf and head down the path spotted with mosaics of tile fragments and sea glass.

I wind through flowering bushes and herbs to the kitchen palapa, an open-sided shelter with tables made of cross-sectioned tree trunks tucked beneath a thatched palm roof. The kitchen itself is basically a counter with a mini fridge, some shelves, and a two-burner stove. One by one, in response to Layla's bell, groggy backpackers emerge from their cabana doorways. Meanwhile, I heat water for tea and cinnamon coffee. Some of the guests need a little caffeine to make it safely down the jungle path to the beach.

Once I'm fully awake, I can appreciate this time of morning, when the air is misty and cool, the dew lingering, the sun still hidden, when the world is all green shadows and flitting birds. I perch on a stool behind the counter and take out my notebook. It's jade, my favorite shade of the ocean here, the underwater world with sun filtering through. Every year, I write in a different-colored notebook, filling it with thoughts, observations, dreams, interviews, questions, unsent letters, musings. My notebooks are what's kept me sane in my nomadic life.

I open to a fresh page, marked with a small brown bookmark made of *amate* bark, painted with a sun and moon. Another one of the mysterious gifts my father slipped me in France. I set it on the table, then write my plans for the day.

1) check on sea turtle nests

That will be the first thing Wendell wants to do, so why fight it?

2) make plan for nature paths in jungle

This will be tons of work, but I'm excited about it. It's mainly for the guests—a wild garden to enchant them, prompting them to write glowing online reviews. We need something special to set our cabanas apart from all the other rustic little resorts spotting the coast. But there's something deeper, too, I realize. Years from now, I'll walk the paths, knowing that my own sweat went into creating them. In previous countries, I've never bothered to plant anything more than potted flowers. I knew we'd be leaving before I got to see the fruits of my labor. Which reminds me . . .

3) have Layla extend contract to stay

I might feel more secure about her promise if it's in writing. She'll probably resist. She finds rules and contracts and obligations of any sort unsavory. And speaking of unsavory tasks . . .

4) finish chem homework

I rub my fingers over the fibers of my bookmark, thinking of my turtle dream last night, the elusive merman. Why try to find a man who's hiding? Maybe I shouldn't look for my father; maybe I should be content in this paradise. I can't shake the image of him lost in the water, the idea that somehow, he needs me, even if he doesn't know it. I twirl my pen, thinking.

Hesitantly, I add a fifth item to the list. My hand shakes as I write:

5) start asking around about J.C., aka José Cruz, aka Tortue, aka Dad

Whatever his reasons for not contacting me, my paradise will not be complete without my father. If he can't—or won't—find me, I'll find him. Even if it means going against his clear instructions *not* to.

I look up to see Layla returning from her rounds, gliding down the path barefoot in her white knee-length huipil—a rectangular piece of raw cotton with arm and neck holes, decorated with embroidered flowers. She's taken to wearing huipils because they're so comfortable in the heat. She looks completely at ease floating along the trail, as though she's lived here for years and not just weeks.

"Oh, thanks, love!" she says, eyeing the water I've started heating. From the rickety shelves, she plucks mismatched, chipped teacups, wetting her fingertip on her tongue and rubbing the smudges she missed last night—a hazard of dish-washing by candlelight. Luckily, there are no health department inspections here.

I stand up to help her with the coffee. *"Qué onda, güey,"* I say, which roughly translates to, "What's up, dude?" Literally, "What wave, ox?" Go figure.

She glows. "Today I'm tackling the Hummingbird cabana."

The Hummingbird cabana is the most dilapidated one, the one we saved for last for repairs. It's still uninhabitable. I thought we should tear it down and start over, but Layla has been adamant that it can be saved, just as she's felt about every other cabana. Our first day here, Layla gazed at the fourteen neglected huts lovingly and announced, "Now I know exactly how Michelangelo felt!"

"Michelangelo?" I asked doubtfully, watching a gecko scurry over the rotting wood.

"He could look at a stone and see the work of art waiting inside!" She's always fancied herself an artist, specializing in turning junk into art. "This place will be my ultimate project," she said. "Besides you, of course, love," she said, kissing my hair. "And what a perfect name . . . Cabañas Magia del Mar . . . Magic of the Sea Cabanas." A dreamy look washed over her face. "This will be the ultimate eco-resort—a refuge for anyone seeking an oasis of renewal."

She set Wendell right to work designing the website for Cabañas Magia del Mar. I offered to write the copy, but Layla said she'd do it. A good decision, actually. Instead of her description of "a haven of rustic sustainability, sensuality, and spirituality," I might have been tempted to be more direct: "Barely a step above camping, where your run-down quarters feature bugs, lizards, unmatched furniture, patched mosquito nets, no electricity, sporadic cold water, ample mildew."

After she tells me her plan for the Hummingbird cabana, I think of number three on my notebook list. "Hey, Layla, let's contact the owners of this land and extend our contract. Maybe to five years, for starters?"

"Well," she says with a sheepish smile, "I actually haven't even signed the twelve-month contract yet."

"You haven't?" I try to keep the irritation out of my voice. I should've guessed. So Layla. "We've already done all this work, and you haven't even signed the rental agreement?"

"I just arranged it all by email through the real estate agent. That's documentation." She obviously feels proud using the word *documentation*. Something she's famously terrible at, something I always have to force her to deal with so we won't be deported from our country-of-the-year.

"We need a contract, Layla," I say firmly. "Today. For five years. At least."

"Fine. I'll write the agent an email."

"Good," I say, making a mental note to keep on her about this. The only documents she's ever been able to keep track of for any length of time are our U.S. passports and American citizenship papers. And when I was old enough—around seven—she dumped the job on me.

The one piece of paper Layla treasures is her List. She began her List shortly before I was born and over the past seventeen years has been jotting down every new place recommended to her by fellow travelers.

I glance over at the List, which Layla has nailed to the wooden beam over the kitchen sink. At times this List has been the bane of my existence, reminding me of all the places Layla would uproot us to and from. But now, I appreciate the poetry of what I see. The first place on Layla's List might be—no, *will* be—the final place we live. Mazunte.

That was the final clue that led us here—the realization that my father must've been the traveler who suggested visiting this town. Layla started the list eighteen years ago, then promptly forgot who gave her the first recommendation. If only she'd recorded the names of travelers who'd recommended each place—we might've traced my father to this town years ago. It wasn't until I'd narrowed his likely hometown to Mazunte last fall that I noticed the connection.

Layla did scrawl some notes after *Mazunte: sea turtles, jade water, jungle, mole. . . .* As a kid reading this list, I wondered why moles would be an attraction. At some point, I discovered it must be *mole—MO-lay*—which travelers have told me is the world's most delicious sauce. Not surprisingly, chocolate is the main ingredient.

"Layla, have you had any *mole* here yet?"

She shakes her head. "But I want to get my hands on some. Right here in southern Mexico was the birthplace of *mole.* Cacao beans were sacred to the Maya and Aztecs. Food of the gods . . ."

She rambles on, picking up a tray with the pitchers of cream and bowls of sugar, as I flip through the pages of the List, mentally ticking off places we've lived—Senegal, Thailand, India—and noting the places we haven't. I notice, on the last page, some fresh writing, new countries that weren't there last week. Madagascar, Portugal, Mongolia. *What?* She's still adding potential new homes?

Before I can ask about it, Joe the clown straggles into the kitchen. I groan at the sight of him in a pink wig.

"Sweat of the stars," he murmurs with a slight Spanish accent, betraying his Mexican roots, despite his insistence on speaking English with us.

Layla smiles as if she knows what he's talking about.

Maybe she does. "Morning, Joe." His real name is something like Joani, but he likes to be called Joe.

I raise an eyebrow. "Sweat of the stars?"

"Another name for chocolate," he says, rubbing sleep from his eyes and adjusting his wig. How he can wear a wig in this climate is beyond me. To complete the look, he's donned a pair of baggy rainbow patchwork pants held up by orange suspenders.

His first day here, before he understood how sweltering the heat on the coast is—unlike the climate of his native Mexico City—he wore sweat-streaked clown makeup, and I briefly entertained the idea that he might be my father. After all, in France, my father's face was hidden beneath white paint, his hands inside white gloves, his hair tucked into a black skullcap. But while my father seemed gentle, timid, respectful of people's space, Joe the clown bumbles around, always in your face, droning on loudly, practically tripping over everyone's feet, an air of desperation clinging to him.

Layla hands him the tray to take out to the tables. He knows the routine. Joe arrived just a couple of days after us and immediately became enamored of Layla. Her blood must contain some secret clown-attraction potion; Joe is definitely not her first suitor of this profession. He convinced her to give him free room and board in exchange for work as the cabanas' maintenance man. Just until he could wrangle up some clown gigs, he assured us—something I honestly don't see happening, given his utter lack of talent. Apparently, he got hooked on clowning somewhere in the American Midwest, where he studied building design and learned

English. Inept clowning aside, I have to admit, despite his ridiculous attire and annoying personality, he does have skills we need—plastering, framing, roofing, repairing furniture.

"Another day and the world's still here," he says, humming under his breath as he arranges the sugar bowls and cream pitchers on the tables. A few months ago, Joe woke up feeling sure the end of the world was near. So he sold the construction business he inherited from his father in Mexico City and set off on a journey—as he tells it—to spread joy to everyone he meets during these last days of existence. His clowning is apparently tied in with the spreading of joy. Unfortunately, his obsessive rants about the Mayan prophecy—the impending destruction of the world as we know it—put a damper on his clown act.

Layla, an eternal optimist, reassures him that the completion of the cycle will be a new beginning rather than a bad ending. He counters that the world is a horrific mess, that the end is inevitable. She shrugs and says that people have always been certain their world was a horrific mess. But they find a way to tolerate the messiness and survive. "Just focus on the good stuff," she keeps telling him.

"I had another apocalyptic dream last night," Joe announces, picking up three oranges from the counter and juggling them. "Involving torrential storms of geckos."

I make a face. Once Joe gets started with his end-of-the-world prophecies, he can go on for hours. Not to mention, his juggling skills are lacking, and there are plenty of breakables in this kitchen.

When he drops the oranges, I scoop them up and wash

them off, then put them back in the bowl. Unfazed, he keeps talking about the storms of geckos. Before he can grab any more oranges, I shoot Layla a look. She hands him another tray, puts on her Rumi-quoting face, and calmly whispers, *"A white flower grows in the quietness. Let your tongue become that flower."*

Joe presses his lips together in a smile. "So wise," he murmurs. Thankfully, his tongue is quiet as a flower while he fills the tray with coffee mugs and spoons.

Meanwhile, the guests have begun trickling in. Layla greets every one with a huge smile and a *qué onda, güey*. Inappropriately street-talky, but the guests either don't understand or seem amused by the slang.

Our guests are the same breed of backpackers we've hung out with all over the world—the kind who stay in out-of-the-way places and embrace the lack of electricity and hot water. Two twentysomething Norwegian women stroll into the palapa and plunk themselves sleepily on the tree-trunk seats in front of the counter. They're followed by a blind, middle-aged Chilean named Horacio who arrived last night. Even with a guitar strapped on his back, he seems to be navigating the irregular stone path fairly well using his white cane—better than some of the hungover guests who can see, in fact. On his heels are three Australian guys in their twenties with half-open eyes; a bright-eyed American couple, who must have gone to bed early; two Canadian women who've brought their own organic herbal tea bags; and a groggy Spanish man who reeks of stale tequila. Finally, along comes a Brazilian couple, who look elegant from the time they open their eyes.

As the guests work their way through their tea and coffee, they become more chatty. By the time I've served the last person coffee and sat down again in front of my notebook, everyone is relatively perky and lost in conversation.

Joe sits beside me. "What's in that mysterious green notebook of yours?"

"Jade notebook," I correct him, trying to keep the annoyance out of my voice. There's something grating about him . . . or maybe, as Layla would contend, I just have unresolved feelings about clowns.

"Jade," he repeats. "What's in your jade notebook?"

I sigh. I might as well interview him, get it over with. I've already filled a good chunk of my notebook with interviews with our other guests. I grab a pen from my pocket and open to a fresh page. "Okay, Joe, what's your idea of perfection?"

I'm pretty sure he's going to say *Layla*, because his gaze moves right to her in response. But he thinks for a moment, then says, "Perfection is this sick, sad world ending, and a shiny new one beginning."

"Right," I say, regretting that I've given him an opening for another the end-of-the-world rant. I let him ramble on about storms and fires while I zone out and think about my own perfect world. Joe would not be in it. My perfect world would actually be pretty close to what I have now. The people I love—Wendell and Layla—in a beautiful place doing rewarding work, meeting (mostly) fascinating people.

It's like a puzzle that has come together for me, with just one piece missing—my father. Number five on my list.

"But of course," Joe is saying, "you can't have perfection without complete destruction first. Annihilating the ego. Burning up in fire until the sparkling soul is revealed."

I bite my tongue and close my notebook. "Thanks, Joe. Very interesting." I search for some reason to end the conversation. "Hey, look—everyone's heading to the beach now. You don't want to miss sunrise yoga."

Joe jumps up, his wig nearly falling off. Tripping over his baggy clown pants, he rushes in front of the others to join Layla, who's leading the motley crew through the jungle toward the beach. As they go, I catch snippets of Layla's melodic voice quoting Rumi to the eager guests. "*. . . graceful movements come from a pearl somewhere on the ocean floor. Poems reach up like spindrift and the edge of driftwood along the beach, wanting!*"

❖ ❖ ❖

After Wendell finally wakes up—somehow he can sleep through Layla's yoga bell—we eat breakfast, then head to Playa Mermejita. Sure enough, the first words out of his mouth are "Let's check on the turtle nests!" As we walk through the surf, he pauses to take photos of water birds and shells. He plans to photograph the flipper tracks leading to and from the sand-covered, egg-filled holes. And maybe, if we're lucky, a few turtles might still be straggling back to sea. The sun's already blazing, but the water's cool, lapping around our ankles and calves.

"I hope they're okay," Wendell says, twirling his camera

strap around his fingers. "Especially that giant one. She's my favorite. Like some big, wise, old grandmother, you know?"

"*Muy chida*," I agree. Another variation of "really cool." "At the rate she was going, I bet she's still flopping back to the surf."

"She does have two tons of body weight to haul around." He pauses, probably sifting through facts from all the books he's read in preparation for his internship. "She must be decades old, to be that big. It's amazing she survived through the time hunting turtles was legal."

I make a face. "Why would you hunt a turtle?"

"People eat turtle meat." He scowls. "And some people believe the eggs make men more virile."

"Ick."

The closer we get, the more animated Wendell becomes, his gestures excited, his pace quickening. "This'll be *bien padre*. The lighting's perfect for abstract sand patterns. I'll get some great shots of the flipper marks." He spreads his arms. "These leatherbacks dig three-foot-deep holes for their eggs. Then they cover them back up with their flippers. I've seen some incredible videos online." Grabbing my hand, he cries, "Hey, look, there she is, Z!"

Ahead is the giant, dark form of a turtle heading back to sea. I have to admire her. I imagine the hours it took her last night to drag her body inch by inch up the beach, to look for the perfect spot to lay her precious eggs. Now she's on her return journey, clumsily flopping her flippers, scooting back to the surf.

In the daylight, I can admire her color—deep gray,

mottled with white. Parallel ridges line her rubbery shell, and marring the surface are several deep scars. They look old; the wounds must have healed years ago, maybe decades ago. They form a distinct pattern—a rough diamond shape. I wish I could interview this turtle for my notebook, find out what stories lie behind those scars.

"This is her, right, Wendell? Your grandma turtle?"

Wendell nods, adjusting his camera settings as we move closer and station ourselves a few meters away. Then he scans the beach, puzzled. "I don't get it."

I follow his gaze. Dotting the beach are gaping holes. "Why aren't the holes covered?" I ask tentatively, sensing that something is wrong. Very wrong.

"I don't know," Wendell murmurs, looking distressed. He hands me his camera, then runs up the beach, away from the water, following the grandma turtle's tracks. When I catch up with him, he's kneeling, staring at an enormous hole. Empty. He leans over, reaching toward the bottom, sifting through the sand. "Nothing," he says, his voice barely audible. "There should be fifty or a hundred eggs. Big ones, the size of golf balls. Impossible to miss."

"What happened?" I ask, glancing around. "You think some animal dug them up and ate them?" I can't help thinking of whatever made that noise in the jungle.

Wendell doesn't seem to hear. He's studying other tracks in the sand—human footprints leading from the hole up to the jungle's edge. He follows the footprints about fifty meters to a small dirt clearing that leads to the road. As I jog after him, he puts his hands on his hips and kicks the ground. When I reach him, I see what he sees: tire tracks in the dried mud, along with a few cigarette butts.

"You think . . . ?"

He frowns. "Poachers. They must have followed the turtle tracks to the nests, then dug them up. Stolen the eggs."

I feel a pang of guilt that I prevented Wendell from checking out the noise on the beach last night. Maybe we could have stopped this.

In a hoarse voice, he says, "Let's see how much damage they did."

We run through the sand, scanning the beach. No other turtles in sight. Probably the rest completed their journey back to the sea before sunrise. But we see their tracks in the sand, parallel flipper markings, each one leading from the sea to an empty hole, then back again to the sea. And another set of prints—human ones—leading from one raided nest to another.

Racing from hole to hole, we absorb the awful truth: All the holes are empty. All the nests have been dug up and ransacked. There are no nests intact, covered in sand. No eggs left safely buried. Not a single egg remaining in any of the holes. No baby turtles will hatch.

Wendell closes his eyes, rubs his face, says nothing. He stays quiet for a long time.

Finally, I take his arm. "Hey, come on. Let's make sure Grandma Turtle makes it back. Then we'll figure out what's going on, okay?"

He gives a slight nod. There's deep sadness in his expression, but also a fierce protectiveness.

We head back to the lone turtle and watch her lumber back to the sea. She treks along, her pace so slow and patient. We're watching something ancient, I realize, a link in a chain that started millions of years ago. The next link—the eggs that should grow to be turtles—is gone. Now she doesn't seem clumsy, but tragic. Her mission has failed.

Just then, she pauses, maybe to rest. She turns her head, which is the size of a watermelon, and stares at us with her disproportionately small, half-closed eyes. And as if she's spoken to him in some silent language, Wendell responds, "We'll find whoever did this. It won't happen again. I promise."

I could swear the turtle gives the tiniest nod before moving forward once again. We watch her until she's back in the sea, engulfed by waves, swimming gracefully away. I stand up, reaching toward Wendell.

"Let's call the police," he says, taking my hand.

I squeeze his hand. "I wonder how long the poaching's been going on."

He shakes his head. "I thought volunteers guarded the beach during nesting season."

Wendell is quiet for the rest of the walk back to the cabanas. I sneak a few glances at his face, notice he's struggling to hold back tears. I lean against him, kiss his cheek. "We'll figure this out, Wendell."

There is no room for poachers in our paradise.

Chapter Four

A few hours later, I'm lying in the sunshine, an orange glow behind my eyelids, the hammock rocking me. Beneath my cheek, Wendell's chest is rising and falling with his breathing. We've just gone for a swim, and the waves linger inside me, lifting me up and down, up and down. I open an eyelid and see a droplet glistening on Wendell's skin.

"Hi," I murmur.

"Hi." Wendell's voice is a gravelly whisper, his breath hot on my neck.

I push the sand with my toe, swinging the hammock. He's been subdued all morning. "Hey, Wendell," I ask hesitantly, "are you still upset about the poaching?"

He breathes out. "Nothing more we can do about it now. The cops said they'd deal with it. And I emailed my boss at the Turtle Center." He hesitates, then says, "I don't know how to explain it, Z." He struggles to find words. "It's like it hurt me—*physically* hurt me—to see all those nests raided."

I brush a strand of hair from his face. "I should've let you go last night. I'm sorry."

"Not your fault, Z."

I kiss his cheek. "We'll make sure it doesn't happen again. These turtles will be back in a week or so to lay more eggs, right?"

He gives a slight nod.

"We'll protect them next time," I assure him.

He makes an effort to smile, changes the subject. "So, Z, what else do you have planned for us in that notebook of yours?"

"Well," I reply, trying to sound playful, "since you asked . . . I was thinking we could start looking for a certain J.C."

He doesn't look too surprised, not after our conversation last night. "You finally feel ready?"

I take a deep breath. "As ready as I'll ever be."

Wendell grazes my cheek with his fingertips. "Hey, remember the muddy speck of hope." Kissing me, he gives the hammock another push. "Let's start looking today. It'll get my mind off those turtles. At least until we hear what the cops find."

I curl against him, my arm draped over his bare waist. Our skin has darkened to nut-brown, almost indistinguishable from each other's. Strands of our long hair intermingle, mine marked by reddish highlights.

The past few weeks, inseparable from Wendell, I haven't

felt the disorientation I usually get during my first month in a new country. All this time together has made life feel like a hammock, cradling me.

I try not to think about his internship, which will start next Monday. It'll be strange to have him gone every afternoon. Of course, that's nothing, considering we'll be spending the next year and a half together, going to college together, spending our whole lives together. Yet there's a small, scared-little-kid part of me that worries about Wendell venturing out on his own. He could make his own turtle-loving friends, then drift out of my life, like nearly everyone else I've ever cared about.

Suddenly, a distant look comes over Wendell's face, as though he's staring at something invisible.

My muscles tense. I know this look. All I can do is wait for it to end. I focus on his breathing, my breathing, on the sound of the surf rushing out and in, the caws of seagulls.

After a torturously long minute, his face returns to normal. He sits up, his brows furrowed.

I touch his bare shoulder. "A vision?"

After a moment of hesitation, he nods.

"About?"

He rubs his face, squints at the sea. "You know the rules, Z."

I close my eyes, attempt to stay calm. I'm one of the only people who knows that he can catch glimpses of the future. For years, he felt helpless, frustrated, at the mercy of his visions. Then, two summers ago, in Ecuador—where Layla and I were living and where Wendell was searching for his birth family—he found someone who helped him manage his powers. The visions no longer take over his life. He's learned to let things happen without interfering. And he'll only share his visions if someone else is in danger.

"It's not—" I sputter. "I mean, you're safe, right? You'd tell me if you weren't?"

He presses his fists to his forehead, then glances at me, his eyes tired. "I don't know, Z."

I swallow hard, and despite myself, I ask, "Is it about my father?" I dig my fingernails into my palms. "You'd make an exception, right? If it was about him?"

He gives me a pained look. "Z, please. We agreed." Holding his head, he stares again at the sea.

He knows he's everything to me. He knows he needs to stay safe, above all else. Safe and with me. And he knows how much I need to find my father. He's been there himself.

"All right," I whisper, wrapping my arms around him. "I trust you."

❖　❖　❖

Later, Wendell and I trek through the jungle, immersed in green shadows and leaves and rich, dark soil and splashes of bright petals, reds and oranges, explosions of stamens and pistils. Lizards skitter here and there, and every so often an iguana shakes the leaves, crawls up a tree trunk. The humid air presses on us, dense with insect chirps and the intense smell of flowers.

We've officially embarked on the search for my father, heading toward our first destination—downtown Mazunte.

To get there, you can either take the dirt road for a kilometer or hike the shorter path through the jungle. We've opted for the jungle route, which is cooler and prettier and allows for more kissing along the way.

As we approach the Forbidden Territory, none of the usual jokes come to mind. When we pass the sign reading TRESPASSERS WILL BE CURSED I squeeze Wendell's hand, and he squeezes back.

"Want to trespass?" I whisper.

"Really? You're not a little freaked out?"

I shrug, regarding the sign. After the bone-chilling noise, it doesn't seem so much joke-worthy as irritating. And the curious part of me is tempted to forge straight into the dense vegetation, find whatever's hidden there, reclaim my paradise. "First things first," I say finally, moving past the sign. "Finding J.C."

Soon we step out of the forest onto the bright Mazunte beach. A few dozen people are scattered across the blinding sand, most sunbathing or sipping Coronas or wading in the turquoise water. Farther out, people are swimming and surfing. Older local men and women zigzag the stretch of beach, carrying their wares on their backs, chanting in nasal voices, "Hammocks!" "Necklaces!" "Skirts!"

This is the popular beach in the area, where locals and tourists alike gather. Although there are clusters of people here and there, it's far from crowded; you can easily find solitary little stretches of beach. No one seems to venture away from here to Playa Mermejita, where the leatherbacks nest.

It's less than a twenty-minute walk from here, yet people appear content where the bikinis and beer are.

"You think the locals have any idea about the poaching?" I ask.

Wendell considers this. "How would they? That beach is deserted." He steps over a giant wad of seaweed. "It's a good thing too. There's no development there, no electric lights to confuse the turtles."

"Confuse them?"

"The baby turtles always head toward light. For millions of years, the only light came from the sea—the moonlight and starlight on the water. If there were electric lights on the beach, the hatchlings would head in the wrong direction. They'd never make it to the ocean."

I grab his hand, swing it in mine. "And here I thought the no-electricity thing was just Layla's excuse to go crazy with candlelight. Now I know she's just a turtle lover at heart."

"Yup. Your dad would be proud."

"Proud?" I watch a flock of gulls that flies up as we approach and settles a safe distance ahead.

"He loves turtles, right? I mean, that's his nickname. *Tortue*. Turtle. He'd be proud of all the pro-turtle changes since he left."

I try to imagine how my father would feel, returning after so many years away. Would he feel the same sense of homecoming that I do? Would people welcome him? He left Mazunte to escape something. And he supposedly returned to become the person he wanted to be. What problems did he want to resolve, exactly? What made him leave this paradise?

We turn away from the water and head down a path between buildings to downtown Mazunte. I take a deep breath and brace myself to find the answers.

❖ ❖ ❖

Downtown Mazunte consists of a single paved street, with a few dirt roads branching off toward the beach. Wendell and I are planning to combine the father search with grocery shopping. Casually questioning market vendors seems easier than approaching strangers cold. And it will give us a chance to get to know the locals better. So far, in our whirlwind of gathering supplies and equipping the cabanas—not to mention lounging in hammocks—we haven't taken the time to talk to people, introduce ourselves as new members of the community.

"Tortillas," I say, looking at the scrap of paper holding my grocery list.

Wendell points to the *tortillería*, what must be the source of the delicious toasted-corn smell. Breathing in deep, we buy fresh tortillas from an elderly lady whose white braid is woven with a long silver ribbon. Her face is a friendly mass of wrinkles, her eyes clouded behind cataracts. Despite the oppressive heat, she wears a cardigan and a black shawl. A little radio on the table plays sad, romantic songs, all about love and loss, kisses and graves.

Suddenly, it dawns on me: *I might find my father today. Within the next few hours.* I have his name. It might be as simple as asking directions to his house. Am I ready for this?

Wendell must notice how nervous I look. "You sure you're okay, Z? We can wait—"

I shake off his question. "I'm tired of waiting, Wendell. I have to do this."

I peer toward the back of the little shop, where a younger woman collects the steaming tortillas coming out of a machine, quickly piling them on a metal stand. Meanwhile, the older woman sits behind a little wooden table covered in a flowered plastic cloth, tending to customers. She weighs a stack of tortillas on her scale, adds a few extra with a wink, and wraps them in rough pink paper. There's no one else in line, so we introduce ourselves.

She shakes our hands warmly, introduces herself as Elisa.

After some small talk about the weather, I feel more relaxed, braver. I take a deep breath and whip out my notebook. "Doña Elisa, do you happen to know a José Cruz from this area?"

She barks a laugh. "José Cruz? *Pues,* I know lots of them." She tilts her head and hands me the pink package of tortillas. "A mountain of them!" she adds with another laugh.

My stomach sinks. "Well, this José Cruz is probably around forty years old. He left for many years and only recently came back."

Doña Elisa shoots me a smile. "Now, that narrows the possibilities down to about twenty! Many men leave to work in the United States or Mexico City and then return to invest their money. Is that why your José Cruz left?"

I shrug, searching my memory for something useful. "He ended up in Europe at some point," I offer.

She nods, considering this. "Well, I suppose some do.

I've never been farther away than Mexico City, so America or Europe—it's all the same to me. Could be the moon!"

As I jot down notes, Doña Elisa asks Wendell if we're here on vacation.

"No," he says. "We're living at the Cabañas Magia del Mar near Punta Cometa."

A sudden shadow passes over her face. She presses her lips together, says nothing.

"How much do we owe you, *señora*?" I ask, filling the awkward silence.

"Eleven pesos," she answers, her voice tense. She adjusts the shawl around her shoulders, pulls it tight, as if protecting herself from a chill.

As she makes change from my twenty-peso bill, Wendell gives me a confused look.

Before we leave, Doña Elisa leans toward us and says, *"Pues,* good luck to you." She leans in farther, wraps her shawl more tightly at her neck. "And be careful up there, you two. *Tengan cuidado."*

Careful? Flustered, I lift my hand in a small wave, then turn to go, digging the shopping list from my pocket.

"Weird way to say bye," I murmur to Wendell.

"Maybe it's a custom around here," he says unconvincingly. After a silence, he eyes the list in my hand. "So, what's next, Z?"

"Fish." I turn my attention to the fishermen lining the curbs with coolers of shaved ice and freshly caught fish, all silver and rainbows in the sunlight. We stop by the cooler of an aging hippie beach bum who we've come to think of as our fish guy. On our first day here, we saw him fishing off Playa Mermejita in his little boat with peeling pink paint. Of course, Layla loves the idea of buying the most local fish possible, from "our own little piece of sea." So she insists we buy from this guy . . . but secretly, I think she just likes to patronize any disheveled vendor with such wild hair.

Finger-length dreadlocks sprout from his head like it's a crazy agave; in front, they hang in his face, hiding his eyes. His skin is a deep mahogany color, probably from the hours he spends on his boat every day. His clothes are always a mess, carelessly thrown on; half the time his T-shirts are inside out.

He greets us with a subdued smile. He's listening to music in his earphones, so I don't try to get into a long conversation.

"*Qué onda,*" I say in greeting.

He grins at my Mexican slang, and nodding at Wendell and me, echoes, "*Qué onda.*"

As he wraps my order, he asks us in a raspy voice, "How's life up there near Punta Cometa?"

"*Bien padre,*" Wendell answers.

The fish guy nods in approval at our mastery—or maybe butchery—of local slang, then hands me the package of fish. He's fairly quiet, harder to engage in conversation than Doña Elisa.

Taking the fish, I introduce myself and Wendell, and ask his name.

"*Pues*, people around here call me El Loco," he answers with a soft smile.

El Loco. The crazy guy.

I raise an eyebrow. "Any special reason why?"

"*Quién sabe,*" he says with a light in his eyes. Who knows. He tugs on one of his dreadlocks. "Maybe my hair? Or maybe my beachside mansion."

"Beachside mansion?" Wendell echoes.

Fish guy chuckles. "My old pink boat. I just turn it over at night, sleep underneath it on the beach."

Unsure how to respond, I smile, and then get to the point. "*Oiga*, do you know a José Cruz around here?"

He puts his hand to his stubbled chin. "José Cruz. I know many of them." He sweeps his arm toward the market stands. "Maybe a quarter of the men here have that name."

I swallow my disappointment and dig some pesos from my pocket to pay for the fish. "*Gracias.*"

"*Gracias, señorita.*" Then, he adds, "*Tengan cuidado, muchachos.*" Be careful, guys.

The same farewell as Elisa. Is this the first time he's said that? Or has he always ended conversations that way and I never noticed until Doña Elisa gave us the same warning? I glance at Wendell. Judging by his expression, the same questions are going through his head. "Next?" he asks.

"Meat."

We head to Carnicería Ernesto, wait in line for Don Ernesto. At least, I guess that's his name, since he's the only one we've ever seen working here. He's middle-aged and hefty, always dressed in a stained white T-shirt with his ample gut poking out over his leather belt. A small mustache grazes his upper lip like a black carpet scrap. His eyes look small, embedded in his puffy face. We usually get a backup chicken from him, since there are often a couple of guests who don't like fish. *Telenovelas* blare on the little TV hung from the wall of his little cement store. It's somewhat disconcerting to see Ernesto chopping through meat and bone with one eye glued to the crying or kissing or dying on the screen.

Despite a couple locked in an embrace on TV, his attention is fully directed to a customer now. It's a beautiful woman with a curtain of long, dark hair, wearing a black cotton huipil that just grazes her knees. She's about Layla's age, midthirties, although it's hard to tell with her face shaded by a wide-brimmed straw hat and huge sunglasses. She looks different from most local women, who joke around with vendors, their children in tow, comfortable rolls of fat around their waists, fake gold earrings and necklaces, jeans and polyester tanks, bulging plastic shopping bags.

This woman carries herself like some regal water creature—a swan or a heron—her head high, her neck long and graceful. Her fingers are laden with silver rings, her wrists and neck draped with beads of seashell and stone. With her traditional woven huipil and elaborate jewelry, she looks like the Mexican painter Frida Kahlo. It occurs to me this might be someone famous—maybe an artist or writer—on vacation.

"*Buenos días, señora,*" Don Ernesto says, keeping his eyes cast down.

"Buenos días, señor," the woman responds in a low voice.

Hardly any other words pass between them. Don Ernesto knows what the woman wants without asking. From a large bucket behind the counter, he scoops piles of raw, glistening, goopy cow organs—hearts, livers, kidneys, stomachs—and a random assortment of bloody bones. Flies are buzzing like mad. A ripe, foul smell rises from the innards, makes my stomach turn. He dumps them into three bags, each of which must weigh five kilos.

Now, I've observed plenty of people—all over the world—who immediately captivate me. Usually they exude something special, like a zest for life or generous wisdom. This woman radiates none of these qualities. In fact, she appears completely closed off, as if there's a veil between her and the rest of us.

What captivates me about her is how out of place she seems. Too elegant for her surroundings ... and for her bizarre and disgusting purchase. What on earth would a woman like this do with three bags of bovine innards and bones? My fingers are itching to open my jade notebook, grab a pen, and interview her.

With graceful movements, the woman takes the putrid bags, her arm muscles taut, and pays Don Ernesto a few bills. Then she says, *"Gracias, señor,"* in a voice barely over a whisper.

"Gracias, señora," he replies, still making no eye contact, and breathing a visible sigh of relief when she leaves.

I watch her walk away. She even limps like Frida Kahlo—who, as I recall from a movie I saw in France, was hurt in a streetcar accident. I wonder what happened to this woman.

Somehow, her uneven gait comes across as dignified, as if the limp is another accessory, suggesting some hidden tragedy.

Don Ernesto perks up considerably when she turns the corner and is out of sight. His eyes flicker to the TV screen for a moment; then he greets me with a warm smile. "Now, what can I offer you today, *señorita?*"

"Just a small gutted chicken, *por favor.*"

As he prepares the meat and wraps it in the ubiquitous rough pink paper, Wendell and I introduce ourselves, comment on how fresh the food here is, how pretty the beaches, how nice the people. After the usual chitchat, I ask, "Don Ernesto, that *señora* who bought all those cow guts—what will she do with them?"

Don Ernesto's expression becomes heavy. He shakes his head and mutters something incomprehensible.

"*¿Perdón?*" asks Wendell.

Don Ernesto's tiny eyes dart around and he warns, "Not something to talk about. Best not ask questions."

Wendell and I exchange glances. Now doesn't feel like the right time to ask about José Cruz. As Don Ernesto counts out my change, he grows more relaxed, his eyes flicking happily between us and his *telenovela*.

And then I mention that we live in the cabanas near Punta Cometa.

He looks up, alarmed, then blinks a few times and shakes his head. Handing me a few bills sticky with innards goop, he cautions, "*Tengan cuidado, muchachos.* Be careful."

I want to ask him what he means, but now other customers are lined up behind us, and Don Ernesto has already moved on to them, appearing glad to end our conversation.

Wendell and I head down the street, past a few tourist booths selling cheap T-shirts and key chains and toys—all sea turtle–themed. Here and there, stray dogs follow us for a bit, attracted to the meat, until we wave them away. Wendell and I don't say much—it's as if the vendors' paranoia has rubbed off on us, made us watch our words in public. We just shoot each other looks as we walk, limiting our conversation to the tasks at hand.

"What's next?" Wendell says, nodding at the list in my hand.

"Bread, eggs, soap, fruit." Then I add cynically, "And José Cruz."

At each shop, after introductions and small talk, we ask if the vendors know a man named José Cruz who fits my father's vague description. Everyone—the sisters at the bakery, the man at the pharmacy, and the lady selling plastic bags of eggs—has the same response as Doña Elisa and the fish guy: they joke about how many José Cruzes are in this town.

Apparently, José is by far the most popular boy's name, and the custom is to give every child a second name, which is often used instead of the first. José Antonio, José Alejandro, José Manuel, and so on. Of course, we don't even know if my José has a second name. To further complicate things, each person also has two last names—the father's family name followed by the mother's. And the Cruzes are a well-established family who've lived in the area for centuries. The name is everywhere, like weeds sprouting between cement cracks.

The pharmacist chuckles, estimating that there are probably even about a dozen people with the last name Cruz Cruz. I suppress a groan. I'd guessed José Cruz was a common name in Mexico, but this is worse than I'd imagined.

On the way to our last stop, to buy fruit, Wendell puts his arm around me, comforting me. "Hey, listen, Z. You're a seeker. Don't forget it. You'll find him."

I force a weak smile. "Seeker." That's what the name Zeta means. And so much of what I've spent my life seeking, I've found in this place—somewhere I belong, a true home. The only thing missing is my father.

We turn into the fruit shop, where we're welcomed by a young vendor, round and cheerful in a tight yellow skirt and cherry-red top. Smiling brightly with rosy balls of cheeks, she fits in with the mounds of fruit around her—mangos, pomegranates, persimmons, guavas. She offers us a slice of cantaloupe, chitchatting as she weighs our bananas and pineapples and watermelon. In her chipper voice, she asks us where we're from, how long we're here, where we're staying.

"The Cabañas Magia del Mar," I say, watching her carefully. "Near Punta Cometa."

Her eyebrows rise in alarm, and then her gaze falls to the fruit. Her smile disappears.

I study her reaction. There's no doubt—something strange is going on. Quickly, she hands us the heavy bags and bids us farewell, avoiding eye contact. Her parting words are *"Tengan cuidado."*

Chapter Five

On the way home, Wendell and I are dripping with sweat and weighed down with bags of food. The odors of raw chicken and fish mix in the heat. Ahead of us, farther uphill on the dirt road, an old barefoot woman is shuffling along at a slug's pace.

Now that we're alone, Wendell asks, "Okay, Z, what the hell's going on in this town? Why does the mention of Punta Cometa set people on edge? And what's the deal with everyone warning us to be careful?"

I hesitate, adjusting the bags in my hands. I have the same questions, naturally. I just don't want to think about them. I want our new home to be as perfect as it looks on the surface.

"Who knows," I reply with a shrug. Thankfully, I don't have to say anything else because we've nearly overtaken the old woman, who clearly needs assistance.

She's hunched over, nearly buried under the heap of woven hammocks on her shoulders. Her mouth is open and she's gasping for breath, her face damp with exertion. Up close, I realize she was one of the vendors zigzagging the beach.

"*Señora,*" Wendell says, "let me help you."

Before she can refuse, he's moved the hammocks onto his own broad shoulders.

I take the grocery bags from him and offer the woman my water bottle.

She sips, pouring the water delicately into her shriveled mouth without touching the rim. "Thank you, *muchachos,*" she says, rubbing her shoulders. After she catches her breath, she eyes us carefully. "You live up there on the hill, don't you?"

I nod. At least she already knows. I don't have to break the news that would surely freak her out too. "My mom's the new manager of Cabañas Magia del Mar."

The old lady frowns. "Good luck to you, then. And be careful."

This last warning has pushed me over the edge. "Why?" I nearly explode. "Why do people keep saying that?"

She states, as if it's a well-known fact, "*Pues,* that place is cursed."

"Cursed?" I refrain from laughing. "Cursed?" *This* is the cause of all the warnings? Some local superstition? I look at Wendell, barely suppressing my relief.

He's watching her intently, waiting for more. Is he taking her seriously?

She clucks. "No manager lasts there more than a few months."

I stare at her, absorbing this new information. A few months? "Well," I say, almost defensively, "they probably didn't have a good business plan." I start spinning explanations, as much for myself and Wendell as for the woman. "We know what we're doing. We're working hard, being innovative, and we've got this amazing website. . . ."

She shakes her head as I babble on.

Wendell, breathless now under the weight of the hammocks, interrupts. "Why exactly do you think it's cursed, *señora*?"

"How long have you been there, *muchachos*?"

"Two weeks."

"And nothing strange has happened?"

I think of the creepy noise, the poaching, the threatening signs. But I shake my head.

She shrugs. "You'll find out soon enough," she says. "Soon enough."

I glance at Wendell, but I can't read his expression.

"Here's my turnoff." She makes the sign of the cross over each of us, murmuring prayers. "May God bless you. Be careful, *muchachos*, be careful."

Wendell places the bundle of hammocks gently on her shoulders. We watch her go, and then I turn to Wendell. "She's a wee bit superstitious, huh?" I give him a sidelong look. "What do you think?"

He says nothing, staring straight ahead with an odd

expression. His eyebrows are deeply furrowed, his eyes unfocused. He's lost in his thoughts, in a memory of something.

I know this look. He's connecting this old woman's words with a vision he's had. I bite the inside of my cheek, trying to rein in my emotions. I'm not expecting him to tell me anything, but he whispers, "That vision I had in the hammock . . . it didn't make sense . . . but it gave me this feeling . . . this disturbed feeling." His voice is raw, as if he's struggling to put something wordless into words. "There were animals."

"What kind of animals?" I ask tentatively.

"They were jumbled together. Flashes of them. A jaguar. A shark. And a chicken. A dead one."

I wait for him to say more, but he's quiet. "Any chance it's *this* chicken?" I ask, holding up the shopping bag with a feeble smile.

He shakes his head. "In my vision, the chicken had feathers. But no head."

"Bizarre," I say, straining to make sense of this. And then, in a softer voice, I ask, "Are you telling me this because there's danger?"

He hesitates. "I don't know, Z. I can't tell. It's just . . . a feeling it gave me."

I gnaw on the inside of my cheek, thinking. I replay the old lady's words as we turn onto the dirt road to Cabañas Magia del Mar. Even though I don't believe in curses, and even though the heat is sweltering, a chill runs through me.

❖ ❖ ❖

Back at the cabanas, Layla's giving a tour of the grounds to some new Dutch backpacker guests. "You know, I've always wanted to go to Holland!" Layla's saying as she ushers the couple into their cabana. Noticing Wendell and me, she quickly wishes them well, hands them two keys strung on pieces of driftwood, and heads toward us.

"*¡Hola, chicos!*" she sings, greeting us with pecks on the cheeks. "Before I forget, the police called. Said they've been in touch with the Turtle Center. That they'll double the volunteers." Unfortunately, I suspect her cheeriness has something to do with a newfound fascination with Holland. A fascination I'll have to somehow stamp out.

She beams. "So, not to worry! Problem solved!"

I glance at Wendell. He doesn't look completely satisfied. "Maybe we could volunteer ourselves," he says. "Get the inside scoop. Find out what went wrong last night."

"Sure," I say. "I'm all for it."

"All night on the beach—just you and the stars and the turtles! How heavenly!" Layla clasps her hands together in delight, gets on her Rumi face. "*Don't go to sleep one night. What you most want will come to you then. Warmed by a sun inside, you'll see wonders. . . .*"

I zone out as she meanders on, until she says, "So what do you think about Holland, guys?"

My muscles tense. I speak through clenched teeth. "Holland?"

She twirls the strands of seashell beads around her neck. "Just for a visit," she says dreamily. "There are, like, a zillion bikes there!" She catches my glare, and says, "Come on, love, it's not like we're marooned on an island here. We can come and go. Regular people take vacations, you know."

I eye her suspiciously. "Did you contact the real estate agent yet?"

"Not yet, not yet. But I will." She brightens even more. "So, did you find anything out about J.C.?"

Wendell and I exchange glances. "Well," he says, "only that you can't throw a stone here without hitting a José Cruz. The town's crawling with them."

Layla looks at me expectantly, waiting for my take on it. "That's it?" she presses. "That's all you found out?"

I swallow. Looming big in my mind is the warning on everyone's lips: *Tengan cuidado.* Be careful. And the supposed curse. Which I emphatically don't believe in, but which I won't mention to Layla because she's the type who might. And I'm not giving her an excuse to pack up for Holland, land of a zillion bikes, in a few months.

Glancing at Wendell, I tell him with my eyes not to mention the curse. He seems to get it and stays quiet.

Layla tosses an arm around me. "Don't get discouraged, love. He'll turn up." Despite her flightiness and other shortcomings, she does have this innocent optimism—a characteristic that mostly annoys me, but occasionally inspires. For better or worse, Layla doesn't wear the protective mask that most people do. No, her face is wide open, ready for anything.

"Layla," I sigh, "how can you be so"—I pause, searching for the word—"sure it'll all be okay?" I finish. "I mean, how can you trust that everything won't devolve into chaos?" That's as close as I'll get to the topic of the alleged curse.

"Just take what the tide brings you, love." As if it's as easy as that—a beachcombing approach to life.

"But, Layla," I insist, "don't you worry—or at least *wonder*—what we'll find? What J.C. will be like?" Last year, Layla was worried he'd think she was a bad mother. But she's apparently let go of this concern. I study her face, searching for any trace of anxiety. "You think he'll be the perfect man, the one you've been waiting for?"

She gets on a dreamy Rumi-quoting face.

"And no Rumi!" I add quickly.

She smiles. "I'm not waiting for a man, Z. And there's no such thing as perfect. If you have no expectations, you'll be happy with whatever little treasure the ocean brings you, no matter how flawed. If J.C. and I fall in love, marvelous. If something else happens . . . well, we'll make that marvelous too."

I wonder if it's possible to put a marvelous spin on a curse.

❖   ❖   ❖

Some of Layla's optimism must've rubbed off on me. After a restless night, I wake at sunrise with a renewed sense of purpose. I'll prove the superstitions wrong and make Cabañas Magia del Mar a wild success. As Layla's bells and chants create a ruckus outside my window, I open my notebook, determined. I sketch out the plan that formed in my mind as I tossed and turned all night.

Over a quick breakfast of mangos and yogurt, I tell Wendell about my plan, which he deems *"muy padre, güey"* with a half-grin. His eyes light up. "Hey, let's bust out the machetes for this, Z!"

Ever since we discovered the machetes—left behind by former managers in the shed—he's been looking for excuses to use them. Probably a little boy's jungle fantasy come true. We grab two and head through the patch of jungle between our cabanas and Punta Cometa.

Inside the forest, it's cool and dark, like a cave of leaves and blossoms and rich soil. We sit down on a smooth rock, lean our machetes against it. I spread open my notebook, position it under a few hazy beams of sunlight that filter through the layers of leaves. We survey the two-page spread that maps out my plan for the paths, my wild garden vision.

I trace my pen over the lines, excited. "See? There'll be one main circular path with little offshoots."

"Like rays from the sun?" Wendell asks.

"Exactly!" I smile, pleased with the perfect symmetry. "And each of those rays will have a surprise at the end."

"Surprise?" He raises an eyebrow. "Like being devoured by a jungle creature?"

"Very funny." I jab my elbow into his side. "Layla will provide the art."

"Ahh." He nods knowingly. "Her famous trash sculptures."

I clear my throat. "For the guests, we'll call it found-item art." I admit I have a certain fondness for Layla's junk art.

A little tree-stump seat embedded with bits of sea glass and metal soda tops. A seaweed-hair mermaid sculpted from rotting planks and frayed, water-worn rope and faded pink and blue plastic bottles. A driftwood mobile dangling rusted cans. In theory, they ring out a peaceful melody in the breeze, but in reality, it would take a tempest to produce the slightest sound—a grating, metallic rattle.

"And listen to this part of my plan—it's *muy chido,*" I continue, excited. "One of the rays will shoot out toward the cliffs over the beach. See? There'll be an amazing view of the ocean." From my bag, I pull a big ball of twine I found in the shed. "We'll use the twine to map out the paths."

Wendell brandishes his machete. "And then we hack through the jungle?"

"Right," I say, grinning. "Indiana Jones–style."

Once we start, I realize we've got our work cut out for us. Our property is big, mostly forested, with a strip of land on the sea cliffs. On the map it looks like a square piece of cake with a large bite taken out of it—our mysterious neighbor's property. The Forbidden Territory.

First we do the circle, unraveling the twine and staking it every so often. After a couple of hours of hacking through underbrush and tying twine, we're at the end of the last ray. That's when we encounter the sign reading ¡SE DEVORAN LOS INTRUSOS! TRESPASSERS WILL BE DEVOURED!

"*Great,*" I mutter.

Wendell pauses, letting the machete fall to his side. The novelty of the tool has worn off, and now he rubs his shoulder, looking exhausted. I wipe sweat from my forehead, examining the blisters forming on my palm.

"Here, Z." He passes the water bottle to me, and I drink, then squirt my neck and arms to cool off. I open my notebook to the sketch, orienting myself.

Reluctantly, I look back at the sign. "The path should end right about there. At the sign."

"We could just make the path shorter," Wendell suggests.

I close my notebook firmly, shaking my head. "Every path from the center has to be the same length. Anyway, having a weird, scary sign within view isn't part of my vision."

Wendell considers this. "We could cover it with branches so the guests don't get freaked out. Or," he says, in a mock-serious voice, "perhaps we could replace it with a more politely worded sign, something like, 'The management would be grateful if you kindly refrained from wandering beyond this point to avoid risk of unpleasant demise. Thank you.'"

I laugh. "And you could paint it with cheery hearts and flowers." I survey the sign, wishing I could just chop it down with my machete. "This is crazy, Wendell. We've been here for weeks. And we don't even know our neighbors." Bracing myself, I take a step past the sign. "I'm going to meet them."

Wendell steps beside me. "Um, I trust your instincts, Z, but . . ." He trails off.

"What?"

"Just don't get us devoured, okay?"

"No unpleasant demise, Wendell. I promise." I hold his hand, and together we take a few more tentative steps.

About five paces in, I hear it. A low, guttural growl. A noise like the one I heard the other evening, only softer. This close, I can tell it's not from a motor or wave echoes. It's from something alive. Something big.

Clutching my machete, I survey the trees. Movement, the rustle of leaves, a flash of black and yellow. Another growl, even closer.

Wendell tugs on my hand, backing up slowly. He mouths the words *let's go*. I take a step backward as quietly as possible, with my machete poised in the air, ready to strike. At least I'm nimble with machetes. As a little kid in Guatemala, I used one to chop firewood and clear brush. But I've never used one on an animal.

I listen for another sound, but there's only silence. I breathe out and take another step backward, gripping my weapon.

And then we see it. A large, sleek, spotted beast. Its jaws open wide, revealing pointed teeth. It's some kind of wildcat. An enormous one.

Time slows. I see its muscular body lunge through the air. The solid, strong head; the smooth, gleaming fur, gold specked with black spots; the rippled legs stretched out; the sculpted haunches and waist like those of a moving, soaring statue. And rows of teeth like knives. A primal fear grips me, the terror of being prey of a bloodthirsty predator. It's as if this creature has emerged straight from a childhood nightmare. And it's headed straight for us.

Suddenly, there's a loud clang. As if in slow motion, the

wildcat drops to the jungle floor. My heart is booming, my entire body shaking. I look at Wendell, searching for some explanation.

He's the one who realizes it first. "A fence," he whispers, pulling me close. "Thank God." I peer over his shoulder, catch a glint of sunlight off wire. Slowly, through the thick foliage, I see the nearly hidden outline of the high fence topped with coiled barbed wire.

And I can make out the cat's open jaw, the gleam of its teeth, as it releases a roar that shakes the trees. We flee, leaving behind the TRESPASSERS WILL BE DEVOURED sign. Which has a completely new meaning to us now.

❖ ❖ ❖

Back at the cabanas, Layla's in the kitchen hut chopping cucumbers. At her side is Joe, in an orange wig and red rubber nose, attempting to twist and tie balloons together in the shape of what looks like a three-headed pig. The rubber squeaking sounds like a three-headed pig too.

Layla notices our panicked expressions first and drops the knife. "What's wrong?"

Breathless, still holding a machete in my shaking hand, I tell her about the wildcat that would've devoured us if not for the flimsy metal fence.

Wendell grips my other hand. When my voice falters, he picks up the story. "So the signs are actually valid warnings." He closes his eyes for a few seconds. "That animal's teeth, his jaws, his massive head. It was—it was—"

I'm at a loss for words too, so I wait for Layla's reaction.

"¡*Qué padre!*" She gives Joe an excited glance.

He looks a bit more wary, his pink balloon creation still and silent in his hands.

"Layla," I say, "it's not *padre*. It's not remotely cool to have a dangerous predator roaring at guests walking along the path."

"Oh, I don't know. They might find it thrilling." She turns to Joe. "Right?"

Of course, he agrees, but just with a slight nod. "I do have to point out," he says, clearing his throat, "this beast is a sign of things to come. The end of the world as we know it." He stares pensively at the three-headed pig in his hands. "I bet it's a jaguar. They were sacred to the ancient Maya, you know. The culture that lived here, on this very land. The culture that made the dire prediction thousands of years ago—"

"Thanks for your input, Joe," I say, and turn to my mother. "Listen, Layla. We have to do something." I open my mouth to tell her about the curse rumors; they must be related to this beast. But I bite my tongue. It's one thing to tell Layla about a wildcat prowling nearby. She's fearless when it comes to realistic dangers. Curses, on the other hand, are a different matter. Ridiculous threats of negative energy are much scarier to her than any wildcat. There's no telling how she'd respond. She's the queen of letting omens guide her choices. Three different people mention elephants in one day? Must be a sign to move to Thailand. Discover a leech on your ankle after a swim? Better quit your soul-sucking job.

If I tell her about the curse rumors, she might bail out on

our plan to stay here for good. She'd somehow twist it into evidence that we should hightail it to Holland or Mongolia.

I stiffen my jaw. "It can't be legal to own a giant wild feline. Let's report the owner to the authorities and have the creature taken away." I turn back to Layla. "And it might be helpful to have documentation that we live here—like the rental contract."

"Well, I was thinking I'd have Raúl look it over."

"Raúl?"

"You know, the lawyer from Spain."

"That guy's a lawyer?" Raúl has been lost in a tequila-and-pot-induced haze from the moment he got here. His only sober moments seem to be during sunrise yoga. But I have to admit, it does seem like a good idea to have a professional review the contract. "Try to make him do it before he hits the tequila, okay, Layla?"

"Right."

"In the meantime, I'll figure out who owns this wildcat."

"Jaguar," Joe says, resuming his awkward, squeaky balloon-twisting, torturing the freakish pig. "Definitely a jaguar."

I ignore him.

Layla tilts her head. "Why don't we pay them a visit?" Her eyes light up. "I'd love to see a jaguar up close."

The last thing I want to do is go back to the Forbidden Territory, not so soon after this encounter. Not when I'm still shaking. I try to sound composed. "First, I haven't seen any entrance from the road. Or a house. We'd have to find a safe way to get in. And second, I want to do some research before I confront someone who keeps a wildcat"—I pause and flick my eyes to Joe—"*jaguar* on their own property." Mustering up a strained smile, I conclude, "And then it's back to enjoying paradise."

But that's when it hits me. With all the adrenaline rushing through me, I forgot about it. Wendell's vision. About the jaguar.

Chapter Six

Wendell and I amble along the Mazunte beach, past the restaurant huts and palm-thatched cabanas, around clusters of swimsuit-clad sunbathers. Sweat is pouring from my scalp, dampening my light cotton dress and the swimsuit beneath it. It's nearly sunset and still sweltering.

I'm groggy from the long nap I took with Wendell in the hammock. We slept too long, worn out from our work in the jungle and the intense heat of the day. When we finally woke up, we decided to take an evening walk on the main beach to ask locals what they know about a large feline roaming the jungle.

"This jaguar," I begin, wiping a trickle of sweat from my cheek, "is it the one from your vision?"

After a pause, he nods. "I think so."

I wait for him to reassure me that the jaguar in his vision was behind a fence too.

He doesn't. Instead, he says, "I looked up jaguars online. They're native to this area, like Joe said. Only they're rare, and they usually stay well hidden, in remote places. But that animal in the jungle—it fits the description."

Biting my lip, I venture, "Any advice on what to do if you come across one?"

Wendell gives a nervous half-smile. "Don't run. Face it and back away slowly. Don't look into its eyes. Make yourself look bigger." He raises his arms, waves them around, demonstrating. "The jaguar might think twice about devouring you."

"And if that doesn't work?" I ask, not sure I want to know.

"If it attacks, you could try punching it in the nose. Poking its eyes."

A weak laugh escapes me. The image seems a little clownish, like one of Joe's attempted slapstick bits.

"But honestly?" Wendell continues matter-of-factly, "you're pretty much doomed."

"Doomed?" I swallow hard.

"Their jaws are so strong they can crush the skulls of their prey in one bite." Wendell has the scientific detachment of a nature channel narrator when he gives disturbing animal facts. But there's a twinkle in his eye that assures me he's not taking this too terribly seriously. I'm guessing—*hoping*—the jaguar in his vision didn't actually devour anyone.

I breathe deeply and focus on my surroundings—the fiery orange sky, seagulls dipping for fish over the swells, my bare feet squishing in the wet sand, cool water lapping at my ankles, the smells of fried fish and Corona with lime.

I'm searching for a new conversation topic—one that doesn't involve tooth-punctured skulls and curses—when Wendell adds, "They're one of the only predators that can crush the shells of sea turtles."

As Wendell goes on about jaguars, we approach Restaurante Tesoro Escondido—Hidden Treasure—and see that there's a volleyball game in progress on a sand court beside the restaurant. A bunch of people, mostly around our age, are diving and leaping, squealing and laughing, shaking sand from their hair. Most of them look like locals and appear to be friends, judging by the way they casually toss their arms around each other. We've passed these evening games before, and I've always been tempted to join in the fun, feel like part of this town.

"Hey!" I say, interrupting Wendell's list of jaguar prey. "Maybe they can tell us something about the jaguar's owner."

"Can't hurt to ask," he says.

Grabbing his arm, I lead him toward the court. "Let's watch the game till they take a break."

Two younger girls—about eight and ten years old—notice us and wave us over, jumping up and down. "Come on our team!"

Wendell and I give each other why-not smiles, then jog onto the court. As we get closer, I recognize some players from the families that own small local businesses. Added to the mix are a few dreadlocked hippies who sell hemp and seashell jewelry; our fish guy, El Loco, sporting his own short dreads; and the clean-cut, hair-sprayed sisters from the bakery.

They're all friendly, giving us smiles and waves. "*¡Qué onda, chavos!*"

I've played pickup volleyball in at least three countries. It's the same everywhere—all ages playing together, laughing, diving for the ball, getting sand in their hair, joking around. When I score the winning point, thanks to a setup from Wendell, our teammates shower us with hugs and high fives and triumphant slaps on the back.

Even the players on the opposing team are good sports, making fun of their own blunders. The hippie jewelry sellers give us fist bumps. "Good game, *güey*, but we'll beat you next time!" El Loco is quiet, as always, but offers us each a warm handshake.

As we all chat, I learn that the dreadlocked vendors trickled onto this beach months or even years ago, coming from all nooks of the world. Apparently they scrape together a modest living, sleeping on hammocks or under boats on the beach. It seems the locals find the hippies amusing, quirky, and harmless, overall. I admit I feel a sense of camaraderie with these nomads. They're the kind of idealistic, mellow people who've drifted in and out of my life for as long as I can remember. Layla and I have *been* them. When I was four, she put dreads in my hair; I quickly ended up with a bout of lice. After torturous hours of having nits picked from my hair, I insisted on regular showers, brushes, and barrettes.

I can almost see why Layla clings to the feeling that we're bits of seaweed floating wherever the waves take us. There's an appeal to the wandering existence, seen in a certain light.

But it's exhausting, too. And most importantly, when seaweed is miraculously washed ashore in paradise, it should know enough to stay put.

Soon the players scatter, say they'll see each other tomorrow night. Wendell and I stick around, lost in the glow of victory and new friends. A boy about our age passes around glasses of cool *agua de jamáica*—red hibiscus tea, tangy and sweet.

"Gracias," Wendell and I say at the same time.

The boy sprawls beside us, brushing sand from his chunky legs, his jiggly belly. Despite his heft, he's a fantastic volleyball player, and a generous one, always passing the ball, letting other players step into the limelight. "You two here on vacation?" he asks.

Wendell answers. "We just moved here."

"You should keep playing with us." The boy breathes on his glasses, wipes them on his swimsuit. "We're here every night."

I look at Wendell, grinning. "Sure!" we say simultaneously.

Taking a gulp of iced tea, I gather courage to ask about the jaguar. I don't want to spoil the good time, but finding out more about this beast is our whole reason for being here. Reluctantly, I offer the bit of necessary information that's sure to alarm the boy. "We live up at there." I point, and his gaze follows my finger. "In the cabanas right near Punta Cometa."

He nods, sips his red tea. He says nothing more, but his

suddenly blank expression suggests thoughts racing through his mind. Thoughts of the jaguar. Of curses.

I take a deep breath and try to act casual. "So, you happen to know who owns that jaguar?"

He looks surprised at my directness. "A *señora*," he says after a pause. "She lives up there. At the end of a footpath through the jungle. We hardly ever see her. Once in a while she stands on the cliffs of Punta Cometa. Just stands there like a statue." He motions with his chin. "Sometimes I see her in town getting food for the jaguar."

I glance at Wendell.

"Like twenty pounds of raw guts?" Wendell asks, making a face.

The boy barks a laugh, short and uncomfortable. "You've seen her, then."

I nod. "What do you think of her?"

He takes off his glasses again, rubbing them on his swim trunks. "Everyone's afraid of her," he says with a shrug. "When I was little, an older neighbor lady would watch me. She'd warn me that if I was bad, she'd let that *señora* feed me to her jaguar." He shakes his head, barks another nervous laugh. "Now she tells my sisters the same thing," he says, motioning across the court toward the girls who invited us to join.

I lean in, look directly into his eyes. "*Oye,* how come no one wants to talk about her? All they say is that the place is cursed."

"*¿La verdad?*" The truth? He flicks his eyes around.

"Adults are afraid of her too. They say she's a *bruja*—a witch. That if you make her angry, she'll put a curse on you. So people don't talk about her—at least, not to strangers." He lowers his voice. "But they say bad things have happened up there at Punta Cometa."

"Like what?" I ask, unsure whether I want to know.

"Accidents. Tragedies. Deaths."

I swallow, staring at the purple clouds smeared against the dusky sky. "Any truth to the rumors?"

"*¿Quién sabe?*" he answers. Who knows. "But I guess it's enough to scare off managers. There's a high turnover rate."

"So we've heard," I say, deflated. I take the last sip of the *agua de jamáica*. "Hey, thanks for filling us in."

Wendell nods. "We've been waiting for the straight story."

I stick out my hand. "I'm Zeeta. And this is Wendell."

"*Mucho gusto,*" the boy says with a sandy handshake. "I'm José Luís."

"José?" I raise an eyebrow. "Let me guess. Your last name is Cruz?"

He nods, grinning. "That's my second last name. My first last name is Salazar. But my friends call me Sapo."

Sapo. Toad. He does look a little like a toad, stout and wide, in a friendly way.

Overhearing our conversation, one of his sisters pipes in. "Our cousin is José Miguel Cruz Diaz," she says, pointing to a teenage boy diving into the waves.

"And another cousin is José Alfonso Cruz Cruz."

Wendell gives me a meaningful look. "Did one of the

older José Cruzes—a man in his thirties or forties—go away for a long time and come back last fall?"

I hold my breath, waiting for El Sapo's response.

He rubs his chin. "*Pues,* we have some uncles who come and go. My mom would know. You looking for someone?"

"*Sí,*" I say, trying not to sound too desperate.

The older sister points to Restaurante Tesoro Escondido. A waitress in flip-flops walks beneath the palapa, going from table to table, lighting candles. "Our family owns that place. You could ask for our mother, Cristina."

"*Gracias,*" I say, careful not to show too much enthusiasm.

One of Layla's favorite Rumi quotes involves a glass case around every human's heart. Suddenly, I'm aware of this thin, delicate globe in my own chest, something that could easily shatter. Every step closer to finding my father rattles the glass. Every step makes me want to cup my hands protectively around the fragile case.

After Wendell and I say goodbye, promising to come play again, we head back across the beach. He takes my hand, kisses it. "Sounds like a good lead, Z."

"Remember," I counter, "there are twenty zillion José Cruzes around here. It'll be a wild-goose chase."

"That's what we're best at, Z." His mouth turns up into a half-smile, and we look at each other for a while, unsaid things passing between us.

There's the knowledge that two years ago, he was where I am now, searching for his birth father. The knowledge that I might not like what I find.

"No rush, Z," he says finally. "Take the time you need."

I think he gets it, the feeling that my paradise, too, is inside a glass case—a kind of snow globe—a perfect, sheltered little world. Something I'm holding carefully in the palm of my hands, determined not to break.

"But I do have a question." He brushes a finger along my bare arm, causing goose bumps of pleasure to pop up. "*Mi amor*, will you go out to dinner with me tomorrow night?"

"At Tesoro Escondido?" I bump his hip, hard, with mine.

"Ow." Then he laughs and pulls me close and, with his lips in my sandy hair, says, "How'd you guess?"

❖ ❖ ❖

The next night, after a few hours of chem homework, I head down to the Mazunte beach with Wendell, toward the Restaurante Tesoro Escondido. On each table, a candle flame in a red glass globe flickers slightly in the breeze. We choose the seats closest to the ocean, its dark, ever-shifting hills of water laced with moon glow. Above us, glittering fairy lights are strung from the rafters of the palm-frond roof. Smells of sautéed garlic and buttery seafood and fresh lime mingle in the salty air. The breeze glides over my bare shoulders, through wisps of my hair, which I swept into a braid. I'm dressed up, for a change, wearing a cute, fairly skimpy red dress from a secondhand shop in France. Scratching my calves, I note that sand fleas and skimpy dresses don't mix well.

I peer at the surf, not far from our table, then farther down the beach that ends at the craggy rocks of Punta Cometa. Waves pound the cliffs. They make me think of the jaguar roar, and I picture the creature in midair, pouncing at us. I shiver, wishing I'd brought some kind of wrap.

Wendell's gaze follows mine. "I wonder where our grandma turtle is now," he says.

I definitely prefer to think about her instead of the jaguar. I imagine her huge body, graceful in the shadowy depths, swimming around sea fans on the ocean floor. Then I catch a glimpse of a dark form drifting alongside her, through cold waters. My father, lost. The dream image sends chills over my skin. "Somewhere out there," I say. "But she'll be back."

"Hey," Wendell says, "speaking of turtles, want to go to the Turtle Center tomorrow?"

A stab of alarm shoots through me. I'm not ready to let him go. I try to keep my voice calm. "I thought your internship didn't start for another whole week."

"Right, but I want to talk to my boss. Ask if the volunteers have seen any more poachers."

I relax. "And we need to sign up to volunteer ourselves." I can't help smiling at the thought of us spending all night on the beach with the turtles, alone under the starry sky. We can spread out a blanket on the spot we've chosen for our handfasting, have a midnight picnic. . . .

A waiter heading toward us interrupts my daydreams. It's El Sapo, who greets us with a fist bump. "*¡Qué milagro!*" What a miracle! "It's the awesome *bolibolistas*." This funny word for volleyball players makes me grin.

"*Hola*, Sapo," we say together.

"*¡Qué onda!*" he says, then asks eagerly, "You coming back for more volleyball?"

"Sure," I say, glancing at Wendell. "It was fun."

"Good, 'cause you're our lucky charm. And my sisters love you guys. They keep talking about you."

Wendell grins. "Well, tell them they're great *bolibolistas*. And that we'll play again soon."

"*¡Claro que sí!*" Of course! He nods enthusiastically. "So what else is new?"

Wendell looks at me. "We were just talking about volunteering to guard the turtles on Playa Mermejita."

El Sapo twists his face. "*Buena suerte*. I've been on the waiting list for a year. I guess everyone wants to volunteer."

Wendell tosses me a look of disappointment. "Well, that's a good thing, right? People want to protect them."

El Sapo nods, twirling his pencil. "The turtles are the reason tourists come here. Of course we want to protect them."

"You know any of the volunteers, Sapo?" Wendell ventures. "We'd like to talk to them."

With a sigh, El Sapo says, "It's weird. You'd think I'd know some of them. I know practically everyone in town. But I don't know a single volunteer."

"Weird," I agree.

El Sapo frowns. "Whoever the volunteers are, I wish they'd give someone else a turn to guard the nests. I love Playa Mermejita—it's a great beach. But the Turtle Center people make us stay away so we won't bother the turtles."

Wendell and I exchange guilty glances. So we're not even supposed to be on the beach? I have a feeling that won't keep us from going back.

El Sapo flips his notepad to a fresh page. "So what can I get you?"

We order seltzers and the daily special of fresh grilled fish with beans and rice.

"How about the lobster?" he asks. "My mom's specialty. Fresh and local. And I give a half-price discount for awesome *bolibolistas*."

Wendell and I look at each other, pleased. "Sure. *Gracias*."

Fifteen minutes later, we're digging into the lobster, which is buttery and mouthwateringly delicious. El Sapo looks thrilled at how much we're savoring it. After he clears our plates, he returns with two dishes of creamy custard in a glistening pool of caramel. "The flan's on the house."

I'm stuffed, but I can't resist. The first bite of flan melts on my tongue, sweet and smooth.

"Wow," Wendell says, promptly shoveling the rest into his mouth.

I look at El Sapo with gratitude. "Okay, we're at your mercy, Sapo. *Bolibolista* slaves."

He laughs. "I'll tell my mom you like her food."

With a subtle glance at me, Wendell says, "If she's not too busy, could we thank her ourselves?"

"Sure, I'll get her."

I grin at Wendell. "You're so smooth."

"Learned it from you," he says, devouring the last bit of flan.

A few minutes later, a woman about Layla's age emerges

from the kitchen. She's wiping her hands on a blue checked apron she wears over a sundress. Her face shines with the heat of cooking, and she smells of garlic, onion, seafood. As she comes closer, into the glow of the candlelight, the contours of her face become clear: Her almond eyes, brown and inquisitive. The heart shape of her face with its high cheekbones. Full lips moving into a warm smile.

I stare at this face, this face that is an older echo of my own.

Out of the corner of my eye, I notice Wendell looking from her to me, then back at her in disbelief. I can't tear my gaze from her. I'm used to people expressing surprise that Layla's my mother. She's fair while I'm dark. But this woman, if I said she was my mother, no one would ask questions. And it goes beyond the brown hues of our skin and hair. The arrangement of her eyes, her nose, her mouth, the curve of her chin, her cheekbones . . . it's the structure of my own face. Of course, her body's larger than mine, an ample bosom and wide hips that betray having had a few children. But her other features are eerily similar to mine. It's strange that El Sapo didn't comment on this; then again, maybe he's just used to seeing her as his mother instead of the sum of her features.

Her smile widens, and she leans over our table. "I'm glad you enjoyed my meal."

I can't seem to find words, so Wendell responds for us. "Delicious!" he raves. *"Gracias, señora."*

I nod, trying to stop myself from shaking—with nervousness or excitement, I'm not sure. I attempt to make normal conversation, despite the fact that every cell in my body is screaming that this woman and I have to be related. Taking a deep breath, I say, "I've eaten seafood all over the world, and this tops it all, *señora*."

"And your flan was incredible!" Wendell adds.

She glows. *"Pues, gracias, muchachos."*

I open my notebook and hold a pen poised, trying to keep it steady.

Wendell must sense my frazzled feelings, because he launches into the questioning. *"Señora,"* he begins, "your son tells us you know everyone in town, especially all the Cruzes."

She laughs. "Yes, there are many of us!" She smooths her apron. "I've lived here all my life, so I know everyone."

Wendell takes a sip of selzer and glances at me. I shoot him an encouraging smile. "You see, *señora*," he says, choosing his words carefully, "we're looking for a José Cruz from here. He left for Europe about twenty years ago. We met him last year in France."

"He played guitar really well," I chime in nervously. "And loved turtles."

Wendell nods. "His nickname—at least in French—is Tortue. Turtle. El Tortuga."

Cristina stares, and after a moment stammers, "I—I don't understand. You—you say you met him in France. Why are you looking for him here?"

I'm too stunned by her reaction to speak. It's not just her face that's like mine, but her expressions, too. I can see she's biting the inside of her cheek the way I do when I'm worried or scared. Her hands, at her sides, are moving slightly, her fingernails digging into her palms—what I do when I'm overwhelmed with emotion. In fact, my own nails are currently dug deep into my palms.

Wendell takes over. "Last summer, Tortue—er, José—said he was going home. We think this was his home."

Cristina says nothing, staring at the table. I bite my lip, waiting for her response. And then she bites her lip too, the mirror image of me.

"So you do know him, *señora*?" I ask, before I can stop myself.

Cristina studies my face. She must notice how alike we are.

My eyes meet Wendell's. An unspoken question passes between us: should we tell her that José is my father? Wendell is silent, obviously leaving this up to me.

My mouth opens, then closes again. I can't tell her. My father's the one who needs to share this, especially if Cristina is his family. Tears springing to my eyes, I plead, "*Por favor, señora*. We just—it's important that we find him."

"I'm sorry, *muchachos*," she says abruptly. "I can't help you." She takes a deep breath, flustered. "It was—nice meeting you," she says. "I'm glad you liked my food." She turns to go.

Wendell stands up, reaches out his arm. "*Espérese, señora,* wait, it's just that—"

"I have nothing more to say," she replies, her voice turning sharp.

And she's gone.

"She knows him," I whisper to Wendell, my voice shaking. "She knows exactly who he is." I take a sip of seltzer, feeling the fizz on my tongue. I try to focus on the cold, crisp bubbles, on Wendell's eyes through the perfect candlelight on this perfect moonlit beach.

"Definitely." Wendell studies my face. "And you do realize how alike you look, right?"

I see Cristina in silhouette back in the open kitchen, moving quickly, keeping her head down. "Wendell, remember how Tortue said I have the same face as his younger sister?"

Wendell considers this. "She'd be the right age. You think she's your aunt?"

"Maybe," I say, trying to clear my thoughts, make sense of this. "But I don't understand why she was so secretive."

After a pause, Wendell asks, "What about the problems Tortue had to face? Maybe his sister was somehow trying to protect him." Wendell gives me a long, thoughtful look. "You know, Z, even if you don't find your dad, you could at least get to know your relatives. Like El Sapo and his sisters. That's something. That would be huge."

"Maybe," I sigh. "But . . ." I trail off. I think of my snow globe paradise, the crystalline world containing my father, Wendell, Layla, and me in our home. All of us happy. If my father's not in it, there's a glaring space where he belongs. A figure missing from the otherwise perfect scene.

"What is it, Z?"

"I just—if I don't find him, I'll always wonder if he's okay out there. If he's still . . ." I swallow hard. "I'll always feel like something's missing. A part of me will always be searching."

Wendell reaches across the table, takes my hand. "Well,

your name does mean 'seeker.' Maybe you'll never stop searching."

I frown and rub my head. I look away, to the courtyard just beyond the restaurant, a tiny grove of tropical leaves and trees. Two of them have wound around each other, becoming essentially one tree.

Wendell leans across the table and kisses me. "Hey, let's not give up."

I offer him a halfhearted smile through the red-tinted candlelight. Then I ask the question I've been too scared to ask, to even write about in my notebook. It comes out in the softest whisper. "Wendell, what if my father—what if he's lost? Forever?"

"We have no reason to think that, Z."

Wendell stands up, walks over to me, holds me close. "We're doing the best we can. We need to trust that he's out there somewhere. That somehow, we'll find him."

I press my cheek to the fabric of Wendell's T-shirt. "You're right." And suddenly, I feel overwhelmed with gratitude. "I don't know what I'd do without you, Wendell."

He kisses me again, a kiss that tastes of caramel. "I feel the same about you, Z."

"I'm just so glad we won't have to say goodbye again, ever." I imagine us as two trees growing side by side, woven together, solid and inextricable. As long as we're together, I can handle anything, maybe even the worst-case scenario with my father.

Chapter Seven

Later, under the star-studded sky, I'm sitting at the edge of the bonfire, mesmerized by the leaping flames, my toes dug into the sand. Layla's voice is a background, like the rush of waves, quoting Rumi to the guests, who listen with rapt attention. *"Flowers open every night across the sky, a breathing peace and sudden flame catching."*

Meanwhile, Wendell is talking—probably about sea turtles—to the Norwegian women, who are nodding emphatically.

I look at each of the rosy, glistening faces of the backpackers around the fire, watching Layla spout Rumi. *"We are the night ocean filled with glints of light. We are the space between the fish and the moon, while we sit here together."*

People murmur and nod and stare at the sky, then the ocean, then back at Layla. She's found her calling, the perfect, ever-changing community for herself. The kinds of people who choose to stay at a place like Cabañas Magia del Mar all have bits of Layla inside them. They're obviously enchanted to be here with her, with each other. A gathering of strangers who, in a short break from their realities, play and laugh and sing and swim and do yoga and explore the mysteries of existence, with Layla as the Rumi-quoting guide. Symbiosis, that's clear from the sparkles in everyone's eyes.

Earlier, after the restaurant outing, while I was helping Layla carry wood from the shed to the bonfire pit, she asked why I was all melancholy. I explained Cristina's strange reaction, and how she looked just like me, and how, at the heart of it, I feared my father might not even be alive. *"Walk with grief like a good friend,"* she recited softly in response. *"Listen to what he says."*

So here I am, waving away woodsmoke, trying to take Rumi's advice and listen to what grief has to tell me.

Beside me, the blind Chilean man, Horacio, is playing guitar, what sounds like a folk song. His husky voice matches his rough beard, black, peppered with white and gray. I focus my attention on the guitar notes, the way his fingers move over the strings.

The image of a man playing guitar on a beach at night . . . this is how Layla described my father. And last year in France, when he slipped me the CD, I finally got to hear his haunting melodies, soul-touching and breathtaking. There are no words in the songs, but there's so much feeling conveyed in his playing. My father's French band was called

Illusion, which is fitting, because he himself was a kind of illusion. I didn't see through his illusion until it was too late and he'd already left. All I have is his music.

But I want more. I want words, his words, tender words for his daughter. He did offer me some of these back in France, words that comforted me. What kills me is that I didn't pay enough attention. I thought he was nothing more than a kind stranger. There's so much I'd want to ask him if he were here with me. Since I learned to write, I've spent my life filling notebooks with words from strangers. And now, more than anything, I want to fill them with words from my father.

Horacio finishes his song, rests his guitar on his lap, stares contentedly into nothingness. I wave away smoke and open my jade notebook, angling it so that the firelight illuminates a page. Twirling my pen, I say softly, "Hey, Horacio."

"Hey, Zeeta."

Strange that he recognized my voice. We've hardly ever spoken. "You're good with voices," I say.

"Everyone's is distinct. I recognize voices the way you recognize faces."

I think about this, how it would come in handy for me. I've heard my father's voice before, briefly, but I couldn't pick it out of a voice lineup, that's for sure. "*Oiga,* Horacio, mind if I interview you?"

"Sure," he says, tilting his head toward my voice.

I decide to start with the basics, then dig my way deeper. "Do you have any kids?"

"A daughter," he says, still facing the fire.

Something about the way he says "daughter," with so much meaning, makes me catch my breath. What if—? Then I get my thoughts back in check. *He's blind. Your father is not. Stop the wishful thinking.* I jot down *daughter.*

"And a granddaughter," he adds with a proud, grandfatherly smile.

I close my eyes. Of course he's not my father. But I know exactly what I'd want from my father if he were here. "Horacio, what's your favorite bit of fatherly wisdom?"

With an amused look, he says, "Here's what I told my daughter." He chuckles, and adds under his breath, "Even though she never actually asked for it, like you." Enunciating each word, he announces softly, "Your life will be a mess."

I blink, taken aback. "Sounds more like a curse than advice."

His fingers graze over his stubbled, fire-flushed cheek. "Twenty-five years ago, when my wife was eight months pregnant, we were in a terrible car crash. She died. Miraculously, our baby daughter survived. Little Elsa was in the hospital with me as I had surgery after surgery. They saved my life. But my head trauma was too severe. I never recovered my sight."

I swallow hard. He's paused and I feel I should say something, but I just stare at the fire, waiting for the rest.

"In the hospital, the nurses would wheel me into the newborn unit and I'd sit holding Elsa and feel how damaged we both were. She felt so fragile in my arms, so helpless, her tiny heartbeat . . ." His voice crackles with emotion. "I held her and cried for my daughter who had no mother and a blind father. Like all parents, I wanted a perfect life for my child. But of course, this was never a possibility for Elsa. From the time she entered this world, her life was a mess.

"One day, as I held her little bird body, I felt this warmth radiating from her, this strength. That's when the idea came to me. Life is a mess. My daughter would just realize it sooner than most people. So I stopped wishing for a perfect life.

"Instead, I focused on her feather-soft skin, this miracle. And I realized I wanted to travel the world with her." He laughs gruffly. "A blind man traveling the world with his motherless baby. How messy is that? But I was determined. I'd gotten a settlement from the accident, so I had the money. My mother came along for the first few years, but when Elsa was old enough, it was just the two of us. She still travels with me sometimes."

Horacio tilts his head back, as though gazing at the stars. "I'll always remember holding my little girl that day and whispering, 'Our lives will be a mess together. A beautiful mess.' His voice softens, almost inaudible now. "You know, your life will be a mess too, Zeeta."

It's as if he can look right inside to my deepest fear. "Maybe not," I say weakly, staring at the dark ocean.

"Oh, it will, sooner or later. But that doesn't mean you can't enjoy it."

I close my notebook, trying to keep my voice steady. "My life has been a mess for the past seventeen years. There's nowhere to go but neater."

He grins into the darkness. "Life can always get messier."

The next morning, I wake up to faint predawn light filtering through the screen. Layla hasn't yet rung her yoga bell, which means it's still early. Way too early to get up. I squeeze my eyes shut and press the pillow over my head, trying to slip back into sleep. But the rushing waves and buzzing insects are too loud, persistent. I turn on my right side, turn on my left, lie on my back, then on my stomach. Then I sit up in frustration.

For some reason I'm awake. Awake and feeling uneasy.

Maybe if I make some tea and write in my notebook I'll feel better. I crawl out through the gap in the mosquito net. I splash cold water on my face, exchange my nightgown for a sundress, slip on my flip-flops. I open the door, expecting the misty morning air, the fresh dew-covered leaves, the stone path leading to the kitchen hut, lined with red-blossomed hibiscus bushes.

I step outside and scream.

There in front of me is a limp, bloody chicken with its head severed, flies buzzing around it in a thick cloud. I stagger back and shut my eyes, choking on the stench. I've seen dead chickens before, butchered them myself, as a matter of fact, but this is different. It's unnatural to stumble across one on your doorstep.

Wendell calls out from the window of his cabana. "Z, you okay?"

Before I can answer, he's at his door in his boxers.

"Watch out!" I yell just in time, before he steps on his own decapitated chicken.

Warily, I glance over toward Layla's cabana, on the other side of mine. Sure enough, there's another headless chicken with an entourage of flies. A yelp flies from my mouth.

Layla pokes her head to the window. "What's happening?"

"Watch out for the dead chicken!" I shout. And then, realizing that my voice might carry to other guests, I wish I could snatch the words back. Nothing worse for business than a bunch of dead chickens lying around.

"What is all this?" Wendell murmurs, wrapping an arm around me, pushing aside my tangled hair.

"A serial chicken killer on the loose?"

Wendell studies the dead animal. "Just like in my vision," he says in a low voice. His eyes flicker to mine. "What's going on?"

I've lived in enough places where witchcraft is practiced to know what this is. "Look, Wendell." I point to the blood-spotted bones, sharp stones, twigs that form a pattern around each carcass.

"What does it mean?" he asks.

"This," I say, like a doctor pronouncing a dreaded diagnosis, "is a curse."

❖ ❖ ❖

Within minutes, Layla emerges from her cabana. Hands on her hips, she surveys the dead chicken and bones and rocks and twigs on her front stoop.

"Well?" I venture, my voice cautious.

"Well," she announces, "whoever did this has come up against the wrong people!"

Wendell raises his eyebrows.

She brushes her hands together as if washing something off. "Oh, yes indeed. If anyone's equipped to deal with negative energy, it's us, right, Zeeta?"

From the supply shed, she grabs rubber gloves, then disposes of each mess in a garbage bag. This goes fast; luckily, only mine, Layla's, and Wendell's cabanas have been victims. This might be because they're the ones clearly marked with MANAGEMENT signs, the idea being that late-arriving guests can knock on one of our doors to get their cabana keys. I never guessed the signage would make us vulnerable in this way.

Next Layla gathers all the sacred amulets and rocks she's accumulated over the years. She picks up her stash of copal incense, a bunch of clay incense pots, salt, little figurines of goddesses and statue of the Buddha, bells and crystals, gemstones and fresh flowers—her entire arsenal. Then she gets to work, chanting and singing and burning incense.

Hearing the racket, the guests trickle out of their cabanas, asking, "What's going on?" in their respective languages.

Layla calmly informs them, "Sunrise yoga has been canceled due to an attempted curse."

Joe, of course, sees this as more evidence that the earth is on the verge of complete destruction. He pins on his purple wig, muttering, "When the most loving woman in the world is victim of a curse, that's when you know the world's about to end. . . ."

Layla thrusts a bag of salt into his hand and instructs

him to scatter it along the stone paths of the cabana area. She directs the befuddled guests to pick fresh herbs from her pots—*ruda* and basil and rosemary—and teaches them chants to say while waving around bundles of leaves. Oddly enough, the guests seem more than happy to participate. I imagine them sending a flurry of emails and texts to their friends back home about how *padre* it is to dispel an actual curse.

And I imagine an addition to our website: *Another featured attraction of Cabañas Magia del Mar . . . Participate in an authentic spiritual cleaning!* We'd just have to leave out the gory bloody-poultry details, of course.

Thankfully, none of the guests have actually laid eyes on a dead chicken; that image would be hard to shake. They'll just remember the bells and incense—a kind of early-morning party.

After an hour, Layla claps her hands and, as if ending a yoga session, calls out, "Fabulous job, everyone! Now let's celebrate with breakfast!" Only Layla could turn a dead chicken incident into a festive occasion.

To put a further festive spin on the morning, Joe dons his giant shoes and does a clown routine with a rubber chicken and a fishing pole and a watermelon. The other guests carry on with their conversations, periodically tossing confused glances Joe's way. He keeps going, and when he stops and bows, people offer some polite claps, which he takes as a sign to launch into another routine using a wind-up cockroach, a hairbrush, and a can of beans.

Blocking him out, I whip up two dozen eggs for break-fast, thinking of what El Sapo said about the rumors of trag-edies, deaths, and accidents on this land. I think of all the "be carefuls" directed at us. I think of what the old lady with the hammocks said about how this place was cursed. And whether or not I believe in rumors and curses, I have a feel-ing this isn't going to be finished so easily.

Wendell heaves the watermelon from Joe's routine onto the counter and slices into it. He offers me a piece and asks in a low voice, "So, who do you think left the curse?"

I take a bite, sweet and cool. The culprit is clear to me. She may have been terrorizing previous managers with this dead-chicken-curse routine for years. "The jaguar lady," I say matter-of-factly, wiping watermelon juice from my chin.

When Wendell says nothing, I add, "You know, the woman whose signs explicitly state that trespassers will be devoured or *cursed*?"

"That would be the obvious choice," he says, deftly flick-ing seeds with the tip of the knife. "But we didn't actually trespass when the jaguar pounced. We were on our side of the fence."

"I doubt she's one to haggle over details." I take another bite. "So what's your theory?"

He finishes his piece, tosses the rind into the compost bin. "I was thinking the poachers would have a motive too. Maybe they realized we called the cops on them. If this place is unoccupied, they can poach more easily. And if that's why they're doing it, we have an extra motive to stop them." He takes a giant bowl from the shelf, and starts scooping the chopped watermelon into it.

I consider his ideas, toss a chunk of butter into the frying pan, then watch it slide and bubble. "But wouldn't the volunteers stop them anyway?"

He frowns. "Whoever was scheduled the night we were there obviously didn't show. Or wasn't doing their job. Or else was cooperating with the poachers. Or maybe they themselves were the poachers."

"You've really been thinking about this, huh?" It seems like overkill to me, this conspiracy theory stuff. For all we know, the volunteer was sick that night. I just ask, "What time should we go to the Turtle Center?"

He shrugs. "Later this morning?"

I pour in the egg mixture, watch as it slowly firms. I mentally shuffle through my plans for the day. I don't mind an excuse for putting off my world history homework. "Okay. After breakfast."

Wendell looks pleased as he sticks a spoon in the bowl of watermelon.

I whisk the eggs, adding a few pinches of salt. I don't mention that I'd still cast my vote for the jaguar lady as the guilty party. But a visit to the Turtle Center is more palatable than the other option—going into the Forbidden Territory. Of course, it's all a matter of procrastination. If we're going to run these cabanas for years, we'll have to meet the neighbor sooner or later.

❖ ❖ ❖

After washing breakfast dishes, Wendell and I walk down the dirt hill and turn right onto the paved main street. The Turtle Center is just a few blocks farther along the road. On the way, we pass Don Ernesto the butcher and Doña Elisa the tortilla lady and El Loco the dreadlocked fisherman. At first I'm worried they might hold it against us that we live on supposedly cursed land, but they each smile and nod in greeting.

El Loco even waves us over. Holding a giant conch shell out to me, he says in his rough voice, "I found this. Thought you might like it."

I take it, hold it in my hands, study the smooth pink spiral interior. "Thanks," I say, surprised.

He shrugs a shoulder, looks at us through black dreads laced with a few white hairs. "You're my new best customers. Have to keep you coming back, right?"

Wendell asks, "Hey, you happen to know where the police station is?"

"Why?" El Loco's eyebrows shoot up. "Everything all right?"

I realize that the locals have probably just been waiting for something to go wrong at our cabanas. I imagine this is how rumors spread. I give Wendell a warning glance.

He says vaguely, "Just some trouble with poaching is all." Thankfully, he doesn't mention the curse.

But El Loco lets his gaze linger, obviously concerned. "The station's just down the block," he says, pointing to a side street. Then he warns, *"Tengan cuidado."*

"Of course," I assure him as I hold the shell nervously.

Now, after the curse, these warnings have more weight behind them. They're harder to shake off.

We give him the fist bumps that the hippie beach bums around here favor, then head toward the police station.

It only takes three minutes to reach the station, a low, dirty pink cement building. Inside, there's a single room with two unfinished-wood desks and two ancient computers and a few dinged-up gray file cabinets. A single door leads back to what must be a holding cell. A fan spins and clicks overhead, making the worn curtains rise and fall.

Two officers sit at the desks, one about fifty years old, with a mustache and stout build, the other thinner, and not much older than me and Wendell. The younger one is fiddling with his cell phone—texting, maybe—and immediately drops his gaze back to his device. We stand there awkwardly until the older one gets up. "I'm Officer Contreras," he says, gesturing to two wooden chairs. "But you can call me Gerardo. What can I do for you?"

We sit down and introduce ourselves, and then I tell him about the curse and Wendell's theory that the poachers might be behind it. Wendell adds that he already reported the poaching by phone a few days ago.

Gerardo nods, jotting down notes, then turns to the younger man. "Did you file that report, Chucho?"

"Uh—yes," he answers, tucking his phone in his pocket. "Where is it?"

Chucho shuffles through papers on his desk, then opens and shuts some drawers in a file cabinet.

Gerardo presses his lips together and sighs. "When he

finds it, we'll add this latest development, *muchachos*." He stands up, shakes our hands. "Be careful up there. Lots of problems over the years up near Punta Cometa."

"Right," I say, turning to leave.

The younger one calls after us, "And if you see any more poaching, come straight here, right to me. I'm the one in charge of your case. I'm on top of it." He scrawls a number on a scrap of paper and hands it to Wendell. "Don't confront the poachers yourself," he cautions. "They could be armed and dangerous. In fact, you shouldn't even be on that beach in the first place. It's protected. You'll disturb the turtles. You could be arrested yourselves for lurking around there at night."

I bite my tongue during his little lecture. The more he talks, the less I like him. Finally, he dismisses us, then pulls out his phone to resume texting.

❖ ❖ ❖

Outside, the sun is beating down even harder now, bouncing off the stark cement buildings. I relish bits of shade from the palm trees as we make our way down the edge of the road. Soon, signs for the Turtle Center come into view. The tacky little souvenir booths multiply, each with their dangling turtle key chains, baskets of stuffed plush turtles, displays of turtle T-shirts that reek of cheap dye.

As we approach the Center, I shake off the strange atmosphere of the police station. Wendell grows excited, talking about the main part of his internship—taking photos and video footage of turtles at sea for promotional materials.

When he mentions the occasional tours of the Turtle Center grounds he'll have to give, he turns anxious, twisting the hem of his shirt around his finger.

"Want to practice on me?" I ask. "Pretend I'm a tourist in a turtle T-shirt, okay? First in English, then we'll move on to French."

"Okay," he says, a little embarrassed. "Until twenty years ago," he begins, "the whole economy of Mazunte was based on butchering turtles and getting their eggs. Then, in 1990, when the turtle protection laws went into effect, the town had to find a new way to make money. The Turtle Center was created to attract tourists looking for secluded beaches off the beaten path. And although the town's economy is better now than before, there's still money to be made on the black market by poaching and selling turtle meat and eggs. . . ."

When he reaches the end, looking at me expectantly, I assure him, "You're a natural. I'd give you a tip, a big one." I press my lips to his, a quick, salty kiss. "You're off the hook with the French version. Here we are."

At the entrance to the museum, a few people in blue shirts with white Turtle Center logos are standing and talking by the ticket booth. Wendell gives me a nervous glance, then walks up to the group and introduces himself.

One of the men lights up and reaches out his hand. "Oh, Wendell! Yes, we're thrilled you're working with us." He introduces himself as Pepe, the community outreach coordinator, Wendell's main contact.

Pepe pushes his sunglasses up onto neatly gelled hair. He's strikingly handsome, with a chiseled face and smooth skin. As he shakes our hands, his arm muscles ripple beneath a gold watch. After introductions, he takes us on a tour of the grounds, leading us past a flower garden toward a circular building. He has a friendly, easygoing manner that makes me instantly relax, forget the curse and the poachers and the sketchy police officer.

It quickly becomes evident that I'm not the only one who finds Pepe charming. We can barely make it ten steps at a time without someone slapping him on the back, giving him a fist bump, calling out his name, waving. Popular guy.

He leads us into the building, and we enter a cool, dark corridor where aquariums built into the walls are full of turtles of all shapes and sizes. While Pepe and Wendell talk, I hang back, peering through the cloudy glass at the creatures meandering through blue-green water. Wendell's Spanish has greatly improved since Ecuador two years ago, when he could barely conjugate a verb in present tense. His trip must have motivated him to study and practice back home, because now Spanish is rolling off his tongue, even faster than French did last summer.

Pepe compliments Wendell on his Spanish, then switches briefly to English to say he spent the past twenty years going back and forth between here, Mexico City, and the United States. "They hired me because of my English—so I could talk with the tourists." He winks. "But my bosses don't know how bad my English is."

"Oh, it's great," I chime in. "And that's coming from an English teacher's daughter."

He smiles modestly. "Well, my English will just get worse from here on out. I'm home to stay now. I had to leave town to find decent jobs, make money, like most men do. But now that there's this steady stream of tourists, I can stay here and make a living."

"Do you have a science background?" Wendell asks.

"Not a bit!" Pepe laughs. "Just the English. Of course I love turtles, but I'm no scientist. As community outreach coordinator, I just have to make connections, involve folks in town. That means being social, talking, shooting the breeze like we're doing now. My specialty!"

In this heavy heat, it's mind-boggling how he can look so perfectly put-together. He's clean-shaven, sporting miraculously unwrinkled clothes. Even his shoes and belt are polished. Whenever I meet a man around Layla's age who seems nice, responsible, good-looking, well-groomed—like Pepe—I can't help wanting to set them up. It's an old habit I'm trying to break, but it's practically an instinct now.

While Layla has clown radar, I have radar for good dad material. My own father would probably not show up on my radar, though. He's socially awkward, unreliable, unstable, often melancholy—few, if any, outward signs of good dad material.

Soon the conversation turns to the stolen turtle eggs. Pepe says he's been in touch with the police officer Chucho about the case. His face creases in pain at the topic, and he shakes his head mournfully. "It appears the volunteers didn't show up that night. What a tragedy. Hundreds of potential turtle lives lost. Needless to say, I fired those volunteers."

"We could take their places," Wendell offers.

Pepe gives him a hearty slap on the back. "Now, that's the spirit. I'll put both your names on the waiting list."

"Who are these volunteers, anyway?" I ask. "Maybe we could talk with them."

"Sure," he says good-naturedly. "I'll email you their names."

"Gracias," Wendell says as Pepe leads us outside into the blinding sunlight.

Flipping his sunglasses back on, Pepe points out blue pools filled with turtles. They're swimming in slow circles and crawling along the sloped edges. Wendell is able to identify most of them by sight and even describe their eating and nesting habits.

Pepe is impressed. "You've been preparing well, Wendell."

Looking pleased, Wendell thanks him.

"So where are you staying?" Pepe asks.

I tense up as Wendell says "Cabañas Magia del Mar," dreading the reaction. Everything has been going so swimmingly with Pepe, I don't want to ruin the sunny mood.

Pepe pushes his sunglasses onto his head. "Up there near the jaguar?"

Wendell nods.

"We know about the rumors," I say preemptively. "In fact,

we've already been victims of a little curse. Bloody chickens left on our doorsteps."

Pepe looks concerned. "Are you going to move into town?"

"No." I shoot him a giant smile. "We love it there. We never want to leave." I babble on, trying to erase Pepe's worried expression. "Actually, my mom and I are extending the contract to five years. Or more. Maybe someday we'll even be able to buy it."

"Well . . . ," Pepe says gently. "Just be careful up there, *muchachos*."

After a pause, Wendell asks, "What can you tell us about the owner of the jaguar?"

Pepe sighs. "Unfortunately, she has psychological problems. It's a dangerous situation. She's living up there with a predator capable of killing anyone within seconds."

Wendell says nothing, just looks at me.

Pepe rests his arm on Wendell's shoulder. "I don't mean to scare you. I just want you safe. If you decide to move to town, I'll use my contacts to help you find a place." He pulls out his cell phone, checking something. "Gotta get back to work, but feel free to wander around. Meet your colleagues."

He gives our hands warm shakes, looking at us intently. "You're my responsibility. If something happened to you . . . *pues*, I'd never forgive myself. Promise me you'll be careful. *Tengan cuidado*."

Chapter Eight

For a while, Wendell and I croon over adorable baby sea turtles in shallow pools; then we head toward a strip of beach that belongs to the Turtle Center. Across the sand, a wizened man leans against a boat, weaving a net from plant fibers. His skin is the color of a polished coconut shell, his arm muscles sinewy, his face deeply lined, his eyes hidden in the shadows of a worn baseball cap. He wears a threadbare Baltimore Orioles T-shirt and ancient dress pants—clothes that look as if they've spent years in the sun and salt and wind, faded and riddled with holes. He has a peaceful, unhurried air about him as he sets down his net and waves in greeting.

When we approach him, he squints at us, curious. *"Buenos días, muchachos."*

We introduce ourselves, and at hearing Wendell's name,

the man's face breaks into a smile. "I'm Santy." He extends a leathery hand. "Your driver. Every day, I'll be taking you out there to photograph the turtles." He gestures to the expanse of glittering wave tips. "*Oigan,* I've got nothing to do now. I could take you for a quick spin."

Minutes later, in the dazzling blue-green sea, Wendell and I are perched on the boat's bench, sporting mildewed life jackets. I shield my eyes with my hands, wishing I'd brought a hat. As we cut through the water, watching the jungle-lined shore grow smaller, we stay quiet. The motor makes it too loud to talk. When we reach a reef, Santy cuts the engine, gestures over the edge. "Plenty of fish and turtles down there."

I peer into the water, searching. A few dark forms flicker far below.

Wendell points out a school of blue fish, a sunfish darting into a reef, a swarm of tiny silvery minnows.

Santy, meanwhile, tosses out an anchor, briefly exposing a huge, ragged scar on his upper arm. I try not to stare, but I can't help it. Questions about scars nearly always lead to riveting notebook entries. "Mind if I ask you what happened to your arm, Don Santy?" I ask, pushing my windblown hair from my face.

"Well, *señorita,*" he chuckles, rubbing the scar, "that's something I don't usually tell people I've just met." His gruff, sandy voice sounds just as weathered as the rest of him. "At least not until they're safely back on shore," he adds with a twinkle in his eye.

This sounds good. Even Wendell tears his gaze from the water to look at Santy. I whip my jade notebook from my bag, open it, and take out a pen. Giving the pen a little twirl, I say, "Just taking notes."

"*Bueno, muchachos.*" Santy picks up the half-finished net, weaving the fibers with calloused fingers as he talks. "A ways back, years ago, I used to spear fish in these waters. Oh, I was just a young man then, cocky and full of myself, always plotting to make my life better." He laughs roughly. "I grew tired of living all the way out in the boondocks. Back then there were no tourists, you see. *Nada de turistas.* It was just a little backwater fishing town. *Chiquitito.*" Really tiny. He pauses to hold his finger and thumb a centimeter apart.

He resumes his weaving, so nimble he doesn't even have to look. He alternates between glancing at me, Wendell, and the sea, as if it's listening too. "For so many years, every morning, I'd swim far out with my spear, catch a few big fish, and then swim back. Same thing every day. I'd always put the fish into a bag so the sharks wouldn't smell the blood."

He pauses, letting this information sink in, looking us each in the eye before he continues. "But finally, when I saved up enough pesos, I packed my little suitcase and told everyone I was leaving for Mexico City. Oh, I was so excited. . . ." He closes his eyes, shakes his head. "And you see, that made me careless."

He stops to gauge our reactions. I admit, I'm riveted.

"On that last day," Santy says, his voice slowing down, "in the early morning, before dawn, I went out to the beach—to say *adios*, I guess." He adjusts his cap, gazes at the horizon, almost dreamily. "The moon was full. There was something about the way the moonlight was making a path to the sea . . . I decided to go out one last time. I was already far offshore when I realized I forgot the bag for my catch. Any other time I would have turned back, but that morning I felt invincible. I decided to risk it. I caught a huge dorado." He extends his hands wide, showing us the length of the fish. "I strapped it across my back, along with my spear, and headed back on that moon path." He leans toward us and whispers hoarsely, "But, you see, I was leaving a trail of blood."

After a dramatic beat, he says, "I was halfway to shore when the shark came."

At the mention of a shark, I glance at Wendell. So far, all the animals in his vision have appeared except for the shark. The jaguar, the dead chicken. Does this count as the shark? I hope so. I hope his vision just signifies a story about a shark and not an actual encounter. I raise my eyebrows in an unspoken question. Wendell gives a small shrug in response and returns his gaze to Santy.

Santy continues. "I let go of the fish and started swimming away as fast as I could." He pantomimes frenzied arm strokes. Now the tempo of his story picks up. "I hoped the shark would just grab the fish, but he came after me. I reached for my spear, but the shark was too fast." He shakes his head. "I'll never forget how he thrashed at me, his jaws open. His teeth closed on my arm and didn't let go." Santy lifts up his shirtsleeve to reveal the full extent of the damage.

"Ripped off a chunk of flesh. For a moment, he let go. But then his jaws opened again. I was thinking, *This is it, Santy.*"

I interject, "And what did you think about, in that moment?"

Santy rubs his whiskered chin. "*Pues,* in that instant, I wasn't just scared, I was sad, you see. And not sad that I'd never make it to Mexico City. No, I was sad that I wouldn't get to see these waters again. Never again." He barks an ironic laugh. "That's what was in my mind, how I'd miss these waters, these waters I'd thought I was sick of, these waters full of a lifetime of memories."

My pen is racing across the pages, trying not to miss a word.

Santy squints into the sea beneath him. His net lies on his lap, forgotten in the momentum of the story. "So I'm just taking in a last glimpse of my ocean, when *zaz!*" He slams his fist into his palm, making me jump. "Something knocks right into the shark. It's huge. The shark is as long as a man, but this thing is even longer, wider." He stretches out his arms to their full span, lets us wait in suspense for a moment.

Finally, Wendell asks, "What was it?"

"A sea turtle. Leatherback. The biggest I'd ever seen. Oh, I'd heard they could get this big—as big as a boat. But I'd never seen it." He leans in closer, his voice brimming with awe. "And I'll tell you something! That turtle fought off the shark. The shark got a few nips at its shell but then swam away."

Don Santy grabs his scarred arm theatrically. "Now I'm

clutching my wound and feeling light-headed from losing blood, and then a new panic hits me. How will I get back to shore one-handed? Without passing out? How will I fend off more sharks? Just when I decide this is the day I die after all, that turtle swims right under me. She rises, up, up, up." Don Santy motions with his arm toward the sky. "Now I'm on her back. It must have hurt her to have me hanging on, because her back was cut up from battling that shark.

"I hold on with my good arm and press my face against her. As gently as I can, *suavecito.* I tell her thank you. *Gracias, gracias, gracias.* Then my memory goes blank. Next thing I know, I'm on shore, and someone's slapping my face. A fisherman. And behind his head, the sky, all pink and red and gold. Am I in heaven? Or is it the most glorious sunrise I've ever seen? Now this man is shaking me, wrapping cloth around my arm, tying it tight. I look out to sea and say thank you to that turtle again. Thank you. Thank you for giving me a chance to be on these waters more days, more years. Thank you for giving me the chance to live the rest of my life without complaints, but with *gracia.* With grace. And gratitude."

Tears fill his eyes. "I wouldn't be here today if it weren't for that turtle. I call her Gracia."

"Did you ever see her again?" Wendell ventures, his voice cracking with emotion.

Santy nods. "*Pues,* I see her once in a while. Most leatherbacks stay far out at sea, but Gracia likes to show up from time to time. She's become famous around here." He peers into the water. "Look, there's a turtle now."

Wendell lights up. Without a word, he tears off his life vest and T-shirt and jumps overboard.

Santy lets out a whoop. "Now, this is a boy who likes turtles!"

"*Loves* turtles."

Santy and I watch Wendell swim with the turtle. It doesn't seem scared of him. It makes circles around him. Another one comes to join them, and now all three are frolicking. Wendell pops his head up for a breath, his face full of sheer delight. Then he dives under again.

Santy smiles. "Your friend has a way with turtles."

It looks fun, and I'm tempted to jump in and join them, but this is Wendell's moment. He's in his element, completely at ease with these creatures. Not to mention, Santy's shark attack story looms too fresh in my mind. Someone has to keep an eye out for circling fins.

A while later, the turtles scatter, and Wendell climbs on board. His teeth are chattering, but he's glowing, gushing in a mix of Spanish and English. "That was amazing! I can't wait to get photos! I can't believe this is my job! I mean, *qué padre!*"

Santy nods in approval. "You'll be good. You're a natural."

I wrap my arms around Wendell, warming him up and cooling myself off in the process. Santy revs the motor and steers the boat back to shore. We bounce along, leaving a trail of white foam.

Near the beach, Santy cuts the motor and we hop out, pulling the boat through the surf onto the dry sand. As I take off my life jacket, I ask, "*Oiga,* Don Santy, do you know anything about poaching at Playa Mermejita?"

He shakes his head, dismayed. "No, but that makes me sad to hear. Beautiful little beach. Still remote." He pauses, rubs his chin. "Lucky the developers haven't gotten their hands on it yet. There'd be hotels and restaurants everywhere."

"Right," Wendell agrees. "Good thing there are laws protecting it."

Santy chuckles. "Laws don't mean much here. People pay each other off, exchange favors and bribes. That's how things work in a small town. Only reason folks stopped hunting turtles was because they realized they'd make more money from tourism. And for tourism, you need the turtles. There's no development on Playa Mermejita now because the folks who own the land around there haven't let it happen. Good for them."

Bringing us back to the subject, I ask, "Any idea who the poachers could be?"

"Oh, it could be anyone." His voice drops. "You never know what people do in the dark of night." Apparently, Santy's pretty cynical about human nature. He leans against his boat, looking out to sea. "You know, I'm not the only one Gracia saved. There was a young boy. Now, this was about thirty years ago. He loved swimming with the turtles." Santy lets out a low whistle.

I settle in the sand and open my notebook again, jotting this down. The paper flaps wildly in the breeze. Wendell sits next to me, ready for another story.

Santy's scratchy voice continues. "And one day he was out near some coral reefs when he cut his foot. A deep gash. Oh, he'd heard my story—everyone in town had. He started swimming back, but sure enough, here comes a shark." With his hand, he mimes a shark cutting through the water.

"The boy remembered how a turtle had saved me. He called to the sea turtles, asked them for help. And just when that shark's about to grab him, Gracia swims up. She knocks the shark out of the way and dives underneath the boy. The boy hangs on. He feels the scars on her back—from the shark that attacked me. Shaped like this." Santy makes a giant V in the air with his finger and thumb. "And two new gashes, still raw." Now he moves his other finger and thumb to form a diamond. "Gracia swam the boy to shore."

In my notebook I do a quick sketch of a sea turtle with a diamond on its back. Suddenly, I remember the turtle Wendell and I saw. Our grandmother turtle. The one whose eggs were stolen. The diamond-shaped pattern on her back.

Shielding my eyes in the sunlight, I look up at Wendell. He gives a slight nod. Yes, it must have been Gracia!

I'm about to mention this, when Santy says, "Around here, we say that some people have a certain . . . connection to turtles." He looks deliberately at Wendell as he speaks. "Some way of communicating that others don't understand.

"There's more," Santy says, lowering his voice. "The boy swore to Gracia he'd always protect her. And sure enough, when he was a teenager, he pushed to have the Turtle Center built."

Santy shakes his head. "But a strange thing happened.

When he was your age, maybe a tad older, he was working for the Turtle Center, taking out scientists, just like I do now. Then, one day, this young man was charged with poaching turtles."

I interrupt. "But how could he poach turtles if he loved them so much?"

"Oh, he was a moody fellow, had a dark side. He ended up skipping his trial and leaving town. Went to Europe, I heard. Guess he was too ashamed. That's the last anyone's heard of him."

My pen hovers over the page, suddenly motionless. Is this a story about my father? The details fit. A man who broke from his past, left for Europe to escape something, never resolved it. The moodiness—possible bipolar disorder. Maybe his illness wasn't even diagnosed yet. Before he took meds, he might have been in pretty bad shape.

I'm trying to form a question, when Santy says, "Tragic how one mistake can ruin a life, an entire family. Gossip and rumors flew, his family was shamed. Personally, I never understood how someone could betray what he loved most. Especially a boy named El Tortuga."

Tortuga. Spanish for Turtle. My father's nickname. It must be him. I look out at the water, trying to collect my thoughts, rein in my emotions. It's dizzying. I feel as if the beach beneath me is rocking, as if I'm still on the boat. I shut my eyes tight. Wendell finds my hand, squeezes it.

My father. A man who betrayed the turtles who'd saved him. A man who shamed his family, his community. Sure, he had to deal with mental illness, but *still*. It hurts my stomach to think about. And why did he want to return? Redemption? What was he hoping to do here? Would it somehow make him a better father? And did he ever return? Or is he out there somewhere, swimming in circles?

"This Tortuga," Wendell says, squinting at Santy, "you say he never came back?"

Santy shakes his head. "If he does, there's a jail cell waiting for him."

"And his family?" I ask hesitantly, swallowing the giant lump in my throat. "Has he ever contacted them?"

"Quién sabe." Who knows. Santy lets out a long sigh. "His father swore that if he came back, he'd lead him straight to jail. The rest of his family was too pained to talk about it. They still are."

After we've said farewell to Santy, as we're walking back across the strip of beach, Wendell says gently, "What do you think, Z?"

"That my father sounds like . . ." I blink back tears, searching for the right words. *A complete jerk* is what's on the tip of my tongue.

Wendell strokes my hair and finishes my sentence for me. "A good person at heart. But maybe a depressed and confused one. One who just made a big mistake."

I force a weak smile. "You *would* give him the benefit of the doubt."

Wendell pulls me close and buries his face in my hair. "Or maybe," he adds, "your father is innocent."

Chapter Nine

Back at the cabanas, Layla's sweeping the path while Joe's practicing some sort of sock puppet routine. As we approach, she glances at us, revealing the tiniest hint of relief at the diversion from Joe's show. When I fill her in on Santy's story, she cries, "It's exactly what I told you!"

"What?"

"Your father—he's a merman! A turtle merman. That's why he can communicate with them. His special powers!"

I bury my face in my hands. "That's not the take-home message here, Layla."

Joe stuffs the sock puppets in his pockets, and turns to Layla, concerned. "And this man is still in love with you?"

She waves away his question and grabs my hand. "I think it's extraordinary, Z!" A faraway look passes over her face. "I knew I wasn't just drunk on moonlight. . . . I knew there was something . . . magical about that man."

Joe looks crushed. "You're not in love with him, are you, Layla?"

I watch her reaction, curious about this myself. Her expression doesn't give any clue to whether she might love him, or hope to love him. There's just that blissed-out smile that comes with her beachcombing approach to romance, and my father.

Ignoring Joe, she drops the broom, takes my other hand. "It's like that myth, Z! You know, where the seal transforms into a human and has a child, then goes back to the sea."

I look to Wendell for a little help. He's picked up the broom and is finishing up the sweeping, suppressing a grin. In exasperation, I say, "Layla, after decades, stories gain a magical gleam. It's a fantastical tale."

"Oh, I don't think so. You know, one of the guests—that new French guy—said that in parts of Hawaii, turtles protect children from harm in the water. Same thing! It's universal!"

I ignore her flawed attempt at logic. And I ignore the fact that just last week, I had a dream of my father as a turtle merman. I'm tired, and frustrated, and I don't care about excuses like being bipolar. My words come out unexpectedly harsh. "The point is that my father betrayed everyone who loved him. He couldn't face the consequences of his actions. Not twenty years ago and not now." I bite my cheek, holding back tears.

Wendell sets down the broom and puts his arm around me.

I force myself to continue. "I just want to be happy in our

home. Our permanent home." I turn to Wendell. "Maybe you're right. I'll get to know my other relatives here—like El Sapo's family. And if the only part of paradise that's missing is my father, I'll deal with it." Maybe if I say the words enough, I'll start to believe them.

Out of the corner of my eye, I catch Joe nodding emphatically in agreement, murmuring, "Just forget about that man."

Layla pulls me to her, wraps me in her scent of jasmine and sea salt. "I'm sorry, Z." She takes a deep breath and looks at the sky over the jungle, and I know what's coming. Rumi. *"The dark thought, the shame, the malice, meet them at the door laughing, and invite them in. Be grateful for whoever comes, because each has been sent as a guide from beyond."*

❖ ❖ ❖

One way to forget the messiness of life is to play a game, giggle a bit. For the next few days, every evening Wendell and I find ourselves on the beach court with the *bolibolistas*, laughing, diving, jumping, and losing ourselves in sand-spewn volleyball antics. These *bolibolistas'* personality quirks are quickly filling up my jade notebook. There's El Loco's understated humor and funny little bouncing dreads, the sweet bakery sisters' ever-changing crushes, the pink-faced Irish hemp jewelry seller's yodeling, Mayra's prissiness, Xochitl's tomboyishness, El Sapo's geeky athleticism and love of Japanese animé.

And all the while, I know they aren't all just strangers whose paths are briefly crossing mine. Some of these *bolibolistas* are—in all likelihood—my cousins. My cousins! I love knowing that for years we could be playing volleyball together, becoming closer, sharing stories, sharing lives. I love this. It makes me feel full.

Full enough to not obsessively fret over the messy developments in my life. It's much easier to lose myself in the simple thrills of volleyball matches. During these games, El Sapo's mother, Cristina, comes over with cups and a pitcher of something cool and sweet for the players. She always makes sure that Wendell and I are served first. Sometimes she pauses to watch the games, a thoughtful look on her face.

Today Cristina has brought us *agua de papaya*—foamy, sugary juice a light shade of orange. After I thank her, I'm about to head to the surf to cool off, when she asks softly, "Any luck finding that *señor*?"

I shake my head and sip my drink. "Look, Doña Cristina, I'm sorry we were pushy the other night. I mean, with our questions. We shouldn't have—"

She waves my words away. "Oh, don't worry about it."

"Really," I insist. "I'm sorry. José Cruz was just a man we met in France." I pause, searching for a way to phrase this, a way that isn't exactly a lie. I need to tell her something more, though, if I want to have a real friendship with her family. I have to make her feel comfortable. Then maybe one day, she can really be like an aunt to me. "He mentioned Punta Cometa," I continue slowly, "here in Oaxaca. And sea turtles. We—we thought he might be from Mazunte." Again, I hesitate.

She's hanging on my every word.

"He said something about returning home," I finish, taking another sip of my drink.

She blinks a few times, composing her thoughts. "*Pues,* I'll tell you if I hear anything, *señorita.*" Then, almost shyly, she adds, "And you will tell me, no?"

"Of course." I search her eyes, so much like mine. I notice her biting her cheek. "And please, call me Zeeta."

"*Gracias,* Zeeta." She looks like she wants to say more, but Xochitl and Mayra have run over, and they're grabbing drinks from her tray. Cristina gives us a nod, then moves on to distribute drinks.

As we sip our *agua de papaya,* Mayra adjusts her barrettes and asks eagerly, "So has she tried to kill you yet?"

Wendell and I look at each other. Who?

"*¡La bruja!*"

The witch? I pause. "You mean the jaguar lady?"

Mayra nods, her eyes wide.

"Not yet," I say, grimacing.

Folding her arms, Xochitl says authoritatively, "I heard she killed her daughter. And then her husband."

Mayra gives a solemn nod. "And kids who go on her land—she feeds them to her jaguar."

"*Sí,*" Xochitl agrees. She scratches a bug bite on her scabbed-over knee, adding, "That's how she kills people."

"Hmmm," I reply. "I'll keep that in mind if I hear any bloodcurdling screams."

Once the girls leave, distracted by their friends who've arrived, Wendell murmurs, "Somehow this doesn't get me excited about heading into the Forbidden Territory."

"We'll have to go sooner or later," I say, finishing off my *agua de papaya*. "The murderous *bruja* needs to know we'll be here for the long haul."

We're getting closer to signing the deal. Layla finally had Raúl the lawyer, in a rare sober moment, look over the contract and plans we drew up. Now she just has to meet with the owners and sign the papers, and that's it, we'll be here for five years. At least. And by then we might have enough money saved up to buy the land. Our guess is the owners will be more than happy to sign. After all, they've had to deal with such a high turnover of managers in the past.

My only concern is Layla, whether she'll back out at the last minute. Who knows what will happen if she gets cold feet, right when one of our guests tells her she simply *has* to go to Bora Bora or Timbuktu. I need to make sure Layla stays convinced that this place is perfect, despite the pesky curse and jaguar. I'm not going to mention the rumors of a child-killing witch, that's for sure.

I'm guessing we'll be stuck with this *bruja* for a long time. But in the meantime, I can at least find a way to get rid of the jaguar. Contain the mess.

❖ ❖ ❖

Sunset at Punta Cometa calls to me. I give myself excuses for not visiting my favorite place: the evening volleyball games, helping Layla with dinners, a world history test. But the real reason is this: going to Punta Cometa for sunset requires a walk through the jungle. And the last time I ventured into the jungle, the jaguar pounced. Even remembering it sends my heart racing.

Still, Punta Cometa calls to me. And I need to go alone, to think.

As I tiptoe down the path, the breeze sneaks between the thick trees, and I wrap my sarong around my shoulders. It's from Thailand, silk, woven with shiny threads the color of moonlight. I feel like a magician when I wear it, protected. It's nearly sunset, golden sunbeams angled through the trees. This hazy light makes the Forbidden Territory less menacing. Beyond the signs, I make out the pattern of wire mesh through the leaves. The gentle light reveals something almost sad about these signs, the fence, the wild animal inside.

Soon I'm walking along Comet Point, listening to my father's music on Wendell's iPod. The notes are plucked so delicately, so nimbly. The melody pulls me up, up, up, as though a wave is lifting me, and then down again. His music is like ocean currents. Most of it must be music he composed himself; I've never heard it anywhere else.

The only song I recognize is an instrumental riff on a Jimi Hendrix tune. I can supply the words to this one. *"Butterflies and zebras and moonbeams and fairy tales . . . that's all she ever thinks about, and riding with the wind . . ."* A very fitting song for Layla.

Many of the songs have a classic, romantic feel, a Spanish or Mexican flavor. I can only imagine what the words might be. Some songs are bright, sparkling like wave tips; others are shadowy, haunting, bringing to mind ocean depths. Maybe my father wrote the lively ones during a manic time, the heavy ones during a depression.

Listening to his music is kind of a bipolar experience

itself, jumping between extremes of heart-soaring and incredibly frustrating. I can't help searching for clues in the notes—clues to who he is—and wondering how someone so flawed and troubled could have made such breathtaking music.

Couples are scattered across the peninsula, facing the orange sun that's falling closer to the water by the minute. At a distance, El Loco is fishing on the cliffs; I can tell by the silhouette of his short dreads against the glowing sky. It's a mystery to me how he reached that spot, smack in the middle of rock crags. Gulls fly overhead, circling and diving for fish. And I stand on the edge, asking myself if, despite everything that's happened lately, I still want to stay here for good.

I do. The connection is stronger than ever. My body, my mind, my soul—everything comes together perfectly in this space. I watch the sun drop below the horizon, then sit for a while longer, until a cool breeze makes me shiver.

I stand up and stretch, looking around. The couples have left. Even El Loco is gone. Quickly, wrapping my shawl around my shoulders, I head toward the jungle, scrambling up the steep part in the half-light, loosening pebbles and dirt. Walking past the Forbidden Territory in the dark seems highly unappealing.

But inside the tree shadows, dusk has already fallen, an indigo blanket.

There's a rustling in the forest ahead of me. I freeze. I haven't reached the Forbidden Territory yet. It must be something harmless—a raccoon or rabbit. Or maybe Wendell. I take a tentative step forward, squinting into the dark shapes of leaves and branches.

I see the eyes first—small yellow globes staring me down. And then I make out the form of the head, the strong jaw, the sleek silhouette of its body. Light reflects off its thin whiskers, silvery in the faint glow of twilight.

The creature is just a few meters away, easily within pouncing distance. In one tiny moment, I take in every last detail—the enormous paws, the tufts of hair in its ears, the flat, feline nose, the angled ovals of its eyes boring into me. For a flicker of a moment, I'm mesmerized by its stealthy beauty, its force. It exudes mystery, embodies the night.

Then its lip curls up ever so slightly. A low growl creeps out, like the putter of an engine revving up.

The noise makes me realize the most essential fact: the jaguar is not behind the fence.

The jaguar is not behind the fence.

I hold completely still, my gaze fixed to this creature's. My heart is thrumming wildly, my mind racing. What to do, what to do. *Don't panic, Z.* Wendell's words come to me. *Make yourself appear bigger. Back up slowly. Don't make eye contact. If attacked, fight back.* I quickly avert my eyes, raise my scarf in the air, stretching my arms up and out. I brace myself for its attack, for the force of its body to slam into me. I tense my muscles, prepare my feet and hands to kick, punch its nose, poke its eyes, whatever it takes. I risk another peek at the creature's eyes. It's still staring at me. Forcing my gaze downward, I wave the scarf above my head and tiptoe backward. Another step and another.

And then, in my peripheral vision, I sense another pair of eyes. And another shape emerging from the shadows, almost imperceptibly.

My eyes flick toward the movement and rest on the slim silhouette of a woman that melts into the night. Her black dress ends above her knees; her legs are long, and she's barefoot. Her feet look oddly delicate beside the jaguar's thick paws. Her hair is as shiny black as the jaguar's spots, her eyes catlike, the whites glowing around a circle of brown with a hint of fiery gold. Her cheekbones are strong, her face wide. She's suddenly still as a statue, staring, her body lithe and taut. Wary.

The jaguar lady. *La bruja.* Even though her face was hidden by the shadow of her hat brim and sunglasses that day at the butcher's, I recognize her easily now. It's the way she holds herself with such astonishing grace.

She stops beside the creature, puts her hand on its haunches. He sits obediently. She takes another step forward and rests her hand on its sleek head. Its ears go back, and the growl turns into a purr that fades into silence.

I realize I've been holding my breath. I exhale slowly. We both stand perfectly still, staring at each other. In the fading twilight she seems like an apparition, a ghost, something conjured up by the jungle. The dream of a tree.

I notice her face glistening. Tears? Is she crying? She moves slightly and lets out a soft sob. Her hands reach toward me. I realize my arms are still high, the scarf stretched above, as though it's a parachute and I've just descended here. Slowly, I lower my arms, keeping my eyes locked on hers, aware of the jaguar seated beside her. I swallow hard, searching for words. What is she? She doesn't quite seem a person of this world. More like something my mind has created. A jaguar in the form of a woman.

I'm afraid if I say something, the moment will shatter, devolve into chaos. The jaguar will pounce. Or she will.

She takes a step toward me. Another. Another. Her voice is a husky purr, but I think I hear the word *mija*. My daughter. She's right in front of me now. It's hypnotizing, the silvery tears flowing down her cheeks, her whispered laments. *"Mi-jaaaa . . ."* Over and over. She's so close now, I'm breathing in her scent—pine, honey, roasted corn. Searching my eyes, her hand moves toward my face, cups my chin. The cool touch of her hand breaks the spell. I take a step backward, extricating myself, one eye on the jaguar at her side.

"Who are you?" I whisper in Spanish. "What do you want from me?"

At my words, her eyes grow wide. She blinks, confused, as though she's waking up. Silently, she backs up a few steps, touches the jaguar's head. The cat rises. Together, they turn and walk into the night shadows. The jaguar gives me one last look before disappearing between the trees.

I stare after them, my heart racing. "Wait!" I call out weakly.

But she's gone.

Stunned, I put my hand to my face, which she cupped so gently, so lovingly, as though I were indeed her daughter.

❖ ❖ ❖

"The thing is," I tell Wendell later, staring at pinpoints of stars, "it wasn't exactly scary. Not scary like the jaguar pouncing at us." I give the ground a push with my toe. We're lying in the hammock outside my cabana, the length of our torsos touching, our feet tangled together.

"So what was it like, then?" he asks, his face close to mine.

I search for the right words. "It was more—spooky. Like in a supernatural, ghost-story way. I mean, I'm not entirely sure this lady was real. Part of me feels like I imagined the whole thing. You know, after all those rumors. If she hadn't touched me, I would've believed she was a ghost."

Wendell cups my cheek with his hand, the precise place the woman touched my face. "You know what we have to do, right?"

Our gazes lock for a long moment. It's time. "Okay," I say, breathing out. "Let's do it. Find out what's inside the Forbidden Territory."

"When?" he whispers.

"Tomorrow." I shut my eyes. "We should bring Layla along. The more of us, the better."

And then I feel his lips on mine and his warm, solid arms pulling me closer. I press myself into him, grasping the realness of his flesh.

Chapter Ten

"La Llorona," Joe announces the next morning at breakfast. An expert eavesdropper, he's just overheard me telling Layla about the crying jaguar lady. He's like a piece of gum stuck to your shoe, impossible to peel off.

I ignore him, but Layla asks, "What's that, Joe?"

"The Weeping Woman. From a famous Mexican folktale."

"Why's she weeping?"

"For her drowned children. The children she drowned herself."

On instinct, I recoil. "Sounds messed up." But I remember what Xochitl and Mayra said—that this lady killed her own daughter and husband.

"Terribly sad," Layla sighs.

Sad isn't the word that comes to my mind. More like *creepy*. Extremely creepy.

"All over Mexico," Joe continues, authoritatively hooking his thumbs on his rainbow suspenders, "there are stories of La Llorona. She lives near rivers, bodies of water. Parents warn their children to stay away. When people hear the wind howl at night, they say it's La Llorona, calling '*Mis hijooooos. . . .*' My children . . ."

I catch my breath. The echo of the jaguar lady's words comes back to me. *Mijaaaa . . .* My daughter . . .

I shake off the shivery feeling, and say matter-of-factly, "I'm finding this woman. Today. With Wendell."

Joe stares at me as though I'm crazy.

"Of course, we'll all go together!" Layla cries. "We'll bring charms and amulets for protection." For Layla, magical tokens are cure-alls.

Joe looks unsure until Layla rests her hand on his arm. "You should come too, Joe."

"Me?" he asks doubtfully.

She beams at him. "Clowns exude positive energy."

At her words, he lights up. "Of course I'll go." Softly, he adds, "For you, Layla."

I barely restrain myself from rolling my eyes. "I'll get Wendell," I say, starting for his cabana.

I have to wait a few minutes while he gets out of bed, groggy, and throws on some clothes. Ten minutes later, when we get back to the kitchen, Layla is cheerily whipping egg whites while Joe is stirring something on the stove and doing clownish impressions.

Frustrated, I peer into the pot. Red chunks bob in deep-pink bubbling liquid. "Beets?" I give Layla a puzzled look. "You're cooking? I thought you were coming with us."

Layla beams. "Oh, we thought it would be good to bring a cake!"

"A cake?" I sputter, eyeing the bobbing beets.

"A pink one, for good heart energy. Angel food cake, pure and light. Topped with fresh whipped cream. And all dyed with beet juice."

Wendell raises an eyebrow.

Joe elaborates. "See, our plan is to gush a tidal wave of love at her." He spreads his arm wide, grinning at Layla. "The best strategy against *brujas*."

An hour and a half later, we're in the woods, on the path toward the Forbidden Territory, taking turns carrying the unwieldy pink angel food cake. Layla chatters nonstop, while Wendell and I stay quiet, on alert for the slightest sound or movement in the foliage. When we reach the fence with the first sign, TRESPASSERS WILL BE DEVOURED, Layla begins waving the incense around while Joe rings the bells. Layla hands Wendell a sack of herbs and instructs him to scatter them here and there. He complies, looking a little embarrassed.

I shift the cake in my hands. It seems to have grown heavier and bigger. Annoyed, I blink at the thick cloud of incense smoke, walking right into the trajectory of a bundle of *ruda*. I frown at Layla. "A can of pepper spray might be more effective."

"Z," Layla murmurs between chanting, "try to give good energy to this space. Open your heart and let the love pour out." She barrels off the path, into the thick of the jungle, following the perimeter of the chain-link fence and sprinkling murky green water from a jar.

Joe tosses rose petals through the fence and rambles on about jaguars, how sacred they were to the ancient Maya. Somehow he connects this fact with the jaguar lady and the impending end of the world.

Rolling my eyes, I lean against Wendell and keep scanning the fence.

Wendell squints into the mass of leaves. "There must be a gate," he says in a low voice. "The lady has to get in and out somehow, right?"

"Unless she flies over on a broomstick," I say with a wry smile.

On the other side of the fence, the leaves and trees are so dense, I can't see far. The jaguar could be crouching in there, just meters from us, waiting to pounce. I take a breath and focus on the insect songs, the birds flitting and calling, the comforting sounds of the jungle. Of course, it's not easy to block out Joe's bell-ringing and Layla's chants.

"Let's follow the fence," I suggest.

Wendell and I walk briskly and quietly, while Layla and Joe straggle behind, making a racket.

Until a noise cuts through their voices. A squawk. Shrill and loud. Then another and another. A cacophony of what sound like disturbed chickens, dozens of them. Following the commotion, we spot a henhouse. It's tucked inside its own protective wire cage within this fence. A few chickens are visible through the leaves, their white feathers bright against layers of thick foliage. Wendell and I look at each other.

"The dead chickens in the curse," I murmur. "You think this is evidence?"

"Maybe," he says slowly. "But lots of people keep chickens."

And then there's a deep purr like a roll of thunder, or a saw slicing through wood, tooth by tooth. My head snaps in the direction of the noise.

Joe stops ringing his bell.

Layla's stick of incense freezes in the air.

Another purr sounds, almost a groan, or maybe even a yawn—an animal rumble that could only come from the jaguar.

We stand motionless, waiting, listening. The only movement comes from the spiral of fragrant smoke twisting through the air. After a stretch of quiet, just insects and bird sounds, we resume our path around the fence perimeter, now with tentative steps.

Through the leaves, a tin roof glints in sunlight. "Look," I whisper, pointing with my chin.

The house is small and wooden. There's a garden in the back, with blossoming herbs and shiny red chiles and huge tomatoes. Sprawled beside a tomato plant, licking its fur casually, is the jaguar. Again, it yawns, revealing its teeth, yellowed points. I pray that the fence is strong enough to hold the creature in.

"Wow," Joe breathes.

"Wow," Layla echoes. "*Qué chido.*"

This is the first time I've seen the creature relaxed and unaware of my presence. It's beautiful, like a polished gem or wood sculpture. Its fur has the smoothness of glass. For a moment, we all stand still, transfixed. Thankfully, Joe has enough sense not to ring the gong.

Meanwhile, Wendell walks farther along the fence, treading carefully. After just a few meters, he glances back, motions for us to come. "A gate," he mouths, pointing.

The gate is held shut with a tangle of thick chains fastened by a heavy padlock. A path runs up to it through the jungle from the direction of the dirt road. And inside the gate, the trail continues to the house. With its potted flowers and blooming bushes, it looks surprisingly cheerful for the home of an alleged *bruja.*

Wendell glances around. "No buzzer or bell."

My eyes scan the gate. Nothing. Nothing but a sign that reads TRESPASSERS WILL BE ELIMINATED. Suddenly, I have the nearly irresistible urge to go back. No, *run* back. Even thinking about another jaguar encounter makes my legs weak, my hands so sweaty I nearly lose my grip on the cake platter.

"What next?" Wendell whispers.

I glance over at the big cat lolling in the sunshine. The last thing I want to do is wake it up by calling out hello.

Which is exactly what Layla does. "*¡Buenos días!*"

The jaguar leaps to its feet in one swift motion. It takes three giant bounds to the gate and hurls its body against it. The chains and locks and metal rattle. And the creature roars.

I nearly drop the cake. We all stagger backward.

"Well," Joe says shakily, wiping sweat from his face, "that's one alternative to a doorbell."

Wendell squeezes my shoulder. "You okay, Z?"

I nod, even though every instinct in my body tells me to toss the cake and run. Far away. But curiosity wins out. I force my legs to stay steady.

"Hello!" Layla calls out, unruffled by the growls from the enormous predator just meters away. "We're your neighbors!"

A movement is visible through a crack in the curtain. Then, slowly, the door creaks open.

And here she is, the jaguar woman—the murderous *bruja*—in full daylight. For the first time I have a clear view of her. Smooth, brown legs extend from beneath a short black sundress. Her arched feet are strangely elegant in red flip-flops and silver anklets. A river of satiny black hair spills over her shoulders, the stuff of shampoo commercials. Her full lips are closed, her hands graceful on the door's edge, her feline eyes boring into us.

"*¡Hola!*" Layla calls out, followed by quick introductions in Spanish. "We're your new neighbors! We're managing Cabañas Magia del Mar!"

The woman saunters toward the gate. "Meche," she says through the gate in a low voice, eyeing our bags of spiritual paraphernalia. She hugs the jaguar's neck, whispers something in his ear, and presses his haunches down beside her.

Layla sparkles. *"¡Mucho gusto, Meche!"* Good to meet you!

When Meche doesn't answer, Layla goes on. "We brought you a cake, pink angel food! Made with all-natural beet dye!"

Meche looks at the cake in my hands but makes no move to open the gate. Gratefully, I set down the platter and back away, as if she herself is a wild animal.

Although Meche hasn't asked, Layla says, "Oh, things are going wonderfully for us. It's such a magical place, isn't it? I lead yoga every morning at sunrise on the beach. You should join us sometime!" Layla rambles on as Meche stands there, impassive.

Even in her own home, this woman maintains a distinct aloofness. The only cracks in her façade are the glances she sneaks at me. I try not to meet her eyes, looking down at the soil, then over her head at the sky, then at the lonely pink cake with its droopy whipped-cream topping, then at the jaguar. Anywhere but at her beautiful, disturbing eyes. They remind me too much of our encounter last night.

She asks no questions; no *Why are you toting bells and incense?* or *Why is that man wearing a blue wig?* After waiting a polite moment for Meche to volunteer information about herself, Layla gets even more direct. "So you live here?"

Meche gives a slight nod.

"Just you?" Layla pushes.

Another nod.

Joe takes a stab at casual conversation, explaining his wig, his calling to travel the world spreading joy as a clown before the end of the world. He's obviously nervous, but I have to give him credit for trying. And at least he hasn't tried doing a juggling routine to break the ice.

Meche gives another nearly imperceptible nod. Every few seconds, she glances in my direction.

"So tell us," says Layla, "how did you end up living with a jaguar?" She's never had qualms mentioning the elephant in the room.

Meche kisses its head, smoothes its fur. "He's Gatito."

Wendell shoots me a confused look. "Kitty?" he whispers in English.

I nod, just as bewildered. Kitty is the last name I would've guessed.

"It's a baby?" Joe asks, unconvinced.

"Oh, no. It's just that—I've had Gatito since he was a kitten."

"So jaguar pets are legal here?" Layla asks.

I suck in my breath, hoping Meche won't take this as a confrontation. The last thing I want to do is provoke an alleged *bruja* with a pet jaguar.

She shakes her head. "Gatito had been poached. He was being sold on the black market." Her voice is so low, I have to strain to hear.

After a pause, she continues. "I bought him so I could bring him to a wildlife sanctuary." Another silence.

"And then?" Layla prompts.

Meche's voice grows quieter still. I crane my head forward to catch her words. "We discovered he—he had a health problem. His kidneys. The vet didn't think he'd live long." Her voice trembles. "They didn't have resources at the sanctuary to care for him. They would have put him down. So I volunteered to nurse him." Something close to a smile passes across her face. "It's been ten years and my baby's still alive."

It's this unexpected tenderness that gives me courage to address the other elephant in the room. I swallow hard and keep my voice casual. "I saw you and—Gatito—on a walk last night."

She stares at me, her bottom lip quivering. Finally, she blinks and says, "I should prepare food for my kitten now. He gets grumpy when he's hungry." Abruptly, she turns and disappears into the house. Gatito lies down just outside the door, licking his chops. Our cake sits untouched on this side of the fence.

After a stunned moment, Layla says, "I bet she's waiting for us to leave before she takes the cake."

I'm doubtful, but I don't feel like carrying it all the way back to the cabanas. Not to mention, the cake is the least of my concerns. As we tromp along the fence, Gatito watches us but thankfully stays put.

Once we're well out of earshot, Joe lets out a low whistle. "I wasn't expecting her to be so . . . pretty." Quickly, he adds, "But not as pretty as you, Layla."

"I couldn't get a handle on her," Layla says thoughtfully. "Usually I get vibes, but she was closed off." She lets out a breath. "Maybe she's lonely. She probably just needs time to warm up around new people. Hey, let's invite her over for dinner! Or a bonfire."

"What do you think, Z?" Wendell asks under his breath.

My mind is buzzing. "For starters, Meche's our prime suspect for leaving the dead chicken curse. Second, no matter how much she dotes on this jaguar, he's not good for our business. And third, the way she kept looking at me was . . . *weird*."

Wendell processes this, running his fingers along the fence. "So what's our next move?" He shoots an amused look at Layla and Joe, who are already burning incense and scattering herbs. "Besides gushing love and pink things?"

"Well," I begin, "I don't believe in witches. Or curses. But I do believe in strange neighbors. In this case, one who doesn't want anyone interfering with her bizarre pet relationship."

"She seems to really love him," Wendell says, grinning. "It's cute."

"Now you're getting all sweet and cuddly too?"

He tosses an arm around my shoulders. "Maybe Kitty's harmless." He suppresses a smile. "As long as he gets his five pounds of cow guts a week."

I cross my arms. "And what happens when our guests run into Gatito? What would they say on the review websites? Paradise . . . except for the deadly predator that gets grumpy when he's hungry?"

My heart starts racing just imagining this disaster. Anything further jeopardizing my home in paradise is nothing to joke about. I turn to Wendell. "We have to find out more about Meche. We have to get rid of that jaguar."

Chapter Eleven

I've never been the clingy girlfriend type. I've always been comfortable on my own, navigating my way through life. But after this taste of being so close to Wendell, I can hardly remember how my life felt before.

The thought of him starting his internship today stirs up melodramatic feelings. Ridiculous feelings. Feelings I'm embarrassed to have. It's not like he'll even be gone nine to five, just for a few hours in the afternoon. But as I walk with Wendell to the Turtle Center to see him off on his first day of work, I admit, I cling to him.

We're passing the tacky souvenir booths as he tells me his schedule: he'll be going out on the boat every day with Santy, taking underwater photos and video footage for promotion and exhibits. On an as-needed basis, he'll guide English- and French-speaking tourists around the aquariums and pools on the grounds. He's nervous in an endearing way—his hair neatly braided, his blue Turtle Center shirt looking humorously official over his worn swim trunks, his new waterproof camera strapped around his neck.

"You'll do great," I assure him. I don't say a word about this lonely feeling that's come over me, this black hole of four hours without him looming ahead.

When we reach the gates to the Turtle Center, Wendell waves to the guard and asks for Pepe.

"You get to work with Pepe?" the guard says, instantly warming to us. "Great guy. He's right over there." He points to a cluster of informational signs.

I walk right in beside Wendell, thankful that the guard doesn't mind me tagging along. I'm still not quite ready to say goodbye.

Tourists are crowded around Pepe, laughing appreciatively at a joke. When he catches sight of Wendell, he holds up a finger, then walks over to us. "Zeeta! Wendell!" he says, offering friendly handshakes. "How's everything up near Punta Cometa?"

Wendell's forehead wrinkles. "Have the volunteers seen any more poachers on Mermejita?"

"Not one," Pepe says, patting Wendell on the shoulder.

"Good," Wendell replies, obviously relieved. "We've been staying away from the beach. Don't want to disturb the nests."

I know it hasn't been easy for Wendell to stay off Playa Mermejita, with the turtles so close. But his desire to leave them in peace has won out. So far, at least.

"Great," Pepe says, and tells us to head over to the boat.

After our goodbyes, we find Santy leaning against his boat, weaving his net by the surf.

"*Buenas tardes,* Zeeta," he says cheerily.

I return the greeting, pleased he remembers my name.

"You coming out with us?" he asks.

Of course I want to, but that would push me too far into clingy girlfriend territory. "No," I force myself to say. "I have work to do at the cabanas." For a moment, I wallow in silly self-pity, thinking about the four lonely hours ahead of me. Just me and the jaguar, I think ruefully.

"See you in a few," Wendell says, giving me a peck goodbye. He starts helping Santy drag the boat into the water. I stay on the beach, watching the white boat grow smaller, until it's a distant pinpoint in the vast ocean.

❖ ❖ ❖

Feeling oddly empty and thirsty, I decide to swing by Restaurante Tesoro Escondido on the way home. The restaurant is deserted now, at this time between lunch and dinner. El Sapo's perched on a table, intent on his sketchpad of manga cartoons.

He lights up when he sees me. "Zeeta!"

I order an *agua de horchata*—blended rice-cinnamon water—and ask him to join me. He pours us both drinks, and as we sip, we talk. I might as well accomplish something this afternoon, I decide. And number one on my list is the jaguar. "*Oye,* Sapo," I say. "Have any ideas how we can make Meche get rid of her jaguar?"

"Meche?" He pauses. "Oh, you mean the *bruja*." After

some thought, he says, "I guess you could call the police, see if she's violating any laws." He looks around, moves his head closer to mine. "But to tell the truth, I think the cops are scared of her too. They don't want her to curse them in retaliation."

I grin. "Um, honestly? I wasn't too impressed with the cops here anyway."

He laughs. "Chucho and Gerardo. They're goofs. Of course, their salaries are supplemented by bribe money."

"Really?"

He shrugs. "That's how small-town life is. We're used to it." He glances around and asks with a smile, "So where's your *media naranja*?"

"Half-orange?" I ask, confused.

With a laugh, he says, "Wendell!"

Media naranja. Must mean my better half, or something along those lines. Is it that obvious I feel like only half of something without him? "At the Turtle Center," I say. "His first day of work."

I tell him about Wendell's internship, how Santy said he has a connection with the turtles.

"Some people do." El Sapo nods. "And some turtles are special too. Like Gracia. She's the superhero of turtles around here."

El Sapo regales me with local turtle tales until a couple sits down at another table. Apologizing, El Sapo excuses himself to attend to them, just as Cristina, carrying an armful of laundry, emerges from a doorway at the back of a small courtyard. This restaurant, I realize, is attached to their family compound—a bunch of cement rooms painted aqua, wrapping around a patch of potted plants, flowers, and palm trees.

She waves to me, then starts hanging up sheets on clotheslines strung between trees.

I take the last sweet sip of *agua de horchata,* leave a few pesos on the table, and walk over to her. "Can I help you with that?"

"Really?" she asks, amused. "You want to do laundry?"

"Sure," I say. "To thank you for the drinks during volleyball games."

"Pues, adelante," she says with a smile, motioning with her chin to the basket of damp linens. "If only my daughters had your enthusiasm for doing laundry."

I start pinning up the linens, enjoying our easy conversation as birds chatter and whistle in the trees. The parakeets and parrots are perched outside their cages like bright blossoms, preening themselves on top of the bars.

After a while, Cristina looks around, and asks, "Where's your boyfriend?"

"Working." I wonder if I should confide in her. Why not, especially if she's my aunt? And haven't I always wanted an aunt? A woman to give me advice . . . advice that isn't peppered with Rumi quotes.

My voice softens. "It's barely been an hour and I miss him. There's this tight feeling in my chest. Like he might not come back." Heat rises to my face. This is embarrassing. I shouldn't have said anything.

But her face holds only sympathy. "You love him. Of course you're a little worried."

I breathe out in relief. She understands. "But how can I deal with it?"

She takes a clothespin from her mouth, gestures to the birds. "While I'm out here, I leave their doors open. They always come back. This is their home, where their food is, where they're loved."

"Really? They always come back?"

"*Pues,*" she says, with a devilish grin, "except for when a cat gets them."

A look of horror must come over my face, because she quickly adds, "But that hardly ever happens!"

I feel myself loosen up and laugh. The ice between us has been broken. She launches into stories about the changes she's seen in this town—from a sleepy little village of fishers and turtle hunters to a haven for hippie travelers. It's not hard to work Meche into the conversation—it turns out they went to high school together. Tentatively, I ask Cristina if she has advice on how we can make Meche get rid of the jaguar.

She takes a clothespin from her mouth and studies it, frowning. "I haven't talked to Meche for years. She keeps to herself. But frankly, I can't see her giving up that jaguar. It's like a child to her. From what I can see, her life revolves around that creature."

She gives a little shiver. Apparently, she doesn't like talking about Meche any more than other people do. "Now *dígame,* Zeeta, tell me, you must speak a lot of languages, you lived so many places."

I decide to drop the jaguar lady subject and let myself bond with this woman who might be my relative. When I mention I can hold simple conversations in a few dozen languages, her mouth drops open, and she asks me to teach her some. I give her a mini lesson of seafood menu items in French, instructing her to pout out her lips to pronounce *poisson.*

This throws her into a fit of giggles. Once she catches her breath, she says, "Speaking of France, you mentioned that *señor* you met—he was in France?" Her voice has turned deliberately casual.

I swallow and nod, suddenly alert.

"Was he—was he all right?"

I want so badly to tell her who I am. But more than that, I want my father to be the one to tell her. I don't want it to feel like a dark, strange secret revealed. I want it to be a joyful occasion.

Still, there are things she needs to know in order to understand, to be patient. "This *señor,*" I begin, "he has bipolar disorder." I say it in English, unsure of the Spanish translation.

"Bipolar?"

"He has ups and downs, manic and depressed periods."

A damp sheet falls from her hands to the laundry basket. She stares at it, absorbing the full meaning of my words. Then, her voice quavering, she asks, "Is he in trouble?"

"He wanted to reconnect with his home, his family.

Wanted to resolve something." I measure my words, not wanting to reveal more than my father would want. Only what's necessary. It's a fine line. "He felt he had to do this before . . ." I search for the right words. "Before he could move on."

Cristina picks up the sheet, pins it to the rope. She does the same with the other sheets and pillowcases. She's biting the inside of her cheek, I can tell.

I grab a sheet and hang it on the line that crisscrosses hers.

Eventually, she speaks. "He'll return to his home. Sooner or later. Like the birds. The important thing is that his family keep the doors open, welcoming."

When the baskets are empty, she brushes her hands together. "Now come back tomorrow for more laundry, Zeeta!" She winks. "You can teach me Portuguese!" Then she bids me farewell in the French I taught her. *"Au revoir."*

I take her hand in a lingering handshake. Our eyes lock, and I wonder if she has the sensation I do, of looking into a mirror. *"Au revoir,"* I say, and leave the cool courtyard, heading toward the sunny stretch of beach.

As I wave goodbye to El Sapo, he calls out, "Sunset volleyball tonight, Zeeta! Be there!"

How much longer can I keep this secret? It's all I can do not to call back, *Sure thing, cuz!*

❖ ❖ ❖

In the kitchen hut, battering fish for dinner, I can't stop glancing up at the path, waiting for Wendell. When I finally do catch sight of him, my heart leaps, as if we've been apart years instead of hours. He's jogging up the path, his camera bouncing on his chest. I'm just trying to find a towel when Wendell throws his arms around me, despite the bits of egg-and-bread-crumb goop stuck to my hands.

"Good first day?" I ask, laughing.

"Incredible!"

I can't stop kissing his neck as he shows me the photos on his digital camera. Even though they're tiny, I can see what he's excited about: close-up after close-up of sea turtles that appear to be posing just for him. Santy was right—Wendell's a natural. I look from the images to him, and it's one of those flashes, when you see someone so familiar in a different light. Wendell has things to share with the world that have nothing to do with me. It's a mostly happy feeling, tinged with something like sadness.

I kiss him again. "*You're* incredible, Wendell."

After dinner, we head to the beach for sunset volleyball. Approaching the court, I notice a commotion of flying sand and people yelling. It's a fight, centered on a guy I haven't seen before—a large, bare-chested guy about my age with a buzz cut and cutoff camouflage pants. He's waving his fists around, his face red and furious. El Sapo's gesturing for him to calm down. Other people are holding back another guy who's struggling, calling out curses and threats.

"What's going on?" Wendell asks Mayra. She's huddled at a safe distance with Xochitl.

"That *vato*," she says, scowling. "He keeps picking fights."

"Who is he?" I ask. "I haven't seen him before."

"He came to town a few months ago," Mayra says. "From

Mexico City. Sometimes he crashes our games. He thinks he's so tough."

Xochitl nods. "See how he's missing a finger?"

I catch sight of his right hand as he runs it over his stubbly head. The ring finger is just a small stump.

Wendell raises an eyebrow. "How'd he lose it?"

"He says it's from a gang fight with machetes. Says he ended up killing the guy."

I shiver, trying to imagine this. Then trying not to. Joe has talked about the gang violence in Mexico City. Not to mention the kidnappings and drug cartels. I'm not surprised to hear this guy's involved in violent crime. "You think his story's true?" I ask hesitantly.

Xochitl gives a devilish grin. "*Pues*, we say he stuck his finger in a blender while it was running. While he was doing kitchen prep in some restaurant. He just blamed it on a gangster."

Mayra laughs. "He's not the smartest guy."

I glance over at him on the court. Things appear to have calmed down. El Sapo walks toward us, breathing hard, frowning. After greeting us, he mutters, "Man, I wish El Dedo would stay away."

"Dedo?" I ask. Finger?

"He's never even introduced himself, so we call him El Dedo." El Sapo glares at him. "That *vato* doesn't talk much, communicates with his fists."

"He doesn't get that this is a peaceful place," Mayra says. "*Muy tranquilo*. We don't fight around here."

"What's he doing in town?" Wendell asks.

El Sapo shrugs. "Maybe he got into trouble in Mexico City and he's lying low here."

We jog onto the court, making sure El Dedo is on the opposing team. Whenever he's upset, he gets in someone's face or kicks sand or hurls the ball, hard. He doesn't direct his violence at the girls, but I do overhear him making crude comments.

During the break, Cristina comes over with *agua de tamarindo*—tamarind water, caramel brown and tangy and cool. She distributes drinks to everyone but El Dedo, instead, scolding, "You're lucky your mother doesn't live around here, *muchacho*. If she did, I'd tell her exactly how rude you are."

He narrows his eyes at Cristina but says nothing.

She walks away, muttering, *"Qué cochino."* What a pig.

I turn to El Sapo. "El Dedo's completely outnumbered. Why don't we stand up to him, tell him he can't play?"

El Sapo frowns. "We're just hoping he'll get tired of our games, decide not to come back. A little while ago, there were a couple other *vatos*, friends of his, who just got bored and stopped coming." He digs his feet in the sand, shaking his head. "But if we kicked El Dedo out . . . guys like that— they get revenge. And for them, revenge means death." He lowers his voice. "Death by machete."

Sounds even more unpleasant than death by jaguar.

Chapter Twelve

A week later, El Dedo still hasn't made another appearance. Wendell and I haven't missed a single sunset volleyball game. We've settled into a new routine. In the afternoons, he works while I help Layla at the cabanas, trying to ignore Joe's clown antics. He's begun performing in the kitchen hut every day at four. This coincides with happy hour, when he has a captive audience sipping Coronas and crunching tortilla chips. His schtick involves chasing a paper airplane around the hut, tripping over chairs and tables. Most guests ignore him, tossing a concerned glance when he falls particularly hard, unsure whether it's a slapstick part of the act. He takes this attention as encouragement.

On Friday, I've reached my limit of his clowning and apocalypse warnings. Normally, I'd head to Tesoro Escondido, but Cristina and El Sapo have gone to the nearby city of Puerto Escondido to run errands. When I consider working alone on my jungle paths, the thought of facing Gatito again makes me shudder. As a last resort, I set up my laptop in the kitchen hut and try working on my English paper. After staring blankly at the screen for ten straight minutes, I shut the computer down and stand up.

On my last visit with Cristina, as I was lamenting Wendell's absence, she asked me what I loved best before I even met him. Doing notebook interviews, I said with no hesitation. "Then do some notebook interviews," she suggested. "Meet your other neighbors."

Maybe she's right. Maybe I should reconnect with notebook-writing Zeeta. It is, after all, what I *do*. Wendell or no Wendell.

Plus, our neighbors might have inside information and ideas on how to get rid of Meche's jaguar. Tossing my notebook and pen into my bag, I head down the dirt driveway. After a brief pause, I turn left, toward the other entrance to the Playa Mermejita, the road the poachers took that night. I've never gone this way, have always taken the jungle route.

The road rises into a hill, with trees and flowering bushes arched over the road, making a green canopy of dappled light. Since there are no cars, I walk down the center of the road. It's peaceful. Ahead of me, a blue butterfly dances, and I'm about to point it out to Wendell until I remember he's not here. It's a hard habit to break.

I shift my bag to my other shoulder as a cheery graveyard comes into view, overflowing with flowers, blue and green painted crosses, Virgin Mary shrines. The butterfly weaves among the graves and disappears into the jumble of colors. I set down my bag, sweeping my gaze over the cemetery.

Someone's moving among the graves. Dark hair, slim body, long legs. A white huipil. A slight limp. Meche. She's farther up the hill, on the other side of the cemetery, holding an armful of flowers.

When she glances up, I raise my hand in greeting, noting that there's no jaguar in sight. I also note that this is neutral territory, a good place to discuss her finding a better place for her pet. I bend over to pick up my bag, but when I stand up, she's gone.

I jog around the graves to where she was standing only moments earlier. There's a blue painted cross with a sign on it: MARÍA VIOLETA RAMIREZ GARCÍA. Breathless, I peer at the dates. The girl died when she was two years old. A heap of fresh white flowers—calla lilies—are scattered on the grave. Meche must have dropped them before she ran off. I pick them up and arrange them in the vase, which is half filled with water. I prop a few rocks against the vase to keep it stable if the wind picks up. This girl would have been twenty now if she'd lived, three years older than me.

Who is this girl to Meche? Is this the daughter she supposedly killed?

❖ ❖ ❖

Feeling off-balance, I head back toward the beach. Flanking the road are falling-down signs advertising home-made tortillas, healer services, fresh eggs. Every dilapidated shack seems to be selling something. Randomly, I choose a house marked by a hand-lettered wooden sign for firewood and walk down the driveway.

Three dogs race toward me, barking and growling. I pick up a stick to defend myself, and peer past them. An old man totters forward, holding an axe. He calls back the dogs, then shouts, "*¿Sí, señorita?*"

"*Buenas tardes, señor.* I'm Zeeta, and I live in the Cabañas Magia del Mar. We're neighbors."

"You live up there?" he says, shaking his head, as if it's a war zone. "You here for firewood, *señorita?*"

"Uh, maybe another time," I say diplomatically. I don't mention that we've already got a stockpile of bonfire wood by our shed.

"So how can I help you?" he asks, his voice impatient.

"Well, I wanted to ask you about the jaguar—"

"None of my business," he interrupts curtly.

Dejected, I thank him and head back to the road, toward the sea that shimmers ahead through the trees. If Wendell were here, we'd be joking about it. We'd probably say screw it and go for a swim. Which is what I decide to do.

I'm nearly to the patch of jungle lining the ocean, when I see a sign half-hidden behind a clump of magenta bougainvillea. Uneven letters are burned into the wood. SE VENDE MOLE.

Mole. What did Layla and Joe say about *mole?* Something about sweaty stars? And food of the gods? Food of paradise? Perfect. Anyone who makes food of the gods has to be cheerier than grumpy firewood guy. And I'll get to see if *mole* lives up to its reputation.

I decide to pretend I'm only here for the *mole*. I won't reveal where I live. They'll be more likely to trust me that way. I take a breath, then turn past the pink bougainvillea, down the dirt driveway.

A house comes into view, a patchwork of blue-painted wood and palm fronds, as though the house itself is another bloom emerging from the foliage. The courtyard out front is bursting with color—birds-of-paradise, hibiscus, roses. The pink-painted gate is flung open, wide and welcoming. Butterflies of all colors flit through the sweet air.

"*¡Buenos días!*" I call out, unsure what *mole*-purchasing protocol is.

In response, a woman's voice sings, "*¡Buenos días!*" through the leaves. Echoes of her words sound through the little forest. They're parrots, I realize, singing out her greetings. I weave around kittens prowling like miniature tigers and a few old dogs lying in the shade and a litter of bouncing puppies. Quite a menagerie.

"Come in, come in," she calls out.

I follow a ribbon of path toward her voice. Soon I reach a clearing and find her perched on a tree stump. Spoons, ladles, knives, pots, pans, strainers, and unfamiliar utensils hang from nails on the tree trunks. At the center is a large fire pit, hot gray coals beneath cooking irons. A thick, dark liquid bubbles in a giant blackened vat.

The woman is leaning over another vat—a cauldron,

really—of something even thicker and darker, more a paste than a liquid. I watch as she deftly scoops some into a plastic bag, knots it, then places it on top of a pile of similar bags.

When she senses my presence, her face lights up. "Ah, *muchachita!* Did you come for my *molito?*"

I smile. Molito. *Cute little mole.* The older locals tend to tack *-ito* on the end of words, making everything cute and little. This woman is cute and little herself—little in height, not width. All her features are wide—her nose, her cheekbones, her smiling mouth, her ample hips, her muscular hands. She's wearing a yellow dress with purple flowers beneath a blue checked apron. Looped twice around her neck is a long strand of green crystal beads. Her hair, deep black streaked with white, is braided into a long, thin rope down her back.

"Sit down, sit down." Emphatically, she pats a worn-smooth stump beside her. She gazes at me, pleased, as if I'm a long-awaited visitor. An old friend. Her gaze feels like a sip of hot milk, a spoonful of soup. Nourishing.

"Gracias, señora." I sit down, basking in her glow.

"Now, you look familiar, *muchacha!* You must have family around here, no?"

Avoiding a direct answer, I simply say, "I just moved here, actually."

"Ah, and where are you from?"

"Everywhere and nowhere," I say, making myself comfortable. "I've lived all over the world."

"Oh! How exciting!" She clasps her hands together, presses them to her chest, as if her heart might just leap out from too much joy. "The farthest I've been is Mexico City!"

Her name is Lupita, she informs me, and proceeds to ask me about every detail of my life up until now. Over the next few hours, she listens to my stories of living in Thailand, Brazil, Laos, throwing her head back in waterfalls of laughter at the funny parts, wiping her teary eyes at the sad parts.

The only pauses in the conversation come when a customer buys a bag of *mole* paste, makes some small talk, and then leaves. Lupita apologizes and picks the conversation up exactly where we left off. She wants to hear about the food from each place I've lived, the mixes of spices, fruits, meats, nuts, vegetables. "Ohh, ahh, hmm," she comments, bright-eyed, encouraging me to go on.

When she discovers I've never tasted *mole*, she jumps up—she's surprisingly agile—lights a fire in the pit, and grabs a pan from a tree. "Oh, you're in for a treat, *mi amor*!"

She beckons me to follow her into a small hut containing a fridge, a wooden table, and rough-hewn cabinets—apparently the indoor section of her kitchen. With a flourish, she hands me a bottle of cooking oil and three tomatoes. She carries out a pot of chicken broth. I follow her back to the fire pit.

She grabs a black and blue mottled spoon from the tree, then oversees me chopping tomatoes and amid the sizzle of oil and aromas of roasting chile and chocolate sauce. "*Sí, mija, así es,*" she murmurs in approval. Yes, like that, my daughter. She heats up rice, and we talk more about food—tagines in Morocco, peanut stew in Senegal, mango-chile salad in Thailand. Spicy, sweet smoke wraps around me, saturating my hair, my clothes, seeping into my skin, making my eyes water.

Time whirls by, until finally, Lupita dips a wooden spoon into the dark sauce and tastes it. "*Ya*, finished!" She ladles chicken and rice onto a plate, then drizzles *mole* on top.

"*¡Come, mija!*" she says, handing it to me. Eat, my daughter!

I take a bite. It's shocking how delicious it is. So delicious my eyes close in deep appreciation. The *mole* heats up my blood, warms my heart, reaches into the very center of my being. An unearthly experience. I force myself to slow down and savor the intermingling flavors. The combination of chocolate and chile gives me some kind of endorphin high. I'm dancing inside. My face feels damp with sweat from the stars now, too. This is crazy. How can a food have this effect?

When I open my eyes, I see Lupita watching me with delight. Her face is aglow. Sweat of the stars. I want to hug her. Now, sitting here, eating this *mole*, I really, truly feel it— I've found home.

❖ ❖ ❖

Two platefuls later, I find myself opening up more and more, telling Lupita how I've always longed for family, for home, how I've always felt a certain loneliness inside, even around other people. I tell her about Wendell, who makes that loneliness subside, but how being apart from him scares me.

Lupita clucks sympathetically and piles more *mole* onto my plate. I'm stuffed, but I don't stop her.

"You know, *mija*, it's good to be away from your loved one sometimes. It makes you love him more. It's like *mole*. I don't eat it for every meal. Just on Sundays, or birthdays, or when I have a special visitor, like you." She nods, patting my shoulder. "It's the same with my husband. I love him more when I miss him a bit."

She lowers her voice, letting me in on a secret. "I send my husband to work at his little store every day. There aren't many customers anymore. He just sits there and watches TV and snoozes. But he feels useful." She giggles, clasping her hands together. "And when he comes back home, I'm happy to see him and he's happy to see me."

I laugh, thinking of Wendell. He'll love hearing about all this. Suddenly, I realize how much time has passed. Wendell will be home soon. I'd better get going. Then I remember my whole reason for coming. "Doña Lupita," I begin, "people in town warned me about a jaguar. And a crazy lady—"

"Oh, *mija*, people are such gossips." She waves her hand, brushing away the rumors. "The truth is that Meche is a lovely woman."

"Lovely?" I pause. "But—what about the jaguar?"

"She adores him! She gave him all her *cariño* after the tragedy."

"What happened?" I whisper.

Doña Lupita clucks. "It was so sad, so sad. Meche was a doting mother, but one day her daughter wandered off, through the jungle. Meche found her just as she was teetering on the edge of the sea cliff. She ran to her, but couldn't reach her fast enough. The little girl fell. The ocean took her, *pobrecita*."

For a moment I'm speechless. "But—then why don't people like this woman?"

"*Pues*, envy. She was so beautiful. When she was your

age, she met a man visiting from Mexico City. He was older, fair-skinned and wealthy, and he charmed her. Soon they got married, and not long after, her belly grew. People gossiped that she became pregnant, then forced the man to marry her. So Meche and her husband moved to Puerto Escondido. She and her daughter came back here after her mother's death to settle paperwork. It was then that her daughter died."

Doña Lupita gives the pot one more stir, then settles back into her chair. "Meche was so distraught. The child's body was never found. Still, people gave her no sympathy. They said she never wanted the baby, only used the pregnancy to lure in her husband. Some went so far as to say she killed her own child."

"Like La Llorona," I murmur.

"Exactly." Doña Lupita waves the idea away with her hand. "Ridiculous, of course. If you ever saw Meche with that little girl, you'd know how much they adored each other."

"And her husband?" I ask, remembering how she was rumored to have killed him, too.

"Who knows. Maybe a divorce. To tell the truth, Meche was so devastated, she couldn't be a wife anymore. She moved back here to live alone on her family's land."

Doña Lupita is silent for a moment, stirring the *mole*, inhaling its scent. "I brought her my *mole*—this can cheer up anyone, I thought—but it didn't help. *Pobrecita*. Poor thing. Even now, after all these years, I'm her only visitor. But I admit, now that the jaguar's no longer a kitten, it scares me. So now I just leave *mole* outside the gate."

I stare at my empty plate of *mole,* wondering what to make of her story. Have I misjudged Meche? Or is Lupita just delusionally kind and open-hearted?

❖ ❖ ❖

The sun drops in the sky, signaling late afternoon. Wendell might be home already, wondering where I am. But as much as I want to see him, I'm in my element here, sharing stories with Lupita. Wendell can wait a few more minutes.

I open my jade notebook. "Doña Lupita, can I interview you?"

"Why?" she asks, surprised. "I'm just an old lady. My life is simple."

"Trust me," I say with a smile. "You're plenty interesting."

She giggles like a little girl, then folds her hands in her lap.

"What would make your life complete?"

She thinks for a moment. "*Pues,* I'd like to teach someone my *mole* recipe. From scratch. It's an ancient recipe. My grandmother taught me. She learned it from her grandmother. I'd like to continue the chain."

"Your children and grandchildren aren't interested?" I find this hard to believe.

She clucks. "The ingredients must be roasted on a handmade clay plate over the fire. My daughter likes to cook, but only with a stove. Too much work to gather the firewood, she says. Too much time. My granddaughters are the same. They like to do things fast." She snaps her fingers. "*Todo rápido, rápido, rápido.*"

I jot this down in my notebook, and then, almost shyly, I say, "Well, if you ever get desperate, I'd love to learn the recipe."

She studies me. "Really? You'd have the patience?"

"*Sí, señora.*" There is no doubt in my mind.

"Wonderful!" She hugs me, pressing me into her soft shoulders. "Come back tomorrow and I'll teach you."

I breathe in one last whiff of *mole*. This is what I've longed for—to be part of something old and important, something tied to this place. A link in a chain. Like the line of sea turtles that nest here—grandmothers, granddaughters, stretching in either direction, past and future. Something that proves this is my home.

I leave, feeling full of *mole* and something else. Strength— enough to deal with a bizarre neighbor, a jaguar, and poachers. Maybe even enough to deal with Wendell-less afternoons.

❖ ❖ ❖

By the time I get home, Wendell's in the kitchen hut, staring at the blue glow of his laptop. I run up to him, plant a kiss on his mouth, glancing at his email in-box. "And how was your day, dear?"

He closes his laptop quickly. "Okay." His voice is oddly flat.

I know I should ask him more, but I want to fill him in on Doña Lupita and the *mole* and the revelation about Meche. I gush for a little while, and he nods distractedly at the wrong places. This isn't like him.

I stop myself and ask, "Hey, are you okay, Wendell?"

He nods unconvincingly.

"Are you mad at me?" I venture. It would be ridiculous, but I can't think of any other explanation. "I mean, because I wasn't here when you got home?"

He glances at me. "Of course not."

I wait a few beats to see if he'll say more.

Nothing.

I take another stab. "Did something happen at work?"

A slight shake of the head. "Got tons of turtle pictures."

After a pause, I ask, "Did you have to do tours today? Speak French? Did it go all right?"

"Yeah," he says, almost impatient. "French and English. It was fine."

Biting my lip, I lower my voice. "Did you *see* something?"

"No, no. Look, Z, I'm okay." But there's an undercurrent of something in his voice. Irritation? I can't tell.

He stands up. "I'm going to lie down awhile. I'm tired."

I blink, not sure what to say. "Okay. Do you want me to—"

"No, stay here, tell Layla about your *mole* thing." And before I can respond, he's gone off to his cabana, laptop tucked under his arm.

I stare after him, hurt. We've been sharing everything since we got here. Only one week at the Turtle Center and he has secrets? It only took one week for him to drift away from me? Just when I'm feeling strong enough to handle our hours apart, he starts slipping away?

Chapter Thirteen

At sunset, Wendell and I are walking along Comet Point, past carpets of pink-blossomed succulents and clusters of cacti. He's kicking small stones from his path, almost angrily. Our gazes aren't on the glittering ocean; his is glued to his feet, and mine is on his distressed face.

Earlier, Wendell stayed in his cabana for nearly an hour while Layla and I whipped up a scrumptious chicken dinner using the *mole* paste. After the preparations, I swung by his room to see how he was feeling. Terrible, by the look of him. It took some work to convince him to take a walk with me, but here he is. Wearing a tortured expression.

"Everything okay?" I ask for the third time tonight.

"Huh?"

"Are you okay, Wendell?"

"Oh, yeah. Just—yeah."

I dig my fingernails into my palms. "Is it something I said? Something I did?"

"What? No." He shakes off his gloom, and kisses me. "No, you're great, Z."

The sea rages against jagged rocks on the west side, where the sun falls toward the horizon like a glowing tangerine. I scan Playa Mermejita in the distance, trying to see if any more leatherbacks are coming to shore to nest. From here, it's hard to tell, but it looks like a clean stretch of uninterrupted beach. When I squint, I think I can make out the faint marks of flipper tracks crisscrossing the sand.

I wish we were allowed to walk there, the site of our future handfasting. By the date of our handfasting—August second—the leatherbacks will have finished nesting, and another species of turtles will probably be there. Wendell and I will have to break the stay-off-the-beach rule, just that once, to honor the promise we made each other. It's just a ritual, but somehow, it seems essential to complete it. Especially now, with this disconcerting feeling that our relationship is inexplicably on the rocks.

By now we've reached the tip of the point. White foam slaps against cliffs, forming violent whirlpools around the boulders below. I wonder if this is where Meche's daughter fell. I shudder, imagining the terrible scene Lupita described.

Wendell and I stand for a moment, watching the chaos of water; then I tug his hand and we continue to the opposite side of the point. A few other couples are scattered, watching the sunset. The sky has turned to liquid gold and pink, melting into the ocean.

Now is the kind of moment when our lips usually find each other, when our eyelids fall shut and we get lost in our own sweet, dusky world. I reach for Wendell's limp hand. "This sunset looks delicious, doesn't it?" I'm desperate to lighten things up, to somehow connect with him. "Like *agua de papaya*. Oh, and wait till you try the *mole*. It tastes like sweaty stars." I force a smile. "In a good way."

He doesn't laugh or even question me.

The sun disappears completely into the ocean, and I lean against him, tuck my head into the nook of his neck. Without warning, he leans away, sticks his hands in his pockets. "Speaking of dinner, we should go back. Layla probably needs our help."

"Okay," I say, swallowing my hurt.

We walk back along the pensinsula, scrambling up the hill, then through the jungle. We're halfway to the cabanas when something rustles in the trees.

Last time I heard something rustle in these trees, it didn't end well. I pick up the pace. We should have brought a flashlight. Dusk has fallen fast in the forest. It's all shadows. We take a few more steps. Another noise, maybe the snap of a twig. My eyes flicker to the sound. I catch a glimpse of movement in the trees nearby. Is it Gatito? Meche?

"Let's hurry," I say, breaking into a jog.

"What's wrong?" Wendell asks, barely keeping up with me.

"Didn't you hear that?"

"What?"

I glance at him. He probably wasn't paying attention, lost in whatever he's been thinking about. I thought I felt alone before, with Wendell at the Turtle Center. It's even worse when he's right beside me but galaxies away. "I don't know. But hurry."

Soon we step into the kitchen hut's candlelit glow. I breathe out in relief. The tables are packed with guests talking and eating *mole*. More like *devouring mole*. Some look up to greet us and compliment me on the dinner, then quickly return to stuffing their faces.

Layla glides over with two plates for us. "Eat up! This food really is fit for the gods!" She kisses us each on the head, then moves on to the blissed-out guests who are begging for seconds.

Wendell finds a seat, not in his usual spot in the middle of the hut, but at a table on the edge. I sit down next to him, watching his reaction as he tastes the *mole*.

"Yum." His smile is strained. He takes another small bite, then scoots his rice around with his fork. Something is definitely wrong, so wrong he can't even talk about it.

I take a bite of *mole*, urge the chocolate and chile to send endorphins through me. Not working. Not with Wendell acting like this. Mindlessly, I stare into the darkness falling on the jungle outside the hut. A movement in the branches catches my eye. My eyes adjust, and now I'm certain. Something—or someone—is there. Tiny lights reflect off a pair of eyes. Not the yellow glow of animal eyes. No, they're human.

My fork clatters to my plate. I stand up.

The eyes meet mine. And then disappear.

I rush out to the trees, calling, "Who's there?"

No answer.

Wendell's at my side now. I put my finger to my lips and wait for a minute, until Wendell says, "Come on, Z," leading me by the elbow back to the table.

"Someone was watching us, Wendell." Composing myself, I sit back down, hearing my heart thud. I unclench my fists, try to relax into the warm candlelight and *mole* smells and happy faces. Such a comfortable little island. Comfortable, yet vulnerable. "It might've been Meche," I whisper.

"Well, there's no one there now," Wendell says, giving me a strange look.

"No, but—"

He pulls me close, wraps his arm around my shoulder. For the first time tonight, he actually looks at me. It took someone spying on us in the jungle to do it, but at least he's not obsessing over whatever's been upsetting him. He's focused on me now. His voice comes out tender. "You're still shaken up, aren't you, Z? From the jaguar? The curse?"

"But, Wendell, I wasn't imagining it. . . . I saw eyes. . . ." My voice trails off. I press my lips together and shut my eyes. I sink into him, breathing in his fresh-laundry-and-cinnamon-soap smell. What matters most is being close to him. That's all I want right now.

❖ ❖ ❖

But by the middle of the next morning, Wendell's distant again, light-years away. We're clearing the network of paths through the jungle. I've been using my machete to chop through brush and dead trees for hours. Wood splinters cling to my hair, my tank top, my pants. Soil spots my ankles and arms, leaving the smell of earth. I pause, wiping my forehead. Except for the distant surf and the echoing boom of Wendell's machete, it's quiet. Too quiet.

I watch him chopping a dead log, breathing hard, wordless. We still have a few hours before he leaves for work. I can't stand this awkwardness anymore. I walk over, wrap my arms around him, let my lips graze his neck.

No response.

I turn him toward me, cupping his face in my hands, kiss him long and hard on the mouth.

He pulls away, looks down. "We should get some work done."

My face hot, I walk away and pick up my machete. There's no explanation for his acting like this. It must have been a vision, an intense one. But what if it's me? What if for some reason, he's not into me anymore?

I glance around at the giant leaves, the flowers spilling out everywhere, the beginnings of my path network. My little paradise. None of it matters if Wendell isn't part of it.

I set down my machete, stand in front of him, look straight into his eyes. "Wendell, the truth. What's going on?"

He brushes the stray hairs from his face. "Yesterday I . . ."

The dread in his voice scares me. "What?"

"After work I got an email." He sighs.

I brace myself. What if it was from an old girlfriend? Or worse, a death in his family? "From?"

"From California College of the Arts."

"What?" This is the last thing I expected him to say. I feel a wave of relief that it wasn't an old girlfriend or a death. Then I wonder where he's going with this.

"I didn't mention it to you before because—well, I didn't think anything would happen."

"What are you talking about, Wendell?" Something in the tone of his voice makes my stomach clench.

"I was sure I wanted to follow our plan, Z. Stay here while you finished school, then go to CU Boulder together . . . but in the fall, my parents made me apply to at least one college. In case I changed my mind."

I'm motionless, listening.

He picks up a dead stick, snaps it in half, and in half again. "I applied to this art school in San Francisco, sent them my portfolio of Ecuador and France photos. There's a famous photographer who teaches there—international nature stuff. I thought there was no way I'd get in, and even if I did, there's no way we could afford it." He pauses, rubbing his head.

"And you got in?"

He lets out a long, somber breath. "All tuition paid, plus a dorm room and meal plan." You'd think he was telling me his dog died. "I'd have to take some prerequisites as summer classes. Starting in June."

A whole succession of thoughts flies through my mind. First, I'm grateful that his news doesn't involve weird animals or creepy visions or terminal diseases. Then I envision him in San Francisco having gallery openings and getting his photos published in magazines, and my heart swells with happiness. Then I wonder why he's so down about it.

It slams into me like a punch in the gut. June. He'd have to leave a year earlier than me. The other realizations hit me like a storm. A dorm room and meal plan. No place for me. No way could I afford to live in San Francisco, especially on my own, doing my senior year in high school. And even after I graduate, I wouldn't be going to an arts college. I need something more practical—international relations, maybe—so I can pay back student loans. And a harder punch in the gut: if he's leaving in June, he won't be here for our handfasting on the beach. The thought of our perfect spot of beach, empty and abandoned on August second— that's what makes my lip tremble.

It takes all my concentration to hold back tears. A hummingbird buzzes by. There's the distant roar of a motorboat or maybe a truck engine. The insect songs rise and fall. He's waiting for me to say something. I wish I could kiss him and say congratulations, but if I open my mouth, I might start to cry.

He takes my hand. "Hey, listen, Z. I'm not gonna take it. I just—" He shakes his head. "I want to be with you. Help with the cabanas. Protect the turtles. I love it here."

I find words, make my mouth move. "Did you tell your parents?"

He nods.

"And?"

He answers quietly. "They think I'd be crazy not to take it." Rubbing his temple, he adds, "They say it's a once-in-a-lifetime opportunity."

I try to wrap my head around this. "Why? Couldn't you postpone it? Till next year? Maybe I could save up money, find a way to go too."

He lets out a long breath. "The prof who's offering me the scholarship—he's leaving next year. He'll be working full-time for National Geographic. It's a one-shot deal, Z."

I absorb this. Wendell's parents are right; he'd be crazy not to take it. But our year together would be gone. And who knows what would happen at college? He could meet anyone, he could change, he could . . . anything. I bite my lip. I know what the right thing to say is. So I force myself to say it. "Maybe you shouldn't refuse it yet. Just email them back. Say you need time to decide."

"Z, I don't think—"

"Just email them, all right?" My words come out almost angry.

"All right."

We clear the rest of the portion of path in silence. My insides are spinning, a whirlpool of emotion. It's another mess. A mess that makes my stomach hurt, my chest ache. A mess that makes me realize I can't count on anything. Not my father, who's hiding from me. Not my mother, who'll leap at any excuse to make us leave. Not Wendell, the person I thought I could depend on more than anyone.

❖　❖　❖

By the orange glow of the bonfire, three Australian backpacker girls are dancing as a long-haired Norwegian architect, Sven, plays a wooden flute and Horacio, the blind man, strums his guitar. It would be pleasant if Wendell—a happy Wendell—were here instead of moping in his cabana. If only he'd never gotten that scholarship offer. And if only Joe weren't sitting next to me, staring at the leaping flames and ranting about the inevitable incineration of the world. "Actually, Joe," I tell him, "at the moment, I wouldn't mind if the world burned to ashes."

That silences him.

Then, inspired, Layla stands up, Rumi written all over her face. *"Rise into the atmosphere, and even if the whole world's harp should burn up"*—and here she looks pointedly at Joe and me—*"there will still be hidden instruments playing."*

A few guests applaud, murmur appreciation. They tilt back their heads, watching the smoke rise into the sky. Horacio and the architect give an appreciative nod toward Layla and keep playing.

She sits close beside me and whispers, "What's wrong, love?"

I stare at the fire. Layla wouldn't understand. She's used to guys flitting in and out of her life. She'd have no clue how I feel. If she were in my place, she'd take it as a sign—or excuse—to move to another country, most likely. "Nothing," I whisper.

"Is it about your father?"

I glance up. I could let her think that.

"You're upset you haven't found him?"

I pause, listening to the lone flute notes spiral up. "It sucks looking for someone who doesn't want to be found. Someone I'm not even convinced I want to find anymore. Not now that I know more about him." I shrug. "I've given up for the moment."

"Really, love?"

I wave the smoke from my stinging eyes, forcing my mouth into some semblance of a smile. "I've found my cousins and aunt. At least, I think I have. And I've met some cool locals—Lupita and Santy and El Loco and the other *bolibolistas*. Maybe that's enough." But even I can tell I'm not convincing.

"There's more, isn't there, Z?" She gives me a sheepish look. "Are you mad I haven't signed the contract yet?"

"You haven't?" I'm too depressed to get angry.

"I promise I'll do it soon, Z." She reaches out, tilts my chin up, studies my watering smoke-stung eyes. "But there's something else, isn't there?" Glancing around, she asks, "Where's Wendell been hiding?"

I wince, as if she's just touched the tender skin around a splinter.

On occasion, Layla can be surprisingly perceptive. She pulls me toward her. I blink back tears, let her hold me.

"He got a scholarship," I sputter, my voice muffled in the cotton of her huipil. "He'd have to leave in June. He says he doesn't think he'll take it but . . ." I let my voice fade, and wipe my tears.

I brace myself for her to assure me it doesn't matter, there are more boys out there, on every continent, a world of boys just waiting to meet me. In fact, she'll probably offer, *Hey, why don't we go find one for you now?* Instead, she says, matter-of-factly, "He's the love of your life, Z. We all know that."

I pull away from her and stare. This is the last thing I expected.

"You've just hit a rough patch. Hang in there, love." She squeezes my hand and says confidently, "It'll work out."

"What if it doesn't?" My voice sounds so small and vulnerable. Usually, I'm the strong one around Layla. The one with my feet solidly on the ground, pulling her back to earth. "What if everything's ruined?"

She pulls me to my feet. "Dance with me, Z!"

I groan. Dancing is Layla's solution to just about anything. I glance around, searching for a way out. Joe is passing out Coronas to the guests. Sven and Horacio set down their instruments, clink their bottles together, and sip. The Australian girls are heading back to their cabana, their laughter tinkling behind them.

"Come on, Z!" Layla insists, her bangles clinking as she snakes her arms through the smoke. "Let's dance!"

"Layla, the absolute last thing I want to do is dance." I scowl, folding my arms tightly. "Anyway, the music's over. There's no point."

She lets go of my hands and begins dancing herself, just the rush of ocean for music, the metallic tinkling of her bracelets. She whispers Rumi. *"We rarely hear the inward music, but we're all dancing to it nevertheless."*

❖ ❖ ❖

The next morning, when I show up at Doña Lupita's house, I'm groggy from a sleepless night. She gives me a big hug that smells of smoky chile and cinnamon. Today she's wearing a silvery dress with a pink flower pattern under her checked apron. I wonder if every dress she owns looks like her garden.

She sits me down on a tree stump and immediately places a steaming cup of chamomile tea in my hands.

I force a smile, determined not to let my bad mood put a damper on our cooking lesson.

She claps her hands. "*¡Empezemos!*" Let's start! Then she takes out a large clay plate—"our *comal*," she says, patting it. She balances it on cement blocks over the cooking fire. Then she plucks an array of dried chiles from a basket and drops them on the *comal*. As they roast, she pours a heap of almonds onto one area, cacao beans on another, then sesame seeds, cloves, pumpkin seeds, and cinnamon sticks in other areas. From time to time, she stirs each ingredient with a wooden spoon. The smell is heavenly—sweet and spicy and earthy. I jot down the ingredients as fast as I can.

Over the next few hours come plantains, raisins, onions, peanuts, garlic . . . so many ingredients, I can barely keep up. It feels good to focus on this smattering of smells and tastes and textures and heat. Lupita shows me how to turn over the chiles and stir the seeds, until everything is almost to the point of burning, but not quite. Then she has me scrape the roasted ingredients into a giant stone bowl, add a little oil, and, with a big pestle, grind everything together in a paste.

"So how's your boyfriend?" she asks, watching me work.

For a moment, I tense up, not wanting to break the spell of the chocolate and chile and spices. Struggling to control my emotions, I tell her about his art school news, how cold he's been acting.

"Will he take the scholarship?" she asks solemnly, understanding the gravity of this situation.

"He claims he doesn't want to," I say, pounding the pestle with more force than necessary. I wipe the sweat from my brows. "But I know I'm the only reason he wouldn't take it."

"And what did you tell him?"

"To tell the school he needs more time to decide." I pause to stare at her. It's as if she can see through me, right into my selfish center. "I want him to stay," I admit. Then, glancing at our *mole*, I add, "He's the main ingredient in my paradise."

She considers this. "Is he happy staying?"

"Not since he got the email. If he passes on this opportunity . . . I think he'll regret it."

She hands me a cacao bean. "Bite."

I do, and grimace. "Bitter," I say, instinctively spitting it out. An old dog moseys over to inspect it. After a few sniffs, he deems it not worth the trouble, and settles back down under a tree.

"Yes, bitter," she says, "but if you add the right ingredients, this bean becomes *mole*. You only need to add the right thing—tanginess, spice, sweetness. Then it transforms."

Once the *mole* paste is smooth, she scoops it into plastic

bags, which I knot and pile into a small mountain. "Now, my husband," Lupita says, "he's a cacao bean! Stubborn, set in his ways. For years, he's run that little corner shop I mentioned, Abarrotes Rogelio."

"Hmm." I mentally scan downtown Mazunte's cluster of stores. "I haven't noticed it."

"That's because it's hidden up there on that hill!" she cries, pointing. "Years ago, people stopped by his store on the way to Playa Mermejita to hunt turtles and gather their eggs. But once the laws changed and the Turtle Center was built, other shops cropped up, in more convenient places for tourists. No one comes out this way to Playa Mermejita anymore. Except the turtles," she adds with a giggle.

"Couldn't he change locations?"

"Oh, that's what we all told him, but he wouldn't listen. Of course, the store started losing money, but he refused to change. And he sells exactly the same things, year after year—canned food, powdered milk, dried goods like salt and sugar, soda, beer. *Cositas* like that. Some of those cans must be ten years old!" She titters again. "But he dusts each can every day. I argued with him at first, then just accepted it."

She moves her head close to mine, letting me in on a secret. "You see, I changed my attitude, added sweetness and spice. I decided to be grateful he wasn't around to bother me, happy I could talk to my friends and customers in peace! He stays busy all day, dusting those cans until he dozes off in front of his *telenovelas*. It's fine with me now. We own the property, so we're not losing money on it. And we earn enough through renting some properties and selling my *mole*." She leans back and folds her arms across her chest. "See, now our lives are a big heaping plate of *mole*."

"Sounds perfect," I say.

"Oh," she clucks, "far, far from perfect! But still delicious."

❖ ❖ ❖

Sweetness and spice. How can I transform Wendell's news into something delicious? It's beyond me. Wendell and I are walking along Playa Mermejita, our moon shadows stretched long across the beach, which is spotted with leatherbacks. Some are lumbering up the beach, some digging nests, their back flippers blindly going deeper and deeper. We keep our distance, careful not to disturb them. Of course, we're not supposed to even be on this beach, but I figured being around the giant turtles would put him in the best possible mood to talk about the scholarship.

Wendell's been quiet ever since I dragged him out of his cabana earlier tonight. Suddenly, he stops and says, "This is it. Our handfasting spot."

In the moonlight, I can make out the landmark—a large driftwood log riddled with holes, soft and worn.

"I don't want to miss it, Z." He cups my face with his hand. "I'll be here on August second, with you. I promise."

I know what I need to say. The words taste as bitter as raw cacao, but I force them out. "Don't stay for me. You'd regret it, Wendell."

He presses his face into my hair, speaks in a muffled

voice. "I emailed the prof, said I needed to think about it."
He draws me to him, kisses me, pulls me gently down to the
sand. "I'd be miserable away from you, that much I know,"
he murmurs, his breath warm on my cheek, my neck. "And I
won't miss our handfasting."

I bite my quivering lip. "We'll figure something out,
okay?" And even though we haven't figured anything out yet,
it seems better, now that we're talking again, touching again.

As we kiss, there's a new urgency to it, since we know
our future is, once again, uncertain. I focus on his fingertips brushing over my skin. The night breeze, soft. Starlight,
moonlight, the waves. The salty, delicious feel of our lips,
together. At some point, we fall asleep, curled up into each
other in the sand.

Chapter Fourteen

Some time later, my eyes open. I take in the rush of nearby surf, the moonlit beach, the dark forms of turtles in the distance. I'm covered in goose bumps. I press myself against Wendell, savoring his warmth. Then I notice voices up the beach. Men's voices. And far-off headlights shining onto the sand.

"Wendell," I whisper, shaking him gently awake.

His eyes open, and his lips, automatically, find mine.

"Wendell, look." I gesture in the direction of the voices. "There are people nearby. Probably the guards."

Furrowing his eyebrows, Wendell rubs his face and sits up. His voice comes out scratchy. "Then why are the headlights on? Any volunteer should know that lights bother the turtles." He pauses. "Let's check it out."

"But we're not supposed to be here. We could get in trouble." I stand up, arranging my clothes, brushing the sand from my legs, combing my fingers through my tangled hair. My lips still feel tender from so much kissing.

"Just a peek, Z," Wendell urges.

I relent. As we walk, I glimpse the large forms of leatherback turtles. I can just barely make out human forms farther ahead. And the hulking shape of a truck. Low, hip-hop salsa beats grow louder as we move closer. We slow down, still in the shadows, but close enough to the headlight beams to see what's going on.

There are silhouettes of three men with shovels. They're digging into holes and plopping the contents into a bucket.

"Poachers," Wendell whispers fiercely. "What the hell?"

My insides freeze. "No one's seen us," I say, glancing around, feeling exposed in the middle of this stretch of sand. "Let's go."

He nods. "We'll call the cops."

Suddenly, one of the men yelps. He drops the bucket and his hand flies to his arm.

Another yelp, louder; more of a scream, actually. A second man drops his shovel.

A third man cries out, clutching his thigh and cursing.

It's as if they're getting hit by invisible punches. One man grabs his arm, the other his leg, the other his stomach. Then the first clutches his head, the next his cheek, the next his back.

The men look around, panicked. One runs into the jungle. "Who did that?" another man calls out, shielding his eyes in the beam of headlights.

I squeeze Wendell's hand, wondering if we should run now or if that would attract attention. I glance at my clothes. I picked the wrong night for a white sundress. At least Wendell is wearing dark colors.

"It came from the trees!" another man cries.

The others follow. "Who's throwing stones?"

When I see the glint of steel in one man's hand, I gasp. Slowly, I back away. "A machete," I whisper.

Wendell's arm tightens around me. "Let's leave," he says, "quiet and slow."

When we're far enough down the beach, we tear up the jungle path toward the cabanas. With shaking hands, Wendell uses the phone in the office hut to call the police. The clock reads three a.m.

Over the phone, Wendell launches into an explanation of what's just happened. When he hangs up, he still looks worried. "It was Chucho. He said he'll drive there himself right now."

"Great," I say flatly. "The most competent guy on the force."

"He was mad." Wendell scowls. "At *us*. Said we could've been killed. Told us to stay off that beach."

I take his hand. "Well, at least we did something."

"Right," he says, "which is more than we can say for the no-show volunteers."

"Did Pepe ever email you their names?" I ask.

He shakes his head, looking ready to tear his hair out in frustration.

"Hey," I say in a soothing voice. "We probably saved some eggs tonight."

We lie in the hammock outside Wendell's cabana, tucking the mosquito net around us, swinging slowly, talking. When my eyelids are nearly too heavy to keep open, I ask, "Who do you think was throwing stones?"

"Whoever it was has great aim," Wendell says sleepily. "He might've even scared off the poachers."

I snuggle closer to Wendell, losing myself in his cinnamon-soap smell. "Or she," I point out, dozing off, vaguely wondering what Meche knows about the poaching.

❖ ❖ ❖

The next morning, we wolf down breakfast and head to the police station. Gerardo is there, eyes fixed on a TV on one of the file cabinets. When he hears us come in, he straightens up and shuffles some papers around on his desk.

Wendell gets straight to the point. "Officer, *buenos días*. We're checking on what happened last night."

"Last night?" He stares up at the clicking fan, obviously clueless.

"We called in another poaching incident," Wendell says impatiently. "Chucho said he'd drive over there and catch them in the act."

Gerardo frowns and unlocks the file cabinet. He flips through folders for a few minutes, then turns to us, puts up his hands. "Chucho must not have finished the report yet. Maybe he went straight home after checking out the beach. It was probably the end of his shift. My guess is he's asleep now."

Wendell whispers to me, "Are we supposed to bribe this guy? Just to get a report filed?"

I shrug. I've met my share of corrupt small-town cops, enough to know that offering a bribe could get you in more trouble. It's best to be cautious. "Maybe they're just really inept," I whisper back. "We can always go over their heads later."

In the meantime, being pleasant is probably our best strategy. "Officer," I say, forcing my voice to stay polite and steady, "could you tell Chucho to call us when he gets in?"

"And tell him we want to see his report," Wendell adds with a scowl. Before he can say another word, I drag him by the arm out the door.

❖ ❖ ❖

Next stop, Pepe.

We spot him just as he's walking into the Turtle Center. When he catches our eyes, he waves. "*Qué onda*. What brings you here so early today, *amigos*?"

Wendell delivers the news. "We saw poachers on Playa Mermejita again."

Pepe raises his eyebrows in alarm. "Really?"

"They were digging up the nests. And no guards in sight."

"What did you do?" Pepe asks, wrinkling his eyebrows.

"Called the police. Chucho dealt with it. Supposedly. We haven't heard back from him."

Pepe rubs his forehead. "Well, I'm sure he'll handle it. In the meantime, I'll talk with the volunteers, make sure they stay on task."

Wendell still looks distraught. "Is that it?"

"Don't worry. But remember, *muchachos,* stay off the beach. Not just for the turtles. These poachers could be dangerous."

"What about the volunteers, Pepe?" I demand. "Isn't it dangerous for them?"

He closes his eyes for a long moment. "They're specially trained."

"Then where are they? We need to talk to them. The police need to talk to them!" I'm getting so worked up, sweat is pouring down my face.

"I'll put the police in touch with them," Pepe assures us in a measured voice. "It's not your job to interrogate them, *muchachos.*"

Wendell's jaw stiffens. "We have to stop these guys, Pepe. Every night of poaching—it's thousands of eggs gone."

Pepe rests his hand on Wendell's shoulder. "I appreciate your passion, man. We'll take care of it. I promise." He gives us a stern look. "But *you* have to promise to keep off the beach, stay safe."

Wendell looks at me. "I can't promise that, Pepe."

"What?" Pepe's obviously not used to people disagreeing with him.

"Sorry," Wendell says, "but I'll do whatever it takes to protect the turtles."

"Me too," I add in a gesture of solidarity. "Playa Mermejita—it's like my backyard. This is my home now. My responsibility."

❖ ❖ ❖

Early the next evening, I'm trudging down the path to the cabanas, laden with bags of chile and cheese and eggs from the market. I'm planning on trying out *chiles rellenos* for dinner. But Layla isn't in the kitchen. She's supposed to be making cream of squash soup, but the squashes are sitting on the counter, abandoned. I glance at the clock. Nearly six. We have to get cooking soon.

On the way to Layla's cabana, I pass Linda from Venezuela in her black bikini and straw hat. "Hey, have you seen Layla?" I ask.

"There she is," Linda says, gesturing toward the beach. "Building a sand castle."

A sand castle? I breathe out in exasperation. "Thanks."

I jog toward the beach, not sure what to make of this.

Sure enough, there she is with Joe, kneeling in the sand. The sun is low on the horizon, the water silvery. The last rays of sunlight illuminate a moat around a lopsided castle. What's she doing playing around when we have fifteen guests to feed in an hour?

Annoyed, I storm up to her. "Having fun?"

Her hair covers her face like a golden curtain.

"Did you think dinner would make itself, Layla?"

"Stay playfully childish," she says, quoting Rumi in a shaky voice. *"Your face will turn rosy with illumination like the redbud flowers."*

Joe pats her on the shoulder, then quietly offers to juggle shells. When she shakes her head, he murmurs that none of this matters anyway because we're all doomed.

Words of comfort? I pull back her hair. She's crying. I should have realized something was wrong. When the going gets tough, Layla builds sand castles. My voice softens. "Hey, what's wrong, Layla?"

She looks at me, her hands covered with wet sand. "The real estate agent sent me an email."

My muscles tense. "And?"

"The owners decided to give this land to their son. They're not renting it to be managed anymore."

"What?" I sputter. "If you'd done the contract on day one, this never would've happened!"

"I know, love. I'm sorry. I just haven't gotten around to it, I've been so busy."

I explode. "You did this on purpose, didn't you? You wanted some excuse to move on to the next country, right?"

"Of course not, Z!" Layla shakes her head, and then dissolves into sobs. "I love it here. It's our home."

I study her face. She looks truly miserable. "Really, Layla? What about the new countries you've added to the List?"

"They're places to visit, love. For vacations." She cups her hand to my cheek. "I promised you. And if I could make it happen, we'd stay in Mazunte for good. But now we have to leave."

"Leave? We could find a property nearby—"

"There's nothing, Z. I've looked. No English-teaching jobs either." She wipes her eyes and starts with more Rumi. *Don't let your throat tighten with fear. Take sips of breath—*

"Layla," I say firmly. "Have you talked with the owners?

I mean, you had a verbal agreement. Maybe we can convince them to honor it."

She shakes her head. "Apparently, the owner's son has been asking for the land for years. For whatever reason, they decided now's the time to give it to him."

I consider this. If we leave, where would Wendell go? And what if I never connect with my father? What if he's somewhere in this town? What if he needs me to draw him out? What if he's on the verge of showing himself? My mind sifts through all the possibilities.

"I'm going to talk with the owners," I say, my voice hard. To make Layla feel on board with my plan, I add, "Give me some of your amulets, Layla. And a bunch of pink from your heart chakra."

"Oh, love . . . ," she sighs, pulling me close.

"We're meant to be here, Layla. It's perfect. And I'm not letting a ridiculous curse or flaky owners mess it up."

Layla gives me a weak smile, brushes the sand from her hands. "Ready to make dinner?"

We walk back through the jungle, my arm around her shoulder, Joe the clown at our heels.

"Let's go in person," I suggest. "That's our best hope. A personal plea."

Layla squeezes my shoulder. "I'll email the agent to let the owners know we're coming. And get their address."

Barely holding back tears, I whisper, "I've finally found home." I look over her shoulder at the sun, glowing orange through the trees, dropping behind Punta Cometa. With new resolve, I whisper, "There's no way I'm letting it go without a fight."

❖ ❖ ❖

The next morning, I wake to a steady drizzle and faint watery-gray light through the window. It must be before dawn. Layla hasn't made her rounds with the bell for sunrise yoga yet. I'm about to close my eyes again when I hear a noise outside my door. I try to ignore it, but there it is again. I untangle myself from the mosquito net, and in my bare feet, I pad across the floor and peek out the window. A wet raccoon is pawing at something on my front stoop.

I open the door, which sends the animal scurrying. Then I look down. There's a pile of bloody bones encircled with sharp stones, sticks, broken chicken eggs. Flies buzz like crazy around it.

Another curse.

After a wave of disgust, rage fills me. This is the last thing I need today. I'm already anxious about our visit to the landowners. And this curse—even though I don't believe in this stuff—it reeks of a bad omen.

"Layla!" I call out, noting that her front stoop also holds a fly-infested mess. "Who's on curse cleanup duty this morning?"

She comes out, frowning and shaking her head.

On the other side of my hut, Wendell pokes his head from his doorway. Not surprisingly, his front stoop also holds curse remnants under a swarm of flies. He wrinkles his nose. "Gross," he groans. "Not again."

"Hey!" Layla says. "There's a note here."

Wendell and I head over to Layla's hut while she runs to the shed and returns with the rubber gloves. She plucks the note from under a stone and unfolds it, fumbling.

It's written in block letters on notebook paper. *LÁRGUENSE DE AQUÍ . . . SI NO SE QUIEREN MORIR.*

Silently, I take in the meaning. "Get out of here . . . if you don't want to die." For a moment, my heart freezes. Then anger surges through me. "Layla," I say, "come on, let's clean it up. Get out the incense and amulets."

"I don't know, love." Layla looks at me gravely. "The owners want us to leave, and whoever's leaving these curses wants us to leave . . . maybe we're not supposed to be here." A tear snakes from the corner of her eye. "Maybe we should go with the flow, stop resisting, just leave."

"No!" The force of my voice surprises me. "This is our home. And this job, Layla—it's perfect for you. And Wendell—you're a natural with the turtles."

"But who's doing this?" Layla whispers.

I glance at Wendell, remembering his poacher theory.

Slowly, he says, "This curse happened soon after we saw the poaching. So did the last curse, right?"

"But," I point out, "the poachers didn't know we saw them."

Wendell chews on a thumbnail. "They might've figured it out once they saw the cops investigating."

"Well." Layla draws in a breath. "For the moment, there's nothing to do but clean up this mess, right? Wendell, get the buckets and trash bags and cleaning stuff. Zeeta, help me with the amulets and incense."

As we gather the materials and dispose of the curse remnants, Layla regains her spark. And as the guests trickle out of their cabanas and offer to help, Layla grows even more energized. Soon she's quoting Rumi with happy abandon, humming as she works. I take in the rain plastering her blond hair to her face, her dripping-wet huipil, her cheeriness in the face of this thoroughly unsavory task.

As I light some incense, a laugh escapes my mouth.

Layla grins at me and says in a Rumi-soaked voice, *"You laugh like the sun coming up laughs at a star that disappears into it."*

"Hey, let's go talk to the owners now, Layla."

"I should really stay and finish cleaning up, love."

I glance over at Wendell, who's hosing off the paths. He'll need to make coffee and breakfast for the guests. I hesitate. Do I want to face the owners alone? Maybe it would be best this way. I can devise a strategy, stick with it. "I'll go by myself," I say finally.

"You'll do great!" she assures me. She disappears into her cabana and comes out with a scrap of paper. "Here's the address. It's not a long walk."

The paper reads *José and Guadalupe, Camino del Mar #22* in Layla's swirling scrawl. That's our street. The number is higher, so it must be farther along, toward Playa Mermejita, near Lupita's. Hopefully, that grouchy firewood vendor isn't one of the owners.

In the increasingly heavy downpour, I walk up the hill, my palms sweaty even though it's cool. Clutching by bag, I pass the dirt driveways and their crooked wooden signs, follow the rising numbers. A few dogs bark halfheartedly as I pass, and one follows me for a while, until he stops, looking bored. The flowers and leaves hanging over the road glisten, their colors more vibrant in the rain.

I'm shivering by the time I reach number twenty. Maybe the owners are Lupita's neighbors. Maybe she can help me convince them. And then I reach it, number twenty-two. But here's the sign about *mole* for sale on Sundays, and here's the bougainvillea. I pause, confused.

Then I realize: number twenty-two *is* Doña Lupita's house. And a split second later, I remember that Lupita is a nickname for Guadalupe. And chances are her husband, Rogelio's, first name is José, like most other men here.

I stand still, stunned, as rain drips down my cheeks, clings to my eyelashes. Finally, I take a deep breath, cross my goose-bumped arms, and walk forward.

The gate is closed, padlocked. The birds sound more subdued today, only occasionally calling out. The courtyard looks sad and empty without sunshine, without tea bubbling over the fire pit, without Lupita's cheery presence bringing it to life. My finger shaking, I ring the buzzer.

"*¿Quién es?*" Lupita's voice calls.

"Me, Zeeta!" I shout.

"Zeeta!" Her voice rings out, full of delight. She appears through the leaves with a ring of clinking keys. "Zeeta!" she says again, beaming. "How good to see you! Come in! I'm expecting some people to stop by soon. Business stuff. But you and I can still chat for a bit." She ushers me inside. "Oh, you're soaking wet!" She takes off her shawl and wraps it around my shoulders. Clucking about how I'll catch cold, she leads me into the kitchen hut.

I set down my bag. I'm shivering more now, and I don't know what to say, so I stay quiet, letting her fill the space with her chatter. "Sit, sit, *mija!*" She bustles about, heating water for tea on the stove. She pulls a handful of fresh chamomile from a basket and tosses the blossoms into the water.

"Wait, Doña Lupita," I say, swallowing hard. "I'm not here to chat. I'm here—you know the Cabañas Magia del Mar near Punta Cometa?"

She nods, puzzled. "Of course. That land has been in my family for years. My husband and I rent it out."

I force myself to continue. "Well, I didn't realize until just this morning, but I live on your land. My mom is Layla, the new manager for the cabanas."

Her eyes widen. "Really? That's your mother? You . . ." She blinks, confused. "You're the one who's supposed to come by this morning? You?"

I look at her imploringly. "We love it there. It's perfect. And we've been doing renovations, and I'm building paths with my boyfriend, and we have big plans. We're doing everything ecologically soundly, following all the laws, no electric lights, so the turtles stay protected." I'm rambling now and can't stop. "It's the first time my mom and I have ever felt so attached to a place. And it was all perfect until . . ."

Doña Lupita puts her hand over mine. "Until we decided to give away our land."

I nod.

She shakes her head, dismayed. "I had no idea you lived there."

"Whenever I tell people, they say the place is cursed. They act like we're doomed. I was tired of hearing it. I decided not to mention it to you."

She rubs her face. "I must be honest with you, *mija*. It's true, the land seems to be cursed. . . . Oh, at first I thought it was just rumors and people's imagination. But I have to admit, I've had more managers than I can count for those cabanas. Within months, they're gone. I'm ready to give up."

"But, Doña Lupita! It's just that someone wants us off the land. Whoever left the curses and the note."

"What curses?" Her eyes widen. "What note?"

"We found dead chickens outside our cabanas. And the second time—this morning—there was a note telling us to leave. Or else."

She frowns, thinking.

"Listen, we're not intimidated." I sound more confident than I feel. "We just want to find out who's trying to scare us away and stop them. We want to stay here for—" I almost say *forever*. Instead, I finish with "a long, long time."

Doña Lupita is quiet as she stands up, stirs sugar into the tea. My hands clutch the warm mug, and we stare at each other through the steam.

Finally, she speaks. "*Mira, mija*. For years I've been saving that land for my older son. Against the wishes of my husband. I thought that renting the cabanas to managers was a way to make use of the property. At least until my older son could claim the land. But . . . things haven't worked out as I'd hoped."

She runs her hand over her braid, distraught. "For years my younger son has been asking for the property. But most of the time he was living in Mexico City. He made enough money there, and now he's ready to settle here. Over the past few months, he's been telling us constantly how much he wants the land. I've grown tired of arguing about it with my husband. I decided he was right. Why hold the land for our older son, who might never claim it?

"So finally, a few days ago, my husband and I decided to give it to our younger son, for his birthday coming up. He doesn't know about it—we figured it would be a surprise. Of course, we felt bad breaking our agreement with the new managers—you and your mother, it turned out—but our son is so desperate for the land. He might leave again if he doesn't get it." She lets out a wavery sigh. "I want my family together. If the land will keep him here, then I have to give it to him."

"Doña Lupita." My gaze hangs on to hers, intense. "Could you put it off a little longer? Give him the land next year for his birthday? Or the year after that? To give us time to find another place to manage?" My voice crackles with emotion. "Please, Doña Lupita. *Por favor.*"

For a long time she stares at me, as if she's taking in every strand of hair, every eyelash, every last skin cell.

I sip my tea, anxiously waiting.

Once I've made it through the entire cup, Lupita says, "Listen, *mija*, I will try to convince my husband to wait a bit longer." She pauses. "I'll see if I can gain you a few months."

"*Gracias.*" I exhale with relief, but what I really want is years—five, ten, maybe more. And I don't want another piece of land. I want this one, just at the edge of Punta Cometa. This place that draws me to it like a magnet, as if I were a sea turtle finally coming home, to the place programmed in the deepest parts of my cells. At the risk of seeming pushy and ungrateful, I make a last-ditch effort. "Is there any other option? Some way we can stay on the land for more time? Like . . . for years?"

A far-off look passes across Doña Lupita's face. "If my older son returned. If he claimed the land. He always had a special connection with the place. You see, life has been a struggle for him. I wanted to keep him near me to help him, protect him. Of course, my husband has always said we should give the land to our younger son, to reward his successes. But I've held out for the one who needs us, needs the land. Most people—like my husband—don't understand him. But I do. He's tenderhearted, the kind of person who might let you stay there."

"Where is he?" I ask hopefully. "I'll talk to him."

She shakes her head sadly. "He's—he's not . . ." She begins again. "He'd have to convince his father. And . . ." Her voice fades again. "There's more. It's a mess."

Through the doorway, I see that it's raining harder now.

Thunder is booming, lightning flashing. She doesn't finish her explanation, simply busies herself with washing dishes, and when the rain lets up and I say I should be going, she doesn't object. She only gives me a long hug goodbye and says she hopes a few months is long enough for Layla and me to find some other property nearby. Her eyes tear up. "I've only just gotten to know you, *mija*. I don't want you to leave."

Chapter Fifteen

I know what I have to do next. Find Doña Lupita's husband, convince him to let us stay. I need him on board, but I'm guessing it won't be easy. Didn't Lupita say he was stubborn, and bitter, like a cacao bean?

Remembering where Lupita said his store is, I take a narrow turnoff from the main dirt road and walk uphill, past shacks of wood and tin and cane leaves, tangles of flowering bushes. The pitter-patter of raindrops surrounds me, tapping on the leaves, the rooftops, a soft *shhh*. I start running, the rainwater streaming from the tips of my hair, down my cheeks, my bare arms. The road has turned to mud now, a network of tiny ravines and rivulets. Breathless, I skirt puddles, even though my sandaled feet are already coated with mud.

On the hilltop perches a small green cement building,

with an awning and garage-door-style front, wide open. ABARROTES ROGELIO, the sign reads. Shivering, I hurry toward the shop. At the front, there's a wooden table with an ancient cash register. A man sits behind it, dozing.

I wipe my feet as best I can, then enter the store quietly. He keeps snoring. He's Lupita's age, wearing a button-down cotton shirt and a sweater vest and dress pants, all worn and, at closer look, darned. His feet are encased in old leather sandals. His face looks vulnerable, his jaw slack, his head tilted back in complete abandonment to sleep.

An old, romantic tune plays on the small radio, what sounds like a classic Mexican song. Rubbing my arms, trying to warm up, I poke around the store. The two sparse aisles contain neat rows of cans and boxes, every one dust-free. Canned chiles, toilet paper, pasta for soup, cubes of beef broth, bags of rice, shampoo, pink bars of laundry soap. Remembering what Lupita said, I pick up a can and examine its expiration date. May, eleven years ago. Everything exudes oldness, loneliness. Like a museum that no one comes to anymore. In the corner is a pink feather duster, and beside that, a guitar.

I put down my bag and study the guitar. It looks old but well cared for, the wood oiled, all the strings intact. I run my fingers over the instrument, admiring its smooth curves, polished sheen. On an impulse, I pick it up and strum.

The man jerks awake with a start and a snort. Abruptly, he looks around, until his eyes land on me.

"Sorry, *señor*," I say quickly. "I was just waiting for you to wake up and ..." My voice fades. Really, there's no excuse for touching his guitar. My mind reels. "I just— How much is this guitar?"

He blinks, orienting himself, and coughs. "Not for sale."

"Oh." Relief. What would I do with a guitar? I set the instrument gently back in the corner. Searching for some way to remedy this awkward start, I ask, "Do you play?"

"Not anymore. I just keep it clean and in tune in case . . ." He clears his throat. "Can I help you with something, *mija*?" he asks, his words kinder now.

I glance around and name the first thing my eyes land on. An ancient roll of toilet paper. I pick it up, make a show of looking for change in my pocket, wondering how to broach the subject of the land, when he says, "I'll let you play it. But it can't leave the store."

I stare at the toilet paper, and finally sputter, "The guitar?"

He breaks into laughter. "Yes, the guitar! Not the toilet paper."

I smile, embarrassed. "Oh, I don't know how to play."

He studies my face. "Want to learn?"

I set down the toilet paper, trying to think of some logical answer. Nothing comes to me, so I say, "Yes."

Through a film of cataracts, his eyes glitter. "You get a free guitar lesson with every purchase."

"Really?"

He laughs, slapping his knee. "It's a new promotion I just thought of now." He nods toward the toilet paper. "Three pesos, please."

I count out three pesos—about a quarter.

"*Bueno*," he says. "Let's begin! Here, sit down." He scoots a wooden chair my way, then takes a wool blanket from behind the counter. "Put this around you, *mija*. You can't play well if you're cold and wet."

I sit down, wrap the scratchy blanket around my shoulders. *"Gracias, señor."*

He sits on the chair across from me, picks up the guitar, rests it on his lap as if it's a small child. He tilts his head as he tunes it.

"Mind if I ask you some questions?" I ask, pulling my notebook from my bag, thankful that just the edges are damp.

"About guitar?" he asks.

"Um, sure. Guitar." I poise my pen over a blank page. "What do you like best about teaching guitar?"

He chuckles. *"¿Quién sabe?* Who knows. You're my first student, *mija*." He pauses, tightening a string here and there, listening to the tone and making adjustments. *"Pues,* maybe not the first, but the first in a long time."

"Did you teach it to—your children?" I hazard. A good way to bring up his son.

He looks down at the strings, plucking one, then twisting the knob. Then he says, "To my older son. He was talented, but he didn't want to play the ballads I taught him. He only wanted to play rock music. *Pura música de rock,*" he says with a sigh and a shake of his head.

He starts playing a romantic ballad, singing in a raspy voice, sad and sincere and full of yearning. There's something vaguely familiar about the melody. I pay attention to the words, catching snippets here and there.

"You say I have no pain, because you never see me cry,
There are the dead who do not cry, and their sorrow is
     much greater than mine. . . ."

Part of the refrain goes *Llorona, Llorona*. Weeping Woman. This song must be about that legend Joe mentioned, the woman who killed her children, who cries, "*Mis hijooooos . . .*"

I'm like green chile, Llorona, spicy, but delicious. . . .
I have already given you my life, Llorona,
What else do you want?

"Beautiful," I say when the last note fades. "I just heard the story of La Llorona for the first time."

"It's a Mexican folk song. Hundreds of years old. The kind of music I love."

"I can't believe your son would choose rock music over this," I say. "I mean, I'm a teenager and I think it's *padre*."

He considers this. "*Pues,* perhaps my son has grown to love it too."

"You miss him," I observe. Doña Lupita implied that they haven't seen him in a long time.

Rogelio plucks a few dissonant notes, then shakes his head.

I remember what Lupita said about her husband's stubbornness. "You could ask him to play guitar with you again," I venture. "See if his taste in music has changed."

He stops playing, wrapping his arms around the guitar. His eyes are deeply lined, with bags beneath them, tugging them down.

Suddenly, I feel guilty about my deception. *"Señor,"* I begin. "I didn't come to buy toilet paper."

He raises an eyebrow.

Rain drums on the awning, plops into puddles outside. I choose my words carefully. "I came to ask you a favor. My mother and I manage the cabanas near Punta Cometa. We love it there. We want to stay. Your wife told me that your younger son wants the land now, but she wants to save it for your older son. She thinks the older son might let us stay."

He studies my face, disappointed. "So you're not really interested in guitar, are you?"

My eyes flicker away, to the sheets of rain pouring down on the muddy street. I stammer, "No—well, yes, I mean. I am. Absolutely. I do want to learn." I hesitate, then take a deep breath. "But I can only take lessons if I'm here. If I can stay on the land." I watch him anxiously.

He runs his hands over his face. "It's a much messier situation than you can imagine, *mija*."

"Messes can be beautiful," I say with a smile.

"Oh, really?"

I nod. Thinking of the flavors of Lupita's *mole*, I quote the song he played me. *"Picante pero sabroso."* Spicy but delicious.

He laughs. "So if I want to teach you, I must let you stay on the land?"

"Maybe you can hold off till next year? Or the year after?"

He stands up, creaking, then sets the guitar in my arms. He guides one hand to the neck, positions my fingertips over three strings. "I'll think about it," he says. "Now strum."

I do as he says, and a sweet, sad sound emerges.

"That's A minor," he says. "*¿Ya ves?* See? This, this is beautiful. And simple."

He teaches me D minor, E, and G next. He's patient as I struggle to remember where my fingers go when I switch notes. Despite my bumbling, I like the feel of the taut strings beneath my fingertips. I like making these chords that resonate through my bones, make my chest feel full and vibrating.

Whenever I grow frustrated, Don Rogelio cracks some silly joke that makes me laugh. At the end of an hour, he says, "Now, *mija*, go home and practice. These four chords are all you must know for 'La Llorona.' Come back when you've mastered them." He chuckles and adds, "Or when you need more toilet paper."

I'm excited to practice, but I'll have to borrow a guitar from one of the guests, maybe Horacio. Grinning, I hold out the guitar to Rogelio.

"Espérate," he says—wait—and disappears into a back room. A moment later, he emerges with a worn black case. He places the guitar in the case, snaps it shut, and hands it to me. "I'm lending it to you."

I blink, not sure what to say. "But I can't—"

"I know I can trust you." He laughs. "My wife and I know where you live!"

"*Gracias,* Don Rogelio. I'll come back soon." I pick up the guitar, heavier than I expected in its case. I reach my other hand out to shake his.

As our hands meet, he says, "There are other cabanas you could manage." He searches my face, curious. "Why does that land matter so much?"

"I—I've lived all over the world and never felt this way before." I try to keep my voice steady. "It's home."

He nods, handing me the toilet paper in a small blue bag. "*Que te vaya bien, mija.*" Go well, my daughter.

"*Gracias, señor. Hasta luego.*" I walk out into the rain, which is letting up a bit. In the drizzle, I half run down the hill, skidding on the slick mud, the guitar case banging against my leg. At the base of the hill, I turn around to take one last look at the lonely little shop. I see him through the rain, standing beneath the awning, watching me go.

❖ ❖ ❖

Over dinner, I explain to Layla that my tentative deal with Rogelio involves me learning guitar, and a roll of eleven-year-old toilet paper. "Our lucky roll!" Layla announces. She's plotting to incorporate it into her next found-art project. I refrain from pointing out the soggy mess it'll be in the next rainstorm.

Lingering late in the kitchen hut, I practice my four chords over and over while Wendell touches up digital photos for a visitors' guide. Eventually, the guests stumble back to their cabanas. It must be around one or two in the morning, but I don't feel like sleeping.

Wendell must not either. "How about a walk?" he asks, closing his laptop.

I raise an eyebrow. "Had enough of my four chords?"

He laughs and tugs me up. "Let's go."

"Isn't it a little late?"

"We have to make up for afternoons apart, right?"

"Let's go to Playa Mermejita," I suggest. For some reason, I want to go to the site where our handfasting will be. If Wendell stays, that is. There are so many things unsaid between us now, an undercurrent to every conversation. Whether he'll stay or go. The knowledge that our future together hangs in limbo.

"We can't tell Pepe," he reminds me.

"Right."

My heart pounds as we cut through the jungle, practically tiptoeing past the Forbidden Territory. And once we're on the beach, my heart continues to beat fast. We're not supposed to be here, which makes it feel thrilling, dangerous. Hand in hand we walk, tentatively. The beach is dark, but stray bits of light bounce off fog, creating a fuzzy glow. We make a wide arc around the leatherbacks in various stages of nesting, careful not to disturb them. I scan the beach ahead for any sign of poachers or volunteers. There's no one.

Suddenly, Wendell stops, staring ahead. "Z," he says, wrinkling his forehead. "Something's weird."

"What?"

"The flipper tracks—they're usually really clear, right up to the nest. And the sand over the buried eggs—the flippers leave special marks when they pack it down." He gestures to the tracks in front of us. "But look."

The tracks are messed up. And the sand over the covered nests—it's too neat, flattened into a firm circle, with spade-shape indentations of a shovel. A human covered these holes.

"I think the eggs are gone, Z," Wendell says, rubbing his face.

I notice rougher tracks headed in the other direction, toward the jungle. Human footprints that have been tamped over with a shovel, leading straight to the patch of mud off the road.

Wendell's gaze follows mine. "They must know the cops are on to them. They're covering their tracks. To make it look like the turtles are burying their eggs. Business as usual. That way, the cops will stop investigating."

"Let's check, Wendell."

He takes a breath. "If Pepe knew we were touching the nests . . ." Then, making a decision, he drops to his knees.

I join him. On all fours, we scrape away the sand. When we've gotten well over a meter down, we still haven't found a single egg. "Stop," Wendell says, wiping sand from his face. "There's nothing here."

For a few minutes, Wendell sits still, head in his arms. Maybe mourning the lost eggs. Maybe holding in his rage. Finally, he stands up. "I'm coming here tomorrow, Z. With my camera. I'll catch them in the act."

"How? It's too dark."

"They had their headlights on last time. I'll hide in the

jungle, find a good angle, get a few shots. They'll never know I was here."

"But they're dangerous, Wendell. And what if Pepe finds out? You might lose your job."

"I don't care."

"Then I'm going too."

"Z," he says carefully. "No. You could get hurt."

"So could you," I counter. "I'm going."

"Z, I really don't think—"

"If you're going, I'm going."

And it's decided. We'll do this together. On the walk home, I wonder what new kind of mess I've just gotten myself into.

Chapter Sixteen

The next night at midnight, Wendell and I creep down Playa Mermejita, wearing black pants and shirts. With our flashlight off, there's barely enough moonlight to see. My pulse is drumming, my gaze skimming the sand ahead. Nothing. Maybe the poachers haven't arrived yet. Maybe they're not coming tonight. I'm hoping for that possibility. I've had all day to think about everything that could go wrong with our plan.

Just up the beach is the dirt patch where the footprints led. We stand still, watching. A few giant turtles straggle up the beach, and others are the middle of digging holes and burying their eggs. Still no sign of the poachers. Or the guards.

"What's going on with the volunteers?" Wendell whispers. "Where are they?"

"They could be the ones poaching," I mutter. "Or maybe the poachers are paying them off." Then I add, frustrated, "And you'd think the cops would be out here investigating."

Wendell frowns. "Remember the corruption people keep talking about? The bribes and favors?"

I consider this. Maybe that's what's going on here. The cops and poachers and volunteers could all be in cahoots. Who can we trust? Pepe doesn't seem to share our suspicions about his volunteers. "Maybe we should go over Pepe's head," I whisper, "straight to the directors of the Turtle Center. Tell them our doubts."

We walk from the sand into the jungle and find a protected spot not far from the patch of tire-marked dirt. I sit down, leaning against the rough bark of a tree. For a while, we talk in whispers, watching the shapes of the turtles at work far down the beach. Soon I doze off.

At some point, a noise breaks through the rush of surf. It's the faint thumping of distant music and the roar of an engine. The headlights are on the road; it looks like they're coming straight toward us. I hold my breath, hoping we're not visible. Suddenly, the lights cut off. The music continues for a moment, then stops.

I nudge Wendell, but he's already awake, holding his camera. Together, we watch through the vines.

Three men get out of the truck. They light cigarettes and converse in loud, brazen voices, smoking and looking at the waves. I can't see their faces in the dim light. Squinting, I try to make out some details. One of them is wearing a cap.

The way they move, their baggy clothes, and their slang and the rhythms of their speech, suggest that they're teenagers. After they toss aside their cigarettes, they grab shovels and start digging.

Wendell draws in a sharp breath. It must take all his will-power not to run out there and stop them. I put my hand on his arm firmly.

Soon the poachers are dumping the eggs in buckets and carrying them to the truck. Bits of conversation float toward us between crashes of surf. "Remember to cover the tracks, *güey*!" one of them calls out.

"I know, *güey*! I heard Chucho."

Chucho? Could it be Chucho the cop? Did he warn them?

More snippets of talk: "Can't we turn on the *pinche* head-lights? I can't see, *güey*!"

"Chucho said not to, *güey*!"

Wendell lets out a string of curse words under his breath.

I squeeze his arm and whisper, "Don't lose it. Just take the pictures."

"I can't," Wendell murmurs. "It's too dark."

I bite my lip. "Then what do we do?"

"I'm using a flash. I just need to get closer. You go back to the cabanas, Z."

"It's too dangerous, Wendell. They'll see the flash. They'll come after you."

He moves closer to the edge of the trees, out of hiding. All the men would have to do is look this way.

"Zeeta," Wendell hisses, "go home."

My heart is thudding. "This is crazy, Wendell. Let's just leave. Together."

He shakes his head. "It'll take them a few seconds to even realize what happened. And by then, I'll be halfway up the path. Please, Z."

"I'm not leaving you!"

He lets out a long breath. "Fine. But, Z, the second you see the flash, run! Along the jungle and up the path. We can do it in the dark. They won't be able to keep up."

I'm not so sure. I brace my muscles.

Wendell moves even closer to the men, then steps out of the trees, exposed. He holds up the camera and presses the button.

The flash goes off, lighting up the trees, the stretch of beach, the gaping nests, the shovels, the men's faces.

They're looking straight at Wendell. Within a second, they're running at us with shovels. One pulls a knife from his belt, another a machete.

I run, and Wendell follows on my heels.

And then, from behind us, there's a cry of "*¡Ay!*"

I glance back. Stones are flying, hitting each man square in the forehead. "*¡Ay!*" The men fall to the ground one after the other, like dominoes. From somewhere above us, high in the branches, comes a man's voice. A loud, urgent word. "*¡Corre!*" Run!

We tear through the jungle, turning onto the path heading toward the Forbidden Territory. No tiptoeing past it this time. My legs are moving at top speed, my lungs and chest burning.

We've got a big lead, but the guys must have recovered. Soon they're crashing through the underbrush behind us. "Stop!" they cry. "You're dead!"

We keep running. It occurs to me that our lead isn't big enough. If we keep going to the cabanas, we'll lead them straight to the innocent guests. And there's no telling what these guys would do. Why didn't we think of this before? But there's nowhere else to go. Unless . . .

"Wendell," I say, breathless. "Follow me."

I look back, see flashes of their clothes through the trees behind us. Their shouts grow louder, closer. I'm running as fast as I can, tripping and stumbling over bushes, ducking under branches, my heart about to explode. I take one more look behind me, see the glint of a machete, catch their words: "You're dead!"

I dart past the TRESPASSERS WILL BE DEVOURED sign, bolting toward the Forbidden Territory. I hurl my body against the wire fence, making a clang. I hope Gatito's a light sleeper. But if that didn't wake him up, the men's shouts will.

I grab Wendell's hand, pull him along the fence in the direction of the gate. *Come on, Gatito, come on!* Three seconds later, when the men have nearly reached the fence—which they wouldn't know is there—Gatito roars and pounces.

The men scream in utter terror. I keep racing along the fence, with Wendell at my side. My lungs are aching, blood pumping wildly.

Meche's house comes into view. We're nearing the gate

when she appears on the doorstep. A black satin robe flows around her, grazes her knees. Her feet are bare, her hair in a loose braid over her shoulder. "What's going on? I heard Gatito, and—"

I'm doubled over, struggling to catch my breath.

"Meche!" Wendell shouts. He reaches his arms out in a pleading gesture.

Meanwhile, Gatito bounds to Meche's side. A guttural growl escapes the cat. Meche puts her hand on his back, silencing him. "Is something wrong?"

I find words. "We're being chased." I'm so breathless and terrified I can barely get the sentence out. "By poachers."

In a few quick strides, Meche is at the gate, unlocking it with a key from her pocket. She swings the gate open, motions for us to enter.

Wendell and I hesitate, eyeing the jaguar.

"Come in, come in," she urges in her husky voice. "You're safe here. Go inside. Quickly."

As she locks the gate, Wendell and I scuttle past Gatito through the door to Meche's home. Thankfully, the animal stays outside.

The room is small, aglow with a bright lantern. Firelight flickers over bare walls and unpainted wooden furniture that looks like Meche might have made it herself. In contrast to the simplicity, in the center of the room is a red velvet sofa. Following us in, she motions for us to sit. "I'll make you tea," she says, oddly composed, and walks into a tiny kitchen.

I collapse onto the soft cushion, trying to calm my thrumming heart, my shaking legs. Wendell sits beside me, wraps his arm around me. I bury my face in his shoulder, and we hold each other for a moment. "Think the poachers were scared away?" I murmur. "Or you think they realized Gatito was behind a fence?"

He breathes into my hair. "Who knows."

"They wouldn't be able to get in here, would they?" I ask, biting my lip.

Wendell tightens his arm around me. "I don't think they'd get past Kitty. I think we're safe, Z. For now."

Soon Meche comes out of the kitchen with clay mugs of fragrant chamomile tea. I note that our cake platter serves as a tray.

"*Gracias,*" I say, wrapping my hands around the cup, breathing in the sweet steam.

Meche perches on a wooden chair across from us, tightening the sash on her black robe. I stare at her, her gorgeous face, bare of makeup, in the golden lantern glow.

I'm struck by a wave of gratitude. "*Gracias,* Meche," I say again. "I don't know how to thank you."

She looks at her lap, embarrassed. *"De nada."* It was nothing.

"You saved us," Wendell says.

She waves away our thanks.

I wait for her to ask what happened, but she just sits there, watching us. Watching me, mostly. She seems curious, and something else, some emotion I can't put my finger on.

Finally, I say, "We wanted to catch the poachers in the act. So Wendell took their photo. They chased us with machetes and knives. All the way up here." I study Meche's concerned face. "Do you have any idea who they are?"

Wendell turns on his camera, and the photo appears on the screen. It's too small to make out much detail. Two of the guys' faces are visible; the other guy had his back to us. Maybe on a bigger computer screen we'll get something useful. We pass the camera to Meche, who examines it carefully.

"Look familiar?" I ask.

"No," she says, stirring her tea. "But I keep to myself. Gatito is enough for me." Her eyes shine in the firelight. "I'm sorry I can't help you more."

Wendell tries another avenue. "Have you noticed anything strange on the beach? Truck sounds? Music?"

"Listen, *muchachos*," she says with a sigh. "I have only one suggestion: Be careful who you trust. Especially on the police force."

"What?" Wendell says. "How—"

She cuts him off. "I don't feed rumors." She gives a bitter laugh. "Unless they're about me, that is."

I glance at Wendell, puzzled. "Meaning?"

Meche raises an elegant eyebrow. "Years ago, when I married an outsider, gossip flew. And then . . . when a certain tragedy happened in my life, the rumors multiplied. I decided not to fight it. If people thought I was a scary *bruja*, they might leave me alone. In peace here with my memories, with my Gatito."

"Is that why you put up those signs?" I venture.

She laughs. "I admit, I had fun making those signs."

I can't quite gather the courage to ask if she also had fun sticking dead chickens on our stoops. Instead, I ask, "And what about the managers before us? You never—got to know them?"

She shakes her head. "The rumors they heard were stronger than what they saw with their own eyes." She looks at me, almost fiercely. "Or hearts." She sets her teacup on the table. "They expect a witch, so I give them a witch." She peers out the window to Gatito. "Anyway, I only care about my baby."

I nod, sipping the last of my tea. I want to ask her more, but I'm not sure where to start.

"I liked your pink cake," she says out of the blue.

"Oh, that's good," I sputter.

"Could I have the recipe?"

"Sure," I answer, surprised. "It's angel food. I'll tell Layla."

I remember how, when I first saw Meche at the market, I wanted to interview her. And now's my chance. I sneak Wendell a little smile, then take my notebook and pen from my bag. He gives me a you've-got-to-be-kidding look as I turn to a fresh page. After a moment, I ask, "Meche, can perfect happiness exist?"

She's unfazed. Maybe she's been a recluse for so long, she has no expectations for normal interactions. She cups her chin in her hand and says thoughtfully, "In moments and memories."

"Like what?" I push.

"The laugh of a little girl." She stares into her empty teacup. "Or the nuzzle of Gatito."

"Tell me more about—" I want to say *the girl*, but Meche looks so vulnerable sitting there, I finish with "Gatito."

Tears fill her eyes. "Gatito . . . he's getting old. I've seen the changes. Losing his appetite, tired all the time, trouble walking."

Just when I'm thinking that this creature certainly didn't have trouble hurling himself at the fence, Meche says, "He still has bursts of energy, when he feels he's protecting me." Her voice trembles. "But soon, he'll be too weak for even that. Soon, he'll leave me here alone. Then I won't have those moments anymore. Only the memories." Her voice lowers, nearly inaudible. "And I don't know if that's enough happiness to live on."

I stay quiet, glance over at Wendell. His eyes glisten with tears.

Meche is wiping her face on her sleeve, composing herself. "Sorry. I'm not used to talking to people. And it's the middle of the night. And you've been kind. Kind enough to bring me that pink cake. Angel food."

She takes a quivery breath. "The truth is, I'm afraid. I'm so afraid of what will happen when Gatito leaves me."

I meet her gaze. I think about how Doña Lupita said she was a sweet girl, a caring mother. I think about Layla's plan to gush pink waves of love. "After Gatito," I begin, "I mean—anytime, now even—you don't have to feel alone, Meche. Come visit us. There are always people coming and going. They're friendly, interesting. Travelers who've never heard the rumors."

"Zeeta," Meche says softly. "That night in the woods,

I thought you were my daughter. She'd be a young woman now, like you. Sometimes . . . when you spend so much time alone . . . it's as though you see things, talk to ghosts. I thought you were—I hoped you were . . ." She shakes herself and says, "Would you like Gatito and me to walk you home?"

I look at Wendell.

"I think we'll be okay," he says. "But thanks."

I nod. "It's been quiet out there. I think enough time has passed. Seems like the poachers gave up the search."

"It's probably for the best," says Meche. "Gatito has trouble walking more than a few paces at a time now."

On the way out the gate, Meche hands Wendell the cake platter.

As he takes it, he says, "Come over soon, Meche. Layla can teach you to make that cake."

I chime in, "Or you could come to sunrise yoga. Or how about a bonfire? You'd like it." Impulsively, I reach forward and offer Meche a hug. At first, her body is rigid beneath my arms, but after a moment, she softens.

Wendell raises a hand in farewell and says, "Give Gatito a hug for us too."

"And a kiss on the nose," I add. And I actually mean it.

❖　❖　❖

Back at the cabanas, Wendell slides the camera's memory card into his laptop. When the photo comes up on the screen, we study it. Two of the men are unfamiliar to us—teenagers in baseball caps, white T-shirts, and jeans. Their faces are generally nondescript—the same dark, square, handsome faces as most teenage guys around here. The third man has his back to us, just a black T-shirt and cutoff camouflage shorts visible. He's not wearing a cap, and he has a buzz cut, a fairly common hairstyle. His hand grips a shovel.

I stare at this third man. Something about the thick neck and stubbled hair is familiar. And those camo shorts . . . "Hey, Wendell. Zoom in on this guy's hand."

Close up, it's obvious. The guy's missing a finger. His ring finger.

At the same time, Wendell and I say, "El Dedo!"

Chapter Seventeen

After just a few hours' sleep, Wendell and I grab quick cups of coffee, then head straight to the police station. Chucho and Gerardo are there, sitting on their desks, watching TV. "What can we do for you?" Gerardo asks.

"Actually," I say, taking a deep breath, "we'd like to speak with you, Officer. In private."

Chucho bristles. Then he stands up and walks outside. I see him hovering by the open window, imagine his ears straining.

Wendell talks to Gerardo in a low voice. "We were chased by poachers. Last night, at Playa Mermejita. They had machetes. They threatened to kill us."

Gerardo's face fills with alarm. He opens the file cabinet, flips through it, mumbles, "Still can't find your other report." Opening a fresh folder, he pulls a pen from his pocket and starts filling out the form. With concern, he asks for details—estimated times, exact locations. Wendell hands over a copy of the photo on a memory stick.

Gerardo studies the image on his computer screen. "Bet they're from the city," he comments. "The trouble-makers always are. Not like our local boys."

I wish he would keep his voice down. I'm very aware of Chucho lurking outside the window.

Wendell zooms in on the four-fingered hand. Keeping his voice just above a whisper, he says, "There's a guy here, from Mexico City. He's always picking fights. He's missing the same finger on the same hand."

"Well, look at that!" Gerardo practically shouts. "Missing a finger!"

I notice Chucho's form outside the window, shifting. I imagine him texting El Dedo about this right now.

"His nickname's El Dedo," I whisper. "We can try to find out his full name."

Gerardo rubs his mustache. "All right, but be careful. This kind of guy can be vicious. And leave the rest to us."

I glance toward the window. "Actually, we—" How to phrase this delicately? "We're concerned that Chucho might be involved. The poachers mentioned his name."

Rubbing his mustache again, Gerardo says, "Well, you are aware that Chucho is a nickname for Jesús? One of the most common names here, next to José and Juan."

I look at Wendell and take a deep breath. "They said Chucho told them to cover their tracks, be careful. A

Chucho with inside information. And we think the curses we reported might've been left by these guys. With Chucho's knowledge."

Gerardo nods, says, "I'll keep this from Chucho. For now. Until there's more information. But you understand, I have to trust my fellow officer."

I press my lips together, not sure whether to trust Gerardo.

He copies the photo file to his computer, hands back the memory stick, and shows us where to sign the forms. "Is that all, *muchachos*?"

"There's one more thing," I say, and tell Gerardo about the second curse, the threatening note.

He nods briskly, then shakes our hands and tells us to be careful.

As we walk outside, Chucho glares at us. A chill sweeps through me. Probably not a good idea to have made an enemy on the police force.

❖ ❖ ❖

Next, Wendell suggests we swing by Tesoro Escondido to see if El Sapo has any ideas about El Dedo's full name.

"No clue," says El Sapo, shaking his head. "I don't think any of us know his name." He pauses. "But man, I'd love to see that *vato* behind bars. And his buddies."

"His buddies?"

El Sapo nods, peering at the image on Wendell's camera. "Two more guys from Mexico City. These guys here," he says, pointing to the image. "Supposedly in his gang. You're lucky you haven't met them. They're almost as bad as him."

"Well, if any of them turn up," Wendell says, "tell us right away, okay?"

"Sure. And I'll spread the word." El Sapo gives a satisfied grin. "If El Dedo shows his face on this beach again, he's as good as in jail."

Next stop, the Turtle Center.

We breeze across the grounds, straight to Pepe's office. The door's open; he's absorbed in his cell phone, until he notices us and tucks it away. When we give him the latest news about the poachers and how we suspect Chucho's involved, Pepe runs his hand through his hair, obviously upset. "I'm just glad you escaped," he says gravely.

Deep creases form at his forehead. "Let's see the photo," he says.

When the photo shows up on the computer screen, Wendell points out the four-fingered hand and explains our theory that the poachers are El Dedo and his buddies.

Pepe draws in a sharp breath. "Anything else?" he asks, handing the memory stick back to Wendell.

Wendell nods and lowers his voice. "We don't know how far the corruption goes, Pepe. We're concerned that the volunteers weren't there again. We think someone's paying them off. Or maybe they're the ones poaching."

Pepe sighs, shaking his head. "What a mess. Listen, leave this to me, *muchachos*. I'll look into all of this. Just don't try anything like last night again. You could've been killed. Stay away from that beach."

Wendell shakes his head, his jaw set firm.

"Wendell," Pepe begins, his voice sharp.

"I told you," Wendell interrupts. "I'll do whatever it takes to protect the turtles."

I cross my arms. "We've faced danger before. We can handle it." I keep my gaze steady. "We're investigating this ourselves."

Pepe stares at us for a moment, frustrated. Then his expression softens. "Hey, you two must be exhausted. Why don't you go home and take a nap? We'll talk more about this later."

As we leave, he calls out, *"Tengan cuidado, muchachos."*

❖ ❖ ❖

Pepe's right about the nap. I wake up feeling refreshed. Sunlight streams through my window and a song loops through my head—my favorite song from my father's CD. The melody moves through me as I crawl out from under the mosquito net and walk into the bathroom. Surrounded by glass starfish mosaics, I splash water on my face, then braid my hair and throw on a sundress. On the way out the door, I grab Rogelio's guitar. If I want to master those four chords, I'd better practice every moment I can get.

I settle on my hammock, squinting at the silver light reflecting off the ocean in the distance. One by one, I play the chords. A minor, D minor, E, and G. I switch from one to another, with only a small pause in between. Hard-won calluses have sprouted up on my fingertips. My hours of practice have paid off.

I savor the feeling of my fingers switching instinctively

from one pattern to another to another, without my mind interfering. It's like learning a new language—at first it's such a struggle it hurts my brain, but after I say the same phrase fifty times, it becomes part of me. Without looking down, I just let my fingertips lead the way. I stare at the ocean as the notes repeat, like one wave after another.

Rogelio said these were the only four chords I needed to know to play "La Llorona." I start humming the tune, singing a few phrases here and there, slowly fitting it all together. My fingers cooperate, finding the notes that correspond to the melody. And soon, to my complete shock, I'm more or less playing the song.

Yesterday, I was a wonder, Llorona,
And today, I'm not even a shadow . . .

Suddenly, my fingers freeze on the strings. "La Llorona." It's the song that's been running through my head. My favorite song from my father's CD. My father's version had a different arrangement, but still, it's the same song, the same basic four chords.

I'm staring at the waves, trying to comprehend this, when Wendell calls, "Hey, Z!"

He comes out of his cabana, yawning and stretching. Running his hand through his tangled hair, he plops down beside me with a kiss.

Then, seeing my odd expression, he asks, "You okay, Z?"

"The music Rogelio played for me," I say slowly. "'La

Llorona,' the song I've been learning those chords for . . . it's on my father's CD. The first song."

Wendell wrinkles his eyebrows, trying to remember. "Hold on, Z. I'll grab my iPod."

A minute later, Wendell's back. We each take an ear bud, listen with our heads close. The song sounds like diving below the sunlit surface into cool, dark shadows, and deeper, into the fierce currents of longing and regret. As I listen, I sing along softly, filling in the words I remember.

When it ends, I take out the ear bud and stare at Wendell. "That's definitely it, Wendell. 'La Llorona.'" Still caught in the music's spell, I try to think about this logically. "Rogelio did say it was an old folk song. Probably everyone here knows it." I bite my lip. "It has to be a coincidence."

Wendell twists the cord around his finger. "Didn't Rogelio tell you his son played guitar? And liked rock music?"

I nod.

His gaze intensifies. "He didn't mention Jimi Hendrix, did he?"

I shake my head, but I see where he's going. I try to recall the stray bits of information from conversations with Rogelio and Lupita. My words come out slowly. "But this son did leave as a young man. Years ago. And he never returned." I search my memory for more. "And he was troubled. Different. But he loved Punta Cometa. He loved sea turtles." Excitement is welling up inside me. Not sure if I'm getting carried away, I turn to Wendell. "What do you think?"

"It could be your dad, Z. Everything fits."

I clutch the guitar neck. It's just a possibility, I remind myself. Not a sure thing. Cautiously, I let my mind go down that path, and little by little, more realizations hit me. "Wendell, if this is true, then Rogelio is my grandfather! And Lupita's my grandmother!" Now I can't help it. I let the sheer happiness of this idea overtake me. My mouth, my face, my entire body turn into one giant smile. Even my toes tingle with excitement. I throw my arms around Wendell. "My grandmother!"

Lupita already treats me like a granddaughter, without even knowing who I am. Who I *might be*, I correct myself. She's trusted me with her secret *mole* recipe, showered me with hugs and advice. And if Lupita were my grandmother, and Rogelio my grandfather, then of course they'd let me stay on the land.

Wendell cups my face in his hands, looks into my eyes. "Will you tell them?"

After a long pause, I shake my head. "My father has to. We have to find him." What I don't dare to say out loud is *If he's even out there. If he's still alive.*

"Maybe Lupita knows," Wendell suggests.

I nod, my mind racing. "I'm supposed to meet her this afternoon. I'll find out everything I can."

A thousand emotions swirl around inside me, until I'm nearly exploding. I need some outlet, or I might start jumping around and squealing. Or sobbing and screaming. Instead, I pick up the guitar and play those four chords, over and over and over, as if their currents might carry me to my father.

Lupita greets me in her blooming, buzzing courtyard with a hug. "*¿Qué me cuentas, mija?*" she asks cheerily. What do you have to tell me, daughter?

Oh, just that I'm your granddaughter, I think. Swallowing hard, I compose my thoughts. I mention my visit with her husband, which she's already heard about—and which utterly delights her. Then I go into the events of last night—El Dedo and the other poachers chasing us, Meche and Gatito saving us, the incompetent cops.

"*¡Ay, pobrecita!*" Poor thing! Lupita folds me again into her great bosom. "How terrifying!" She insists on giving me a shot of what she calls *agua de espanto*—fright water. She pours dark liquid from a dusty, ancient bottle into a small glass. "Here, *mija,* so you won't get sick from fright."

Fright. That about sums up last night. The liquid burns going down but warms my insides. It tastes like sugar cane liquor laced with rich spices—cloves and cinnamon.

As I let the heat seep through me, Lupita says, "You're right about the police. They're paid off, some more than others. It's all about exchanging favors and bribes in this town." She shoots me a devilish look. "Why, even I've been known to give the cops some *mole* to stay on their good side!"

Not surprising. It's how things work in most parts of the world. Little networks of favors—with a fine line between generosity and corruption. Especially in small, out-of-the-way places like this.

Lupita leads me to the outdoor kitchen area, where bulging burlap sacks sit by the table.

"I'll teach you how to make *pozole* today!" she announces.

I peer inside one of the bags. It's full of large, hardened corn kernels. Another contains dozens of dried red chiles. Lupita disappears into the kitchen and emerges with a pot containing a large pig's head. Not quite what I was expecting.

After Lupita starts boiling the water, she places red chiles gently on the comal, one by one. *"Mija,"* she begins. "I'm so glad my husband agreed to give you more time. But you shouldn't count on my older son saving you."

"Why?" I ask, helping her with the chiles, hoping she doesn't see my hands shaking. I try to sound casual, but an electric charge is surging through me. I'm grateful for the *agua de espanto's* calming effect; without it, I might jump right out of my skin.

She lets out a long sigh. "It's a long story."

"I'm not going anywhere," I say with a hopeful grin.

Another sigh. "My oldest son was my joy. His music made me smile. He sang and played guitar so beautifully. But he was very . . . fragile. Not like most people. He would swing between extremes. He was excited about his latest plans one moment, but then he fell into this sadness, for no reason I could see. Oh, how this frustrated his father! And other people. They had trouble understanding him. He was the opposite of his younger brother. Now, that one has always been friendly and upbeat. But I always paid special attention to my eldest because he needed me."

My father, I think. *She's talking about my father.*

She stirs the corn kernels into the vat of water, then stokes the fire beneath the enormous pot. "Keep an eye on those chiles, *mija*," she instructs. "Turn them once they're about to burn."

I nod, moving my gaze to the comal, my heart thumping. I try to absorb what she's telling me. It sounds like my father's bipolar wasn't diagnosed until he left home. Of course it would have been confusing and upsetting for them.

"José was nineteen," she begins. "One night, very late, we were woken up by the police chief banging on the door. He said that someone had taken my husband's truck and filled its bed with turtle eggs and freshly butchered turtle meat. Then, when the cop pulled him over, he leapt from the driver's seat and ran away, abandoning the truck. The police didn't see the driver's face, but they recognized the truck as my husband's. Of course I vouched for my husband. He'd been sleeping next to me. The chief asked to speak with my sons. My younger one was asleep in his bed." She pauses, rubbing her eyes with her wrist. "Don't forget to turn the chiles, *mija*."

I blink and look at the chiles, which are starting to burn. Quickly, I nudge and flip them over, one by one, with a wooden spoon.

Eyes watering, she continues. "But my oldest son wasn't in bed. An hour later, with the police chief still there, José came into the house. He told us he'd been alone on a walk. But he was covered in sand and blood."

The ground is shifting beneath me. This is the story Santy told me. My father's story. Any lingering doubts disappear. Lupita's son is my father. Which means Lupita really is my grandmother. Without a doubt. She's my grandmother! And this land I'm living on, this land I love so much, this land is my grandmother's land.

She's looking at me strangely now. All my feelings must be visible on my face. I swallow hard, force myself to act normally, try to recapture the soothing feeling of the *agua de espanto*. "Did you think José was telling the truth?"

"Of course not." She stirs the corn kernels and pig's head in the now-bubbling water.

"Oh." I stare into the pig's eye sockets, my heart sinking. Part of me has been clinging to the idea that he might be innocent. But if even his mother doesn't believe him . . .

"He was with a girl," she says, frowning, flipping a smoking chile.

"A girl? How do you know?"

"A mother senses these things. I smelled perfume on him." She shakes her head with conviction. "There was no poaching that night. He was meeting a girl."

I'm not sure what to make of this. Is it just the hopeful explanation of a devoted mother? "Couldn't this girl provide an alibi?"

"He wouldn't admit he was with anyone! I pleaded with him, but he wouldn't change his story. He was protecting the girl."

"Why?"

"Who knows? The police said there was enough evidence to book him. And my husband believed our son was guilty. Rogelio was furious. It was too much for poor José—

the gossip and dirty looks—and the worst of it from his own father." She shakes her head sadly. "José left town before his trial. A foreign researcher from the Turtle Center helped him get a work visa for somewhere in Europe. She believed he'd been falsely accused. I kept thinking he'd come back, but . . ."

My voice comes out in a whisper. "Has he?"

She pulls a tissue from her apron pocket, blows her nose. "José told us he planned to leave before the trial. Rogelio was so angry, he told our son never to return. He warned that if he did, he'd bring him straight to jail himself. Oh, he's so stubborn, even after so many years."

"Are you the only one here who believes he's innocent?"

"Probably," she admits, her face scrunching into a frown. "People thought he was delusional, depressed, capable of anything. It's not true. He loved the turtles more than anything. His nickname was El Tortuga!"

I flip a few more chiles, wondering if there's any chance she's right and my father is in fact innocent. "Then who did it?"

"Who knows."

"But who would've had keys to the truck?" I ask softly.

She shrugs. "Anyone could have taken them. Even back then, Rogelio always fell asleep at his store, leaving his keys on a hook. And we never locked our gate. Friends and relatives and customers were always coming and going."

Hoping she doesn't find my curiosity suspicious, I ask, "Are you in touch with him?"

She makes a small sound. I can't tell if it's a yes or a no or just a sigh. She's lost in her thoughts, pushing coals around with a stick. "You know, years ago, I went to every girl in the community, trying to figure out who he'd been with that night. Begging them to tell the truth. But no luck."

In France, my father did seem tenderhearted, kind, timid. I can't imagine him being cruel, especially to the turtles he loved so much. But I've done plenty of online research on bipolar disorder. Delusions and erratic behavior fit the profile, especially in someone whose condition was untreated. I remind myself that when I met him, he was on meds and therapy. Who knows what he was capable of as a teen, struggling with an illness he had no name for?

Without talking, Lupita and I watch the water boil, the pig's head half submerged in bubbles. It bobs, its eye sockets gaping, its mouth wide open. My father might be majorly flawed, I realize, even more flawed than I imagined.

But he was obviously loved, too. I open my notebook. "Doña Lupita, tell me about your son. The good things."

"Oh, there are so many! Let's see . . . he was the best tree climber you've ever seen—he'd scamper up and pick papayas, oranges, lemons. And he had the best slingshot aim—could hit a target a kilometer away! He loved Punta Cometa. He'd bring his guitar there and play at sunset. And let me tell you, the only thing more beautiful than that place at sunset is that place at sunset with my son playing his music. Heaven on earth. Oh, and he was always diving—he could hold his breath for ages. He'd dive deep and come up with little treasures for me—shells and sand dollars and starfish." Lupita's face darkens. "But like I told you, he was . . . moody. He had big ideas and a lot of passion, but when it came time to see his ideas through, he'd feel overwhelmed. He wanted to start a rock band, tour around the world, but then he fell into such a terrible mood he just roamed the beach alone." She holds her head up proudly. "But even in his dark times, José brought me little treasures from his walks."

She disappears into the kitchen and comes back outside with a cloth-covered basket. Ceremoniously, she reveals the contents. It's full of beautiful shells, red and purple and orange, some tiny, some huge. One by one, she picks them up, turns them over in her hands, places them in mine. "Look at all these!"

Little by little, as I run my fingers over the smooth shells, I start seeing my father through his mother's eyes. Everyone should have someone who defends them when no one else will, sees them as forever innocent, the bestower of endless treasures. I try to see him this way, which isn't too much of a stretch, since he's given me little treasures—the Jimi T-shirt, the jar of sand, the bookmark.

Over more stories about my father, Lupita and I grind the chiles, add garlic and oil, then toss oregano and other herbs into the boiling corn kernel–pig's head mixture. Finally, we eat our *pozole,* which is rich and delicious, sprinkled with cilantro and chopped onions, drizzled with spicy chile oil. When my bowl is empty, I ask, "How can you not be bitter about all this?"

"Oh, years ago, I was, but then I looked at the lives

around me. None turned out how people planned. I'd always thought El Tortuga would be an important turtle researcher here, live on the land by Punta Cometa, find a nice girl who understood him, get married. . . . I had his life planned out in my head. And then, after one terrible night, it was gone. Life takes its own path. And it's never neat and predictable. The best I can do is trust that I can handle whatever life brings me." She reaches out and touches my cheek. "And look what it's brought me . . . you!"

I want so badly to tell her who I am. I hug her, and when I pull away, I whisper, "What's your son's full name?"

She wrinkles her eyebrows at my direct question. "José Carlos Cruz Castillos."

I whisper those long-awaited words, repeating them under my breath, all the way home. And they stay inside me, a kind of undercurrent, throughout my excited dinner conversation with Layla and Wendell, and our bonfire circle, and even my dreams.

Chapter Eighteen

"*¡Incendio!*" I'm deeply asleep when the word penetrates my brain. Shouts of "*¡Incendio!*" over and over. I struggle to wake up. Now there's a banging. Someone pounding on my door? More yelling. "Fire! Fire!"

I push up onto my elbows, orienting myself, as an acrid smell fills my nose. I clamber out of bed, tangled in my mosquito net, and stagger to the door. The Brazilian couple is running down the path, shouting "Fire!" Behind them, smoke and flames are rising.

My heart's racing. Is it one of the cabanas? Is anyone hurt?

As I move closer, squinting through the smoke, I see Wendell running toward me, his arm shielding his mouth.

Layla is heading my way with Joe on her tail. She's coughing, gasping, "Zeeta!"

Relieved, I watch them, blinking my watering eyes. "Everyone okay?"

They give dazed nods. "What happened?" Layla asks, bewildered.

Joe puts his arm around her protectively. He looks strange without a wig—his messy, thinning black hair is exposed—and with his face bare of the rubber nose and fake eyebrows. He's wearing loose sweatpants and an old undershirt, no rainbow suspenders in sight. He points toward the smoke. "It's the supply shed." He tilts his head, frowning. "Was there anything combustible in there?"

Layla shakes her head slowly. "Just tools and buckets and natural cleaning products."

Rubbing his eyes, Wendell offers to call the fire department and heads for the phone.

This propels us into action. Layla jogs toward the kitchen hut, calling over her shoulder, "I'll get the extinguisher."

"Okay, and I'll get the hose," I shout, turning to run in the other direction.

"Wait, Zeeta!" Joe calls after me. "I smell gasoline. We shouldn't use water. And we can't get too close."

I concentrate. Now I smell it too. Gasoline ... that means someone set this fire. And the shed could explode any minute.

"I'll take care of it," he says, taking the extinguisher from Layla. "You two go back to the kitchen hut. Make sure the guests are safe."

Joe heads toward the fire, stands as close as he dares. An

arc of chemicals spews from the extinguisher. It doesn't put much of a dent in the blaze but at least seems to contain it.

As Layla and I head to the kitchen hut, Wendell rushes over. "The fire truck's on the way," he says, breathless. "It's coming from nearest big town—Puerto Escondido."

The guests are huddled at the dining tables, in shock, murmuring expressions of disbelief in their various languages. I note that Sven the Norwegian architect has gotten Horacio safely from his hut and is explaining what's happening. I join the little group, and together, we watch the shed burn.

At some point, I realize tears are streaming down my face—whether from smoke or shock, I'm not sure. I lean on Wendell, pressing my face into his shoulder. The stench of burning wood has saturated our hair, every bit of skin and clothing.

A few minutes later, Joe runs toward us, coughing. His eyebrows are singed, his face blackened with soot. "Ran out of chemicals," he gasps.

Layla fusses over him with cool washcloths, and I bring him a glass of ice water, regarding him with appreciation for the first time.

Soon sirens are shrieking in the distance, and red and blue lights flash through the trees. With the truck come four firefighters. They put out the fire fairly quickly with heavy-duty fire extinguishers, then inspect the site, digging through the smoking rubble. Eventually, all the firefighters leave except for the chief. Their truck is pulling away just as Gerardo arrives.

In the kitchen hut, over glasses of lemonade, the fire chief—a burly, middle-aged man named Alejandro—gives his assessment. "The blaze was fueled by gasoline," he announces. "Just as you suspected. It was intentional. Arson."

Arson. The word ripples through the guests in their various languages. Then come the questions—"Who could have done this? Why?"—and the waves of gratitude: "Thank God no one was hurt. Someone could have died!"

I wrap my arms around Wendell, whispering silent thanks that he's okay, Layla's okay, the guests are okay, even Joe is okay. I realize, with more intensity than ever before, that we are in danger. Real danger. Danger beyond the scope of herbal remedies and charms and sprinkled salt. Sure, Layla and I have survived some sticky situations during our travels—sandstorms in Morocco, earthquakes in India, thieves in Thailand. But this feels different. This isn't a wild force of nature or a random criminal out for quick money. This is someone plotting against us. Someone who wants us seriously scared, or hurt, or even dead.

"Any idea who did this?" Gerardo asks, rubbing his mustache.

I look at Wendell and Layla, sure we're all thinking the same thing. I say it first. "Whoever left us dead chicken curses and a threatening note."

"A threat?" Alejandro asks, alarmed. "You have it in writing?"

We shake our heads, not mentioning that Layla burned the note in her purification ritual. At the time, it hadn't seemed that serious. We could handle a few curses. But this fire, this destruction—it's taken everything to a new level.

"We mentioned the curses in our police reports," I say. "Chucho has them on file." I can't resist adding with an edge of cynicism, *"Supposedly."*

Alejandro frowns. "Chucho, huh?"

There's something in his tone of voice—scorn? doubt?—that tells me he doesn't trust Chucho either. Alejandro turns to Gerardo and murmurs, *"Oye,* maybe you should take over the case."

Wendell and I sneak looks at each other. Apparently, Chucho's incompetence—or corruption—is common knowledge. And although I get the feeling Gerardo isn't exactly upstanding, he seems better than Chucho. It's good to know, at least, that the fire chief seems on top of things. Alejandro is based not in Mazunte, but in the bigger town of Puerto Escondido. Maybe that gives him enough distance to see the local police department's major shortcomings.

Alejandro turns back to us. "Any idea who's trying to scare you?"

Wendell motions with his chin toward the ocean. "Maybe the poachers."

Alejandro's head snaps up. "Poachers?"

"On Playa Mermejita," I say, swallowing hard. "We've seem them twice. The police know about it," I add, eyeing Gerardo.

Alejandro raises an eyebrow at Gerardo, whose gaze flickers away.

"We were down on the beach at night," I continue, my heartbeat quickening with the memory. "The poachers chased us with machetes, but we got away."

Alejandro scribbles some notes, then hands us a piece of paper. "You have any more trouble with the poachers, come straight to me. Here's my number. We'll take this to the state level if we need to."

Gerardo looks away, obviously insulted.

From there, Layla takes over, signing forms. Meanwhile, Joe sneaks his arm around her, and again, she lets him. I'm just grateful he's not in his clown getup. And not using this fire as an excuse to rant about the end of the world or do a comedy routine. I like him better this way.

I spot the Brazilian couple huddled with Horacio and Sven the architect, sipping chamomile tea, chatting in a mishmash of English, Spanish, and Portuguese. Walking toward them, I call out, *"Obrigado,"* digging up the Portuguese word for thank you, which I remember from my year in Brazil.

"Oh, don't thank us," the woman replies. "Someone knocked on our door. He yelled 'Fire!' in English and Spanish."

"Really? Who was it?"

Her husband answers. "By the time we opened the door, he was gone. We assumed it was Joe or Wendell."

I shake my head. "No, it wasn't them." I glance around at the other guests. "Anyone know who knocked on the doors?"

Horacio taps his cane thoughtfully on the tile. "No idea.

But it was the same for me. I heard pounding on the door. And a strange man's voice shouting 'Fire.'"

The other guests murmur in agreement about a man's voice shouting warnings and fists pounding on their doors. But none of the men here takes credit.

Wendell looks at me. "Who could it have been?"

I shrug, mystified. "It's weird. I don't know." I go into the kitchen to make a pot of tea, turning the possibilities over in my mind.

Ten minutes later, setting out cups and saucers, I still can't figure it out. I move from table to table, pouring tea, checking on everyone. Thankfully, our guests aren't typical tourists. They're shocked at the idea of arson, but no one's been traumatized. In fact, they're treating this as another bonding experience. There's even an air of excitement as they buzz about the mysterious hero who saved us.

Soon dawn comes, lighting up the putrid mess of what used to be our shed. I calculate what we've lost—some gardening supplies, tools, equipment. Nothing irreplaceable or expensive. We might even be able to rebuild the shed with some scrap lumber. I peer past the smoldering pile to the ocean, glowing silver and misty in the light of dawn. Letting out a long breath, I focus on what matters most: everyone is alive.

❖ ❖ ❖

After the fire and police chiefs leave, Layla announces that she won't charge the guests for their stays last night. Not only does everyone refuse this offer, but after conferring with the others, the Australians shout, "It's unanimous, we're all in the mood to build a shed!"

The other guests chime in, "Hear, hear!" Sven offers to draw up plans, and Joe and Wendell volunteer to go to town to buy tools and lumber. Layla beams, quoting Rumi left and right. I take the eggs from the fridge and start getting breakfast ready. After all the commotion, I figure people will be hungry soon.

As the sun is just peeking over the sea, I make out two figures walking up our path from the road. It's Lupita and Rogelio, rushing toward us, reaching out their arms. "We heard the sirens!" they cry, embracing me. "We were so worried about you, *mija!*"

After assuring them we're safe and introducing them to everyone, I invite them to have breakfast with us. When the guests hear that Lupita is the genius behind the *mole,* they gush compliments. Layla hugs Lupita for so long, I practically have to pry her away, worried that she might not be able to hold in my secret. Layla's clearly as enamored of my grandmother as I am. And before long, she's kidding around with Rogelio about how many rolls of toilet paper she'll have to buy for her own guitar lessons. With all the bubbly conversation and laughter, you'd never guess there'd just been an arson attack.

After breakfast, Lupita and Rogelio swing by their house to gather supplies while Wendell and Joe head downtown. The rest of us choose a flat area for the shed, prepare the ground, and stake out the perimeter with twine.

I'm just tying the last stake when Meche appears. All heads turn toward her. She's as glamorous as ever, wearing a black huipil, her fingers laden with silver rings, her hair in an intricate network of braids. She offers brief nods to the guests in greeting, then approaches with her oddly dignified limp. "I smelled smoke and heard sirens," she says, looking around. "What's going on?"

Delighted, Layla greets her with a kiss on the cheek. "A shed-building party!"

"What?"

Layla sweeps her arm over the worksite. "We're building a new and improved storage shed." She laughs. "A little fire last night gave us the excuse."

Joe nods. "Complete destruction of the old, making way for the new. Just like the Mayan prophecy, you know—"

Layla cuts him off. "Meche, if you have time, we'd love your help."

Meche blinks. "Well . . . all right."

"*¡Maravilloso!*" Layla cries, ushering Meche to the pile of wood. "Just talk to our architect!" She points to Sven with his long blond ponytail, who's holding a ruler and a notebook.

We've just finished leveling the building site when Wendell and Joe return with El Sapo and his sisters in tow, all carrying heavy bags.

"Ran into them downtown," Wendell says cheerfully. "They volunteered to help out."

"*Qué chido.*" I show them where to put the bags and direct them to Sven.

Meche's already started cutting the wood to size for framing. I remember the rustic chairs in her house and wonder if they're the result of her carpentry skills. Guests trickle over to her, introducing themselves, admiring her jewelry, her braids, her handiwork with the saw. At first Meche seems overwhelmed with so much positive attention. But soon she relaxes, even begins joking around with the others.

The girls, Mayra and Xochitl, are helping to mix cement for the foundation. "Zeeta!" they call in an urgent whisper.

"That's the jaguar lady, isn't it?" Xochitl asks, motioning with her chin.

I nod. "Her name's Meche."

Xochitl looks triumphantly at Mayra. "See, I told you!"

Mayra twists her face, doubtful. "Where's her jaguar?"

"He's sick at home." I lean in and whisper, "You should be extra nice to Meche. She's been sad about Gatito."

I grab a glass of lemonade from a tray, hand it to Mayra. "Here, take this over to her. It'll cheer her up."

The girls look at each other, eyes wide. Giggling, they walk over to Meche and offer her the drink. She quickly engages them in conversation, asks them questions, makes them laugh. She's surprisingly great with kids. I can imagine how she was with her own daughter.

When Lupita and Rogelio appear, toting supplies, the girls run over and hug the old couple.

"Zeeta!" Lupita calls out. "I didn't know you knew my grandchildren!"

My heart flutters as I take in this fact. So these girls

are my cousins. El Sapo, too. And Cristina *is* my aunt. She must be my father's sister, who he mentioned looks so much like me. It's all I can do not to throw my arms around them with unrestrained joy. "They're my fellow *bolibolistas*," I tell Lupita, forcing my voice to stay steady.

"Where's your mother?" Rogelio asks the girls as he hands them lollipops from his shirt pocket.

"At the restaurant," Xochitl replies, unwrapping her loot. "But she'll bring us all lunch later, enough for everyone here."

It's a strange feeling to see these people who are my family—yet don't know it—gathered here at my home. A delicious feeling. It could only be more delicious if they knew who I was. Again, I'm tempted to blurt out the truth.

But if I do, I'll never get to see my father make the announcement himself. Somehow, if I told them, it would mean giving up on the idea of finding him. And I'm not ready for that. Not yet.

Barely keeping my joy contained, I start hammering the frame together, with Layla's and Meche's help.

"So, Meche, how's your adorable little Gatito?" Layla asks, holding a beam of wood.

A cloud passes over Meche's face. "Doing worse," she says, wiping sweat from her cheek with her forearm. "It's a matter of days now. . . ." Her lip quivers. "I don't know what I'll do without him."

Layla rests a hand on Meche's shoulder, puts on a classic Rumi face. *"Keep knocking, and the joy inside will eventually open a window and look out to see who's there."*

Meche gives a small smile. "Thanks for the cake . . . and for everything."

As Layla spouts more Rumi, I glance around at the guests working, a happy sight. Beyond the little crowd, at the edge of the jungle, there's a movement. I keep my eyes glued to that spot.

There it is again, between the branches, a flash of clothes, faded orange. A blur of dark flesh, shiny eyes. Black hair. I can't tell if it's a man or woman. But someone's there, watching us. And as soon as our eyes meet, the person flees. A chill moves over my skin. Is it the arsonist? Or the man who saved us?

I search for Wendell, to tell him what I saw. Immediately, I realize something's wrong. He's gazing at the wood he's in the middle of sawing, a distant look on his face. A vision. I hurry over, watching him carefully. I've nearly reached him when he shudders, drops the saw, and clutches his hands to his throat, gasping for breath, his face wild with panic.

My pulse racing, I rest my hand on his shoulder. "Are you okay?"

His eyes are wide, terrified, his breathing ragged. No one but me seems to have noticed.

"It's okay," I whisper, "it was just a vision."

But as I hear myself say this, I know it's not okay. Not remotely. Because as far as I know, every one of his visions has come true.

Once his breathing is steadier, he says, "Zeeta . . ." Fear fills his eyes. His hands remain at his throat.

"What happened, Wendell?"

He gradually moves his hands away from his neck, stares at them.

"Wendell, just this time, please tell me."

He opens his mouth, then closes it again.

I grab his hands. "There was danger, wasn't there?"

Slowly, he speaks, his voice hoarse. "You weren't in it, Z. I was alone."

"But, Wendell—"

He pulls me toward him and rasps, "I can handle it, Z."

My heart's banging, my head a jumble of panicked thoughts. "Wendell," I whisper, "you looked like you were"—I struggle to say the word—"dying."

He rubs his face, closes his eyes. "I can't—I can't let this freak me out, Z. If I do, I'll be a slave to the visions."

I fight to control my voice, hold back tears. "Wendell, you have this amazing future ahead of you. A full scholarship to the art school of your dreams. You can't lose that." I choke back a sob. "And I can't lose you."

He holds my chin, moving my face close to his. "Trust me, Z." He gives me a shaky kiss. "I'll be careful." Offering a pained smile, he adds, "And anyway, life's a mess, right?"

I wipe my eyes and manage a weak grin. "Sounds like Horacio's told you about his beautiful-mess-of-life theory." For a while I'm silent, willing my heart to calm down, struggling to trust him that everything will be okay. "Whatever happens," I say finally, "I got your back." Then I add, "On one condition."

"What?"

"You let Layla load you down with a few kilos of amulets."

Half smiling, he whispers, "So now you believe in that stuff?"

I graze my lips over his red-streaked neck. "Whatever it takes."

Chapter Nineteen

The next day, Sunday, we put the finishing touches on our new shed. Layla's painted an ocean view on the door, lining every cloud with glitter. Of course she snuck in a Rumi quote: *We're clouds over the sea, or flecks of matter in the ocean when the ocean seems lit from within.*

"Just to put our little troubles in perspective," Layla says, satisfied.

El Sapo and Xochitl and Mayra arrive right when we're burning incense for the shed's ceremonial blessing. Joe hands them some bells. After his heroic efforts during the fire, his purple wig doesn't bother me so much.

The girls get into the ritual, ringing their bells and belting out chants. Afterward, Xochitl turns to me. "Where's Meche?"

"At home with Gatito."

"We like her!" Mayra declares.

Xochitl's eyes light up. "Let's make a present for her jaguar."

"I think she'd love that," I say, showing them the brushes and extra paint and scraps of wood.

Half an hour later, while I'm cleaning the Iguana bathroom, the girls burst through the door, proudly hold up a piece of scrap wood with a painting of a smiling, sparkling jaguar framed by jungle flowers.

I admire it. "*Oigan,* I have an idea!" I find a stake in the pile of leftover lumber and nail it to the back of the painted wood. "I'll hammer this into the ground just outside Gatito's fence. Then he can enjoy it, okay?"

The girls smile, pleased.

Later, when Wendell and I walk down the jungle path carrying the sign, for the first time, I'm not scared at the idea of seeing Gatito. Not that I want to cuddle with him, but I do have sympathy for the creature. Next to the TRESPASSERS WILL BE DEVOURED warning, we set up the girls' cheerful portrayal of Gatito. I'm sure that pounding in the stake will rouse him, but there's no sign of him. We peer through the fence, scanning his patch of jungle. Nothing.

"He must be really sick," I say to Wendell.

He nods. "Poor guy."

I take Wendell's hand, lean into him as we walk back. Now that he's shaken off the darkness of his vision, he tells me about online research he's done on poaching regulations. "We need to go higher than the local police," he says, determined. "Mexico has an agency that protects wildlife—PROFEPA. I'm going to talk with Pepe, suggest we contact them. Maybe PROFEPA can send people to investigate. Maybe even train a whole new volunteer force."

I nod in encouragement, but inside, I wonder how the poachers will exact their vengeance. What was it El Sapo said about El Dedo's revenge style? Death by machete? I remember the threats El Dedo yelled as he chased us through the jungle. Then I remember how Wendell looked clutching his neck, gasping for breath, as though he were dying.

I tighten my grip on his hand, wishing I never had to let it go.

❖ ❖ ❖

On Monday, under the blazing afternoon sun, Wendell and I head to the grounds of the Turtle Center. There's a bulge beneath his blue shirt—the pouch of amulets he's agreed to wear, after pointing out that I'm turning into Layla.

We head past the turtle hatchery, straight to Pepe's office. Wendell is holding a packet of information and a list of agencies to contact about the poaching.

"*Hola*, Pepe," he says, poking his head in the doorway. He's trying to sound casual, but his voice is brimming with tension.

"Wendell!" Pepe stands up with a look of concern. "I heard about the fire. I'm glad you're all right."

"Thanks." Wendell chooses his words carefully, trying not to sound accusatory. It can't be easy. "Zeeta and I—you know we're concerned that the volunteers aren't able to protect the turtles. And—"

"Oh, don't worry, *muchachos*," he says. "I replaced the volunteers who were slacking off."

Wendell and I exchange glances. Pepe would be offended at the suggestion that his entire volunteer program is part of a cesspool of corruption. "Actually," Wendell says diplomatically, "we're thinking the police aren't doing the best job of it either."

"Really?" Pepe says, his brow furrowed.

Wendell sets his printouts on the desk. "We have to notify PROFEPA. They can investigate."

Pepe leans against his desk, rubs his temples. "*Mira,* Wendell. Look. As much as I appreciate your enthusiasm, you still have a lot to learn." He rests his hand on Wendell's shoulder. "You get farther in life by making friends, not enemies." He sighs. "If the police find out that a representative of the Turtle Center has gone over their heads, they won't be happy. We'll pay for it. You see, we have a relationship going. You can understand that, right?"

Wendell is quiet. I can almost feel the outrage he's holding inside.

"Leave it to me," Pepe continues. "I have friends on the police force, friends all over this town. I'll handle this in a way that won't upset folks. All right?"

Wendell's face hardens. He looks Pepe in the eye and says evenly, "I have to protect the turtles . . . even if it means losing friends. Or my job."

Pepe presses his lips together. "Don't contact PROFEPA yet. Just give me time to deal with it."

Slowly, Wendell shakes his head. "Every day means

thousands more turtle eggs stolen, Pepe." He takes a deep breath. "One day. That's the most I'll wait. Unless the poachers are caught, I'm contacting PROFEPA on Wednesday."

Pepe rubs his temple, looking disappointed, as if Wendell has let him down. An uncomfortable silence settles in the room. Finally, Wendell says goodbye and leaves. I follow, not sure what to think. Maybe Pepe's right; maybe there's an easier way to deal with this. One that doesn't involve making enemies. The last thing I want is another enemy at this point, especially not after Wendell's terrifying vision.

Flushed with emotion, he leads me past the shallow pools toward the beach.

Under my breath, I say, "Wendell, be careful. Please."

He taps on the bunch of amulets under his shirt. "That's what these are for, right?" His words are light, but I know him so well, I can sense the fear in his voice, his downcast eyes, the set of his jaw, the way he walks. He's scared, and trying hard not to show it.

I try again. "Wendell, why don't you just give tours around the grounds for a while? Stay off the water?"

"I have to go on the water, Z. That's my main job." He squeezes my hand and says, "Just trust that it'll be worth it, Z. It'll be okay in the end." I suspect he's saying it to calm himself as much as me.

On the beach, Santy is washing his boat, and waves to us in greeting. After some small talk, he and Wendell push the boat into the water. Hugging myself in the wind, I watch from shore as they hop in and rev the engine. Wendell waves as they go, calling out something I can't hear over the motor, probably something like "Don't worry." As the boat grows smaller and smaller until it's just a pinprick of white, I do exactly that. Worry.

❖ ❖ ❖

The afternoon drags on. I can't stop thinking about Wendell out there on the water, vulnerable. To distract myself, I work on the jungle path, even wishing Gatito would make an appearance—from behind the fence, of course. Later, I bring a bowl of *mole* by Meche's house, guessing she's too distraught over Gatito to cook. She doesn't answer when I call out, so I leave the dish at her gate, not willing to risk an encounter with the jaguar, even if he is sick and weak.

At home, I check the clock. Still two hours until Wendell gets home. Time is crawling so slowly, I could scream. I practice my "La Llorona" chords: A minor, D minor, E, and G, until I think I might go crazy. Then I swing by Don Rogelio's shop, where he helps me put the chords together more smoothly, clapping out the rhythm. Now the song is discernible when I play, but remains patchy, spewing out in fits and starts.

His company calms me a little, but when I get home, there's still nearly an hour to kill. I help Layla cook chicken in *pipian* sauce, a recipe Lupita gave me. As I grind the pumpkin seeds, I keep checking the clock and looking up to see if Wendell is coming down the path.

Finally, when five-thirty comes, there he is, heading toward me. Relieved, I let my muscles loosen, and greet him with a giant hug. "Your amulets worked!"

With a grin, he pats them. "You need to relax, Z."

"True," I admit.

Glancing up from the sauce she's stirring, Layla says, "I'll finish making dinner. You two go for a swim!"

As if by silent agreement, Wendell and I head to Playa Mermejita. At this point, we're blatantly disregarding Pepe's warnings about staying off the beach; we can protect the turtles better by keeping tabs on them and their eggs, since no one else seems to. As we walk, we stay close to the surf, giving wide berth to any mounds that could be covered nests. No turtles have emerged to lay eggs yet tonight.

We haven't actually swum on this beach before, because of the riptides, but the sea looks especially calm tonight, glassy, with gentle waves. It's nearing sunset, the light golden and soft, a few seagulls roaming in the surf, leaving sticklike tracks in the wet sand. I pull off my sundress, and he pulls off his shirt, and in our swimsuits, hand in hand, we wade into the ocean.

The water soothes my tense muscles, quiets my thoughts. We swim farther in as Wendell tells me about his day.

"I got lots of good turtle footage," he says. "But afterward, when I swung by Pepe's office, he was still acting weird."

"You think he just wants everyone to get along?" I speculate. "That it's clouding his judgment?"

"I guess." Wendell sighs. "But I told him I'm sticking to what I said. Even if I have to leave the Turtle Center."

I hate thinking Wendell might lose his job. That would be another reason for him to take the scholarship in California. One less thing holding him here. But he's passionate about the turtles, and honestly, they need him. I kiss him, a salty seawater kiss. "I'm here for you, Wendell. And the turtles. Whatever happens."

We leap over waves until we're past the breakers. I flip onto my back, closing my eyes, letting the water carry me. Wendell floats beside me, his hand in mine. The light is amber behind my eyelids. It's easy to lose myself in the effortless drifting, letting go of worries. I'm vaguely aware of the sun setting, the light fading, the air growing cooler.

At some point, I sense the waves picking up and the breeze turning into a cold wind. I open my eyes, shake off my daze. It's growing darker by the second, but not just with dusk. On the horizon, dark clouds are rushing toward us. And gusts of wind are blowing violently. Farther in the ocean, a huge wave is rolling toward us.

"Wendell!" I cry, rousing him from his own dreamy state. "A storm's coming."

At my words, a jagged line of lightning slices the sky.

Wendell splashes upright, taking in the situation. "Let's go in, fast."

"That wave," I say, looking over my shoulder with growing panic. "It's gigantic."

"Hold my hand," he says as thunder rolls. "Swim for shore."

We struggle against the rough currents, glancing at the wall of water behind us. The sky is steely gray and heavy now, the wave black and towering.

"It's gonna crash!" Wendell yells over the ocean's roar.

"It's too big to ride in!" I shriek.

"Dive under!" he calls back, tightening his grip on my hand.

We take deep breaths, squeeze each other's hands, and dive under, deep, close to the sandy bottom. But the wave grabs me and tears my hand from Wendell's. The force thrashes my body against the ocean floor. The sea pounds me, flips me over, my head smacking the sand, then my shoulder, then my leg. I've become a tiny piece of driftwood in this angry expanse of water. Sand scrapes my skin; salt water fills my head.

My mind is screaming Wendell's name. My whole body is shouting for him. Thoughts tumble through my mind—Wendell's vision, his gasping and choking. Is this it? My lungs are burning. My mouth opens, searching for air but only sucking in more salt water. *Wendell!* I scream inside.

Finally, after what seems like forever, the wave passes and recedes. I fight toward the surface, but it's hard to tell which way is up. It's dark on all sides. This water has swallowed me. But somehow, I emerge, gasping for breath, coughing, gagging. I look around desperately in the darkness. The ocean is all seething foam. No sign of Wendell.

"Wendell!" I call weakly. The ocean swells devour my voice. "Wendell!" I try again, louder, scanning the water desperately. A flash of lightning briefly illuminates the ocean. No sign of him.

"Wendell!" My voice is stronger now that I've caught my breath, but it's still no match for the stormy sea.

I start swimming toward shore. Maybe he's already there. I glance around, seeing nothing but waves. My body throbs and aches from battling the sea. A current keeps pulling me back, sucking me toward the open water. I swim and swim, making no progress. I'm stuck out here. And utterly exhausted.

Then I see another giant wave heading to shore. Not again. I can't handle this. There's nothing to do but dive under. This one nearly knocks me out, bashing my head against the sand, whipping my body around and around. But now, when I break the surface, coughing and gasping, I'm closer to shore. The wave must have caught me, carried me head over heels. The inside of my head stings with salt water. I look around for Wendell. Nothing but the dark, raging sea.

Now I'm driven by a survival instinct. My arms muster up every last bit of energy and propel me toward shore. I stagger through the foam onto the beach, just before the next wave. This wave smashes my body against the sand, but at least the water's shallow here. I find the gritty floor with my hands and knees and push myself to my feet, force my legs to carry me through the surf. Once I'm ankle-deep, I turn back to the ocean, searching for Wendell. It's dark, so dark. Another enormous wave comes, swirling around my waist, knocking me back a few steps.

"Wendell!" I yell, cupping my hands around my mouth. "Wendell!" I stand there, shaking, barely keeping my knees from collapsing. Rain is pelting me, stinging my flesh, making it even harder to see. What should I do? Stay here and yell? Or go back in? Or run for help? I don't know. There's not enough time. I'm sobbing, choking out screams. The wind's whipping my wet hair, smacking it against my skin. "Wendell!"

I squint through the downpour and gradually see a shape coming out of the water. I keep my eyes glued to it, hoping, hoping. I splash and trip toward it. *Please, please, please.*

As I'm closer, I hear his voice, weak, gasping "Zeeta." He's staggering toward me, but then another giant wave swells behind him.

"Watch out!" I scream.

It knocks him over, and for a moment, he's under again. I keep my eyes stuck to that spot and fight my way toward him. Finally, he comes up, and the wave recedes in a chaos of foam. I stumble toward him, my arms outstretched. "Wendell!"

We grasp onto each other and stumble out of the surf. The rain and wind are driving into us as we forge our way up the beach toward the jungle. At the edge of the trees, we collapse. I kiss him, all over his damp face, his neck, his shoulders. "Thank God you're okay."

"You too," he says hoarsely, his trembling arms wrapped around me.

Here, the trees shelter us from the worst of the storm. We lie in the sand, shivering, holding each other. Gradually, I notice the time between lightning and thunder growing longer, the rain letting up, the wind calming.

This must have been Wendell's vision, I realize. How

horrible, the weight of this, the knowledge that he might die. The helplessness. And he was carrying this alone. "This was your vision, wasn't it?" I ask softly.

He looks as if he's struggling to decide whether to tell me something. "In the vision, I was drowning. I was exhausted, scared. It was dark, stormy. Just like tonight."

"You survived," I say, rubbing his shoulder. "It's over. And now everything's okay, right?"

He stares out into the ocean. "It's just—"

"What?" I ask, panicked.

"Nothing. You're right. This must've been the vision." He turns to me, kisses me.

But something about his tone doesn't convince me. There's something he's not telling me. "And if it wasn't?"

"Z, come on. I'm not gonna cower. Not for every scary vision. I have to live my life."

I pull him toward me again, wrap my arms tightly around him. As I peer over his shoulder, I see a movement in the jungle. A pair of eyes. Someone's there, watching us. This time, I don't try to catch the person. I simply raise my hand in strange greeting, hoping for the best.

Still, whoever it is runs away.

Chapter Twenty

The next day passes more quickly. I take it easy, doing home-work and lounging in the hammock, nursing my bruises and scrapes. I nap for hours, exhausted from last night's ordeal. In no time, it's evening, and I'm chopping cucumbers for the side salad, chatting with Layla, who's stuffing *chiles rellenos*. At some point, I glance up at the clock, and I'm surprised to see it's 5:32. "Isn't he usually back by now, Layla?"

"Who, Wendell?" She glances at the clock. "I think so. He's probably running a little late."

Distracted, I continue chopping the cucumbers, nearly slicing my finger. I take a deep breath, try to calm down. Now each chop on the cutting board makes me think of machetes, and El Dedo, and death threats. And was that an extra-long, dramatic kiss goodbye he gave me when I dropped him off at the Turtle Center today? The kind of kiss you'd give before . . . *Stop, Zeeta!* I try to control my wild, panicked thoughts. Wendell's vision already came to pass. And he survived. Nothing to worry about.

When six-thirty rolls around, the sun is setting. I've assembled the salad and the guests are trickling into the kitchen hut. Wendell's always here in time for dinner. Always. Last night, when I asked if his vision had been realized, he hesitated. Why? What did he know that he wasn't telling me? I set out the glasses and plates as fear builds inside me.

Stop, Zeeta! I put down the pile of dishes and blurt out, "That's it, Layla. I'm going to look for him."

"He's probably resting in his cabana, love."

True; he got so battered from the waves last night, he might have come home and gone straight to bed. Hoping that's the case, I race toward his cabana, bang on the door. No answer. I peer through the window. No sign of his having come home.

I jog down the dirt road, heading to the Turtle Center. I'll run into him on the way there, I tell myself. He'll be perfectly fine, with some good reason for being so late—maybe lugging groceries. My hopes rise when I see a figure toward the bottom of the hill, carrying bags. But at closer look, it's a woman with a slight limp. Silver necklaces and bracelets glitter in the angled sunlight.

"Meche!" I call out, picking up my pace. "Have you seen Wendell?"

"No, Zeeta. Is something wrong?"

My heart's pounding, my breathing hard. "He never came home from work . . . I—I think something bad happened."

She doesn't question my concern. "I'll search the

jungle and the beach," she says calmly. "I'll meet you at your kitchen hut."

"Thanks, Meche," I say, already running again.

"Be careful, Zeeta!" she calls out.

By the time I reach the Turtle Center, I'm exhausted, with a stitch in my side. It's nearly dusk and the Center is officially closed. The place is deserted, the gates open just a crack. I call to the guard. "*¡Señor!* I need to get in!"

He saunters over, frowning. "Yes, *señorita?*"

"Have you seen Wendell?" I ask.

"Not since you walked him here today."

"He never left?"

Frowning, the guard shakes his head.

"What about Pepe? Is he here?" I poke my head around the guard. A group of men in blue Turtle Center T-shirts are walking toward the gate, laughing and chatting. Thankfully, Pepe is one of them.

"Pepe!" I call out. "Pepe!"

His head snaps up; his hand rises in greeting. I dart around the guard, make a beeline for Pepe. "Have you seen Wendell?" My voice is brimming with desperation.

"He left a while ago," Pepe says, waving goodbye to his colleagues.

"You saw him? Where'd he go?"

"Who knows. Home, I guess."

"No, he didn't, Pepe. Tell me every detail. What time did he leave? Which way was he headed?"

"Sorry, I don't remember, Zeeta. Maybe he's running errands."

"No, he's missing! He wouldn't—"

Pepe shakes his head, a gesture of pity and impatience. "Zeeta, when a *muchacho* has another girl, the first sign is not coming home on time. The second sign is when the girlfriend invents scenarios. Excuses that feel better than the truth."

"What?" I sputter. "What are you talking about?"

"Zeeta, all I'm saying is that there are many beautiful girls around here. Any one of them might catch a young guy's eye."

I glare at Pepe, suddenly seeing him in a different light. He's actually accusing Wendell of cheating on me? It takes all my restraint to not slap this man, or at least curse at him in about twenty different languages. I'm shaking now, searching for words to tell him off.

He puts his hand to my shoulder. I wince, stepping away. "Keep your dignity, Zeeta. Go home now."

My eyes bore into his. "I have to look around the Center for Wendell."

Pepe shakes his head, then signals to the guard, who takes a step forward. "The Center is closed," Pepe says. "Go home, Zeeta."

With no other choice, I walk out the gate and head down the main street. Pepe calls out, *"Hasta luego."*

I ignore him. Halfway down the street, I turn around and see that the guard has returned to his little booth. My pulse racing, I double back. Staying hidden from the guard's view, I run around the perimeter to where the fence ends and the beach begins.

Across the dusky violet stretch of sand, I spot a white boat. Beside it, a man crouches by a bucket, gutting a fish.

"Santy!" I feel like hugging him. "Thank God you're here. Where's Wendell?"

"Who knows. I didn't take him out today."

"But you always take him out!"

He nods, frowning. "This afternoon, two *muchachos* beached their boat here. Pepe said they were researchers, told me they'd be taking Wendell out today. He gave me the afternoon off. Seemed strange to me, but I left. Spent the time fishing."

I run my hand through my hair. "Do you have any idea where they took him? Or who they were? What they looked like?"

He shakes his head. "I didn't know them. They were teenagers, around your age. Not from around here. City boys. Oh, and one of them was missing a finger."

Panic rises, nearly suffocating me. It's El Dedo. And his buddy. The poachers have Wendell.

"Santy," I say, my voice trembling, "we need to look for Wendell."

Santy's eyes widen in alarm. "Didn't he come back?"

"No," I say, struggling to keep my tears at bay long enough to tell Santy about the threats, curses, the poachers. "They must've realized that Wendell's on to them." I don't say anything about the vision, but what I've said is enough for Santy.

"Vámonos," he says, pushing the boat out into the surf.

Once we jump in, he speeds up the coastline, zigzagging

along the shore. I wish I'd thought to bring binoculars or a flashlight. There's a small light on Santy's boat, but it doesn't help much. It's getting darker by the minute. I think of Wendell's vision. Nighttime. Darkness. His hands at his throat. Gasping for breath. El Dedo's words: *You're dead.*

After we've gone a few kilometers up the coast and we still haven't spotted Wendell, Santy gives me a sympathetic look. "We should turn around, maybe go the other way down the coast."

I nod, swallowing hard. As we speed off, I scan the water, shivering, and notice that no other boats are out. Darkness is moving in fast, not just because it's twilight, but because another evening storm is approaching. The wind's blowing harder, dark clouds racing in, covering the moon. In the distance, thunder pounds, lightning flashes. Soon the boat is rocking violently. I want to throw up, not from seasickness, but from pure terror at the possibility that Wendell's somewhere in this ocean, struggling to stay alive.

"Zeeta," Santy yells over the roar of the engine and waves. "We have to go to shore. It's not safe out here."

I want to beg him, but I know he's right. I can't risk his life too. My only hope is that Wendell's boat came to shore and he's gone home. Maybe he's in the kitchen hut with Layla waiting for me. Maybe I'll get home and everything will be all right.

Once we're on shore, we jog across the beach. "I'm sorry I don't have a car to take you home," Santy shouts over the howling wind.

"It's okay, Santy. You need to go to your wife." I give him a quick hug. "Thanks for everything."

"I can't leave you like this, *señorita*."

"I'll be fine, Santy," I reassure him. Unfortunately, he'd just slow me down with his creaky joints. "Please, go home."

"Call the Coast Guard," he says after a pause. "All right?"

I promise, and then, reluctantly, he turns away, shielding his face from the rain. Immediately, I run down the path toward the road. The wind whips at me and the rain stings, but I focus on moving my legs. Tree branches are cracking and flying, and I dodge out of their way. In the flashes of lightning, I see that the uphill road ahead has transformed into a brown river. I head straight for it, bracing myself. My lungs burning, I slip and fall and scramble back up, smeared with mud. Finally, at the top, I turn left at the cabanas sign and tear down our driveway, shaking with cold and fear. *Please be here, Wendell. Please.*

I approach the kitchen hut, breathless, soaked to the bone. The trees shelter the dining area from the worst of the wind, but the candles are all blown out. The tables are empty; the guests must have retreated to their cabanas. Layla and Meche are huddled behind the counter, washing dishes by lantern light.

"Layla!" I call out as I enter.

"Zeeta! Are you okay?"

I nod quickly. "Wendell? Is he—?"

She shakes her head, drying her hands on the dish towel. "He's not back, love."

Meche grabs a black wool shawl from a hook in the kitchen. It must be hers; I've never seen it before. She wraps it around me, despite the mud clinging to my clothes and skin. Gently, she sits me down on a bench. "I couldn't find him, Zeeta. Are you okay?"

I nod. "But Wendell—" I stifle a sob. "I think he's out there on the water. Santy and I couldn't find him."

Meche and Layla shoot each other looks of alarm. Layla asks, "Should I call the Coast Guard?"

I hate that it's come to this. "Yes," I relent. "And the fire chief. Hurry, please."

As Layla disappears down the path toward the phone, I catch a glimpse of movement at the edge of the jungle. My eyes scan the dripping-wet trees, their branches blowing in the wind. It's dark, shadowy, but I'm sure of it: someone's behind a tree. A branch covers most of his face, but I can tell it's a man. A man in a dark shirt and pants.

As I stand up, he turns and disappears into the forest.

By the time I make my legs move a few steps in his direction, I realize it's too late. He's probably long gone.

I drop back down to the bench and look at Meche. "Did you see him?"

"Who?" Her gaze flickers around.

"A man watching us. In the jungle."

"No." She squints at the rainy foliage. "Who was it?"

"I don't know. Maybe the same person I noticed before. One of the poachers?" I shiver, trying to think of a less scary scenario. "Or maybe the guy who warned everyone about the fire. Maybe the one who threw stones at the poachers." I like this explanation better. The one involving an invisible protector.

She ponders this, staring into the jungle, then puts her arm on my shoulder. "Zeeta, why are you so convinced Wendell is out there? In danger?"

I pause. I can't tell her about Wendell's vision. "Santy described the guys who took him on the boat today. One of them fits the description of a poacher in Wendell's photo. This guy named El Dedo."

As I'm talking, I remember Santy's words. If Pepe was the one who sent Wendell out on the boat today, he must know El Dedo. And he must have known that El Dedo was one of the poachers in the photo we showed him.

My mind is reeling. I sputter, "And this guy, Pepe—Wendell's boss at the Turtle Center—he's acting weird. Lying to us. Wendell wanted to report the poaching to PROFEPA even though Pepe told him not to. . . ." I struggle to compose my thoughts, which are leading me to some disturbing conclusions about Pepe.

Meche looks bewildered. "Wait, this Pepe from the Turtle Center . . . you mean Doña Lupita's son?"

I glance up. "What?"

"Her younger son?" Meche asks. "The so-called community coordinator?" Uncharacteristic sarcasm has crept into her voice.

I try to make sense of this new information. "I guess that's him."

"Lupita told me about his new job," Meche says.

My heart's racing. "What do you know about him?"

She laughs wryly. "I'm not surprised he got the job, even with no science background. Everyone loves him. He's charming, all about exchanging favors. He tried to involve me in his little network, but I refused. And I suspect he fuels the rumors about me, hoping I'll leave and sell him the land." She pauses. "Of course, he's never been interested in turtles. He's only been interested in—"

I stare at her. "What?"

She shakes her head. "I've said enough already. I hate gossip."

"I have to know, Meche. Wendell's in danger."

After a long pause, she continues. "Money. That's what he was always all about. Impressing his friends. Whatever it took to do that."

I blink, fighting to rearrange my assumptions about Pepe. "What do you mean?"

"He came over a few months ago, pressuring me to sell my land. Said he'd let me in on an investment, a fancy hotel he wanted to build here." Meche's voice hardens. "My land is smack in the middle of his plans. And he's assuming he'll get this land you rent from his parents. Apparently, he met some investors in Mexico City. It all sounded shady to me. Of course, I refused. Which didn't make him happy."

"But how could he build a hotel? Wouldn't the electric lights endanger the turtles?"

"Exactly. Why would he be working at the Turtle Center

if he cares so little about the turtles?" Meche furrows her eyebrows. "Maybe he thought he'd have more power if he worked there, being on the inside. I wouldn't put it past that man."

I shut my eyes tight, not wanting to believe it, but it makes sense. Slowly, I say, "Pepe wants us gone. He's always wanted us gone. With us gone, his parents will give him the land. And he'll develop a hotel. And knowing him, he'll get the support of his friends, the cops, and everyone else. He'll find a way to avoid following the turtle protection laws. That's why he doesn't want Wendell going to PROFEPA—he doesn't want anyone else interfering. If PROFEPA gets involved, they'd stop him."

I hesitate, putting together the rest of the information. "El Dedo and the others must be Pepe's friends from Mexico City. Maybe he does them favors—like letting them poach on this beach. And the volunteer force—it's a sham, nonexistent. El Dedo and his buddies do Pepe favors in return, like leaving curses and committing arson, to try to scare us off."

Meche listens intently, nodding.

The more I talk, the more pieces come together. "The first curse came after we reported the poaching. The threatening note came after Lupita found out that we wanted to stay for years. The fire came after I convinced Rogelio to let us stay. Lupita and Rogelio probably mentioned these things to Pepe, and he instructed his buddies to do the dirty work. And now this incident with Wendell—it came right after he told Pepe he'd go to PROFEPA."

Each of Pepe's attacks has escalated, gotten more serious,

more destructive. And now, this latest one—would he actually try to kill Wendell?

I turn to Meche, a sinking feeling in my stomach. "Wendell's in serious danger, isn't he?"

Solemnly, she nods. "It appears so."

And then there's the big question, which I can't tell Meche about, because it involves my father: What if my father really is innocent of the crime he was accused of as a teen? What if his brother, Pepe, was the guilty one? Pepe would've had access to the keys to his father's truck. He could've escaped from the truck, taken a shortcut home, and slipped into bed, unseen. He could've easily pinned it on his brother, who was out with a girl. Maybe everyone was so charmed by Pepe that they just assumed his troubled brother did it.

My insides are still spinning over the revelations about Pepe when Layla comes down the path. "I reported him as missing at sea," she says, breathless. "The Coast Guard is out looking. The fire department too." Twisting her face, she adds, "And supposedly those inept cops."

"You called them, too?"

"The Coast Guard did. Said it's protocol." Sitting down beside me, she hugs me and looks back and forth between me and Meche. She must see the new wave of fear in our eyes. "What is it?"

"Pepe," I say shakily. Between the two of us, Meche and I tell her about Pepe's shady side.

Once Layla understands the meaning of this, she jumps up and runs to call in this new information to the authorities.

Now there's a search on for Pepe as well as El Dedo and

Wendell. For what feels like hours, I wait in the kitchen hut, watching rain drip from leaves, praying that Wendell will make it back. But with every minute that passes, it seems less and less likely.

After word of Wendell's disappearance spreads, the guests stop by the palapa, trying to comfort me. They adore Wendell too. Many of them have gone on a tour with him at the Turtle Center, become enchanted by his turtle enthusiasm. There's no bonfire tonight, only a solemn mood as people offer me sympathetic hugs, then, after midnight, trickle off to their cabanas.

Eventually, the only ones left are Layla and Meche and Joe, drying dishes behind the counter, and at a table, Horacio and me. He sits beside me in the flickering light of a small lantern. Knowing that he can't see my face is liberating. Finally, my tears stream down, unrestrained. Hearing my muffled sobs, he reaches out, finds my arm, rests his hand there.

I sniffle as he pats my arm rhythmically. "You were right, Horacio," I say in a shaky voice. "My life could get messier. It did."

"Trust . . . ," he begins softly, his voice fading.

"Trust what?"

He sighs, searching for words. "Trust you'll handle the mess. Trust you'll even, somehow, love it. Trust that in the end, it will all be fine. More than fine. Beautiful."

I wipe my eyes. "My friend Lupita—she told me the same thing. She said life is like *mole*. Not all sweet. Spicy with chile, bitter with cacao. All these flavors that jumble together and make it delicious."

He gazes into the night, his expression pensive. "And now, tonight, we're living through the bitter part, or maybe the painful, burning chile part." He pats my arm some more. "But more sweetness will come, sooner or later. Trust that it will."

I think about all the sweetness Wendell has brought into my life. The sweetness this new home has brought into my life. And how terrified I've been of losing it all. My home, Wendell, my perfect paradise.

But it's not a perfect paradise. It never was and it never will be. The only real perfection is the miracle of simply being alive. Suddenly, I understand this with every cell in my body. There will be storms, scares, beasts, heartache . . . and I'm strong enough to deal with it all. *As long as he's alive.*

All this time I've been worrying he'd leave and I'd lose him. And now, I might lose him in a way I never dreamed possible. Lose him for good.

No! I scream inside. He will come back. *He will.* He has to. I have to believe that he'll return. And even after he does, there will always be uncertainty, a string of obstacles to overcome, the pain of being apart, the elation of being together. Our paths will fork here and there, unexpectedly, double back, take detours. And I'll give him freedom to fly, to be his own person. I'll trust that in the end, we'll be together. Trust in the sweet parts and the bitter parts—trust the whole delicious mess.

Then I think of my father—the depth of his music, the tenderness that comes through in his mother's stories. He might be innocent of the crime. If so, how tragic that a false accusation shaped his entire life. But if he hadn't left and gone to Greece and met my mother, then I wouldn't exist. I think of all the regret and sorrow and anger he must feel . . . and maybe hope, too, like a speck of mud that starts a world anew. I have to believe that he's still out there, with enough hope to meet me halfway. His life has been the ultimate mess, but there's been beauty in it.

Suddenly, Horacio grips my arm. "Listen," he whispers, motioning with his chin. "Someone's coming from the jungle, over there."

I look up. Two figures are stumbling through the battered path toward the kitchen. They push through broken branches and rain-pelted leaves, huddled together beneath a blanket.

I jump up, squinting to make out the faces. One of the figures pulls back the blanket. It's him, Wendell.

Chapter Twenty-One

I explode with relief. In three bounds I've reached him, I'm hugging him. His body shivers in my arms. I lead him to a table, vaguely aware that the other figure has stayed at the edge of the woods. On seeing Wendell, Meche and Layla and Joe run from the kitchen and crowd around us. Wendell's teeth are chattering violently; his face is a strange gray color, his lips deep purple.

Layla sits on his other side, putting her arms around him, sharing warmth. "Should we call an ambulance?"

Wendell shakes his head. He doesn't seem able to speak.

"I'll get some tea," Meche says, hurrying into the kitchen.

Joe offers to get blankets and heads for his cabana.

I keep my arms around Wendell, willing my heat into his icy body. "Are you okay?"

He nods, trembling, and I press him against me.

In a few words, I tell Horacio what I see, giving him a visual to go with the sounds.

"And the other person?" he asks in a low voice, gesturing with his chin to the forest.

I'd forgotten about him. I peer over Wendell's shoulder at the figure in the shadows. I can barely make out the silhouette. "Hey!" I call out. "You okay?"

The person nods, pushes back the blanket, just a little. But it's enough. Dozens of little dreadlocks sprout from his head. Our fish guy.

"El Loco?" I murmur.

"Come on over," Layla shouts. "Have some tea, warm up."

The man shakes his head, raises a hand in a gesture of no thanks. I catch a flash of his bare chest. He must have given his shirt to Wendell—a damp black T-shirt peeking from Wendell's blanket. El Loco starts backing up.

"Wait!" I call out. "Where'd you find Wendell? What happened?"

He continues backing up into the tree shadows.

Meche comes out of the kitchen holding two steaming mugs of tea. "Here, *señor*," she urges. "Please, sit down."

"I can't stay," he rasps. "But keep the boy warm. And safe. He's been through a lot." He turns and disappears into the jungle.

I face Wendell again, holding him tight. I'm dying to hear what happened, but at the moment, he can't seem to talk. Joe runs over with a heap of wool blankets. I peel off Wendell's wet T-shirt, then wrap the blankets around our bodies and press against his bare chest, desperate to warm him up.

Wendell sips the tea as the rest of us watch anxiously. I'm just thinking maybe we do need to call an ambulance—what if this is hypothermia?—when he sets down the cup and says in a hoarse whisper, "Th-thanks."

Everyone murmurs relief at his speaking. "Wendell," I say, searching his eyes, which are glassy from shock. "What happened out there?"

"Th-that man saved me."

"El Loco?"

He nods.

"But where were you?"

"I-i-in the ocean. For a long time. B-but then Gracia came."

"Gracia?" Horacio asks.

I explain. "She's a—turtle we know."

Horacio makes a puzzled face, and then Meche chimes in. "Yes, Gracia! She's famous around here."

I turn back to Wendell. Thankfully, he seems to be thawing out. "Then where'd our fish guy come in?"

Wendell makes a visible effort to calm his chattering teeth. "Wh-when I couldn't tread water any longer, I called to Gracia. She came up under me. Brought me to his boat."

I glance at Layla, who doesn't seem to find this at all strange. "You have a way with those turtles, Wendell," she says, nodding. "Just like Zeeta's father."

Meche appears to accept this bizarre explanation too.

"Gracia has saved people for years, from the time our *abuelitos* were young."

I close my eyes, trying to hang on to something logical. "Well, what was El Loco doing out so late?" I ask. "And in the middle of a storm?"

When no one offers an answer, Horacio clears his throat. "When I heard that man speak—El Loco as you call him—I knew his voice. He was the one who pounded on our doors. The one who warned us the night of the fire. The one who saved us."

❖ ❖ ❖

Once Wendell is warmed up and feeling more clear-headed, we call the fire chief, Alejandro, to file a report. Wendell gives the basics as I sit beside him, holding his hand and listening. He explains that he went out to the Turtle Center beach in the afternoon. Instead of Santy, two men were waiting for him, baseball caps pulled low over sunglasses. They said they'd be taking Wendell out today, that Santy was sick. It wasn't until they were on the water that Wendell noticed one of them was missing a finger. El Dedo, he realized.

Wendell knew he couldn't take them both on, so he stayed quiet and kept his eyes open for a chance to escape. They took him far out from the usual reefs, into the open sea. Finally, they cut the motor and pulled machetes from under the seat.

At the mention of machetes, I cringe, remembering what El Sapo said about death by machete—El Dedo's preferred method of killing.

As I dig my fingernails into my palms, Wendell continues. El Dedo ordered him to jump overboard. They were surrounded by ocean—no land, no other boats. But Wendell had no choice. He jumped.

They took off, leaving Wendell there, treading water in the open sea.

As he tells his story in such stark detail, a wave of panic rushes over me. It's painful imagining him abandoned in the cold ocean.

I squeeze his hand and force myself to listen. He says that after hours of swimming, he was exhausted. Night was coming, and so was the storm. The waves grew rougher, higher, the water colder. He thought he was going to die.

That was when he started noticing fins—shark fins, moving toward him—and teeth, glinting in the reflected lights of the clouds. Then a giant leatherback turtle rose beneath him. He hung on as it carried him away from the sharks, toward shore. By now, the thunder and lightning were wild, the waves crashing. But the turtle swam him all the way to a little fishing boat.

A man reached out, pulled him in. El Loco.

I want to interrupt and ask again what our fish guy was doing out in his rickety little boat in the middle of a storm. But I hold my tongue and listen as Wendell continues.

El Loco took off his own T-shirt, put it on Wendell, wrapped him in a wool blanket, and motored the boat to Playa Mermejita. Then he half carried Wendell up the path through the jungle to our cabanas.

Once Wendell finishes his story, he asks Alejandro to promise he'll go over the heads of the local police, right to the state police, to investigate. Looking reassured, Wendell hangs up with a weary sigh.

I give him a long hug. "Come on, Wendell. You're exhausted." With my arm firmly around his waist, I walk him down the path to his cabana. Inside, I help him onto the bed and lie down beside him, arranging the mosquito net around us.

I move my face close to his on the pillow, stroke his damp hair. "Wendell, when you were missing, I thought about our future. I always wanted it to be easy—like a perfect, predictable path." I pause, looking into his half-closed eyes. "But I realized it's okay if we take detours."

"What are you saying, Z?" he asks sleepily.

"Take the scholarship, Wendell. This time I really mean it. I want you to. I was scared before."

"Scared?"

"Scared you'd go off and start a whole new life, one without me." I pause to swallow my tears.

"Oh, Z . . ."

"But I'll let you go, Wendell. And trust that you'll come back."

He twirls a strand of my hair around his finger. "Listen, Z, I know we'll be together again . . . even if it might not be for a while." He kisses me, then whispers, "It's like those turtles that always come back to the same beach. You're my beach."

"And you're mine," I manage to say, my voice breaking.

We kiss again, and just before he slips into an exhausted sleep, I say, "So you'll take the scholarship?"

"Yeah," he murmurs.

And despite the stab of pain, there's a rightness to this decision. A decision made from a place of love, not fear.

I stay awake, listening to the rush of ocean, wondering where we'll be in a year, ten years, what we'll be doing, whether we'll be together. My mind wanders to Gracia, swimming around out there, full of old secrets. And to El Loco. I picture those crazy dreadlocks half covering his eyes, his earphones playing unknown music, his sandy, salty voice, his ratty old clothes, his weatherworn pink boat, his cooler of shaved ice and shiny fish. My eyes rest on the huge conch shell he gave me, sitting on my bedside table.

What was he doing out in the ocean? Looking for Wendell? But how did he know Wendell was out there? And how did he know about the fire? Is he the one who's been watching us from the jungle? Why? Who is this man?

I manage to sleep for an hour or two, restlessly, waking often to check Wendell's breathing, his heartbeat, his temperature. At the first light of dawn, I climb out of bed, not bothering to try to sleep more. Now is usually the time Layla rings the bell for sunrise yoga, but with the events of last night, everyone's sleeping in.

I take a quick shower to wash off the dried mud still coating my legs, then throw on a yellow sundress. Wendell is still sleeping soundly. From the back of my wooden chair I pick up the shirt El Loco lent Wendell. It's still damp, and coated in mud. I'll wash it and bring it downtown later today, I decide. El Loco is usually at his spot behind his fish cooler on the street by midmorning. He can answer my questions then.

I carry the shirt outside into the chilly dawn air. Stepping over storm debris, I head down the stone path to the big washbasin under a small, open-sided hut. I fill the sink with water, pour in powdered green soap. Rays of morning sun peek through the sugar cane roof overhead, illuminating the bubbles. As the shirt soaks, I survey the destruction from the storm. Tree limbs have cracked, their leaves torn off and matted on the ground. A few palm fronds were blown off the roofs, but overall, the cabanas held up well.

I scrub the T-shirt, then rinse it with clear water and wring it out. I hold it up, inspect it to make sure all the mud is out. The T-shirt lettering is swirling script that spells out *Illusion*. The name of my father's performance troupe in France.

My head spins. It's him. El Loco, Tortue, El Tortuga, J.C., José Carlos Cruz Castillo. My father. Is he the one watching us in the jungle? The invisible one protecting us? The one who saved us from the fire? Pelted the poachers with stones? Defended the sea turtles? And defended us? I remember, suddenly, that Lupita said her son was an expert tree climber, with amazing slingshot aim. And the treasures and shells he gave her—he gave one to me, too: the smooth conch shell. My mind scrambles to put together the pieces.

For a second, I consider bursting into Layla's and Wendell's cabanas, telling them to get dressed and come with me to find my father. But that would mean waiting. And explaining. And after waiting so long already, I can't bear to wait any longer. Not even for ten minutes.

I tear through the jungle, heading toward the cliffs of Punta Cometa, toward the tiny crescent of beach where he keeps his pink boat. Fallen branches litter the path, but I crash through, clutching the dripping T-shirt, not caring about the scratches on my legs.

As I run, I try to conjure up my father's face, the shape of it, its expressions. But in France, it was covered in white paint; the only image I see is a mask. What I remember more clearly is his voice, so tender. I try to recall El Loco's voice. There's a raspiness to it, a sandiness, as if he's just crawled to shore. Now that I replay it in my mind, it sounds as if he's been holding back waves of emotion, just barely. The hoarseness of a man about to cry. Or cry out. Was he ever teetering on the verge of telling me? Why didn't he?

I pick up my pace, determined to find out.

Finally, I emerge from the jungle onto the rocky peninsula of Comet Point. As I run, skidding down the steep part, dashing around cacti, these details work themselves out in my mind, the bits of random knowledge I have of this man, my father. And by the time I reach the edge of the cliff, the only question left is *why?* Why hasn't he shown me his face? If he knows I'm here, looking for him, reaching out to him, why hasn't he met me halfway?

I skid to a stop at the edge of the cliff, sending a few

tiny pebbles soaring into the surf below, smacking against the cliffs. There's the pink boat, upside down on the beach, surrounded by flotsam from the storm, piles of sea-worn garbage. Cupping my hands around my mouth, I shout, "Tortue!" The ocean swallows my cries. Louder, I try "Tortuga!"

Nothing. He must be asleep. I'll go down to his boat, wake him up, I decide. But how do I get there? The little beach is surrounded by steep cliffs on three sides.

I could turn back, look for him downtown later today. That way, Layla and Wendell could come with me. But what if we've scared him off? What if he's planning to run again? Now that I've figured out who he is, and know that he's so close, I have to find him. *Now.*

My heart racing, I scan the cliffs for some kind of path. Finally, my eyes rest on what might be a trail, with a few spindly trees and a smattering of cracks in the rock that could serve as foot- and handholds. I head toward that section of the cliff, darting around cactus outcroppings and hardy shrubs.

When I reach the top of the path, I tie the damp shirt around my waist. I'll need both hands for this. Looking down the steep incline, I feel my heart pound even harder. Sharp rocks and cacti and dried tree branches jut up everywhere. And at the bottom, waves crash against the thin crescent of sand. I glance at the pink boat, which looks tiny so far below.

It occurs to me that no one knows where I am. Everyone is sleeping. If something happens . . . Biting my lip, I look at the dazzling ocean, the silvery blue sky. I should go back, get some help. But I'm so close. I'm not letting him get away again.

I try calling out again. "Tortue!"

No response. I take a deep breath and turn around, positioning myself to face the incline and climb down backward. I go slowly, finding solid spots for my feet, grips for my hands. I'm about halfway down when I stop to rest. The drop is almost vertical here. Now it's even harder to find a place to hold on. When I've caught my breath, I grasp a slender tree and lower myself, stretching my right foot into a rock nook below. Then I let down my left foot and an arm, wedging my fingers into a ridge. My knuckles are white, gripping the rock. My left foot has nowhere to go. I search the stone face for somewhere to put it.

Nothing. Sheer rock. And then my right foot slips.

I shriek. An animal scream of sheer terror. I'm hanging by my fingers now, my feet scrambling desperately to find something to step on, a root, anything. I scream again, in words this time. "¡Ayúdenme! Help!" The ocean swallows my sounds but I keep screaming on instinct. "¡Ayúdenme!"

As I scream, thoughts race through my mind in a loop. *I'm going to fall, I'm going to fall. What if I die? What if I die just moments before meeting my father? How can I die after seventeen years of waiting for this?*

An image of Wendell comes to my mind. Someplace deeper than my mind, somewhere in my center, inside my chest. All our moments together, our breaths close, our lips grazing, the comfort of his arms, his chest, his cinnamon smell. And then, the image of our spot on the beach, our handfasting place, empty. His confidence that we'll be together in the end . . . but what if I don't make it to the end?

All this time, I'm crying for help as the waves drown out my flimsy words. I don't know how long I scream—seconds, minutes—all I know is my hands ache, and I'm terrified to adjust my grip. I need all my fingers to hang on.

And they're slipping. One by one, as if in slow motion, the fingertips slide off.

My feet flail wildly, searching for anything solid. Again, I scream.

And now I'm falling, sliding down the rock face, stones and pebbles and cactus thorns ripping into my skin. The world becomes a spinning blur of rock and sea and sand.

Then, somehow, there's an arm around me, holding me securely. My body is still, my head still spinning. But I'm safe—yes, I am. Someone's caught me. I look up, focusing. A pair of deep brown eyes meet mine.

It's him. He's breathing hard, sweat glistening under his dreadlocks, holding me firmly with his muscled arm, his hand gripping a tree root. His eyes peek through his hair, relieved, tender. Without a word, he sets me on my feet, then guides me down the rest of the cliff, knowing exactly where to step. He leads me to the crescent of beach, where he sits me down gently in the shade of the pink boat. *Gracia*, it reads in peeling, faint white letters. Named after the turtle who saved him so many years ago?

Or it might simply mean "Grace."

He watches me, surveys my wounds.

I realize how much my body aches, stinging and throbbing. "You heard me," I manage to say, hoarse after so much screaming.

He nods. He looks like he wants to say something, opens his mouth and closes it again.

"Your shirt," I say, flustered, unwrapping it from my waist and handing it to him. "I washed it but—it's covered in dirt again." It's crazy that this is all I can think to say, talking about a shirt at this moment I've dreamed of all my life.

He takes the damp shirt.

I run my fingers over my scrapes and bruises, waiting for him to speak. He doesn't. I want to hear his voice, because now I'm starting to wonder if he's an apparition. If I fell and died and he's some kind of silent angel. Hugging myself, trying to stop shaking, I say, "I know who you are."

No reply. I strain to see his expression beneath his wild hair.

A wave of something is rising inside me, some oceanic feeling that makes the pain from my wounds fade into the background. "I know you. I know you've been protecting us." I suck in a breath. "I know you're innocent. I know you're scared and sad. And full of regret." Again, I wait for him to say something.

He doesn't.

I feel like a sea turtle, battered and beaten by the currents. Finally making it onto the beach. Exhausted, wanting. Something. A word, anything. I look at him, pleading. "I just—I don't understand why you never—why—" And the tears break loose, like a dam opening, streams of tears.

He sits there watching me, awkwardly. Why isn't he talking, hugging me, comforting me? Something. Anything. Anything remotely fatherly.

"Tell me why!" I shout. My words echo off the cliffs, fade into the ocean.

He lowers his head. "Zeeta." His voice is a whisper, barely audible over the crashing of waves on the cliffs. He buries his face in his hands. "This isn't how I imagined it. Us finally meeting."

He speaks in Spanish, the Spanish of the locals, I realize. Maybe that's why I didn't recognize his voice. In France, he spoke to me in French.

"It's not how I imagined it either." I look at the debris washed ashore, surrounding us, plastic bottles, an old flip-flop, frayed rope, heaps of trash.

He takes a wavery breath. "I wanted—I wanted to be strong for you. Complete. I wanted to be someone you could depend on. Someone you'd be proud of." He pauses. "I came back here last summer. I thought I'd reconnect with my family. Let go of old hurt. Fix myself. Become the father you deserve."

"What happened?" I ask in a small voice.

"I—I realized it wouldn't be easy. I couldn't tell my family I was here. I disguised myself as a beach bum, thinking I'd find the courage any day. Then I ran out of my meds, didn't bother to get more. I thought, *What's the point?* I fell into a dark place. And I didn't have my friends here to pull me out. I was at a real low. I even considered . . ." His voice trails off. "But then I saw you and Layla and Wendell in town. I wanted to run up and tell you who I was. But I felt too broken. I decided I had to get better first. Seeing you every day—it gave me motivation. I even started taking my meds again. And when I saw you were in danger, I knew I had to protect you."

"Then why didn't you show yourself?"

He lets his dreads fall over his eyes. "Look at me, Zeeta. . . . I sleep under a boat. I forage fruit from the jungle and fish from the sea. I have nothing to give you. I'm so sorry. I'm a mess."

He stares at me, his arms outstretched, his palms turned up, empty. Surrounded by broken and worn things from the sea. The sunlight shines through his graying dreadlocks, illuminating his face.

I reach out, push away the hair to reveal his eyes, which are red, shining. I muster up all my courage and say, "You know, I kinda like messes."

Chapter Twenty-Two

Since I can't make it up the cliff trail, Tortue takes me in his boat around the cove to Playa Mermejita. Then we hike up the beach and through the jungle, arm in arm, him supporting me. We don't talk much; I'm in too much pain as we hike. And shock. It's like a dream. I'm in a state of disbelief, struggling to absorb everything.

Once we reach the dining hut, I'm thinking more clearly. I stop by the freezer for some ice packs, and Tortue helps make coffee. It's still early; everyone else is asleep.

He carries our mugs of coffee to the table. I sit down, propping up my sore leg and icing it. Across from me, through lit-up spirals of steam, my father sips his coffee. I sip my own, watching a line of ants crawl over a few stray sugar crystals. I sneak awkward glances at him. One moment I want to throw my arms around him, and the next I want to shake him.

"I don't get it, Tortue," I finally sputter. "Why did you stay? Why didn't you just go back to France?"

"Money. I had none left." He smiles. "And the turtles."

"The turtles?"

"In the fall, I knew the leatherbacks would be coming to nest. I'd come this far and I didn't want to miss them. I remembered I'd left my boat, *Gracia,* under a rock ledge on the little beach. She was still there." He smiles again. "I took it as a sign. I camped on the beach, caught and sold fish to support myself. And I started saving pesos to get back to France. I figured by the end of leatherback nesting season I'd have it saved up. But it wasn't easy. Some days I was too depressed to even roll out from beneath my boat."

He brushes the hair from his face, his eyes filling with tears. "Zeeta, when I saw you here . . . I was filled with so much emotion. I couldn't believe you cared enough to cross an ocean to find me. But I knew I'd only disappoint you."

He wipes his eyes, and after a moment, continues his story. He says that as he watched the turtles on Playa Mermejita and kept an eye on us at the cabanas, he became aware of the dangers. So he became the protector of the turtles . . . and of us.

My heart swells when I hear this. My father isn't a coward after all, but a kind of hero turned on his head. In his own backward way, he's been a dependable father, one who's kept me safe. What I've always wanted in a dad. Suddenly, I'm filled with warmth, gratitude, *gracias.*

When he pauses to sip his coffee, I say, "That was you with your slingshot, shooting stones, wasn't it?"

He nods. "I was in the trees, hiding."

"And you were the one I kept seeing in the jungle? The one who ran away?"

"Yes." His gaze falls to his lap. "That last time—I suspected the poachers were plotting something. I'd overheard them talking about it the night before last. I came last night to warn you."

"That was you I saw," I murmur.

With a nod, he continues. "I heard you tell Meche that Wendell was out at sea in the storm. So I ran to my boat to find him."

I'm on the verge of asking him more about the poachers, about the plot against Wendell, but he looks exhausted. He rubs his eyes and says, in his soft, raspy voice, "But tell me about you, Zeeta."

I take a deep breath, staring at the wood-grain pattern in the table. Where do I begin? How do I fill him in on seventeen years? I don't have to do it all at once, I remind myself. There will be time to fill in the gaps. We'll have the rest of our lives together, especially if Layla and I get to stay on this land, make this our real home.

After another sip of coffee, I settle on giving him the highlights of my seventeen years roaming the planet—a recap of the countries we've lived in, how Wendell and I met, the multitudes of clowns and musicians Layla has dated. This last one elicits an ironic chuckle from him.

Mostly, he nods, trying to take it all in, looking a little overwhelmed. Finally, he sets down his coffee cup and offers a tentative smile. "I don't know what to say. You're—you're amazing, Zeeta."

I bite my cheek. Of course, this is exactly what I've always wanted to hear from my father. Still, I flush, embarrassed.

"You're everything I've wanted in a daughter," he continues. "You're smart, you're kind, you're strong." His hands twist nervously on the table. "And I'm none of those things. I don't deserve you. . . ."

"Stop saying that, Tortue." I study his face, taking in the features that are so similar to my own. Again, this feels like a dream, as if I'm watching a movie of Zeeta meeting her father. "Tortue," I say quietly. I consider calling him Dad or Papá, but I'm not ready for that. I'm most comfortable with the name I've known him by best, his French nickname. "I still don't get it. Why couldn't you reconnect with your family? I'm friends with your parents, you know. Your father regrets how he acted. He's a sweet man. And of course, your mother adores you."

"She adores everyone," he says. "I've been in touch with her over the years. Phone calls, letters."

"Really?" I wonder if it was hard for Lupita to resist mentioning this fact to me. "And?"

He sips his coffee thoughtfully. "She says people have forgotten about the scandal. She says my father would forgive me."

"He would! So what's stopping you?"

Tortue shakes his head. "My brother. I contacted him

when I first got here. I thought he'd give me honest advice." He rubs his face, too upset to continue.

His brother. Pepe. And he actually thinks Pepe's honest. How can that be? "And what did he say?" I urge gently.

"That my family would turn me over to the cops. That my father's grudge has only grown stronger over time. That my sister has finally let go of me. That I'd hurt my family if I tried to come back home—"

"That's not true, Tortue! Cristina still misses you. Just like your father." My heart is racing. "Your brother's wrong." I try to compose my thoughts. "I know Pepe. He's Wendell's boss."

Tortue raises his eyebrows. This must be new information for him. "I see you've met my entire family."

"I don't trust your brother, Tortue." I pause. "How can you?"

He shrugs. "He's my brother. He's always been a friendly guy. Wants everyone to love him. That's his weakness. It was hard on him to have his family be victim of a scandal." Tortue forges ahead slowly. "He said he left town in shame, that I nearly ruined his life. Now that he's settling back here, he wants a clean reputation. He's got a good job at the Turtle Center, and—"

I can't stand it anymore. "Tortue," I practically shout, "that man—your brother—he had something to do with Wendell nearly being killed last night. The poaching on Playa Mermejita—Pepe's involved somehow. He lied to us. He's been lying to everyone." I look at Tortue and say, almost fiercely, "Including you."

"What—how . . . ?"

"He's been pressuring our neighbor to sell her land—a piece of jungle by Punta Cometa. He wants to build a giant hotel here."

Tortue clutches his head. "Then—" He must have a million questions. Finally he settles on, "But the turtles—why does Pepe work at the Turtle Center?"

"Why not? It's one of the best jobs in town. All he has to do is be friendly. And coordinate volunteers—*nonexistent* volunteers. That way he can let his buddies poach. And in exchange, they do his dirty work. Like leaving curses, setting fires, making threats, trying to kill people."

The pained look on Tortue's face makes me remember his fragile emotional state. The last thing I want to do is make things worse. More softly, I ask, "Tortue, is it possible that Pepe committed the crime years ago? And framed you?"

After a long moment, Tortue answers. "When Pepe was a teenager, he was always trying to impress people, especially the kids he thought were cool. Some of his buddies were a little sketchy. Honestly? I figured they manipulated him into giving them the key to our father's truck. I didn't want him to get in trouble." Tortue runs his hand over his dreadlocks. "But maybe Pepe was the one manipulating his friends all along. And his family."

I'm quiet for a while, thinking. Pepe managed to keep his own brother and mother and father blind to his shady nature. Wendell didn't see it either, and they worked together. Even I didn't start seeing through Pepe until last night, when he suggested that Wendell was being unfaithful. The man has this entire town wrapped around his finger. So many people owe him favors—including the police—it would be easy for him to break the law and build the hotel. I could even imagine him flaunting his authority, assuring people that the hotel beach would be a safe haven for the turtles. And of course, everyone would believe him. They love him.

Ultimately, the only obstacle to building his hotel would be this land we're on. And his plan to get it was threatened by Tortue's reappearance, and then by Meche's and my determination to stay here.

Almost all the pieces fit together. There's just one thing I don't understand. "Tortue, why did you take the fall for Pepe? You had an alibi. Proving your innocence wouldn't place the blame on Pepe. Not then and not even now."

He stares into his coffee. "I had to protect someone."

"Who? The girl you were with that night?"

Just then, the leaves in the jungle rustle. With a wave, Meche emerges from the path and walks toward us with her somehow regal limp. *"Buenos días,* Zeeta. *Buenos días, señor."*

She doesn't appear to recognize him as the fish guy. Or the cloaked man who saved Wendell. She must assume he's just a new guest who woke up earlier than the others. *"Buenos días,* Meche!" I call back. "Grab some coffee. Join us."

Tortue stands up, mumbles that he should be going. Letting his dreadlocks fall over his face, he starts backing up.

I reach out and grab his hand. "Please stay," I whisper.

He takes a long breath and sits back down, lowering his head.

"How's Wendell?" Meche asks, bustling behind the counter.

"Still asleep. I think he'll be fine."

"Thank God," she says. "I could hardly sleep I was so worried."

"Well, you're the only one," I say. "Everyone else slept in." Then I notice the dark circles beneath her eyes. "Hey, how's Gatito?"

She takes a long breath. "He's not eating. He doesn't want to move."

"I'm so sorry, Meche." And I am. As much as I wanted that jaguar gone, now I'm rooting for him to pull through. "Anything we can do?"

Meche pours sugar into her coffee. "Actually, I was hoping I could use your phone later. I need to call the vet, see how much time my baby has left."

Walking over with her coffee mug, Meche takes in my ice pack, the scratches and welts from my tumble down the cliff. "Zeeta! What happened?"

"A little fall. Nothing broken." I motion with my chin to Tortue. "He saved me. And he's the one who saved Wendell last night."

Meche sits down beside me and regards Tortue from across the table. "And you're a fisherman?" she asks, confused.

"This is—" I begin, and hesitate. How do I introduce him? Definitely not as El Loco—The Crazy Guy. And Tortue—that's French—would be hard for her to pronounce. El Tortuga isn't a possibility either; it would betray his hidden identity. "José," I finish, turning toward him. "And this is my neighbor, Meche."

She offers him her ring-laden hand. *"Mucho gusto."*

Tortue pushes the dreadlocks from his face and shakes her hand.

Suddenly, Meche's eyes grow wide. She doesn't let go of his hand. "Is that you?" she whispers. "Tortuga?" Tears well up in her eyes and she places her other hand over his. "Tortuga?"

He meets her gaze. "I—I've missed you, Meche." His voice cracks with emotion.

"¡Qué milagro!" What a miracle! Meche blinks, bewildered, and turns to me. "El Tortuga and I—we've known each other since we were children. We were good friends, *grandes amigos!*" Turning back to him, she says, "I'm so glad you're back! Lupita didn't mention—"

"I asked my mother not to tell anyone."

"Why not? That scandal? But it was so long ago."

When Tortue doesn't answer, I ask her hesitantly, "What do you know about the scandal, Meche?"

"Pues, not much," she says, flicking her hand. "I heard some rumors after I returned home from Puerto Escondido, but I refused to pay attention. You know I hate gossip." She looks back at Tortue. "Tortuga, all I knew was that you were my friend, a man with a good heart." Almost shyly, she adds, "I never got to thank you for that night, Tortuga."

He swallows, looks away. "It was nothing."

"You saved my life, Tortue. Just like you saved Wendell's." She reaches out again, takes his hand. *"Gracias."*

I flick my eyes to El Tortuga then to Meche. "What happened?"

Meche looks at me. "I've never told this to another soul. But lately I've been thinking about it . . . with Gatito so close to passing away. Thinking about being alone again, thinking about people in my life who've shown me kindness, people I'd like to have around."

She's quiet for a moment, then says, "My daughter fell off the cliffs of Punta Cometa when she was two. We weren't living here at the time, just in town for a visit. When I returned to my husband in Puerto Escondido, I was too devastated to eat or talk or do anything. On the year anniversary of her death, I came back to this property—my family's property. That night, I sank into such despair, I decided I couldn't live anymore. I walked to Punta Cometa and threw myself off the cliff."

My muscles tense.

She gives a wry laugh. "Obviously, I didn't die. I broke my leg and got banged up. The surf tossed my broken body onto Playa Mermejita. I lay there, moaning in pain. I couldn't move. The water washed over me. It's strange how clearly I remember it, the moonlight reflecting off the bubbles, the way the sand glistened. Strangely beautiful.

"And then an odd thing happened. A sea turtle came to shore right beside me, an enormous turtle, and it looked at me, right into my eyes. At that moment, for some reason, I decided I didn't want to die. I don't know why . . . something about the moonlight, the turtle, the sand, the water. It was as if they all held little bits of my daughter. I don't know how to explain it."

Her voice quavers. "But I knew I wanted to live. The tide was coming in. I'd lost a lot of blood. I was too weak to move. I could only lie there watching the turtle drag itself from the surf onto the sand. Every wave brought the tide higher, nearly covering me. That's when I saw someone on the beach. El Tortuga."

She looks at him across the table, keeps her gaze fixed on his as she speaks. "Without asking questions, El Tortuga took me in his arms and carried me all the way up the jungle path to my house. I don't know how, but he did it. He wanted to take me to the hospital. I told him no. I was ashamed I'd tried to kill myself—and failed. I didn't want to give people more ammunition for gossip. And most of all, I didn't want to drag poor Tortuga into it. He was already . . . misunderstood. And I had a terrible reputation. I knew people would invent their own stories about why Tortuga and I were alone together. I made him promise not to tell a soul. He agreed. He bandaged my wounds and set my leg with wood splints."

She pats her leg. "You did a pretty good job, Tortuga. It's a miracle I can walk at all."

She doesn't know, I realize. She doesn't know she was his secret alibi. I have to break it to her, gently. "Meche, was this the same night he was accused of poaching?"

She wrinkles her eyebrows, confused. "I—I don't know. I went back to Puerto Escondido after that, back to my husband. It wasn't till later that we divorced and I returned here. The scandal had mostly blown over by then. Since I kept to myself, and I never really asked—" Her hand flies to her mouth as the realization hits her. "Tortuga? That was the night . . . ?"

He nods ever so slightly.

She searches his face. "But how? How on earth did they think you were guilty?"

Tortue looks too distraught to speak.

I answer for him. "He came home with sand and blood on his clothes. The police thought he was the guy who'd run—the poacher who fled the truck loaded with turtle eggs and meat. It was his father's truck; the evidence pointed to Tortue—El Tortuga. His mother believed he was with a girl. But he refused to name her or give an alibi."

Meche's jaw drops as the full significance sinks in. "You mean—it's my fault? That you were falsely accused? All this time I could've cleared your name? All this time you honored your promise? Despite the sacrifice?"

Silence. His eyes fill as he looks at Meche.

"We have to tell your family! And everyone else!"

"Tortue," I say, surging with emotion. My voice sounds so strong and certain, it surprises me. "Tortuga. I'm not disappointed in you. Just the opposite. I'm proud you're my father."

Meche's head snaps up, and just as she whispers, "Your father?" Layla comes down the path, followed by Wendell.

❖　❖　❖

Layla enters the kitchen hut wearing a wrinkled huipil that she probably slept in, her hair a mess and wrapped in a silk scarf. She's yawning and rubbing her eyes when she catches sight of Meche. "*¡Amiga!*" she cries, embracing her with a kiss on the cheek.

Meche is still speechless, absorbing the revelation. In confusion, she looks at my father, then at me, then at Layla.

Wendell, meanwhile, notices Tortue and walks over, extending his hand. "Thank you so much. For last night. I'm glad you came back."

Layla turns to him now, and echoes, "Yes, thank you!"

Then she looks at him, really looks at him. His dreads are pushed away from his face. Her eyes flick from mine to Tortue's. A long ray of angled morning light, fresh and silver, illuminates his face. Her eyebrows furrow as she studies him. I can almost see it dawning on her, who this man is. It's as if she's digging deep in her mind for the memory of his face, asking herself, *Is it . . . ?*

She looks at me and whispers, "Zeeta?" Her eyes are intense. I know the question she's asking.

I nod. I take a deep breath, and say, "Meet my father."

Layla falls back onto the bench. Wendell steps to my side, holds my hand tightly. In the stunned silence, a blue butterfly flutters into the kitchen hut, hovers, and breezes out the other side, toward the ocean. For once, Layla is speechless. I expect her to spout off Rumi, but she sits silently, her hand over her mouth.

Meche speaks first. "I don't understand. How—?"

That revives Layla. She stands up, moves toward Tortue with outstretched arms. They hold each other, a little awkwardly, but gently. I watch to see if there's any trace of the passionate love that Tortue declared for her in his letters years ago. Any lasting spark. I can't tell.

Now come the tears—Tortue's, Layla's, Meche's, mine—and the cries of happiness, of disbelief, of regret. Then the explanations. The earnest, eager stops and starts in the conversation.

Soon the guests trickle in, groggy and hungry. Layla grabs some tomatoes and I grab peppers and Meche grabs onions. Together, we whip up a breakfast of *huevos a la mexicana* with tortillas and heaps of pink sugar-coated sweet rolls, mounds of pineapple and cantaloupe and watermelon. Meanwhile, Wendell and Tortue sip coffee, discussing the details of last night.

Throughout breakfast, Layla keeps staring at Tortue. It's the first time she's seen my father's bare face in daylight—knowing it's him, at least. She's uncharacteristically shy, asking him hesitant questions. He answers just as shyly. They're strangers with a sudden, intimate bond. Layla said she had no expectations—that he'd be a treasure from the ocean. And that's what he makes me think of, a salt-soaked piece of driftwood, battered by life and the sea, gnarled but soft, and oddly, in his own tender way, tough.

Meche watches this unfold, regarding us curiously.

And all the while, Wendell holds my hand, anchoring me, solid and warm.

I continue to watch for any signs of attraction between Layla and Tortue. As a little girl I dreamed of my parents being reunited, their passion rekindled and transformed into lasting love, the three of us forming a happy family. And Tortue is even Layla's type—musical, scraggly-haired, homeless. But now, looking at them, I see something unexpected—a tentative affection.

There's none of Layla's usual flirtation, her unconscious effort to charm. And even more surprisingly, this doesn't disappoint me. It's actually reassuring to know that my father is not being relegated to fling status.

And Tortue doesn't seem love-struck by Layla. Not in the least. In fact, most of the time as they're talking, he looks at me, exactly the way a father would look at his daughter, his eyes full of pride, love.

At one point in the conversation, Layla's fork clatters to the plate, and she says, out of the blue, "Thank you for our daughter."

El Tortuga's lip quivers. "Our daughter."

And then, as if the spell is broken, Layla launches into the story of my life—the long version—starting with my babyhood in Italy and rambling through country after country.

Tortue listens with rapt attention. It's a strange feeling to witness my father laughing at the things I did as a toddler. Now that I've found him, I have the same feeling I get standing at the tip of Comet Point—that this is the edge of the world as I've always known it. The promise of something new stretches ahead, something that's certain to be smooth at times, choppy at others, something shimmering with the delicious unknown.

❖ ❖ ❖

After breakfast, the guests scatter, leaving me, Wendell, Meche, Layla, Tortue, and Joe sipping our third cups of coffee. Bit by bit, we've filled each other in on our suspicions about Pepe and the developments in the poaching scandals—both the current one and the one that's decades old. Meche wants to go to the authorities immediately and clear Tortue's name, but he insists that his family should be the first to know. "I want to tell my whole family at once," he says earnestly. "Not just about Meche, but about Zeeta. That she's my daughter. And that I'll be claiming my land, *our* land." He casts a hopeful look at Layla and me.

"Gracias," I say, grateful for this moment, the morning sunlight on the ocean, the glittering aftermath of the storm, everyone I love here in this place I love. Finally.

"I know!" Layla says, clasping her hands together. "Let's invite your family here tonight—Lupita, Rogelio, Cristina and her kids. . . ." Her voice trails off. She must be remembering Pepe and the probability that he had something to do with Wendell's nearly dying last night.

Tortue looks at his lap and says, "Maybe you should check in with the authorities. See if they have any leads on Pepe."

Wendell nods. "I'll call the fire chief," he offers, heading to the phone in the office.

Tortue lets out a long breath. "Let's not tell the rest of my family about Pepe. Not just yet. I want tonight to be a festive occasion." He gazes at me, the loving gaze of a father. "I've waited years for this day."

Chapter Twenty-Three

We assign tasks to prepare for the celebration tonight. Layla will buy ingredients for dinner; Tortue will head out on his boat to catch fresh fish; Wendell will go to Restaurante Tesoro Escondido to invite El Sapo and his sisters and Cristina to the party. I'm in charge of inviting my grandparents.

I swing by Lupita's house and manage to catch Rogelio just before he leaves for his shop. I'm nearly bursting with giddiness as I give them the mysterious invitation. I simply say there will be an important gathering at our cabanas tonight at sunset. A big announcement will be made. Rogelio and Lupita pelt me with questions, but I press my lips together in a contained smile and say, "You'll see!"

Meanwhile, Meche has gone to check on Gatito. But on the way home, I run into her on the jungle path. Her hair is mussed, her face puffy and tear-streaked.

"What's wrong, Meche?"

"It's Gatito. The vet came over. My baby's kidneys are failing."

I reach for her hand. "What does that mean?"

"He can't filter out the toxins in his blood. He's in terrible pain. He might have only a day or two left." She breaks down into sobs.

I lead her to the bench at the end of my sun-path ray and sit her down. Suddenly, a stream of pent-up words tumbles out. She reminisces about how she first met Gatito, recounts his cute antics as a cub, the adorable tricks he learned. I listen, offering comforting words here and there. For the first time, I really get it—Gatito was her baby, her child, the closest possible replacement for her daughter. And now, she'll have to live through the sorrow of her baby dying all over again.

Finally, after she's cried out, she draws in a long breath and glances around. She takes in the GET WELL sign that Xochitl and Mayra painted for Gatito. It's right next to the TRESPASSERS WILL BE DEVOURED sign. Looking at the signs now, I get a lump in my throat. It's as if they're memorials to Gatito.

Meche regards the smiling, sparkling jaguar and sniffles. "Where did that come from?"

"Mayra and Xochitl painted it. For you and Gatito." I squeeze her hand. "You have people who care about you. We'll help you through this, Meche."

She gives me one more hug. "I'd better get back to Gatito.

I'll come over for a little while this evening. Just long enough to explain to everyone that I was with El Tortuga that night. But after that I need to get back to my kitty."

After saying goodbye, I head back home, passing Wendell and Joe, who are cleaning the storm debris from the gardens and stone paths. Wendell sets down the broom and drapes his arm around me. "I did it, Z."

Instinctively, I know he's talking about accepting the scholarship. There's something about his tone—a mixture of sadness and excitement. "Good," I say, determined not to mope, to just enjoy our last few months together. And to trust that some time after that, we'll be together again. Somehow.

"I start in June," he says a little wistfully.

"You'll do great, Wendell." Swallowing hard, I add, "You'll love it there."

From the kitchen hut, Layla catches my eye and waves me over. "Hey, Z!" she calls out, tying on an apron. "Come cook with me!"

I join her, taking a bag of *mole* paste from the fridge. She's making flan using Cristina's recipe, humming as she whizzes around the kitchen. "Well," she says, "I talked with the fire chief. Pepe and his friends haven't been found. They might've left town."

I breathe out slowly, trying to stay calm. Layla doesn't seem concerned, but I'd feel better if we knew where Pepe and El Dedo were.

She interrupts my worrying. "I hope J.C. gets here soon

with the fish. Especially if we have to gut it and everything." She's taken to calling my father the name she first knew him by.

I glance at the clock. Four o'clock. "He'll probably be here soon," I say. But a little part of me wonders, what if he doesn't come back? What if he freaks out again? What if I can't trust him after all? I shake off my questions, try to relax and sink into the smells of sizzling chile and chocolate and the excitement about the party. After all, tonight will be the culmination of nearly two decades of longing for family and home. Mine, and—I realize—my father's.

❖ ❖ ❖

Where is he? An hour later, Tortue still hasn't shown up. I've showered and changed into a sundress and tucked a pink flower, which I can't stop fiddling with, behind my ear. What's going on with him? At this point, it's too late to cook any fish he might've caught. Layla assures me it's fine, there's plenty of *mole*. She doesn't seem worried about him getting cold feet.

Shortly before sunset, Lupita and Rogelio show up, sporting fancy clothes—a flowered dress and woven silvery shawl on Lupita and an old-fashioned, neatly pressed suit on Rogelio. Then come Cristina and the girls, their hair brushed and slicked back into ponytails tied with ribbons. El Sapo is wearing dress pants and a long-sleeved shirt, and every strand of hair is gelled into place. Even his glasses sparkle. The first words out of the girls' mouths are "Where's Meche?"

I crack a smile at how fast they've embraced the so-called jaguar lady, the feared *bruja*. "She'll be here soon," I assure them. "She's with Gatito. And you know, your sign cheered her up." I try to sound natural, as if my insides aren't in knots.

By dusk, everyone is sipping lemonade and speculating about the mysterious announcement. Everyone but Tortue. To stall, I bring out the guitar and play a butchered version of "La Llorona" for Rogelio. Although he acts impressed, my heart isn't in it. *Where is my father?*

I pass Rogelio the guitar and make an excuse about checking on the *mole*.

Lupita stops me, her face lit up. "So when will we hear the big announcement, *mija*?"

"Soon," I stall, glancing nervously at Wendell.

Wendell gives me a sympathetic look and follows me behind the counter. Little by little, the sun has slipped farther toward the horizon, painting the sky dusky hues of violet.

Wendell strokes my hair. "Hanging in there, Z?"

Under my breath, I ask, "You think he ran?"

Wendell pulls me close, kisses my ear. "He has to have a good reason for being late."

Our cabana guests have started trickling in, looking hungry. Layla breezes over to us. "Well, we might as well feed everyone now. *Mole* seems like a perfect distraction till J.C. gets here."

"You really think he's coming, Layla?"

"Of course, Z." She offers a conspiratorial smile. "You know, I heard that guys who sleep under boats aren't the most punctual. And he had a rough night last night. He's probably dozing under his boat now."

True . . . or he could be on a plane somewhere.

That's it. I can't stand waiting another second. "I'm going to look for him."

Quickly, Wendell says, "I'm coming with you, Z."

Before Layla can protest, I turn to the expectant faces of my family. Barely keeping my voice steady, I say, "Wendell and I are going to get our guest of honor. After dinner, we'll make the announcement." I take a deep breath, attempting to inject enthusiasm into my voice. "In the meantime, enjoy the *mole*!"

Wishing us luck, Layla begins heating up the food as Wendell and I bid everyone farewell. We hurry in the opposite direction, down the dark jungle path. "Let's see if his boat's there," I say, breathless.

When we emerge from the jungle, we peer over the cliff into the crescent-shaped cove. The full moon illuminates the beach. No boat. Just piles of storm debris. I look at Wendell, my heart sinking. "He's not here."

Wendell puts his arm around me. "Maybe he's out fishing and lost track of time. I mean, Layla's right. He's not the kind of guy who wears a watch. Hey, maybe his boat's still on Playa Mermejita. That's where he beached it this morning, right?"

"Worth a shot," I say, biting my lip.

We head through the jungle, around the rocky cliff, toward Playa Mermejita. Bits of moonlight filter through the tree leaves, just enough to show the way. When we reach the beach, I exhale with relief. There's his pink boat, upside down on the sand.

We hurry to it, peer underneath. No one. Only the blanket strapped beneath the seat. We glance around, calling out all the various names he goes by. "Tortue! Tortuga! José! J.C.! Loco!"

No response.

I slump on the boat. "Where could he be?" I let my head fall into my hands. Emotions crash and tumble inside me— anger, disappointment, fear. Maybe he changed his mind, decided he wasn't ready to see his family, to be my father. Maybe he decided he'll never be ready. Things look so bleak, it's all I can do not to sink into the sand and cry.

Wendell's voice breaks through my misery. "Hey, look, Z!"

My head snaps up.

He's pointing to something on the sand, on the other side of the boat. Slowly, we stand up, walk toward the movement. Small, dark shapes crawling down the beach. I see their flippers first, moving, determined, surprisingly large on their small bodies.

"Hatchlings!" Wendell cries. "Some of the eggs must've made it!"

A tentative path of baby turtles stretches from the nest to the surf. Near the nest, tiny noses poke out from the sand, and flippers flop, full of effort and hope. Once the hatchlings are out, they take a moment to get their bearings, then head toward the reflected light of the sea.

Despite my despair, I can't help smiling at these tender creatures. By silent agreement, Wendell and I move obstacles out of their way—stones and bits of driftwood—making their journey a little easier. We watch them row themselves into the surf and disappear into the sea. Something about this, their survival against all odds, gives me hope.

As the last ones are flopping into the surf, a giant form emerges before us. Huge and oval. A turtle head pokes up, adult-size, its tiny eyes gleaming.

"A leatherback," Wendell says, moving closer. "Full-grown."

We wait a moment, expecting the turtle to crawl to shore, but she simply circles there, in the water.

"Strange," I say. "Is she watching her babies?"

"I've never heard of that happening," Wendell says, puzzled. He splashes carefully into the surf, his eyes glued to the enormous turtle.

"What?"

He walks closer to the turtle. "Z, it's Gracia!"

"Really?" I ask, squinting. "You see her scars?"

"No. I just know her. It's like Horacio recognizing voices. I can recognize turtles, especially the one who saved me."

I follow him into the water. Gracia swims closer, close enough that Wendell can rest his hand on her back. "Feel her scars," he whispers.

I run my hand along the ridges of thick, healed-over flesh, stroke her leathery back, thinking of the lives she's saved. Abruptly, she turns and swims out to deeper water. Then she circles back to us.

"She's acting weird," Wendell says, staring into her little eyes. "I get the feeling she wants us to follow her."

I bite my lip, give him a dubious look. "Wendell, come on. I'm in a dress. My whole extended family is waiting for us to make a big announcement. I can't just swim after a sea turtle. And you shouldn't either. You nearly drowned last night. You need to rest and—"

"The boat!" Wendell cries, and before I can argue, he's running to the pink boat, flipping it over, pushing it out onto the water.

"You're serious, Wendell? We're following Gracia?"

"Z, remember, she has a connection with Tortue. If something happened to him, maybe, there's a chance . . ." His voice fades into the surf.

"Something? Like what?" And then I realize. Pepe is still on the loose. And Tortue is the main obstacle standing between Pepe and this land.

I swallow hard. "Okay, Wendell, let's go."

I help him push the boat into the water and then jump in and wring out the hem of my dress. Luckily, Wendell knows how to operate a motorboat from his outings with Santy. He revs up the engine, switches on the front light. Gracia watches us for a moment, then swims straight out to sea. We follow her around the cove to a rock outcropping not far from the coastline, one that looks like a jagged sculpture. The waves crash wildly against the stones, shooting sea spray, drenching our skin and clothes.

Soon Wendell cuts the engine so the blades won't get caught on the rocks. I keep my eye on Gracia, who's gliding right beside the boat, so close I could reach over and touch her. Wendell and I scan the rocks illuminated by the boat's light.

And then, ever so faintly, a hoarse voice calls out. It's barely audible over the ocean's roar. *"¡Ayúdenme!"* Help me!

Wendell adjusts the light, and we squint in the direction of the sound. No one. I strain to listen over the pounding of my heart, the ragged waves. There it is again. *"¡Ayúdenme!"* It's a ghostly sound, unearthly, hollow and echoing.

Gracia swims around the outcropping as Wendell paddles behind her.

Another shout for help, eerie and distant-yet-close.

I cup my hands around my mouth. "Where are you?"

"¡Aquí! Here! In the cave."

My gaze sweeps over the rocks. They're riddled with nooks where water rushes in and out. Any of them could lead to a cave. In desperation, I turn to Gracia. "Help us!" I plead.

Gracia glides through the rough current toward a gap in the rocks, an opening too small for her, too small for the boat. "Anchor the boat, Wendell! I'm going in."

Before he can object, I jump overboard. The water's cold and violent, battering me against rocks hidden underwater.

"Z!" Wendell calls out. "Let me go instead!"

"Not after last night!"

"No, Z!"

"I can do this!" I take a deep breath and swim after Gracia. The tidal current is strong, smacking me this way and that. Gracia slows down. I reach out and hang on to her, pressing against her scarred back. She carries me to the edge of the cave, as far as she can fit.

"Wendell," I call, "over here! Give me some light!"

He positions the boat lamp to light up the cave. I grab a rock, steadying myself, and peer inside.

There, up to his neck in water, is Tortue. He sputters, coughing in wide-eyed panic. "*Apúrate,* Zeeta—hurry, the tide's rising!"

"Tell me what to do," I shout.

"Untie me! My hands, behind my back."

I move along, hanging on to the rocks as I go, struggling against the currents. When I reach Tortue, I feel the thick rope underwater. It binds his hands tightly to a cluster of sharp, rocky protrusions behind him.

Blindly, I tug at the complicated mess of knots.

"You okay, Z?" Wendell calls from outside.

"Tortue's tied up!" I yell back.

"I'm coming in, Z!"

"No, Wendell! Stay in the boat. Keep the light shining here. You might need to go for help." I don't mention that there wouldn't be time for that. The water is rising higher by the second, with each rush of tide. At this rate, within minutes, it'll be over our heads. The knots are so tight and complex, I'm barely making any progress.

"We need the knife," Tortue gasps, struggling to raise his head high enough to breathe. "Strapped under the seat on my boat."

I gauge whether I have time to get back to the boat. "Wendell!" I call. "The knife, under the seat!" I start swimming toward the cave entrance. Another huge wave pushes me back inside. I look back and see Tortue's head underwater now. As the wave rushes out, it exposes his mouth, and he desperately sucks air in.

As fast as I can, I swim to the entrance of the cave, propelled by the outrush of water. Wendell holds the fish-gutting knife out toward me. I just manage to grab it and swim back inside with the next rush of tide. The wave smashes me against the back wall. There are only a few inches of air at the ceiling of the cave now.

I can't see Tortue at all now. He's fully underwater. God, is he dead?

I take a deep breath and lower myself, my hands searching the churning foam for his hands. Every second feels like an eternity. Finally, I locate the network of ropes holding Tortue's wrists. He doesn't seem to be moving. In the chaos of white currents, I can't tell if he's still conscious. How long has it been? One minute? Two? Or more?

Adrenaline coursing through me, I tear off the sheath and slide the knife between his wrist and the rope, slicing through the wet fibers, hoping I'm not slicing into his flesh. I strain to cut through the thick strands. *Come on, come on!*

How long can a person go without oxygen? It can't be this long. But Lupita said Tortue could hold his breath for a long time when he went diving as a kid. I pray he still can. *Please, Tortue, hang in there!*

Once, twice, three slices through the rope. And he's free. With all my might, I pull up my father. *Be alive!*

He breaks through the surface, gasping for breath, coughing and sputtering. *Thank God.*

I want to collapse, cry from pure, sweet relief. But there's no time. Another rush of tide pounds us. As it races out, I push off from the wall, pulling Tortue with me, going with its momentum. We're nearly out when another wave heads toward us.

"Grab on!" Wendell shouts, stretching out a paddle. Tortue and I lunge forward and clutch it just as the next waves hits. Wendell grips the oar as the water drags our bodies backward. We hang on, barely. The next lull comes, and Wendell heaves us into the boat.

Tortue is shivering violently. Wendell wraps him in a blanket, then starts pulling up the anchor. "We have to get you to shore, Tortue."

"No, wait!" Tortue gasps. "It might not be safe."

Wendell lets the anchor fall back down. There's enough light to see the fear in his eyes. "Why?"

Tortue's voice is raw. "My brother. This morning, after I left you, I took a nap under my boat. When I woke up, Pepe was standing there."

My heart starts thudding anew.

"He said he wanted to apologize, clear up some things. Told me his friends had tried to get him involved in some shady deals, but he wanted out. Said he realized that his family was all that mattered." Tortue pauses, choked with emotion.

I stare in shock. "And you believed him?"

He nods. "I know, it was stupid of me. But he's my brother. I had to give him a chance. He said he wanted to right his wrongs. Asked if we could go for a ride, for old time's sake." Tortue wraps the blanket around himself more tightly. "As we rode out here, every place we passed held memories. We even laughed, remembering good times. Pepe asked me to stop the boat here. This was a cave we came to as kids when the tide was out, when it was safe. He suggested we swim inside."

I clutch my head. "And you did?" I ask in disbelief.

"Yes," he says, lowering his gaze. "At the heart of it, I just couldn't believe my own brother would harm me."

I take this in. I admit, Pepe had me fooled for a while. He's incredibly manipulative, charming, well-practiced at lying. It's terrible but not surprising that he'd wield these skills on his brother.

"So then what?" Wendell urges.

"Pepe jumped in. I did the same. We swam around, splashing each other like kids. Then I blacked out. Next thing I remember, he's tying my hands. My head ached. He must've hit me with a rock." Tortue's voice breaks. "I kept saying, '*Hermano*—brother, how can you do this to me?'"

I reach out, touch his shoulder, trying to find the right words. "I'm so sorry, Tortue."

He takes a deep breath and continues. "The water wasn't high yet, but we both knew the tide would come in soon. Pepe finished tying me up without a word. His eyes—they were so cold. After he climbed back in the boat, he said, 'You should never have come back. That land is mine.'"

"I asked him if he was guilty of the poaching so many years ago. He laughed and said of course." Tortue pauses. "He said that to reach your dreams, you have to make sacrifices. Or sacrifice others.

"And then, before I could say another word, he left." Tortue wipes away tears with his wrist. "He left me to drown."

"I don't understand," Wendell says after a moment. "Why didn't he just kill you?"

"He's a coward." Tortue spits out the words. "He has his friends do his dirty work. Or the ocean tides." He takes a long breath. "I knew I had to live, Zeeta. I knew you were waiting for me—with my whole family. I had to survive. So I called to Gracia."

He looks down at her, swimming in circles by the boat. "And *qué milagro*—what a miracle—she came! She came to the cave opening and I could just see her head, but she couldn't fit inside. 'Go,' I told her. 'Go to Wendell and Zeeta.' It was my only chance. Hours passed, and I'd almost given up hope when I heard the boat's motor."

He looks at me, his eyes welling up. *"Gracias, mija, gracias."*

I lean forward, open my arms to him. This time, he meets me halfway. And my father and I share our first hug—cold and wet, but somehow, perfect.

After a moment, Wendell asks, "Ready to go?"

"One moment," Tortue murmurs, peering over the edge at Gracia, who's drifting beside us, just within arm's reach. We each stroke her leathery shell, worn and scarred, and whisper *"Gracias."* She meets our gazes with her ancient eyes, then swims away into the darkness.

"Let's paddle back," Tortue says. "I don't know if Pepe's out there somewhere. He might notice my boat's gone. Might be waiting for us at Playa Mermejita. We have to approach carefully."

Wendell flicks off the light and hands me an oar. Slowly, we paddle around the rock outcropping toward the beach. "See anything?" Wendell asks.

"No." I wish we could just turn on the motor. My arms are tired, my whole body throbbing from being bashed against the rocks. And the older bruises from this morning's fall are suddenly aching.

Noticing my exhaustion, Tortue reaches out to grab my oar. "I'll paddle a while."

"No, you rest," I insist.

Suddenly, Wendell whispers, "Look, there, through the trees!"

My gaze follows his finger. Moonlight glints off something shiny. A truck. It's parked on the dirt clearing in the jungle, just beyond the beach. And then, through the trees, I see the bobbing orange glow of two lit cigarettes. I groan.

"Change course!" Tortue urges. "Let's beach the boat in my little cove instead."

"But how will we get up the cliff walls?" Wendell asks. "In the dark?"

"I know the way. You can follow me."

I'm not looking forward to climbing up the same cliff

wall I already fell down once today. But it's the best option. We paddle the boat around, heading for the cove.

"Let's hope they didn't see us," Wendell says, glancing back.

"And if they did," I add, "that they don't guess where we're headed."

Chapter Twenty-Four

The cove looks empty, just the sliver of sand enclosed on three sides by towering cliffs. The rock face on the right rises into the west part of Comet Point, the spot where I've watched many sunsets. The steep incline directly across the beach is where I fell this morning, which seems like ages ago. Briefly, I think of Layla and my new family back at the cabanas, waiting for us. By now, they must have finished the flan. They must be worried.

We drag the boat ashore and run to the base of the cliff. Tortue starts climbing first, showing us exactly where to put our hands and feet. The darkness makes it harder to find secure grips. We feel with our hands, watch Tortue's shadow above us, listen carefully to his instructions. "Put your hand on this root here," he whispers. "Then wedge your foot in here. . . ."

There are a few close calls when I slip, but Wendell

manages to catch me, helps me regain balance. Wendell too skids down a couple times, but he grabs roots to keep from falling farther. Every muscle in my body burns. My bones throb, my flesh stings.

By the time we're nearly to the top, I'm so exhausted I don't know if I'll be able to hang on to the last handhold. Tortue is already there, leaning over, on his knees, breathing hard, watching us. He reaches out to pull me up the final stretch. I'm doubled over, gasping, as he helps Wendell. For a moment, we don't move, just catch our breath, taking in the dizzying height we just scaled.

I give Wendell a depleted grin. "We did it."

But he's not returning my gaze. He's looking at something over my shoulder. Something terrible, by the expression on his face. With dread, I turn around.

Two figures step out from the shadows. First Pepe. Then El Dedo. My heart sinks. They saw our boat and beat us here.

Both men are holding machetes, blocking the path to the jungle, straight ahead.

To our right the land curves into Comet Point. To our left are more rocky cliffs, which descend to Playa Mermejita. I glance down at where we came from. Not an option.

I look at Wendell and Tortue. There's just enough moonlight to see the expressions on their faces. Dismay, anger, fear. We're in no position to defend ourselves. We've spent every last remnant of energy on the climb.

The men step toward us.

It's amazing how sheer terror can make adrenaline kick

in, just when you're sure your reserve is empty. Instinctively, my body wants as much distance as possible from those machetes. The only direction to run is onto Punta Cometa, toward the tip.

"Run!" I shout in English, and take off. In my peripheral vision, I see Tortue and Wendell sprinting, spreading out across the point. I understand the strategy—use our numbers to our advantage. There are two of them and three of us. Maybe someone can escape and get help. It's our only hope.

I'm behind a giant cactus now, looking around desperately, squinting in the darkness. There's nowhere left to run. A few more paces and I'll be off the edge of the cliff. El Dedo is running after me, brandishing his machete. I can barely make out Tortue, racing along the other side of the peninsula, the east part of the comet. Pepe is closing in on him.

No one is chasing Wendell. He has looped around and is scrambling up the dirt hill, heading toward the jungle. He must be hoping to run for help.

Now El Dedo has reached the other side of the giant cactus. I dart one way, he darts the other—a cat-and-mouse game. It's a matter of time, probably only seconds, until I'll no longer be able to dodge him.

A scream flies from my mouth, a raw instinct. Of course no one back at the cabanas will be able to hear—the crash of the waves against the cliffs drowns out any feeble human sounds.

But Wendell hears. He freezes, turns back. In a flash, he's half falling down the hill, then barreling toward us at top speed, yelling, "No! Don't hurt her." He stops a few meters from El Dedo. "Don't touch her! What do you want?"

El Dedo turns, holding his machete up to Wendell. "You had three warnings," he growls. "No more."

Stall, Zeeta, stall. Keep him talking. "You can't kill us all," I say. "You'll be caught. Everyone knows your motives. There's already a search on for you."

Pepe grins. "No problem. They're all friends of mine."

Wendell makes a wide arc around the cactus and takes my hand. I squeeze it, trying to communicate that I love him.

I catch a glimpse of Pepe and Tortue on the other side of the peninsula. Tortue's hands are up and Pepe is leading him toward us, machete at his neck. "Got him!" Pepe calls out.

El Dedo turns to wait for them. I'm grateful for the distraction. Every moment we manage to stay alive counts. Every breath, every heartbeat. If we can just hang on a little longer, we can find a way. . . .

"I told you to go back, *hermano*," Pepe hisses into Tortue's ear. "And you didn't listen! If you'd left, I wouldn't have to do this!"

As Pepe goes on with his rant, I realize he must feel guilty, at least a little. If not, he would have just killed his brother in the cave. He would kill us all right now. He's not acting rationally. The key, I'm thinking, is to keep him talking.

"How could you do this to your own brother?" I demand. "And your sweet mother?"

Pepe glares, lifting his machete. For a moment I wonder if I've pushed him too far, if I've just provoked him to chop me into pieces. But he spits out, "She coddled him. All his melodrama, his moodiness—it was just a ploy for attention. I'm the successful one. The one who deserves the land."

Jealousy? That's what it sounds like. He's actually jealous of his brother. For a brief moment, I have a flash of sympathy for Pepe.

Tortue looks at his brother, eyes full of pain. "I'm sorry, *hermano*. I know it must have been hard for you."

I'm praying that Tortue might get through a chink in his brother's armor, when El Dedo shouts, "Shut up!" He gives us all a look of scorn, his lip curled. "None of you have any idea how much money is riding on these hotels, do you? Tens of millions. More than you can dream of."

"But you don't make much at the Turtle Center, Pepe," Wendell says. He must see my strategy of making them talk. Maybe if we stall enough, help will arrive. "You don't even have starter money."

"I have investors in Mexico City," Pepe shoots back. "*Narcos*. Drug lords. It was all set. I just needed to get Mamá to give me the land. She was hanging on to it. For him." He spits out the words, scowls at Tortue. "She kept renting it, and I kept having my *vatos* cause trouble. And after years of this, I nearly convinced our parents. They were getting tired of renting the land. Giving up hope on my pathetic brother." He glares at Tortue. "Then, out of the blue, you pay me a visit, *hermano,* asking if our parents have forgiven you. I should've killed you then. But I figured I'd just have them sign the land over to me before you revealed yourself."

He focuses his glare on Wendell and me. "And then you two interfered." His face twists into a grin. "But with all of you gone, the land goes to me."

"Your parents will never do that!" I cry, trying to make my lie sound convincing. "Everyone knows what you've done."

"Who're they gonna believe? The most popular guy in town . . . or a few outsiders?"

"You'll never get the land!" I counter. "Just let us go."

"Shut up!" El Dedo yells, making me jump.

Wendell shoots him a fiery look. "Who the hell are you, anyway?"

El Dedo smiles, a terrible, creepy smile. "Business partner. The brother Pepe never had."

Keep stalling, Z. Keep stalling. At some point, Layla and Joe will come looking for us. Maybe they'll bring backup. I rack my brains for some distraction. "Why were you poaching? I mean, you'd only get a few thousand pesos compared to the millions you're talking about."

With a sneer, El Dedo says, "A few thousand pesos for a couple hours of work every night? Better than a real job. Enough to tide me over till the hotel's up."

"But what—?"

"Enough questions," El Dedo snarls. "Time to jump."

Tortue speaks up loudly. "Brother, I'm asking you this one last favor. Kill me. But let them go."

My heart jumps. I shake my head frantically at Tortue.

Pepe doesn't answer.

El Dedo says gruffly, "They know too much."

"They'll leave," Tortue cries. "Wendell and Zeeta and her mother. They'll leave tonight and never come back."

Pepe regards Wendell. "I know this guy. He'll never leave those turtles in danger. And the girl won't leave without him." He shakes his head. "You've given me no choice."

"Move to the edge," El Dedo orders, raising his machete.

There's nothing else to do. I have no doubt this man would take joy in slashing us to bits. In fact, he's probably looking for an excuse. We move to the edge, and I glance down. Below, the cliffs are straight drop-offs, the water churning savagely below against sharp rocks.

Briefly, I wonder if this is where Meche fell. I wonder if there's any chance we can survive with just some broken bones, a limp like hers, or if we'll meet the same fate as her daughter. If the ocean will batter us and carry us away. If our bodies will ever be found.

Tears pour down my face. I lock eyes with Wendell, then Tortue. *Not now, not after I've finally reunited with my father, found my home. Not now!*

I draw a deep breath into my belly, into the wildest animal part of myself, and I scream.

El Dedo smacks my face hard, nearly knocking me right off the edge. Wendell's hand shoots out toward me, steadying me.

El Dedo laughs cruelly, as if he's a cat torturing a bird, drawing out the agony, taking sick pleasure in it.

Wendell holds me close, inspecting my cheek. Then he sends El Dedo a look of daggers.

This violence sets off Tortue. In one swift movement, he lunges toward Pepe, grabbing for the machete. Pepe swings it away and slices into Tortue's arm. Blood spills out. Tortue staggers backward, clutching his wound.

Pepe's eyes are hard, cold, unfeeling. He simply orders, "Jump."

My eyes fix on Wendell's. I know him so well, I can guess what he's thinking. He's not going to jump; he's going to charge El Dedo. I brace myself, get ready to grab the machete in the confusion.

And then, from the tail of the comet, a thin voice calls out, "¡*Hola!* What's going on?" It's a woman's voice. A figure is heading toward us, limping slightly. Meche.

"Help!" I call. "Call for help!"

Another smack from El Dedo. He shoots me an insidious grin. He's enjoying this, watching me teeter on the edge, relishing my pain.

My face throbs. I'm vaguely aware of the iron taste of blood in my mouth.

"Turn around, Meche!" Wendell shouts. "They have machetes!"

"Meche, go get help!" Tortue calls.

But it's too late; Meche is already close enough to see the men. She takes in the situation.

"They're gonna kill us, Meche!" I scream. "Run!"

Meche, keeping perfect balance, steps down the incline, then stops a few paces from us.

The men are watching her and giving each other looks, as if communicating about this new development.

Meche is a vision in a black dress and silvery shawl, her hair piled in braids on her head. Standing tall and regal, she commands, "Drop your machetes." She eyes our captors with utter disdain. "Or else."

I have to admire her ability to bluff. Of course, she's been practicing that witch persona for years now. It's convincing.

"Or else what?" Pepe demands.

She tosses a confident glance back into the tree shadows. I notice a slight movement in the foliage, two yellow eyes.

"Or else . . . you will be devoured," she says, lingering on each word. "Eliminated," she adds, enunciating every syllable.

Pepe and El Dedo glance at each other. Is there a hint of nervousness in their eyes?

Meche folds her arms, draws herself taller still. "My kitty is right there, waiting for me to give the command."

I glance at Wendell, well aware that Gatito is dying, probably almost too weak to walk.

Pepe and El Dedo exchange looks. Under his breath, El Dedo asks, "Is this the *bruja* with the jaguar?"

Pepe says nothing, shifting his machete to the other hand, a gesture of uncertainty, maybe even fear.

Meche sighs. "Death by jaguar is never pleasant. And yes," she adds with the delicate raise of an eyebrow, "I am the *bruja*."

After a pause, Pepe points his machete at her. "Move to the edge."

She stands firm, her arms crossed, giving Pepe a look of

pity. Then she cups her hands around her mouth and shouts, "Gatito!"

I fix my gaze on those eyes burning in the trees. The animal steps out of the shadows and into the moonlight. A sleek, muscular, imposing silhouette. He's walking slowly, a majestic prowl. He pauses, opens his jaws. The moonlight shines off the sharp teeth. He lets out a roar. The most earth-shaking one I've heard yet. Even though I know he's on our side—and nearly too sick to walk—the noise taps into a deep, instinctual terror and makes me shudder.

Pepe's and El Dedo's machetes tremble in their hands. Their eyes are glued to Gatito as he saunters forward.

I try to breathe. Halfway down the peninsula, Gatito pauses. I'm sure he's resting, in pain, exhausted. But to anyone else, it would simply look like he thinks he's too important to be bothered with pesky little tasks like devouring people.

"Gatito!" Meche calls again, her voice booming over the rush of waves.

The jaguar leaps down the hill in a single bound, pauses, then walks closer, a sheen of moonlight on his fur. Now I can see that he's straining himself. Not something you'd notice unless you knew he was dying.

I glance at Pepe and El Dedo. Sweat glistens on their foreheads. They're clutching their machetes, terrified. Gatito prowls closer and closer, appearing cocky, taking his sweet time.

"Call off that cat!" El Dedo demands, his voice cracking with fear.

Meche laughs, a cackling, haunting sound. She's got this witch thing down. "Gatito!" she calls again, this time more softly, because the cat is so close.

As the men's attention is diverted, Wendell and I inch toward Meche. The closer we are to Meche, the safer, at least where Gatito is concerned. I glance at Tortue and Pepe. Tortue also seems to be moving, almost imperceptibly, closer to us.

After another pause, Gatito takes a few more steps. Now he's just meters away. I see pain in his eyes, and strangely, I want to hug him. He must be using every last bit of energy to walk to us.

But when I look at Pepe, I see that he's shaking, sweat pouring down his face, his eyes wide in terror.

And then, in swift succession, several things happen.

The machete falls from Pepe's hand, clangs onto the rocks.

He dashes toward the jungle.

Tortue grabs his brother's machete from the ground.

El Dedo lunges toward Meche, his machete raised high, ready to strike.

And, seeing Meche threatened, Gatito pounces.

It takes just a few giant bounds. Jaws wide, he crashes into El Dedo. The momentum sends them both flying off the cliff.

"Gatito!" Meche shrieks.

Far below, cat and man are thrashing in the violent surf. I watch in horror as a wave picks up El Dedo and slams him into a cliff. His body is sucked under as the wave retreats.

"Gatito!" Meche screams again.

The jaguar lifts his great head upward to look at Meche. His yellow eyes flash, and then the sea swallows him.

Meche clings to me, sobbing. Wendell stands beside us, watching the water below. There's no sign of El Dedo, just the rushing, savage ocean. Tortue makes his way to us, bleeding, his brother's machete dangling from his hand. Now he embraces Meche, murmuring soothing words. His blood soaks them both, but they don't notice. Her eyes are wild with pain—maybe the distant pain of her daughter's death, and her own attempt to kill herself, and now the fresh pain of Gatito's death—all on these very same cliffs.

"Gone," she cries, raising her hands to the ocean. "My baby is gone."

❖ ❖ ❖

We walk through the moonlit jungle, all of us limping from injuries old or new. Still crying, Meche pauses to tie her shawl around the gash in Tortue's arm, staunching the blood flow. Then she wipes her eyes and says in a raw voice, "I was bringing Gatito to Punta Cometa. So he could see the ocean one last time. He was in so much pain, it took us an hour to get there. This was his goodbye."

I pull her close. "He saved us, Meche. He loved you. And so do we. It'll be hard without him, but we'll help you through it."

Tortue nods. "You're not alone."

When we pass by the TRESPASSERS WILL BE DEVOURED sign, I whisper my own words of gratitude to Gatito. Soon the flickering light of lanterns and candles becomes visible through the trees. And as we grow closer to the cabanas, I hear guitar chords. A minor, D minor, E, and G. And a gentle, mournful voice—my grandfather's voice—singing "La Llorona." It almost feels like a tribute to Gatito.

Tortue is listening intently, his expression full of all the longing and regret in the song.

We round the curve and emerge from the jungle, into the glow of the kitchen hut, where my whole big beautiful family is waiting for us.

We're here, home, finally.

❖ ❖ ❖

Don Rogelio sees us first. His fingers freeze on the guitar. The music stops.

One by one, the other faces turn to us. There is a moment of stunned silence as we all walk forward.

Lupita stands up, whispers, "Son?" And then she is murmuring, *"Mijo, mijo, mijo,"* and running toward us. Rogelio stays seated, frozen, clutching his guitar. A tear runs down his cheek. Cristina stares, motionless, as if she's seeing a ghost. Lupita throws herself into Tortue's arms, holding him as if she'll never let go.

Seeing my wounds, Layla rushes to me. "What happened to you, love?" My entire body stings and throbs, but the pain is overpowered by the intensity of this moment.

"I'm okay, Layla," I whisper.

And before anyone else can ask what's happened, Meche steps forward, raising her arms. Her face is tear-streaked, her eyes raw with grief. "Twenty years ago, on the night of the poaching, I was with El Tortuga."

A murmur ripples through the little crowd.

"I'd thrown myself over a cliff," she continues. "At Punta Cometa. I wanted to end my life that night, but El Tortuga saved me. I asked him not to tell a soul. He honored that promise at all costs. El Tortuga would never have harmed the turtles. He's always been a man full of kindness. And courage."

It's as if her words have broken a spell. Rogelio sets down his guitar, walks toward his son, reaching out his arms, palms upturned. "I'm sorry, *mijo*," he murmurs. "I'm so sorry, son." Tortue steps toward him, and then he's in his father's arms. Cristina hugs her brother next, echoing, "I'm sorry, *hermano*, so sorry."

Once they release Tortue from their embraces, he turns to Meche. *"Gracias,"* he says softly. Then he clears his throat. "Many years ago I left Mazunte. I left the people I love most." He takes a deep breath. "I returned in hopes of reuniting with you all. I hoped to be a better son, a better brother, and . . ." He pauses, putting his hand on my shoulder, a sweet, awkward gesture. ". . . a better father."

I flush, a little embarrassed, but secretly savoring this moment.

"Zeeta—who you all know and love—is my daughter."

Stunned silence.

"It's true," Layla says, resting her arm on Tortue's. "We had only one night together. But it was a magical night that gave us our daughter."

Now everyone is up, hugging each other. Through tears, Cristina sobs, *"¡Sobrina!"*—Niece! El Sapo laughs as he calls out, *"¡Prima!"*—Cousin! Lupita and Rogelio hold me in a warm embrace. Through the commotion, I sneak a smile at Tortue, offer him a silent *gracias.*

Soon Meche grabs a first-aid kit from behind the counter and starts cleaning and bandaging wounds—Tortue's machete slash first. Meanwhile, a barrage of questions comes. Mayra asks why we're scraped and bleeding, and Xochitl asks why we're soaking wet and muddy.

I exchange glances with Meche and Wendell and Tortue. I don't want to see his parents' pain when they hear what their younger son has done. Not right now. Tortue can find a way to tell them, later. I keep the explanation short and sweet and deliberately vague. "Some trouble with the poachers," I say. "But we've contacted the authorities. They're on it."

Wendell gives me an encouraging smile, then turns to Rogelio, deftly changing the subject. "How about some live music?"

Rogelio pauses, then hands the guitar to Tortue, whose arm is now neatly bandaged. Meeting his father's gaze, Tortue positions his fingers on the frets and strums the first notes of "La Llorona." Rogelio sings along while Lupita hums. The currents of notes carry me from one emotion to another. I look at the faces of my family and see myself reflected in them.

At the end, Rogelio says, *"Mijo,* I thought you only liked *música de rock."*

Tortue smiles sadly. "*Pues,* I do love Jimi Hendrix, but your music is the best, Papá. All these years away, I've been playing the classics you taught me. Whenever I closed my eyes and played, I could hear the waves, see the sunset off Punta Cometa, smell Mamá's *mole.*"

Chapter Twenty-Five

It's June ninth. Tomorrow Wendell will leave for California. The rainy season has just begun, turning everything dripping-wet shades of green and blue and silver. It's chilly, and we have to wear wraps and coats and use blankets over our sheets at night. The backpackers are still coming, despite the rain, but Layla and I are expecting a lull during the next few months. We'll have enough money to tide us over, and the downtime might be relaxing after the steady stream of cooking and cleaning and fixing of recent months.

Still, I feel an impending emptiness, a distinct lack of sunshine and sparkle.

Today the clouds are heavy, but inside the kitchen hut there's a warm atmosphere. We're throwing Wendell a good-bye party. All our friends are gathered at the tables, eating *mole,* tamales, *chiles rellenos, pescado a la plancha*—a feast that Layla and Lupita and I cooked as Tortue and Rogelio jammed on the guitar. They played one Jimi Hendrix song after another—"Little Wing," "Black Magic Woman," "A Merman I Should Turn to Be." Amazingly, Rogelio can't get enough Hendrix. On a sentimental impulse, I passed along to my grandfather my father's ancient Jimi T-shirt, which Rogelio is proudly sporting now, despite the holes and the fact that it doesn't quite cover his hefty belly.

A new round of guests are here—from Germany, Israel, Japan, New Zealand, Argentina, and South Africa. I take in their blissed-out faces, some freshly arrived, some already familiar. I always miss them when they leave, but I'm glad that I'm not the one leaving. Now I know that staying behind isn't easy either. It takes some getting used to—seeing the oddly vacant space at the table where a friend used to sit, feeling that emptiness.

I glance at Horacio's and Joe's favorite seats, both occupied by other guests now. Horacio left months ago to meet his daughter in the Philippines for more adventures. Joe left shortly after him. He fell in love with a funky clothing designer and followed her back to her home in Malaysia. Before leaving, he informed us that the world wasn't going to end after all. It simply couldn't, he said, now that he was thinking of getting married and having a little pack of children. Before he left, he'd already switched to wearing hip T-shirts designed by his fiancée. He packed away his clown clothes but promised to pull them out for future kid birthday parties. Before he left, he thanked Layla for making Cabañas Magia del Mar a truly magical stop on his life's journey.

Layla's new clown is at her heels, carrying the lemonade as she serves *mole*. In top form, Layla's found a replacement for Joe and the string of spiritually minded clowns before him. This one is a life-coach-turned-rescue-pig-trainer who performs antics and tricks with the pigs onstage. During the summer months, he lets the pigs vacation on a Nebraska farm, taking a break from their show circuit. From what I can tell, he has no intention of leaving Cabañas Magia del Mar until pig show season starts again this fall. Every once in a while, I wonder if this will be the clown Layla will settle down with . . . but I'm not counting on it. At least now, the clown sidekicks come to her rather than us going to them.

Layla continues with sunrise yoga and bonfires and Rumi quoting, always an inspiration to the revolving door of travelers who come to our rustic oasis. On starry reviews on travel websites, guests rave about the cabanas, the nature paths through the jungle—which are now complete—and most of all, about Layla, who has truly found her calling.

For once in our lives, we have money—at least, enough money to let us slide through the upcoming low tourist season even with just a trickle of guests. Not surprisingly, Layla sees this as an excuse to leave. Just for a vacation, she promises. To Malaysia, for Joe's wedding. Just a few weeks, then she'll come back. And Tortue and my cousins can help me run the cabanas during that time.

My gaze rests on Tortue, across the table from me, strumming the guitar, his head close to his father's. Tortue has contributed much to our success. He gives our guests eco-tours, taking them out on his pink boat, where they never fail to spot sea turtles. He's enlisted eager guests to spend nights on Playa Mermejita, side by side with locals, to guard the turtles, their nests, their eggs, and their hatchlings. In the early spring, night after night, we watched hundreds of baby turtles flop down the beach and into the sea—moments that have left everyone, turtles and humans alike, full of hope.

Every night at dinner, Tortue performs, often with his father beside him. I love watching them play guitar together. I especially love it on the busy nights, when Lupita comes by to help cook and serve. All the guests adore my grandmother, and she embraces them all.

After the last guitar notes, Meche walks over to Tortue, kisses him on the mouth, and rests her head on his shoulder. They have fallen in love. For the first few weeks, she and Tortue talked, reminisced, bonded, took long walks and swims together. It became clear that although Layla valued Tortue's help and his new role as my father, their spark of romance was gone. Tortue realized he'd romanticized it over the years and came to understand that it had simply been one passionate night. A night that happened to result in me, and my new home, and my new family.

When Layla saw the love forming between Meche and Tortue, she told them earnestly that nothing would make her happier than the two of them being together. Now Tortue lives with Meche in her little patch in the jungle. He fills the void that Gatito left in her life. More than fills it.

Meche has patiently helped him manage his bipolar disorder, making sure his prescriptions are filled on time, scheduling his therapy sessions. And she's been at his side through the hardest task—coming to terms with the betrayal of his brother.

Pepe disappeared. Maybe he returned to Mexico City. We don't know. Word spread quickly about his crimes. And word spread even faster that Tortue had returned, innocent, having been framed by his brother.

Every opportunity she gets, Lupita makes sure everyone knows that Tortue and Meche are heroes. The sweetness of gaining a son and a granddaughter—and soon a daughter-in-law, Meche—has eased the bitterness of Pepe's betrayal. To their credit, the locals gave Meche and Tortue a chance—and ultimately, embraced them. And, after a federal investigation revealed Chucho's corruption, he was kicked off the police force. If Pepe ever dares to return, he'll be arrested in a flash.

El Dedo's body was never found. Neither was Gatito's. Sometimes Meche and Tortue and I walk to Punta Cometa and stare quietly at the sea. We don't talk, just watch the water. It's impossible to put the feelings into words—so much sorrow and joy, all swirled together, inseparable. Waves crashing, churning. Beyond the chaos, sunlight melting into glittering pools. The beautiful mess of life.

Now Wendell walks toward me, down the stone path from the tiny new office hut, where he just printed his travel documents for tomorrow. Seeing him with the boarding pass gives me a stab of pain. This boy I love is leaving on his own path, separate from mine.

He weaves around the guests, coming toward me, and kisses me. "A walk?" he whispers.

I swallow hard and nod.

We head into the jungle, damp and rich with rain-soaked earth, slippery leaves. The air feels alive, all muted green light, the buzz of insects, the hum of frogs. Our interlocked hands swing between us.

Again, it hits me. He's leaving tomorrow. I stop walking. I could collapse right here, somehow refuse to let time keep going. Make it stop.

Instead, I hold him tightly, as tightly as I can. I shut my eyes and try to savor this moment, find a way to make it infinite. I breathe in his smell, his warmth. Beneath my cheek, I feel his flesh, the muscles beneath, the structure of his bones. I hold on to his long braid. I take in every detail, with all my senses. I'm conscious, suddenly, of the trill of every bird, the beat of every insect wing. I feel as though I'm looking back on this moment, experiencing both my life and a memory of my life. And somehow I know for certain that Wendell will always be part of me.

I feel, all over again, our first kiss in a candlelit crystal cave, our secret swim in hidden springs, our salty, sunlit naps in the hammock. I feel all of these sensations at once, filling me, and I don't know what to do, so I keep holding him, tightly. We stand in the middle of the path, clinging to each other as droplets of rain find their way through the canopy of leaves, dripping down our hair, our eyelashes, mixing with our tears as we hold each other.

Epilogue

I lie in my hammock, alone, swinging slowly, listening to the waves, watching the stars. It's late, close to midnight, nearly the end of August second. A year and a day after the hand-fasting in France. This is the day Wendell and I promised to meet if we want to stay together.

He's been gone nearly two months. With every phone conversation and text, I've felt our paths diverging farther and farther. He's caught up with new friends, classes, ideas. *Hey Z! Gotta run! More later . . . ,* and the later becomes later and later. And there's not more, but less.

But it's not just him. I've become absorbed in life here, helping with the cabanas, meeting new guests, hanging out with my cousins and the other *bolibolistas,* filling up more jade notebooks. It's the same on my side—*Busy now, W! Love you! Thinking about you. . . .*

And I am thinking about him. But mostly just during the quiet times, and those are few and far between. Sometimes a fleeting sadness overwhelms me unexpectedly, like a wave sneaking up on me from behind. The tears come, and I hold on to that feeling from the jungle, the moment I believed in with my whole heart. The moment I still believe in, even now that our handfasting anniversary has almost come and gone.

I push the ground with my toe, giving the hammock a fresh swing, and soak in the expanse of stars. Suddenly, it seems unbearably sad that we picked the perfect spot for the handfasting, yet at midnight, it will be empty.

I sit up. I'll go alone. It will be just me and the sea turtles, but I'll be there. I peek at the clock by my bed. Eleven o'clock. There's still time. I grab a light shawl and head through the jungle toward Playa Mermejita. Emerging from the trees, I see the beach gloriously full of small olive ridley turtles—this season's species—inching up the beach, at various stages of their journey. I breathe in the salty air, wishing Wendell were here to see this.

As I weave around the turtles, careful not to disturb their nests, I ponder their journey, the same one their grandmothers took. This beach is a constant in their lives, over so many generations. This beach, in some way, defies the limits of time.

The moon is nearly full, illuminating the waves, the surf, the determined mass of little shells moving up the beach. I find the spot near the giant log of driftwood where, many months ago, Wendell suggested we renew our handfasting. I sit down on the sand, hugging my knees, grateful for the company of turtles. I wonder if they understand that this journey is just one of many in their lives, in the lives of their ancestors, the lives of their descendants. I wonder if they grasp this miracle.

Gradually, I sense another presence on the beach. A human presence. Someone is walking toward me, skirting the surf. I watch the figure draw closer and closer. The moonlight bathes him, almost ghostlike. A visitor from my past, or maybe my future, slipping into the present.

"Wendell?" I call.

"Zeeta," he calls back.

"You came," I say, my voice breaking.

And now he's here, at our spot, our handfasting spot, and I'm staring at him, wondering if he's real. He leans in, kisses me, wraps his arms around me. "Of course I came."

I want to explain to him what I was just thinking—about the turtles, about so many journeys, about glimpsing the sum of all the journeys in our lives. Instead, I kiss him, until he pulls away, sits in front of me on the sand, his eyes on mine.

"Zeeta," he murmurs. "I could only come for the weekend. But I needed to tell you something. A vision I had."

I close my eyes for a long moment. I'm not ready for more danger. Not after all we've been through. "What is it?" I ask under my breath.

"Something I saw while I was stranded in the ocean.

When I thought I was about to die." He pauses, his eyes growing shiny.

My muscles taut, I reach out and take his hand. "What did you see?"

"I saw you and me, Z. Together. You—you had white hair, and wrinkles, but the same eyes. I could tell it was you. You were crouched down, digging in a garden, planting flowers or something, and you looked up at me and smiled." His voice cracks; his eyes fill with tears. "The way you looked at me—you knew me better than anyone in the world." He swallows, cups my face with his hand. "We'll be together at the end of it all, Z. I don't know how we'll get there, but we'll be together."

And that's when, finally, I trust, deep in my bones, that I can let him go completely. He can go to the far reaches of the sea—or wherever life takes him—but he'll come back. We sit, hand in hand, the miracles of turtles and waves and sky and stars and a zillion grains of sand surrounding us, things you can never quite grasp, things of infinite beauty, pathless mystery, things that are rough yet smooth, simple yet complex, things without end.

GLOSSARY AND PRONUNCIATION GUIDE

Since Mexican Spanish has sounds that don't exist in English, this pronunciation guide is an approximation. Note that the Mexican *v* is often pronounced as a soft *b*. The *-o/-a* ending indicates masculine and feminine genders, respectively.

abarrotes	ah-bah-RROH-tays	groceries
abuelitos	ah-bway-LEE-tohs	grandparents
adelante	ah-day-LAHN-tay	go ahead
agua de espanto	AH-gwa day ays-PAHN-toh	"fright water" (a Oaxacan medicinal herbal brew)
agua de horchata	AH-gwa day or-CHAH-tah	cinnamon-rice water
agua de jamaíca	AH-gwa day hah-MY-kah	hibiscus water
agua de papaya	AH-gwa day pah-PY-ah	papaya water
agua de sandía	AH-gwa day sahn-DEE-ah	watermelon water

agua de tamarindo	AH-gwa day tah-mah-REEN-doh	tamarind water
amate	ah-MAH-tay	a kind of tree bark
aquí	ah-KEE	here
así es	ah-SEE ays	that's how it is
ayúdenme	ah-YOO-dayn-may	help me
bien padre	bee-AYN PAH-dray	really cool (slang)
bolibolístas	boh-lee-boh-LEE-stahs	volleyball players
bruja	BROO-hah	witch
buena suerte	BWAY-nah SWAYRR-tay	good luck
buenas tardes	BWAY-nahs TAHRR-days	good afternoon
buenos días	BWAY-nohs DEE-ahs	good day/good morning
cabaña	cah-BAHN-ya	cabin
cacao	cah-CAH-oh	cocoa
cariño	cah-REEN-yoh	affection
carnicería	carr-nee-say-REE-ah	butcher shop
Castillos	cahs-TEE-ohs	last name; literally "castles"
chavos	CHAH-vohs	guys
chicos	CHEE-cohs	kids; guys
chido/a	CHEE-doh/dah	cool (slang)
chiles rellenos	CHEE-lays ray-AY-nohs	stuffed peppers
chiquitito	chee-kee-TEE-toh	very tiny
Chucho	CHOO-choh	nickname for Jesús
claro que sí	CLAH-roh kay SEE	of course
cochino	coh-CHEE-noh	pig
comal	coh-MAHL	clay plate for cooking

compañeros	cohm-pahn-YAY-rohs	buddies/friends/ teammates
corren	COH-rrayn	run
cositas	coh-SEE-tahs	little things
Cruz	KROOS	last name, literally "cross"
de nada	day NAH-dah	it was nothing (a response to "thanks")
dedo	DAY-doh	finger
dígame	DEE-gah-may	tell me
Don	DOHN	Mr./sir (respectful term)
Doña	DOHN-yah	Mrs. (respectful term)
empezemos	aym-pay-SAY-mohs	let's begin
Ernestino	ayrr-nays-TEE-noh	male name
espérate	ays-PAY-rah-tay	wait (a command; informal address)
espérese	ays-PAY-ray-say	wait (a command; formal address)
Gatito	gah-TEE-toh	Kitty
Gerardo	hay-RAHRR-doh	male name
gracia	GRAH-see-ah	grace
gracias	GRAH-see-ahs	thanks
grandes amigos	GRAHN-days ah- MEE-gohs	good friends
Guadalupe	gwah-dah-LOO-pay	female name (after the famous Virgin, patron saint of Mexico)
güey	WAY	dude, man (slang)
hasta luego	AHS-tah loo-WAY-goh	see you later
hermano	ayrr-MAH-noh	brother
hola	OH-lah	hi
Horacio	or-AH-see-oh	male name

huevos a la mexicana	way-vohs ah lah may-hee-KAH-nah	eggs scrambled with peppers, tomatoes, and onions
huipil	WEE-peel	traditional native tunic
incendio	een-SAYN-dee-oh	fire (in both Spanish and Portuguese)
Jesús	hay-SOOS	male name
José Luís	hoh-SAY loo-EES	male name
La Llorona	lah yoh-ROH-nah	The Weeping Woman (from Mexican folklore)
Lupita	loo-PEE-tah	nickname for Guadalupe
magia del mar	MAH-hee-ya dayl MAHRR	magic of the sea
mamá	mah-MAH	mom
maravilloso	mah-rah-vee-OH-soh	wonderful
Mazunte	mah-SOON-tay	small town/beach in Oaxaca, Mexico
Meche	MAY-chay	woman's name, nickname for Mercedes
media naranja	MAY-dee-ah nah-RAHN-hah	literally "half-orange"; slang for "better half," romantic partner
mi amor	mee ah-MOHRR	my love
mija	MEE-hah	my daughter (contraction of "mi hija")
mijo	MEE-hoh	my son (contraction of "mi hijo")
mis hijos	mees EE-hohs	my children
mole	MOH-lay	traditional Mexican chocolate-chili sauce
molito	moh-LEE-toh	affectionate term for *mole*
muchacha	moo-CHAH-chah	young girl

muchachita	moo-chah-CHEE-tah	affectionate term for a young girl
muchachos	moo-CHAH-chos	kids, guys
música de rock	MOO-see-kah day RROHK	rock music
muy	MOOY	very
nada de turistas	NAH-dah day too-REES-tahs	no tourists
narcos	NAHRR-kohs	drug dealers (short for *narcotraficantes*)
oiga(n)	OY-gah(n)	hey; listen (formal/plural)
oye	OH-yay	hey; listen (informal, singular)
palapa	pah-LAH-pah	open-sided, rustic hut made of natural materials
papá	pah-PAH	dad
Pepe	PAY-pay	male name, nickname for José
pipian	pee-pee-AHN	Mexican sauce made with pumpkin seeds, corn, and chile
perdón	payrr-DOHN	pardon me
pescado a la plancha	pays-CAH-doh ah lah PLAHN-cha	grilled fish
picante pero sabroso	pee-CAHN-tay PAY-roh sahb-ROH-soh	spicy but delicious
pinche	PEEN-chay	damn
Playa Mermejita	PLAH-yah mayrr-may-HEE-tah	Mermejita Beach, a small beach in Oaxaca
pobrecita	poh-bray-SEE-tah	poor little thing
por favor	pohrr fah-VOHRR	please

pozole	poh-SOH-lay	stew made from hominy (corn), pork, and chile
primo/a	PREE-moh/mah	cousin
pues	PWAYS	well
Punta Cometa	POON-tah coh-MAY-tah	Comet Point
pura	POO-rah	only, just, pure
¿Qué me cuentas?	KAY may KWAYN-tahs	What's up?
qué milagro	KAY mee-LAH-groh	what a miracle
¿Qué onda?	KAY OHN-dah	What's up? (slang)
qué padre	KAY PAH-dray	how cool
que te vaya bien	kay tay VAH-yah bee-AYN	take care (literally, "may it go well with you")
¿Quién es?	kee-AYN ays	Who is it?
quién sabe	kee-AYN SAH-bay	who knows
rápido	RRAH-pee-doh	fast
Raúl	rrah-OOL	male name
Rogelio	rroh-HAY-lee-oh	male name
ruda	RROO-dah	rue—a strong-smelling herb used in Mexican spiritual cleansing rituals
Santy	SAHN-tee	male name, nickname for Santiago
sapo	SAH-poh	toad
se devoran los intrusos	say day-VOH-rahn lohs een-TROO-sohs	trespassers will be devoured
se vende mole	say VAYN-day MOH-lay	mole for sale
señor	sayn-YOHR	sir/Mr.
señora	sayn-YOH-rah	ma'am/Mrs.
señorita	sayn-yoh-REE-tah	Miss
sí	SEE	yes

sobrina	soh-BREE-nah	niece
suavecito	swah-vay-SEE-toh	softly, gently
telenovela	tay-lay-noh-VAY-lah	soap opera
tengan cuidado	TAYN-gahn coo-ee-DAH-doh	be careful
territorio prohibido	tay-rree-TOH-ree-oh proh-ee-BEE-doh	forbidden territory
todo	TOH-doh	everything, all
tortillería	tohrr-tee-yay-REE-ah	tortilla shop
tranquilo	trahn-KEE-loh	calm, tranquil
vámonos	VAH-moh-nohs	let's go
vato	VAH-toh	dude, guy, man (sometimes connoting a gang member)
verdad	vayrr-DAHD	truth
Xochitl	SOH-cheel	female name
¿Ya ves?	yah VAYS	See?

AUTHOR'S NOTE

Although the locations in the book are real, I took some liberties with details of the landscape and building layout to fit the needs of the fictional story line. If you do visit Mazunte one day, have fun (it's one of my favorite vacation spots), but don't be surprised at the tweaking I did!

LAURA RESAU lived in Oaxaca, Mexico, for two years, teaching English and doing cultural anthropology research. When she is not traveling, she can be found at home in Colorado, writing in her silver trailer and enjoying life with her young son and husband. Laura's time abroad also inspired her novels *What the Moon Saw,* available from Yearling, and *Red Glass, The Queen of Water, Star in the Forest, The Indigo Notebook,* and *The Ruby Notebook,* all available from Delacorte Press.